THE BORGIA BULL

Pamela Bennetts

Pamela Bennetts was born in London, where she still lives with her husband, a planning engineer, and her daughter. She has a full-time job with a Church of England organisation which means that most of her writing has to be done in the evenings. Despite this, Pamela Bennetts is the successful author of several historical novels.

Also by Pamela Bennetts
and available in Sphere Books

THE BLACK PLANTAGENET
THE BORGIA PRINCE

The Borgia Bull

PAMELA BENNETTS

SPHERE BOOKS LIMITED
30/32 Gray's Inn Road, London, WC1X 8JL

First published in Great Britain in 1968
by Robert Hale Ltd.

First Sphere Books edition, 1972

TRADE
MARK

Printed in Great Britain by
Hazell Watson & Viney Ltd,
Aylesbury, Bucks

Acknowledgements

To write a book about a man whose personality and motives were as complex as those of Cesare Borgia, one needs much help from those who have studied his life with such care, and who have produced biographies and histories of such distinction. To these authors I give my thanks:

William Harrison Woodward	Cesare Borgia
Rafael Sabatini	The Life of Cesare Borgia
L. Collinson-Morley	The Story of the Borgias
John Leslie Garner	Cesare Borgia: A Study of the Renaissance
F. B. Corvo	A History of the Borgias
Carlo Beuf	Cesare Borgia: the Machiavellian Prince
E. L. Miron	Duchess Derelict
Orestes Ferrara	The Borgia Pope
G. Portigliotti	The Borgias
Christopher Hare	Life and Letters in the Italian Renaissance
Charles Yriarte	Cesare Borgia
Jacob Burckhardt	The Civilisation of the Renaissance in Italy
Count Pasolini	Catherine Sforza
Niccolò Machiavelli	The Prince
John Addington Symonds	The Age of Despots

CHAPTER ONE

THE night was not made for death. The oppressive heat of the day had given way to a soft warmth, and a slight breeze carried the perfume of flowers through the beautiful vineyard adjoining St. Martino ai Monti in the Trastevere.

Under the clear star-decked sky, a table had been set for a banquet, the spotless linen a foil for the gleaming gold and silver dishes, the goblets of rock crystal with precious stones set in their stems, enamelled flagons and the jewelled spice holders. In the centre of the table a heavy silver candelabra held scented candles which threw mellow light on the remains of the feast.

Plumb rich pheasants, turtle-doves, ducklings, veal, quince pies, lamb-tongues and a profusion of elaborate sweet-meats and fruits were spread across the board, and the guests had partaken freely of both food and the cool sweet wines, and were now relaxed and contented.

At the head of the table, Vanozza de' Catanei looked with pride and satisfaction at her well-appointed table, and then at her guests gathered around her.

She smiled indulgently at her son, Giovanni Borgia, the Duke of Gandia, as he flirted openly with his sister-in-law, Sancia, a ripe beauty with deep raven hair and long, sly, grey-blue eyes, which now sparkled with mischief as she responded to Gandia's overtures. Her blue silk gown was cut low to reveal a full luscious body, which excited all men but her youthful husband, Jofrè, Prince of Squillace, who was more than happy to allow his brother to claim her.

Gandia ran a seductive finger along Sancia's bare shoulder, and she gave a contented murmur. He was magnificently attired in a doublet of white silk, heavily worked with gold and silver thread and jewels, and trimmed with miniver; on the hand he curved round Sancia's waist were rings of startling quality and value.

His light blue eyes were large if a trifle shallow, and his face, although handsome, shewed the first signs of the dissolute life he led. There were lines under his eyes and round his mouth which should not have been visible on a face which had seen barely twenty-one summers.

Light brown hair curled carelessly about his head, and Vanozza's heart warmed as she looked at him, for she was devoted to him, and was inclined to dismiss as boyish pranks some of the vicious and unpleasant rumours and gossip which were linked with his name.

He is young, she told herself, and he is his father's son, but he will grow to wisdom, and could one blame him for the fact that women found him so attractive. At his age, his father had had the same irresistible appeal, and, indeed, still had it, but now another held his affections. For a moment Vanozza's full mouth tightened as she thought of Giulia Farnese, the beautiful Roman girl who had supplanted her position as Rodrigo Borgia's mistress. The irritation and anger passed quickly, however, for Rodrigo had been generous and had supplied her with all she needed, and had had constant attention to the future of her sons.

He mouth relaxed again, as she turned to Jofrè, her baby, young for marriage, and certainly too young for Sancia, that sophisticated and experienced bride who had been selected for him for political reasons, and there was something child-like and defenceless about him, which made the strong maternal instinct in Vanozza long to protect him from the intrigues and spite which swept about him.

Her glance travelled on to the distinguished upright figure of the Cardinal of Ceverna, who sat quietly sipping his wine, his faded eyes professing to ignore Gandia's blatant efforts to seduce his sister-in-law, and her excited laughter as she encouraged his ardour.

Next to him sat Juan, the Cardinal of Monreale, her nephew, as dear to her heart as her own sons; a thin, spare man, with deep-set eyes and a kind humorous mouth, who now watched Gandia's flirtation with an ironic eye.

At the end of the table sat her remaining guest, and although he was as much a part of the group as the others, he seemed strangely remote, as if he disclaimed all connection with them, and moved in a world detached from theirs.

As Vanozza's brown eyes rested upon him, her heart quickened and her firm mouth took on a softer line, for this was the dearest of her sons, the most beloved, the most cherished, the most bewildering.

The warm glow from the candles threw into sharp relief the beautiful contours of his pale face; the firm sweep of cheek and jaw, the straight nose, the line of the slender brows. His lids were half closed, barely shewing the lovely hazel eyes, and his well-shaped mouth was hard. Against the magnificence of his brothers' elaborate attire, his plain scarlet silk was austere, but he wore his Cardinal's robes with such grace and authority that he dominated his companions for all their grandeur.

Vanozza sighed as she watched his terse face. She knew how bitterly he hated the habit he wore, and how desperately he longed to be free from his priestly trappings and to turn instead to the steel and leather he was convinced he was born to wear. His tall, elegant figure was slim, but even at twenty-two, his shoulders had breadth and power, and his slender hands were incredibly strong. Vanozza's eyes held a momentary gleam of sadness. Rodrigo, who had fathered these three, and who now sat on the throne of St. Peter as Pope Alexander VI, was curiously stubborn about his eldest son.

It was on Gandia that he had fastened all his hopes and ambitions, and for whom he had sought and secured the brilliant alliance and the title which he now bore. Giovanni was the son who was to strengthen the Borgia dynasty, and who was to support and extend the power of the Papacy, and nothing would turn Rodrigo from this course.

For his eldest son he had reserved a career in the Church, and had stilled his protests and rage with vague promises of greatness to come, meanwhile softening the yoke of the unwanted office with vast wealth and the much sought after, and envied, title of Valencia.

Vanozza's mouth tightened again. In her view, Rodrigo, for all his native shrewdness and wisdom, had made a mistake in the disposition of his sons' futures. Gandia, attractive and gay, was also weak. He was a puppet, the strings of which his father could pull without resistance. If Alexander was determined to bring back to the Holy Church the rebel fiefs of the Romagna, and to send Giovanni, the Gonfalonier of the Church and Captain-General of the Papal Forces, to carry out this plan, he would have to direct his every move, and this would not be a simple matter for what could be planned with meticulous detail in the Vatican, could fail utterly and completely on the battlefield, if but one unexpected factor were encountered. Gandia, confronted by such an exigency, would crumble, for much as Vanozza loved him, she recognized the fatal flaw of weakness in him, and was conscious that he had none of the deep reserves of inner strength needed for the task he had been allotted.

Her eyes turned again to the Cardinal of Valencia, still lost in thought, his face the same inscrutable mask. Here was a different proposition. If he could but free himself from the Cardinalitial chains which bound him, there would be no doubt as to his success in combat, for he had in him a power and determination, of which Vanozza was fully aware without understanding it. There would be no need for a hand on the puppet strings here, for this man, for all his lack of years, needed no prop or support. From his childhood he had been self-reliant and self-contained, and something in him made all those about him uneasy, for what they could not comprehend, they distrusted.

They saw the force, but fearing it, they were not easy in his company. Only Vanozza, realizing her son's ruthless ambition, could get near to an appreciation of his frustration and anger as he watched his younger brother's feeble efforts to lead the Papal Forces, whilst he, whom nature had so richly endowed for such a purpose, was forced to take his seat in the College of Cardinals.

Suddenly Gandia turned from the voluptuous body of Sancia, to gaze at the Cardinal of Valencia and there was a spiteful gleam in his light blue eyes as he watched his brother's set face.

"My lord of Valencia is quiet tonight," he said, and the malice deepened. "What ails you, brother? Are you not looking forward to your visit to Naples to anoint and crown Don Federigo de Aragón? Surely you welcome the trust the Holy Father places in you for this difficult and delicate task?"

His face was flushed with the effect of wine too freely taken, and with the excitement Sancia had aroused in him.

For a moment there was silence, then the Cardinal of Valencia turned his head to look at Gandia.

"Nothing ails me." The voice was quiet, but under the softness of the tones there was an unmistakable quality, which angered Gandia, who heard it without being able to fathom its source. He had never understood this enigmatic brother of his, and had never been comfortable in his company, for despite the honours and power his father had showered upon him, in Valencia's presence, he felt himself to be his inferior, and his frustration at this inexplicable feeling lashed his anger to fresh spite.

"No? Yet you do not seem happy, brother. Doubtless you would prefer some less irksome task, such as the conquest of the Romagna, eh brother? What do you say to that? Would you not welcome this? But yet this is just a dream for you, is it not? For this is the brief His Holiness has given me, and for you it is but an idle vision. This is the task I must perform, is it not?"

He leaned back in the chair, and his hand sought Sancia's shoulder again. She gave a responsive chuckle as he smoothed her creamy skin with a careless touch, and he laughed.

"My task, is it not, brother?"

Valencia's amber eyes were expressionless as he surveyed Gandia's face, but there was something of contempt written on his mouth.

"Yours, indeed," he said calmly, "and I shall watch with interest your valour and skill on the battlefield. The chance is yours, my lord; let us see whether you know how to use it."

The scorn in the quiet voice made Gandia's colour rise further, and he jerked upright in his chair, his hand clenched round the stem of his goblet.

"You doubt me?" he asked sharply, "you think me incapable of what I set my hand to? You would do well to watch your tongue, brother, for you forget that I am the Gonfalonier of the Church."

"I do not forget your title," said Valencia laconically. "I have yet to see your measure, for if my memory serves me correctly, my lord, your essays in war have not so far been attended with great success."

Gandia rose in fury at this sly reference to his recent rout in battle, which had driven him back to Rome in great haste, and the slight injury he had sustained was nothing to the blow to his pride, which had done little to enhance the reputation he so eagerly sought.

"You forget yourself, my lord," he said harshly, "must I remind you again of my position? I will not be spoken to by a . . . a . . . Cardinal in this fashion. You forget; I am Giovanni Borgia."

The Cardinal of Valencia's eyes met his brother's, and for a long minute held them locked, then Gandia looked away, and Valencia said softly:

"And you forget, brother, that I am Cesare Borgia, and long after your name is forgotten, men will remember me."

Seeing the black rage on Gandia's face, Vanozza was about to pour oil on the troubled waters which were always stirred as these two met, when a servant appeared, followed by a man clad from head to foot in black, his face covered by a heavy mask. The servant bowed, and Gandia's colour gradually receded, leaving his face oddly white in the flickering candlelight. Valencia's eyes narrowed faintly, and then Gandia turned to his mother.

"You will forgive me?" he asked, and his voice was taut as if held in check by some strong emotion. "I must leave you."

Sancia pouted, and immediately began to protest, catching Gandia's velvet sleeve in a possessive grip.

His teeth shewed in a momentary impatience. "Madam, I have told you; I must go."

He glanced at Valencia, and some of the tension left him as the malice returned.

"I suggest you look to his Eminence of Valencia for comfort, for this will not be the first time, will it, and I am sure you will not mind returning to his arms, since I am to be otherwise engaged."

There was a brief shocked silence at Gandia's contemptuous reference to the affaire which had existed between Valencia and Sancia, and Vanozza said sharply:

"Giovanni! How dare you! If you must go, then be on your way, and God go with you."

She rose, and Gandia, slightly out of countenance by her sharp reprimand, allowed his mother to kiss him fondly on both cheeks.

"I am sorry." He smiled at her in a way which made Vanozza's crossness evaporate, for he was very young and charming, and she could not sustain her anger for long when he looked thus.

She shot a quick look at Cesare, but his face and eyes never betrayed his thoughts, and he appeared to have taken no notice at all of the jibe hurled by his brother, but Vanozza, knowing Cesare, was uneasy. That he shewed no reaction did not mean that he had remained unaffected, for he never gave any indication of his anger, but stored it up until the moment was ripe for retaliation.

Giovanni looked at Cesare and then at the man in black, and for a second, Vanozza had a queer feeling that Gandia was trying to draw from Cesare some of his strength, and she sensed intuitively that he was reluctant to go with the stranger, who stood so silently in the background.

Gandia gave a short laugh. "I must be gone. Cesare, do you come my way?"

Again Vanozza had the feeling that this was not merely a pleasantry; Giovanni wanted Cesare to go with him. Vanozza frowned. Who could this be; this stranger who had come to meet Giovanni? And this was not the first time she had seen him with Gandia. He had been visiting Giovanni regularly for the last month, and her servants, who were in constant touch with the servants at the Vatican, had remarked on the presence of this masked stranger who appeared to cause Gandia some disqiuet.

Cesare nodded. "As far as the Sforza Palace, at least. Mother." He turned to Vanozza. "I will come to see you immediately upon my return to Rome. Meanwhile, God keep you."

He bent and kissed her cheek, and she caught his hand.

"Cesare . . ." she looked into the clear, beautiful eyes and could not go on.

"Farewell, dearest," he repeated and smiled faintly, and then turned to bow to Sancia.

"Madam."

Sancia pouted again. She did not like being put aside by Giovanni and Cesare in this careless fashion, and had no intention of spending the evening with Vanozza, or with her boring young husband, and Juan was hardly likely to give her a second thought. She rose, and came to Cesare's side.

"Cesare, belovèd, you do not have to leave for Naples yet. Let us spend this evening together; you and I, and, of course, Jofrè." She cast a scornful glance at her husband, who was nibbling a sugared coriander seed, his blue eyes untroubled and uncaring of his wife's boredom and contempt.

Cesare looked at her, one brow raised.

"For what purpose, madam? We have made our farewells. What is left?"

Sancia bit her lip. Once Cesare had been passionate and eager for her embraces, and his indifference and coldness infuriated her, for although she had taken other lovers since Cesare, including Giovanni, none had measured up to the tall young Cardinal, who was such a strange mixture of fire and ice.

"T'would be interesting to see if you still amused me," she said, and her voice was sharp, for the light in his eyes was cool and mocking, and her temper mounted.

"T'would be even more interesting to see if you could amuse me, now that you have had more experience," drawled Cesare, and Sancia's eyes sparkled with fury. "But, alas, madam, I have things to do 'ere I leave Rome. I regret I cannot accept your invitation, but no doubt Juan and Jofrè will entertain you."

He bowed again, his lips marred by a faint sneer, and Sancia's colour rose dangerously.

"Cesare," she began, when Giovanni came back to his brother.

"Dio, Cesare, are you not coming; I must be away."

His face was still white and there was a line of sweat on his brow.

"Come, let us be gone," he said impatiently.

Cesare looked at him silently for a second, then bowed again to his mother and Sancia, and raised a hand to Juan.

"Very well; I am ready."

Vanozza watched them go. Both so tall and handsome and young. How lucky she was to have such sons, and lucky that Rodrigo shared this pride, and was prepared to go to such lengths to ensure their future. For Gandia, power, wealth and possessions; for Cesare. . . . Her frown returned. What for Cesare? The triple tiara one day? Even this was possible, but Cesare would reject it as he had rejected his Cardinal's hat, with the same impatience and scorn.

"I was not born for this," he had said of Vanozza, when his father had bestowed upon him the title of Valencia.

"I was not meant for this life, and you know it. I am a soldier, and one day I will free myself from this absurd cage my father has fashioned for me, and then you will see . . . he will see, what is my destiny."

Vanozza remembered the light in his hazel eyes, and the power of his clenched hands, and was frightened.

When Giovanni and Jofrè made predictions and promises, no matter with what heat and determination, she merely smiled indulgently, her placid demeanour unruffled by their words, but when Cesare made a promise, that was different, for what Cesare promised, Cesare did.

She watched them leave the garden with a sigh, and turned back to her remaining guests, her heart and mind sorely troubled by some indefinable worry she could not place.

At the entrance to the vineyard, Vanozza's servants were waiting with Gandia's horse and Cesare's mule, with a few of Giovanni's servants who had accompanied him to his mother's house, and when all were mounted, they set forth for the centre of Rome, the masked man following behind.

Cesare rode by Giovanni's side, and his quick glance noted the tight grip his brother had on the reins, the knuckles white as bone as he held the leather in his fingers. The hazel eyes narrowed again.

"Does something trouble you, Giovanni?" he asked quietly, and for a moment, Giovanni hesitated, as if he were considering confiding in Cesare, but the moment passed and he shook his head.

"No, nothing. What could there be to trouble me on such a night?"

"Only you could answer that," said Cesare, and Giovanni shot him a look.

"What do you mean? I tell you, nothing troubles me."

Cesare shrugged. "So be it. I am glad you are at ease, brother, for it would not do for the Gonfalonier of the Church to be disturbed by matters which do not concern his high task, for all his energies and attention must be devoted to this."

Again there was the slightest hesitation, but Giovanni's eyes dropped and he nodded.

"It will be so, brother; it will be so."

They rode on in silence until they reached the Sforza Palace, where Giovanni reined his horse to a halt.

"I must leave you here," he said, and his voice had lost its arrogance and assurance. "I wish you well in Naples."

Cesare looked at him quickly, but there was no mockery in Gandia's voice or glance now, and it was as if his mind had gone on to what lay ahead of him.

"I shall have no need of you tonight." Gandia waved an

abrupt hand to his servants. "You will come with me," he turned to one of his attendants. "The rest of you may go."

He cast an uncertain glance behind him. "Come sir." He nodded to the masked man, who came slowly forward to stand by Gandia's mount.

"Let us away."

He leaned down and helped the man on to his own horse, and raised his hand to Cesare in salute.

"Farewell, Cesare. God be with you."

"Farewell, Giovanni. God protect you."

Gandia turned sharply at Cesare's benediction, but as their eyes met, his looked away uneasily, and without further words, urged his horse forward into the darkness.

The attendants dispersed, whispering amongst themselves, leaving Cesare alone. After a while Cesare stirred, and turned his mule in the direction of the Ponte S. Angelo, and as he rode home through the still, calm night, he wore a preoccupied frown. He was thinking of Giovanni; of his hautiness and contempt at dinner, and his complete self-assurance which had been so suddenly deflated when the masked man had appeared, and Cesare had not misinterpreted the look in his brother's eyes when he had asked him to accompany him. Giovanni, the Captain-General of the Papal Forces, was afraid.

Cesare's frown deepened. Fear was not an emotion with which he himself was familiar. It was not in his nature or disposition to fear anything, for he never doubted for one moment his ability to deal with any situation which might arise, but he recognized it in others, and the terror in Giovanni's eyes had been unmistakable. For a moment, Cesare contemplated turning back to follow his brother, for despite their quarrels and the ill feeling between them, Giovanni was his brother, and a Borgia, and if he was in fear of his life, then it was incumbent upon Cesare to protect him, and to deal with whatever problem beset him. Then Cesare shrugged. Why should Giovanni be in fear of his life? He had dismissed his servants, which he surely would not have done had he expected an attack, and the whole of the Papal Army was at his command if he needed protection. No, possibly this was some clandestine affair in which Giovanni had become involved, and he had had a momentary spasm of unease at the thought of a husband's irate reaction; no more than that.

The next morning Gandia had not returned, and his servants reported his absence to the Pope, who smiled knowingly, for he was not unaccustomed to Giovanni's nocturnal absences, but when by nightfall, he had still not returned, some of the Pope's confidence disappeared, and he sent for Cesare.

As Cesare came through the Pontifical Chamber to bow low before his father, Alexander studied his son. He noted with a mixture of pride and caution the grace and arrogance with which the Cardinal walked. He loved Cesare, but even to himself he would not admit that his love was leavened with a measure of fear, for he recognized in Valencia something that was completely missing in Giovanni and Jofrè, whom he could control and guide with ease, and it was because of this unacknowledged fear that he kept Cesare safely imprisoned in the College of Cardinals.

Alexander sat upright on his throne, an imposing figure of majestic plumpness, his face still handsome though marred by an excess of flesh. His nose was strong and aquiline, his eyes black and bold, and his mouth more sensual than was fitting to his office.

He stretched out a hand to allow his son to kiss his ring.

"Cesare." He smiled, and his voice shewed nothing of his worry. "You are welcome, my son. Are you making preparations for your departure to Naples?"

Cesare's white teeth shewed briefly.

"Yes, Holiness. All is prepared for my vital and important mission."

The Pope continued to smile blandly, unmoved by Cesare's sarcasm.

"That is good, my child, for the task is an important one, and we send you in our stead, knowing your worth and ability to carry out this mission to our satisfaction."

Two lines appeared at the corners of Cesare's mouth, which

the Pope recognized as the forerunner of trouble, and he went on hastily:

"Now, Cesare, my child, there is another matter."

The lines disappeared, and the hazel eyes became calmer.

"Holiness?"

"Your brother, Giovanni. He has not returned, and his servants are concerned."

"And you, Holiness?" The mockery was slight, and the Pope decided to ignore it.

"And I, although no doubt 'tis one of Giovanni's women who has proved so demanding as to keep him at her side this long."

The Pope smiled, remembering his own youth, but then the amusement vanished.

"Yet 'tis late, Cesare. He should have returned 'ere now. When did you last see him?"

"Last night. We dined at our mother's house. We left together and rode as far as the Sforza Palace. There, Giovanni dismissed his servants, save one, and the man who had called to fetch him."

"What man?" The Pope's urbanity cracked slightly, and Cesare looked at him quickly.

"The man in the mask, Holiness. I understand this was not the first visit he had paid Giovanni. I am told he has called on him many times in the past month."

"Who is this man, Cesare, do you know?"

Cesare shook his head. "No. I do not know him. A messenger perhaps."

"From whom?" The Pope was sharp.

"From his demanding mistress." Cesare's tone was light, but the Pope's worry did not diminish.

"But why should he dismiss his servants? Why should he do this?"

"They are not actually necessary for a visit to one's mistress." Cesare's flippancy paid little heed to the reverence which was due to the Pope, for in truth he held his father in little reverence or respect.

"Yes, but——" Alexander broke off. "You did not see him

again?" he asked finally. "You did not see where he went?"

"In the direction of the Piazza degli Ebrei, and I did not see him again. Why are you so concerned, father; he will be back when he tires of the woman's charms."

"But so long, Cesare."

"Perhaps she is very beautiful, Holiness."

"Even so, time passes and I am worried, Cesare."

Cesare looked at his father with some irritation, for the Pope's passionate concern for Gandia did nothing to placate his fury at the position his father had forced him into, and he thought, somewhat acidly, that had he disappeared for a week, his father would scarcely have noticed it. In this, however, he was quite wrong, for Alexander loved Cesare greatly, and his motive in controlling him within the Holy Church had nothing to do with lack of affection.

"If he is not back by the morning, we must begin a thorough search," went on Alexander. "For if he has not returned by then, something must be amiss."

His black eyes were fearful.

"Nothing must happen to Giovanni, for our future power rests in him."

"Then God help us," said Cesare shortly, and the Pope frowned.

"Cesare! You forget yourself."

Valencia was unmoved by the rebuke.

"Father, how can you be so blind? Can you not see that Giovanni does not have that in him which will make us great? He is no soldier; he cannot win the Romagna for you. Is this not obvious to you?"

"He is the Captain-General of the Papal Army, and is well able to undertake any task I set him," returned the Pope sharply, and Cesare laughed without amusement.

"You delude yourself, Holiness. A title does not arm a man for an undertaking such as this. He must be born to lead; to control, to seize power and use it. Father, Giovanni does not have this in him, and I pray God you will see it before it is too late."

"Cesare! I will not have you talk so. I know well your

desire to set aside your sacerdotal robes and take to the field, but I will not have this. You are the Cardinal of Valencia, and will remain so. Your brother will lead the Papal Army, and he will succeed. I will see that he does."

The black snapping eyes had lost the worry and were almost angry as he met his son's.

"Nothing you say will turn me from this course, and you would do well to reconcile yourself to your lot, Cesare, for I shall not change my mind."

The anger died as he gazed at Cesare, for he could not control the surge of love and pride as he looked at his son's tall straight body and handsome face, now so cold with anger.

"But Cesare, one day . . . one day, you too will have the power you seek. When I die, the Holy Church will need a strong Pope to take my place, and you, my son, who better than you to succeed me?"

Valencia's hands clenched at his side. "Almost anyone would be better than I, father, for my destiny does not lie in the Church. I was not born for this, and one day you will have to accept this, for I will not fill this rôle forever, no matter what you say."

For a moment there was silence between them. The proud despotic Pope, who had met no resistance since he had first ascended the Papal Throne, and who was unused to argument and rebellion, and the determined Cardinal, who met his gaze so fearlessly. Then Alexander's eyes dropped, and a faint smile appeared on Cesare's lips.

"One day, father," he repeated softly, "one day, and not too distant, I will shew you what is my mettle and my intent."

With that, he bowed low, kissed the Pope's ring and strode through the chamber, his scarlet silk whispering softly across the floor. His father watched him go, and his mind was troubled.

He knew only too well that what Cesare said was true. He was no priest, this fiery young son of his. He was soldier through and through, but there was something else in him which frightened the Pope, and which, once released from the bonds of his Cardinalitial robes, might one day swamp the Papacy with its fierceness and power.

Alexander sighed and his worried thoughts went back to Giovanni's mysterious absence, and the nagging fear at the back of his mind grew alarmingly as the night went by.

CHAPTER TWO

On the morrow, Giovanni had still not returned, and the Pope, now unable to conceal his fears, instituted a thorough search of Rome. Most of Giovanni's friends and mistresses were known, and all who were likely to have seen him, were visited and questioned, but none could give any information which helped the searchers.

On the third day of Gandia's absence, the Pope, now frantic, intensified the search, and gave orders that sailors and fishermen should be summoned to drag the Tiber. Cesare watched the activities and frenzy of those about him in caustic silence, but when he saw the agony in his father's eyes, the lines appeared at the corner of his mouth again, and he turned away from the Pope in coldness.

Cesare was in his rooms at the Vatican when the news of his brother's reappearance was brought to him. The servant who carried the tidings bowed low to his Eminence of Valencia, and his face was white.

Valencia's brows rose slightly. "Well, Luis, what have you to tell me?"

The man was shaking, and his mouth could not form the words.

Cesare frowned. "What is it?" he repeated sharply. "My Lord Gandia has returned?"

"Eminence, I fear . . . I fear. . . ."

Cesare rose. "Where is my brother?" he asked shortly. "Speak, unless you wish me to loosen your tongue for you."

The servant's eyes dilated in fresh terror, for Valencia though a fair and just master, was not slow to exact instant obedience.

"My . . . my lord . . . I beg you . . . no . . . no. I . . .

I . . . it is terrible news, Eminence; the Duke of Gandia has been found."

"So? And this is bad news?" Cesare was still, with a deathly quietness, as if he had ceased to breathe.

"He is dead, my lord. His body was taken from the Tiber. The fishermen found him not an hour since; his throat was cut, and his body had been stabbed in nine places."

The silence in the room seemed interminable to the trembling servant, and finally he raised his fear-wracked eyes to look at Valencia.

The Cardinal's face was a mask, beautiful and without emotion. The man shivered, and Cesare looked down at him.

"You may go," he said quietly, and turned to walk to the window. At the door the manservant looked back. Valencia's lithe elegant form was silhouetted against the blazing noon sunshine flooding through the window, one hand resting on the jewelled dagger he wore at his slender waist, an unexpected and unusual adjunct to a Cardinal's garb. The man shivered anew. His Eminence did not move, and there was something terrifying about his controlled silence; with a gasp the man fled the room, his heart beating furiously.

Cesare gazed out of the window, a far-away look in his eyes. Gandia dead. The Gonfalonier of the Church and the Captain-General of the Papal Forces was no more. He smiled to himself, his mouth distorted by the movement. At last, Giovanni was out of the way. The Cardinal's eyes were icy cold. Gandia gone, and thus the way free. Valencia's hand left his dagger, and he turned in a swift graceful movement from the window.

He found his father overwhelmed with grief, tears pouring down his now ashen cheeks. Cesare bent his knee to the Pope, and for a fraction of time their eyes met; the black, stricken, tear-filled eyes of Alexander, and the cool, hazel eyes of Valencia, and the Pope shuddered in horror, for he thought he read in his son's clear gaze something so terrible that his mind could not support it. Then he dropped his face into his hands and started to weep again.

Cesare withdrew quietly and putting aside his Cardinal's robes, he mounted his coal-black charger and set out for a house a short ride from the centre of Rome.

In the gardens he found the girl he had come to see. She was small, but sweetly rounded, and her ash-blonde hair fell to her waist in a silken cloud. Her skin was milky white and smooth, her sky-blue eyes innocent and fringed with dark lashes. Rose lips parted in a smile of welcome as she saw Cesare, and she put aside the basket which held the flowers she had been gathering.

"My lord." Her voice was light and melodious, and she held out her hands to his Eminence, who crossed the trim grass in swift strides.

"Laura." He took the outstretched hands, and for a moment looked down at her. Then he took her in his arms, and his mouth was fierce upon hers.

She gave a faint laugh as he released her. "Cesare, my love."

She took his hand again. "Come, I beg you, let us go into the house, for it is some days since I have seen you, and there is much for us to talk about."

"Talk?" Valencia was mocking. "I did not come to talk to you, Laura, for there are many at the Vatican to whom I can talk. I have come to you for an entirely different reason."

She blushed, and he laughed sardonically.

"Come into the house, by all means," he said, but she hung back.

"Cesare, the news. It is terrible. It is said that the Duke of Gandia has been murdered. But, Cesare, who could have done such a thing? Is it yet known who the assassin is?"

Her azure eyes were filled with concern and pity for the dead Duke, and Cesare's smile vanished.

"No, it is not known, nor will it be. Now come, Laura, I have not come here to discuss my brother's death, unfortunate though it may be."

"But, Cesare, do you not care that Giovanni is dead?"

Cesare's mouth tightened in anger. "Yes, I care," he said,

and his eyes were alight with something Laura Montefiore did not understand, but which filled her with a sudden fear. "Yes, I care very much, for his death will make a great difference to me."

The Cardinal smiled; a smile of infinite terror, and Laura drew back instinctively.

"Cesare, why do you look thus?" she asked fearfully, and would have moved away from him, but his slim strong fingers closed round her wrist and jerked her close to him.

"Do not trouble yourself with this, Laura," he commanded, and his free hand twisted the flaxen hair through his fingers. "It is nothing which need cause you concern. And I feel I have discussed my brother's unfortunate demise enough for one day. I have come here to seek relaxation and amusement, not to conduct an enquiry into Giovanni's death."

The Cardinal's hand tightened on Laura's wrist, and she winced, for his grip was painful, and he knew it.

"Come," he repeated, but still she hesitated.

"Cesare," she began again, when he lost patience and swept her up in his arms.

"Very well, madam, if you will not walk, I will carry you," he said shortly, and without further words, took her into the house.

When he returned to the Vatican, he found the Pope had retired to his private apartments, and was refusing to see anyone, or to accept food or wine.

Cesare shrugged and went about his own business, and started the final preparations for his journey to Naples, whilst about him, the rumours and gossip as to the murderer of his brother grew and grew. Certain names began to emerge. Giovanni Sforza was an obvious target, for he had good cause to hate the Borgias, who had made him the laughing stock of all Italy by their insistence that Lucrezia's marriage to him should be dissolved on grounds of his impotence. Jofrè was mentioned as a possibility, the motive in his case ascribed to his jealousy of Gandia's attentions to his wife, but this was not a rumour which lasted long, for no one seriously imagined the child-like Jofrè either cared enough about Sancia, or had the ability to contrive the murder with such masterly care.

The Orsini were also named, and Cardinal Ascanio Sforza was known to have quarrelled with Gandia, but gradually this gossip also died, and through the silence a new name was whispered. At first it was merely a thread of sound; mentioned cautiously in despatches from those living a safe distance from Rome, but gradually the whispers got louder and more convincing, and all Rome grew cold as it contemplated the suggestion now laid before it, for this theory held water. All were agreed that the murder had been planned by someone who had both skill and cunning, and who feared nothing. There was only one person who fitted this bill, and there was horror and fear in the eyes that met Cesare's. Valencia, however, was unmoved by the gossip, and continued his plans without interruption, but when he left Rome for Naples on the 22nd July, it was noted that he had not seen his father since Gandia's death, and this fact seemed to the scandalmongers a confirmation of the ugly story of fratricide with which his name was linked. The Pope was silent.

After his outburst of grief, and his tortured cry that had he seven thrones, he would gladly have renounced them all in exchange for the life of his son, he had said little, and whether the rumours of Cesare's guilt reached him, none knew, but as he gradually abandoned any pretence of looking for Gandia's murderer, it was assumed by all that in fact he knew the assassin's name.

Thus matters stood until the beginning of September, when Cesare returned to Rome. At the Monastery of Santa Maria Nuova, all the Cardinals in Rome gathered to meet the Papal Legate, and after Mass had been celebrated, a procession was formed, and the Cardinals moved in solemn state to the Vatican.

The atmosphere in the Pontifical Chamber was charged with emotion, and apprehension. Alexander, still drawn and white, sat on his throne surrounded by prelates, courtiers and secretaries, and as the doors were flung wide to admit the

Cardinal of Valencia, the silence deepened and the tension mounted.

As Valencia appeared in the doorway, erect and proud in his scarlet robes, the crowd fell back, to leave a space through the centre of the chamber, and with calm assurance and self-possession, the Cardinal walked slowly to his father's throne.

The Pope's eyes fell as Cesare bowed low, and there was the faintest sigh throughout the chamber as the Pope rose and silently embraced his son.

When the ceremonies were over, the Pope and Cesare were left alone. Alexander's hands were not entirely steady and he had difficulty in meeting Cesare's eyes.

"You have done well, my son," he said finally, "I am told you gave a good account of yourself in Naples."

Valencia bowed slightly. "I am glad that this should be so, Holiness," he said formally. "For it is my will to please you."

The Pope shot him a quick glance, but the Cardinal's face gave nothing away, and the Pontiff's restless fingers twisted his ring about his plump forefinger.

"And now," he began, when Cesare turned to him.

"And now, Holiness, you will attend me," he said, and the startled black eyes met the blaze of his son's amber ones.

"Now, father, you will listen to me."

On August 17th, 1498, the Cardinal of Valencia robed himself in scarlet silk for the last time. On this occasion, he forebore to add the small sharp dagger he was wont to wear, and his manner was grave and solemn, but underneath his unshakable poise, there was a glint of satisfaction which shewed only slightly in his hazel eyes.

A hand strayed to the jewelled crucifix he wore on his breast as he glanced at his gentlemen assembled in his chamber.

"T'will not be long now," he said, "and I shall be free. Free to take up the sword to release the Holy Church from ridicule, and to make her great."

"The Holy Church, Eminence?" asked Pietro Santa Croce slyly, and Cesare laughed.

"But yes, of course. Certainly the Church will benefit from what the Holy Father and I propose. Now 'tis but a matter for laughter in the taverns, and men hold Her in scant respect." The smile was gone. "When I have done, there will be no laughter."

The Cardinal's mouth was hard, and Mario di Mariano looked at him curiously.

"This is in no doubt, my lord," he said, and meant it, for he had a very clear idea of Cesare's ability, untried and untested though it was. "But what of you, Eminence? When the Romagna is taken, what part will you play then, for this action will merely bring back to the Holy Church its fiefs which have so long rebelled against it. What then for you?"

The slight smile returned, and Cesare's hand tightened over the crucifix.

"The world is not bounded by the Romagna, Mario, nor yet by Tuscany. For he who is prepared to seize power, there are no limits."

"Tuscany?" Domenico Sanguigna was startled. "You look beyond the Romagna, my lord?"

"Far beyond." Cesare turned to look at the group of young men, and his eyes were amused as he surveyed them.

Giangiordano Orsini, Pietro Santa Croce, Mario di Mariano, Domenico Sanguigna, Bartolomeo Capranica, Giulio Alberini, Gianbattista Mancini. Young, wealthy, well-born and eager for blood. The smile deepened. This, at least, his father had arranged to his satisfaction; the gathering round his son of the scions of some of the great patrician families. And there was much in them which appealed to Cesare. They had spirit and fire, and were unswervingly loyal, and would be invaluable when he moved against the rebels.

Cesare laughed slightly as he saw the amazement in their eyes.

"You seem surprised, Domenico, but why? Why should I stop at the Romagna? You have seen the folly of divided states; you can see for yourself what Italy is today. She cannot stand against France or Spain for she is weak and feeble and torn by internal strife, but this does not have to be. She could be strong; strong enough to rebuff France or Spain or both, and so she will be. This is no idle dream. I am not playing at war as my brother Giovanni did; I am in earnest, for what Orleans can do, so can I."

His lip curled as he contemplated Louis XII, the Duc de Orleans, who had succeeded to the throne of France when Charles VIII, the stunted, crippled young king, had died suddenly as a result of what had appeared to be a minor accident.

Giulio Alberini gave a quick exclamation. "But, sire, you go to France 'ere long to wed a Princess of the King's choosing. I though you sought an alliance with his Majesty."

The Cardinal smiled again, and there was something of affection in his eyes as he looked at the handsome young man who stared at him in such consternation.

"I do, Giulio, I do, but not for Louis' benefit, but for my own. It will be slow, for this is not a thing which can be achieved quickly. We shall have to be patient and suffer much delay and frustration, but I am convinced 'tis the only way, despite the Holy Father's desire to cling to our Spanish alliances."

He glanced at the group again. "No, through France we will achieve our will, and if it takes time, then time we have to spare, for the years are on our side. Yet I pray it will not take unduly long for I am weary of the rôle Italy plays in the game of power, and I would seek an early conclusion to her subservience."

Pietro Santa Croce smiled suddenly. "When you speak thus, my lord, nothing seems impossible. Italy has not known greatness since Caesar; 'tis time she took her rightful place again, and I for one give you my sword and life most willingly for this task."

"And I, Eminence, and I," broke in Mario di Mariano, and was joined by a chorus of eager voices as his companions moved nearer to Cesare, fired by the strength of purpose they saw in him, and the vision of greatness he had spread before them.

"I thank you," said Valencia quietly. "I shall be in need of men such as you, and I value your loyalty and service. You will not find me ungrateful. And now." He straightened his shoulders. "Now, 'tis time I took the first step."

His fingers stroked the stiff silk. "I will rid me of these dull and useless garments, and then," the amber eyes lit again, "and then, signores, we will begin our task."

Before the Sacred College, the Cardinal of Valencia laid his plea to be allowed to return to the secular life, and for once, the silent Cardinal, who usually had so little to say, pleaded eloquently for his release.

"I have never sought ecclesiastical offices," he said as he confronted the assembled Cardinals, "my father gave me no choice, but forced me into a life for which I was not fitted, as all of you know."

"That at least is true," said Cardinal Ximenes sourly, but in an undertone, to his neighbour, "for this young man is old in crime and sin, and a disgrace to the Church, yet he should not be allowed to set aside his calling in this fashion, and I shall oppose it."

Cardinal Correlli snorted. "Oppose it as you will, it will not stop the Pope, and your opposition is dictated by Spain's interests, and not by a sound judgement of the facts. The Sacred College will be well rid of such a man, for he brings dishonour to us all."

They both turned to listen to Valencia, who had started to speak again.

"It is my desire to return to a secular life, and to serve the Holy Church as a soldier, for in this I will be of some use; in my present office I am not. I therefore beg your Eminences to support my plea to the Holy Father to allow me to put aside my habit and grant me a dispensation to return to the lay life, so that I may serve you in this way, and may also contract marriage, for this alliance will serve you well."

"T'will serve Valencia better," said Ximenes cynically, "for Carlotta of Aragon and a Duchy are prizes which will more than compensate the good Cardinal for the loss of revenues from his benefices. I shall vote against it."

And this he did, but his voice was a lone one, and the Pope, to whom the Sacred College left the decision, was firm but benign.

"My dear Ximenes," he said in his rich, calm voice. "Can it be that you would wish to stand between Valencia and his soul's salvation? You have heard the Cardinal confess that his mode of life is not worthy of his office, and I doubt not that it is too late for him to mend his ways, and thus it seems to me that we have little choice but to release him. And furthermore." The deep voice purred, and the dark eyes were guileless as they raked the indignant Cardinal Ximenes.

"All of the Cardinal of Valencia's benefices will accrue to Spain, for after all, it is right and proper that Valencia's wealth should not be severed from Spanish interests. Now what do you say, Eminence?"

The Pope was not really interested in Ximenes' answer, for his decision was already made, but he did not wish unduly to disturb his relationship with Spain, and the promise of the transfer of Cesare's wealth to Spanish churchmen was to placate the anger of Ferdinand and Isabella, who were far from happy at the proposed union of Italian and French interests.

Rodrigo was not entirely happy either. As a Spaniard, he had a natural affinity to Spain, and distrusted France, and Louis in particular, but from the day Cesare had confronted him and laid his final demands before him, he had found himself unable to withstand his dominant son, and when Cesare had insisted on the French alliance, Rodrigo had no weapons with which to fight him.

The alliance had been made simple in that Louis XII sought an annulment of his marriage with Jeanne de Valois, with whom he claimed a relationship of the fourth degree, and with whom he had never had a desire for marriage.

Furthermore, he pleaded that Jeanne was incapable of bearing a child, and thus the throne of France would have no heir, unless this marriage, which was in fact no marriage at all, were set aside. Louis' eye had already fastened on Jeanne's successor, Anne of Brittany, Charles VIII's widow, who was comely, capable of child bearing, and possessed of rich estates, and he pressed the Pope to give sympathetic consideration to the injustice of his position.

The Pope set up a Commission to consider the case, whilst he withdrew to contemplate the situation from his own point of view. Cesare would need a title when he returned to the lay life, and the Pope was not slow in seeing advantage in Louis' plea for a dispensation, for overwhelmed though he might be by the forceful personality of his son, he was still shrewd and perspicacious, and saw in this entreaty from the French king, a golden opportunity to furnish Cesare with the Duchy he needed.

Valence and Diois, territories over which the Vatican had had control for many years, were, nevertheless, a source of dispute between the Vatican and France, and Rodrigo, with a cunning and astuteness which made even Cesare smile, offered the suggestion that the Vatican should now relinquish its claim upon these states, and that Louis should raise the County of Valence to a Duchy and confer it upon Cesare.

Louis had smiled wryly, but had accepted the terms, throwing in for good measure his own request that Georges d'Amboise, the Bishop of Rouen, should be given a Cardinal's hat, together with a plea that he should be granted a dispensation to marry Anne of Brittany.

Thus, Cesare became a layman, and as he left the Sacred College and walked across the soft green lawns surrounding the mellow brick buildings, his eyes were coolly satisfied. Even in this moment of triumph, when, after so long, he had achieved his greatest desire, there was no emotion in him. Where another man's heart would have sung with joy, Cesare's remained unmoved. Only his ice-cold brain registered his victory, and calculated with frigid precision the effect this freedom would have upon his plans.

In the house in the Trastevere, Cesare removed his robes,

and for one moment held them in his hand, his eyes expressionless as he estimated the time lost by their restrictions. Then he flung them from him, and donned a velvet suit, embroidered and jewelled, and slipped a gem-encrusted belt round his waist. It was ornamental and costly, but also functional, for it held a diamond studded sheath housing a wickedly sharp dagger, which Cesare's hand sought automatically as he moved to the door. He looked back once, to gaze for a last time at the crumpled heap of silk, and with a faint smile closed the door of his chamber quietly behind him.

When news came that Louis' fleet, which had come to escort the Duke of Valence to France, had dropped anchor at Ostia, Cesare went to Laura Montefiore to bid her good-bye.

She received him in the sala overlooking her green, sun-stroked garden.

He bowed gracefully and took her hand, and there were tears in her eyes as she curtsied to him.

"My lord," she murmured, and her voice was low and filled with sadness, for much to her surprise, the affaire she had started with Cesare as an antidote to boredom, had resulted in her losing her heart to him, and at this moment of final farewell, she was desolate.

"Tears, Laura?" he asked, and drew her to a nearby couch. "Come, this will not do. Do you not rejoice that I now go to claim my duchy?"

A tear coursed down her cheek. "Of course," she said, "but you also go to claim your Duchess, my lord."

Cesare smiled. "A marriage of convenience; nothing more. Do you imagine it will affect my feelings for you?"

She looked up into the Duke's handsome face, and read there the truth she could no longer escape.

"You have no feelings for me, Cesare," she said quietly, "you have never had any feelings for me. You merely took me for your pleasure; there was never any more than that." Cesare's brows rose slightly, for he had not thought this pretty, simple girl had the perception to see this somewhat obvious truth.

"My dear, this is not so," he said, and took her in his arms. "You have pleased me greatly, and there is no reason why our association should not continue when I return to Rome."

"If you return." Laura had not relaxed, and Cesare laughed gently.

"Oh, I shall return, cara, never fear. I shall return, and then I will come to visit you again."

"I may not be here, my lord." Laura freed herself from his hold and stood up. "I may be leaving Rome."

"So? Where are you going, cara?"

She raised her chin defiantly. "I may go to Florence, for there my uncle dwells, and he is anxious that I should go to him. He has long desired that I should marry my cousin Ludovico."

Cesare smiled. "It seems we are both contemplating matrimoney. And this union will please you?"

His tone was light, and Laura's colour rose slightly.

"Why not? Ludovico is young and comely, and his family is wealthy. He will be good to me."

For a second there was silence, then Cesare took her hand.

"And this is all you seek, Laura? Wealth, and a personable husband who will guard you well? Do you look for nothing else? For love? For excitement? For passion? Such as you find with me?"

She bit her lip and would not look at him.

"You do not love me, my lord. This much is obvious."

The Duke smiled again.

"But you, Laura. Do you love me; that is what is important."

She turned away with a sob, but his hand still held hers, and he jerked her back, forcing her to her knees in front of him.

"Answer me," he said, and her eyes darkened slightly at his tone.

"I . . . I . . ." she began, when he caught her shoulders and looked down at her pale face.

"Answer me," he repeated, and she felt her will melt as she looked into his tawny eyes.

"Oh Cesare." Her voice broke, and he gave a low laugh.

"You will not go to Florence, Laura; you will wait here until my return. Is this understood?"

Her eyes closed and she was silent.

The iron fingers tightened and she gave a gasp of pain.

"Is this understood?"

Finally she nodded and her bemused gaze met his again.

"Good." The Duke smiled coldly and released her. "When I tire of you, you may go to Florence, but until then, you will remain in Rome. Now come here, for I cannot stay long as there is much to do before I join Louis' fleet. It is important that I prepare well for this journey, for the eyes of France will be upon me, and I must ensure that our estate is well understood."

He took her in his arms again, and this time she did not resist him.

"You were not entirely correct in your assessment," he said gently as he looked down at her. "You are very beautiful, my dear, and if you held none of my affection, why should I wish to seek to keep you with me? Why should I prevent your folly in seeking an alliance with your good cousin?"

She swallowed with difficulty. "Perhaps because you will allow none to cross your will, Highness," she said in a low voice. "Because it must always be you who decides when such affaires shall end."

"You are becoming too astute, Laura," he said, and she heard the steel under his soft words. "It does not become you. You were not made for verbal fencing, and you would be well advised to forswear this pastime.

She shivered, for she was aware that although Cesare was reluctant to terminate their relationship at this moment, should she seriously displease him, her life would be forfeit.

There had been ugly rumours of other women who had rebelled against the careless but demanding Cardinal, and those women had suffered sharp and final punishment at his hands, and she did not doubt that Cesare would deal with her in like fashion should he become angered.

"Yes, my lord," she said submissively, and the anger died in Cesare's eyes.

"Better," he said coolly, and his hand tilted her chin. "Much better."

He bent to kiss her, and she felt the familiar desire leap in her as he drew the silk gown from her shoulders.

CHAPTER THREE

CESARE'S departure from Rome on the 1st October was spectacular. The Pope had spared no expense in preparing his son for the visit to France, and was determined that the French King should fully understand Cesare's status.

All Rome had been agog with the excitement of the preparations, and had exclaimed in awe and wonder at the magnificent clothes and jewels which were fashioned for the new Duke of Valence and his retinue. Even the luxury-loving princes of Rome were startled by the sumptuous display which Rodrigo and Cesare produced to impress the French Court.

The Duke left Rome in the early hours of the morning, and his company comprised a hundred attendants, Ramiro de Lorqua, Master of his Household; Agapito Gherardi da Amelia, his secretary, and Gaspare Torella, his physician. The young noblemen who had pledged their lives and swords to his service on the day he sought release from his Cardinal's vows, formed his escort of honour, and in addition, there was a mounted guard of considerable grandeur and force.

All were richly garbed and splendidly mounted, but none overshadowed the young Duke who rode with such assurance in the midst of this dazzling company. His black steed was caparisoned in crimson silk and golden brocade in a token of respect to the French, whose colours they were, and his servants also wore the red and yellow of France.

Cesare's white doublet was trimmed with gold, and thrown over his shoulder was a black velvet cloak which matched the cap on his auburn head. The jewels he wore would have supported an army for months, the most magnificent being the huge rubies set in the velvet cap, and the diamonds he wore on his breast. His velvet gloves, black as his cloak, were relieved by sparkling diamond drops, and his velvet boots trimmed with gold cord and diamonds.

For all his cold calculation, or perhaps because of it, Cesare had never under-estimated the value of display and pageantry, and even as a Cardinal, had been in the habit of attiring himself and his attendants in lavish style and riding through Rome to excite the interest of the populace, a course which was in marked contrast to his normal reticence and secrecy. By enigmatic silences, and sudden outbursts of brilliant display, did Cesare Borgia hold Rome's attention, and now he sought to entrance the French in the same manner.

The Pope watched his progress from the window of the Vatican, and there were tears in his eyes as Cesare was lost to sight. He had completely recovered from his grief at Gandia's death, for he was mercurial by nature, and the whole of his energy and passion was now devoted to Cesare's cause, and his heart was bursting with pride as he watched his son ride from Rome. If a small, still voice warned him of the lethal nature of his offspring, he quelled it sharply under his affection and exultation at Cesare's beauty and power.

He refused to admit to himself that he was no longer master of Rome; that the young ex-Cardinal had now gained the upper hand, and ruled Rome and the Vatican with an iron fist behind the Papal Throne. He contented himself with joy and delight that his belovèd son was now setting forth to claim his duchy in France, and to wed a French princess, and his heart was too full for words as he turned from the window.

Cesare's cavalcade through France caused a sensation, for the French had none of the glittering extravagance of the Italians, and were overwhelmed by the display which met their eyes. Tongues wagged long over the retinue the Duke brought with him, and they stared aghast at the sumptermules laden with the chests and coffers bound with strips of gold and silver. Their jaws dropped as they beheld the scintillating brilliance of the entourage as it wound its way through the countryside, and the final touch to the magic was the golden shoes with which Cesare's mount was shod, and the mules similarly decked, for as these precious shoes were cast, they were left for the bewildered and bemused peasants to collect.

Cesare's entry into Chinon, where he was to meet Louis, was the finale of a journey which had stirred the imagination of the French, and if there were some nobles who sneered at the effrontry and splendid elegance of the Duc de Valence, Cesare merely smiled, for he knew better than they, the effect and value of such shows, and was in any event contemptuous of the meagre, sparse and frugal court of the King of France.

Louis welcomed Cesare warmly, and hid any scorn he may have felt for the pretentious appearance of his guest's court, but it was not long before Cesare discovered that Carlotta of Aragon was not prepared to bend to the King's will and accept Cesare's hand in marriage. Her refusal was emphatic and final, and in this she was supported by her father, Federigo, a support which ultimately was to cost him his kingdom, and for a time it seemed as if the carefully hatched plans of Alexander and Louis were destined to failure, and that Cesare, who was daily growing more impatient, would return to Italy unwed, but then Louis, with his eye on the tottering alliance of France and the Vatican, contrived to bring about another proposal, that of the hand of Charlotte d'Albret, daughter of Alain d'Albret, Duc de Guyenne, and sister of the King of Navarre. She was seventeen years of age, and famed for her beauty and gentleness, yet she too shrank from marriage with the formidable Italian prince, whose reputation had preceded him to France, but she had none of the determination of her namesake, and furthermore, her father was prepared, for a price, to give his daughter in marriage to the Pope's son.

Thus, when her rapacious father had wrung the last advantage from the marriage bargain, Charlotte, suitably escorted and chaperoned, made her way to Blois, where the wedding was to take place, and as she travelled over the rough, uneven roads, her heart was as heavy as the laden chests and caskets which accompanied her train.

All the rich adornments and clothes which had been provided for the Prince's bride did nothing to lessen to one degree the terror and repugnance she felt at the thought of the forthcoming nuptials. The horrifying stories she had heard of the Duc de Valence filled her with cold fear, and her blue eyes had a frozen look as she gazed at the passing countryside, now bursting with Spring. Her mind refused fully to accept what had been done to her; she could not bring her paralysed imagination to dwell upon what awaited her at Blois. She only knew she travelled towards something so devastating, that life, as she had known it, was at an end.

Her companions, as young and pretty as she, tried to comfort her, but there was little they could say, for they too were aware of the bloody history of the terrible Duc, and shared fully Charlotte's revulsion to the match.

"It is said that he killed his own brother," said Charlotte suddenly, and a tremor of fear went through the party. "He stabbed him and threw him into the Tiber." Her eyes darkened, and Louise Duprès, one of the less excitable and more stable members of the group, leaned forward and patted her hand.

"There is no proof of this chèrie. There were countless rumours about the Duke of Gandia's death, and many were accused. The Duc de Valence was not the only one who had reason to wish him dead, and his guilt is by no means certain. After all," she added reasonably, "is it likely that the Holy Father would have allowed him to escape retribution for such a crime, for he doted on Gandia?"

Charlotte turned her head and smiled faintly at Louise's round, sensible face.

" 'Tis said the Pope cannot control the Duc; that the Duc now rules the Pope and the Vatican, and that the Holy Father did not seek to punish his son because he is afraid of him. And so am I." Her voice fell to a whisper on the last words. "Oh God; so am I."

A tear fell on the clasped hands in her lap, and Louise gave a quick exclamation.

"Oh beloved, do not distress yourself so. It may not be as dire as you think, for he is a powerful man, destined for great things, so they say, and you will be by his side to rise to these heights. Many would envy you your rôle."

Charlotte checked a sob. "Envy me? Envy my life tied to a brute . . . a monster like Valence? He is said to be without mercy or compassion, and is a man of great cruelty and cunning. And so strong that he can snap a horseshoe in his fingers," she added inconsequentially.

Her eyes darkened again, and her lower lip quivered.

"Oh, Louise, how can I bear this; how can I endure this life?"

She buried her face in her hands, and Louise Duprès put her arms round her and held her close, her own heart heavy with the fears she felt for her friend, for talk as she might, she knew only too well the reputation of the Duke, and was sick with dread at the fate which awaited the slender lovely Charlotte at his hands.

Even the May sunshine which greeted Charlotte when she awoke in the apartments at the Château de Blois the next morning did nothing to ease the load from her mind, and she dressed slowly and without interest, brushing her warm brown hair which flowed round her shoulders like satin.

She refused food and wine, and amidst the protests of her maids and companions, left the Château to walk in the gardens.

"I want to be alone," she told them, to still their arguments. "Soon, I shall not be alone; I shall be the prisoner of the Duc de Valence. Allow me this last moment of freedom, I beg you."

And they had no words left to stop her, as she sped quickly over the shallow stone steps to the velvet green lawns which rolled down to a small stream running under a clump of trees.

The morning was cool and shining, with a promise of warmth to come, and in spite of her black depression, something of the beauty of the garden and the soft May breeze lifted the care a little as Charlotte made her way to the stream. Here she found a fallen log, and sat down, her white silk gown falling in graceful folds about her small silver slippers. In the clear water she could see her reflection as in a mirror; eyes large and sad, mouth full and meant for laughter, now set in lines of grief. She shuddered suddenly as she thought of the morrow, when the marriage was to take place, and hard as she tried to blot out the thoughts which crowded into her mind, she saw again, in shadowy imagination, the brute figure of the Duke who was to claim her, and her fingers tore at the silken handkerchief she held in her hands.

Suddenly there was a sound of horse's hooves, dulled by the thickness of the green turf, and Charlotte raised her head quickly to watch the advent of the rider. He swung his horse, a magnificent white steed, round a curve in the path leading to the Château, and the next minute was almost upon her.

She stared up at him, and her eyes widened slightly as she looked at him.

He wore a simple hunting costume, his auburn hair uncovered, and she found herself responding to his warm smile.

"Madonna." He bowed low, and quickly dismounted, with a lithe ease and came to her side.

"Madonna." He bowed again, and his tawny eyes were filled with an admiration which made slight colour touch Charlotte's pale cheeks.

"I had not thought to find such beauty on my morning ride. I account myself the most fortunate of men that my excursion should have been so blessed."

Her colour deepened, and he laughed faintly.

"And you are enchanting when you blush," he added, and she turned her face away in confusion.

The man came nearer and bent slightly to take her hand. She found herself raised to her feet, and with difficulty looked up into the stranger's handsome face.

"But why so sad, Madonna, and on such a morning as this?" His glance was quizzical, and she found it hard to stop her hand shaking in his firm hold.

"I . . . I . . ." she began, when he smiled slightly.

"Can it be, Madonna, that you suffer from an affaire of the heart, for surely only love, or rather lack of it, could bring this look to such an exquisite face?"

Her face blanched, and his eyes narrowed faintly.

"Madonna?"

She shook her head silently, and he led her back to the log and sat beside her.

"Tell me," he said quietly, "what brings this unhappiness to you, for if it is in my power to undo this wrong, my pleasure is only this. Tell me what causes you this grief."

"Sire." She took a grip on her trembling emotions, and met his steady look. "You cannot help me; no one can, for my destiny has been fashioned for me in such a way that no man, however kind or bold, can do ought to release me from the fate which lies in store for me."

"Nothing is inevitable," said the man gently. "That which man contrives, man can undo, if the will is strong enough. What has fate designed for one so beautiful which causes such sadness to mar her face?"

She shook her head. "I . . . I . . . cannot explain, sire, but I can assure you that what has been settled, cannot be undone. It is too late."

"It is never too late, Madonna, and since I am a stranger why should you not tell me the cause of your sorrow, so that I may share it, and perhaps lighten it for you?"

"A stranger?" She looked at him quickly. "Yes, of course, you are not French, although you speak my tongue with fluency. Do you come from . . . from . . . Italy. With the Duc de Valence's train?"

Her voice trailed off, and he saw the pain in her eyes again, and his brows met in a sudden frown.

"Yes. I have come from Italy, but why does the thought of my fair country cause such pain, Madonna? What ill has come to you from my country?"

" 'Tis not your country, sire, which causes me pain, but. . . ."

"But the name of the Duc de Valence," he finished softly. "Yes, I see."

His hand moved to the golden medallion he wore round his neck, the only ornament to break the severity of the deep green habit.

"You are Charlotte d'Albret." It was not a question, and her eyes flew to his, her lips parting slightly.

He saw the amazement and smiled without amusement.

"It is known that the Duc has come to France to wed; that a marriage has been arranged between Alain d'Albret's daughter and the Duc, and now I see the fear and sadness in your eyes, it can only mean one thing. But why do you fear the Duc so much? You have not seen him yet, have you? Why, then, does his name cause you so much terror?"

She shivered. "His name causes many terror. His reputation is well known, sire, for he is a fearful man; wicked and of great strength and cruelty. He is said to stop at nothing to gain his ends, and my father has sold me to him. Do you wonder that I dread tomorrow when we are to be wed?"

The man's mouth relaxed slightly, and there was the faintest trace of amusement in his eyes as he looked at her.

"When a man is powerful, madonna, there are always those who will speak ill of him. Jealousy and fear weave rumours faster than deeds. The Duc may not be a saint, but he is a human being, not a devil, and thus he will be moved by your youth and beauty. You need have no fear; you will come to no harm at his hands."

"But you do not understand." Her blue eyes were agonized as they met his still face. "I am to wed this man. He will possess me; I shall be his chattel to do with as he will, and I am filled with horror at the thought of his huge brutal hands upon me."

The man's slender white hand closed over hers again.

"Someone has filled your head with a lot of nonsensical tales, Madonna," he said gently. "The Duc is not a monster, but a mortal of normal aspect."

"No, no, this is not so, for he is of abnormal strength." Her eyes lit with fresh fear. "He can bend an iron bar and break a new rope in his hands. Consider the strength needed for this, sire, and these same hands will take me tomorrow. Oh God, I cannot face this."

She put her hands over her face to blot out the revulsion, and he caught her wrists and pulled her hands away from her tear-filled eyes.

"This is folly," he began, when she gave a cry:

"No, no! 'Tis not. He is a gross, evil brute; oh how can I expect you to understand?"

"I understand only too well, Madonna," he said grimly. "Your mind is clouded with nightmares which do not exist in reality. Your fears are groundless, and you are torturing yourself for no reason. Now, attend me."

The grip on her wrists tightened, and she winced at his strength. Seeing the pain on her face, he released the hold, and took her hands in his.

"I give you my promise, Madonna," he said slowly. "You have nothing to fear from Valentinois. He will find you exquisite, and as a lover of beauty, will hold you in great esteem, and will care for you for all your days."

"You jest, sire." Her pale cheeks took on colour again. "This man cares for none; this at least is well known. I am nothing more to him than a pawn in the game he and the Pope play for high stakes. They used the Madonna Lucrezia without compassion or thought to advance their plans; why then should they hesitate to use a stranger. I fear, sire," her voice became hard, "you place too much value on the Duc's motives."

The hazel eyes were cold. "Madonna Lucrezia? What have you heard of her?"

She looked up quickly at his tone. "You know her?"

"I know her." The quiet voice was expressionless. "What tale has been told of her?"

"That she is a wanton." Her eyes dropped to her restless hands again, and thus missed the tightening of the man's mouth. "A wanton who would sell herself to any man, and there is a rumour . . ." she flushed and stopped herself abruptly.

"That she sold herself to her brother?" His voice was harsh, and she could not meet his eye.

"It is not true," he said after a pause. "She is gay and lovely, and far from wanton."

"You know her well, sire?" Charlotte found courage to look at him again, and shivered slightly at what she read in his face.

"I know her well," he said without emphasis, and she looked back at the trickling stream at her feet.

"Yet 'tis true that the Pope and her brother arranged her marriage for political reasons, is it not?"

He shrugged. "Such things are not unknown, yet Lucrezia is not unhappy. She is filled with joy and happiness; you need not waste your sympathies upon her, for she needs no tears shed over her."

There was silence between them for a while, then Charlotte stirred.

"I must return to the Château," she said, and suddenly smiled at him, the movement lighting her face to even greater beauty.

"You have been kind to me, sire, and I give you my thanks. I am sorry to have burdened you with my troubles, and I am grateful to you for your patience in listening to my woes."

The hardness had gone from his face as he raised her, and his gaze was warm again.

"It has been no burden, Madonna. And I say again, your fears are groundless, as you will see."

She shook her head. "This I doubt, but thank you for trying to comfort me. I must face what lies ahead with such courage as I can muster, and I pray God I may accept it with dignity."

"I think you will," he said gently, and raised her hand to his lips.

"I have not asked your name, sire," she said, and the amusement in his eyes deepened.

"No, you have not," he said, and there was laughter in his voice. "I wondered when you would."

She looked puzzled, and he kissed her hand again.

"I am Cesare Borgia," he said softly, and with a quick graceful bow, was gone, leaving her to stare after his tall elegant figure as he leaped on to his horse.

As he turned the mount, he raised his hand to her.

"Until tomorrow, Madonna," he called and his white teeth shewed in a brief smile.

She sank to the log, her trembling legs no longer able to hold her, and her hands were shaking uncontrollably.

"Cesare Borgia," she whispered to herself. "Cesare Borgia," and her stunned mind threw up again the picture of the tall stranger as he had sat by her side. Young, straight and fair of face and form. This, the dreaded Duc de Valence; the renegade Cardinal who had come to France to seek a bride for all reasons but love. It could not be; this young man, with such grace and charm, the same accused of fratricide, incest, murder, and many other nameless crimes. It was not possible.

She flushed as she remembered the charges she had laid against his name, and how violently she had expressed her revulsion at the union. Yet he had shewn nothing but amusement, save when his sister's name was mentioned, and then there had been for a brief moment something in those fine eyes which gave a slight indication of the qualities which lay beneath the surface of his beauty.

Her calmness and control was completely shattered by the encounter, for all her preconceived ideas of her betrothed had been set assunder by the meeting. He was so totally unexpected that she could not assimilate the situation; the picture she had drawn for herself of the dissolute Italian prince was so false that she could not adjust to the truth.

Terrifying he might be; ruthless and violent, yet he was the most handsome man she had even seen, and his firm hold on her hand had caused a shiver of something that was far from fear, and suddenly the May morning was beautiful to her, and as she rose to make her way back to the Château, her step was lighter, and her heart, which had been so heavy, was almost gay. Tomorrow she would see him again; tomorrow she would be his bride, and her eyes were bright, her cheeks warm, as she sped back to her chamber to prepare for the morrow.

The marriage of Cesare Borgia and Charlotte d'Albret took place without pomp or extravagance and in almost complete secrecy at the Château Blois. Georges d'Amboise, the newly created Cardinal of Rouen officiated at the wedding which took place in the Queen's apartments, in the presence of Louis XII and his bride, Anne of Brittany.

Before a portable altar of gold, inset with agate and jasper, Charlotte came to stand by the side of the Duc de Valence. She wore a robe of white satin, encrusted with pearls and diamonds, with a panel of cloth of silver falling from her slender waist to the hem. A jewelled diadem was set on her small proud head, and her russet brown hair fell in shimmering beauty to her shoulders.

Cesare turned to watch her move in grace to his side, and a smile touched his mouth.

She gave him a quick shy glance, and her heart beat faster as she saw his tall figure so wonderfully clad in a silk suit of amber which matched his eyes. The jewels he wore were spectacular, and he completely overshadowed the rather drab attire of the King, who was no match for the devastating prince.

The ceremony was short, and in a matter of minutes Charlotte was joined in matrimony to Cesare, Duc de Valence, and her hand placed in his by the jovial Cardinal, who was well pleased with this union, since it suited his own ends in no small measure.

After the ceremony itself there was feastng and celebrating until nightfall, when, amidst much laughter and joking, the bridal pair were escorted to their chamber. Tradition normally demanded that the wedding party should remain in the chamber until the pair were safely bedded, and even after the crowd had left, witnesses remained to ensure that the marriage was consummated, and knowing this custom, Charlotte's heart sank as time drew near to the point when she would have to join Cesare in the chamber. He glanced at her white face and squeezed her hand gently.

"Courage, madonna." His tone was light, but the expression in his eyes made her heart leap in her breast for already the magic of his presence had caught her in its spell.

At the door of the chamber the noisy crowd sought entry, but Cesare barred their way.

There were many protests at this outrage against custom, and even the King raised his voice in admonition.

"It is necessary to ensure that the marriage is consummated

sire," he said in his rather high querulous voice. "Do you seek to stand against this?"

"I do." The Duc's voice was quiet, but again Charlotte heard the authority in it, and the party became still under his cold eye.

"But sire." Cardinal d'Amboise was fussy and irritable. "How shall we know whether this marriage is a true one if it is not witnessed?"

Cesare's mouth was sardonic. "Because I tell you it will be so. Do you doubt my word, or my ability?"

The Cardinal looked abashed, but the King was not satisfied.

" 'Tis the custom," he began again, but Cesare made an impatient gesture.

"And in my country sire, but I will have none of it. Now, I beg you, leave us, for we would be alone."

Charlotte shrank back in dread, fearing the King's wrath would fall upon Cesare for his scant respect, but Louis, after a pause, shrugged and turned away.

"As you will," he said indifferently. "Doubtless time will show if you make good your boast."

His courtiers stared in curiosity at this bold Italian prince who stood his ground so firmly against the King's wishes, but at a sharp word from Louis, they turned and left with him, d'Amboise withdrawing, still shaking his head at the unorthodox procedure.

Cesare closed the door of the chamber firmly and looked at Charlotte.

"That at least you will be spared," he said, and she smiled faintly.

"I thank you, my lord," she said in a nervous whisper, "I am grateful to you for your concern, yet I would not have you anger the King for me."

Cesare laughed shortly. "I am indifferent to Louis' anger, as he will discover anon, and there is no reason why those gaping imbeciles should be present on such an occasion, custom or not."

He put his hands on her shoulders and drew her to him,

and something like panic shot through Charlotte as he bent his head to kiss her.

As their lips met, Charlotte felt a sensation she had never experienced before, and suddenly her fear and trembling ceased, and as Cesare's arms went round her, the tide of desire welled up inside her.

He felt her response, and gave a slight laugh.

"My little Charlotte," he murmured, and held her at arm's length. "You are exquisite, my love, and now you are mine. You have, as you feared, fallen into the hands of the diabolical Duc de Valence. What have you to say now, Carlotta?"

She smiled at the translation of her name to his native tongue.

"It is, as you said, my lord. My fears were groundless, and I tormented myself for no reason."

His hazel eyes were steady on hers. "You are sure, Carlotta mia?"

"I am sure, my lord."

"My name is Cesare." His glance did not waver. "Use it."

"Cesare," she repeated obediently, and he nodded.

" 'Tis well then, Carlotta, for now you are my wife. Whatever my reasons, the fact remains unaltered. You are mine."

He felt her tremble slightly in his hold.

"This frightens you, cara?"

"No." She shook her head. "My only fear is that I shall not be able to please you, my lord."

"Cesare."

She blushed. "Cesare. I may fail in my task."

"I doubt this," he said gently, "but there is one sure way to discover if your fears have any foundation."

He pulled her to him and his mouth was hard upon hers. "Come," he said softly, "let's us see how you please me," and led her to the bed.

The following morning was as bright and warm as their wedding day, and Charlotte hummed softly as she brushed her hair before the mirror. Cesare came to stand behind her, and she turned to smile at him.

His expression was hard to read as he looked down at her, and she felt a sudden moment of uneasiness.

"Cesare! What is it? Why do you look at me thus?"

For a moment he did not answer, then he rested one hand on her shoulder.

"Nothing, cara; nothing."

"Cesare, you looked as if . . ."

"As if what, my love?"

She shook her head. "I do not know . . . but it frightened me. It was as if you had left me. As if you had gone from me. Oh, Cesare, you will not leave me, will you? Oh, I beg you, do not go."

The hand tightened on her shoulder.

"Is this the shy maiden who dreaded the touch of the brutal Duc de Valence?" he said mockingly, and she laughed ruefully.

"How foolish you must have thought me, Cesare. I was so stupid."

"I thought you lovely and desirable," he said quietly, "the more so now you are mine."

He turned away from her.

"Yet, 'ere long, I shall have to return to Italy, for there are tasks I have to perform, and I cannot tarry long in France, much as I should like to do so."

"Cesare!" She rose in panic. "Oh, Cesare, not yet. I beg you, not yet."

She came to his side and caught his hand.

"Oh please, Cesare; do not return yet."

He looked down at her silently, and her eyes filled with tears.

"Do not cry, cara," he said. "I shall not go yet." He held her close. "I shall not go yet."

She laid her head on his breast, and he stroked her hair gently.

"Come, chèrie, enough of tears, for what will the assembled company think if you show such sorrow?"

She smiled tremulously. "I care not what they think,

my lord. They are no longer important to me. Only you are important to me now."

"That is good, cara, yet I would not have you weep on this our first day together. Come, dry your eyes, and we will join the others."

He raised her chin with his forefinger.

"That is better. Now, my love, you are ready?"

She nodded. "Now I am ready, my lord, for anything, so long as you are here."

Cesare frowned slightly, but did not speak, and together they left the room to join the King, but in Charlotte's heart there was the remains of fear and sadness, for she knew that Cesare would not stay long in France, and the thought of his departure filled her with far greater dread than that which had attended her thoughts of the marriage.

The monstrous nightmares which had filled her mind before she had met the Duc were as pinpricks compared to the prospect of life without him, for, from the moment she had seen him dismount and walk towards her, her heart had been lost, and she recognized only too clearly the irony of the trick which fate had played upon her when it sent to her the satanic ex-Cardinal as her bridegroom, whom she would love until the end of her days.

CHAPTER FOUR

On the Feast of Pentecost, at the Château Blois, Louis XII of France conferred upon the Duc de Valence the Order of St. Michael, the most prized and envied decoration of the Christian world, and that Louis elected to bestow it upon the Pope's son, indicated in some small measure his determination to seal the bond between France and the Vatican.

Charlotte was aflutter with excitement as she stood with Louise Duprès, Maude Letour, Anne Chantenay, and other of her companions to watch the Chancellor of the Order begin the ceremony by the celebration of the Mass.

On the altar, the collar and mantle of the new knight lay on a red silk cloth, and as the Mass proceeded, they were duly censed by the celebrant. Charlotte felt a tightening of emotion as the point arrived for the oldest knight of the Order to fetch Cesare for the actual investiture, and her face was pale with the tension inside her.

Her eyes travelled quickly over the assembled company; Louis, King of the most powerful state in Europe, huddled in his robes like a commoner, with none of the majesty his office demanded; Anne de Bretagne, his new Queen, smiling with a quiet triumph, her green eyes barely veiling the satisfaction she felt at her return to the rôle of wife of the monarch, one jewelled hand smoothing the soft velvet of Louis' sleeve. Nearby stood the thirty-six knights of the Order, robed in camlet, trimmed with miniver, impressive and dignified as they waited for the newcomer to their ranks.

There was a slight stir by the door and Charlotte turned her head quickly and caught her breath as she watched the aged member of the Order lead the Duc de Valence by his hand to the presence of the King.

Cesare walked with the supreme assurance of one who

suffered no doubt or indecision, and who accepted without question that his position would be recognized by all. He was the Pope's son, a Prince of Italy, and now a French Duke, and further, he intended to conquer Italy and rule over her as king, and something of his unyielding intent shewed in the way he held himself.

As he came before Louis, he bowed low, but none present had any illusions about his obeisance. He was merely paying lip service to convention; to him, Louis was just a stepping stone to his ambitions, and even Louis recognized this with a spurt of anger, as the Duc presented him with the customary offering of gold.

Louis would dearly have liked to bring about the reduction of this proud young upstart, but he needed him, and swallowing his irritation, he rose to continue the ceremony.

First the collar of the Order was laid round Cesare's neck, an exquisite necklace of gold cockleshells, delicately interlaced with loops of gold, holding a pendant depicting St. Michael and the dragon locked in combat. The cap was high and of crimson velvet; the mantle white damask, which, even on Cesare's tall figure, touched the floor, was richly worked with a border of cockleshells in gold, and trimmed with soft ermine.

Charlotte's heart beat faster as Louis recited the poetical words which accompanied the investiture, and she caught Louise's hand in sudden ecstasy.

"Oh, Louise," she whispered. "Is he not magnificent?"

Her friend nodded, but her eyes were cautious as they regarded the new knight. Magnificent perhaps; dangerous, certainly. The relief Louise Duprès had felt when she had discovered Charlotte's bridegroom was not the depraved, hideous villain they had all feared, had subsequently been tempered with doubt as she studied the Duc de Valence.

That he was gay and charming and fair to look upon was undeniable, but not blinded by love, as was Charlotte, Louise saw him with more perceptive eyes, and beneath the attractive façade she thought she read something else; something which had given rise to the rumours and tales which had heralded the Duc's arrival in France.

Watching him, Louise saw every now and again an expression in those tawny eyes which belied his pleasant and gracious manner, and a small quiet worry began to grow in her. She had feared for her friend, and when she had first met Cesare, something of the dread she had harboured had melted under his spell, but when this initial relief had settled, she began to see that Cesare's particular brand of terror did not lie in a gross, misshapen body and surface violence, but in something more frightening. That he was handsome, strong and graceful, merely made more alarming the indisputable power Louise saw in him, and she looked at Charlotte's radiant face with a mixture of pity and dread.

How long would it be before that look of joy and happiness faded from Charlotte's face, to be replaced by sadness and perhaps worse? How long before that gentle mask of Cesare's was replaced by something which would tear all the love and pride from Charlotte's eyes and leave her stricken and terrified?

Louise shook herself. This was folly. She must put aside such fancies and shew nothing of her doubts which would cloud this time of happiness for Charlotte. Together they watched Cesare bow again to the King, and take his place amongst the other knights as the ceremony proceeded in time honoured custom, and Louise squeezed Charlotte's hand.

"He is more handsome than any there," she said, "and even the King must envy his presence."

Charlotte smiled. "Yes, oh yes! And to think, Louise, how I feared our marriage; how I dreaded our meeting. How foolish I was, for he is so kind and gentle, and I love him greatly."

Again Louise felt a qualm of doubt and unease. Fair and graceful Cesare Borgia might be; kind and gentle he was not. The rumours and stories of this Italian Prince may have been exaggerated, but they had some basis in fact, of this Louise was sure. That Cesare now shewed kindness and consideration was, she was certain, because it suited his purpose; that purpose being to convince the Court and his bride that he was a worthy husband for a French Princess. But when this charade was over, what then would the Duc de Valence do?

Louise shivered suddenly, in spite of the warm May sunshine which flooded the hall, and her eyes closed in a brief prayer that Charlotte would not be too greatly hurt when the Duc's plans began to mature, and his need for her was over.

That night, a masked ball was held, and Charlotte was dazzling in a white silk gown, her rich brown hair threaded with diamonds, one of Cesare's wedding gifts, and her exquisite face touched with the glow of happiness. She sat by Cesare, who was dressed in a style which, as usual, put the French courtiers in the shade, and her eyes sparkled through the slits of her white satin mask as she listened to the talk about the table, particularly the words which passed between the King and her husband.

After the feast, there was dancing and entertainment, and Charlotte was swept on to the floor by some of the gallant young Frenchmen who sought Cesare's permission to dance with his lovely bride.

At midnight she found herself on the moonlit lawns, where the dancers had strayed, and her companions were laughing excitedly as they whirled to the strains of the music from the open windows. Charlotte felt a sudden longing for a sight of Cesare, whom she had not seen in an hour, and would have turned in search of him, but her hand was firmly held by a young chevalier who was dancing with her.

"Sire," she began, when he laughed.

"Mademoiselle," he said, and Charlotte gasped, for she realized that he had not understood who she was, for she had changed partners many times, and in the whirl and excitement, had found herself with this man who was wholly unaware of her identity, concealed as it was by her mask.

"Sire," she said again firmly, "you . . ."

He put one hand over her mouth in a gentle, teasing hold.

"No words, mademoiselle," he admonished. "Tonight is not made for words, but for love."

Her eyes widened in sudden fear, and she tried to wrench

herself away from him, and succeeded in dislodging his hand, only to find herself pulled to him in a fervent embrance.

"You are lovely," he said huskily, and kissed her passionately.

"Stop! Oh, please, stop, stop! You do not know what you are doing," she cried. "I am . . ."

He kissed her again. "No words, mademoiselle; I do not want to know who you are. Tonight is made for mystery. I shall not tell you my name, nor will I seek yours. Tonight we meet; tonight we part. Now kiss me again, for your lips are intoxicating."

She smelt the wine on his breath as he bent towards her, and twisted away in revulsion.

"Oh, please, I beg you let me go; let me go." Her eyes were black with fear as she tried to free herself from his hold, but he had the stubborn determination of those caught in the grip of a potent wine.

Finally she pulled her hand free, and they stood facing one another under the pale light of the moon. The man smiled; this time in a different way, and slowly he removed his mask.

"Forgive me," he said gently. "I have caused you distress, and this was not my intent. I beg you to forgive my impetuous demands which were brought about by the sight of your beauty. It was not my desire to harm you, nor to bring you unhappiness."

Charlotte's heart slowed slightly, and some of her fear abated as she looked at him. He was young and dark, his eyes almost black and slanting slightly at the corners, which wrinkled with laughter lines. His nose was blunt, his mouth crooked, and there was a duelling scar along one cheek. He smiled again, and despite herself, Charlotte found herself responding. He was not handsome, but was possessed of great charm, and as no harm had been done, she saw no reason to call for aid, since his behaviour had been caused by the excitement and magic of the night and the wine he had taken. She said with a pretence of coldness:

"Very well, monsieur, we will forget what has happened.

Now, I pray you, escort me back to the house, for the hour grows late."

His black eyes, which had been alight with laughter, suddenly grew sombre.

"No, mademoiselle," he said slowly. "We shall not forget what has happened here tonight. I crave your pardon for my boorish behaviour, and I beg your forgiveness, for what I did was inexcusable, but I shall not forget tonight. Will you?"

Charlotte flushed slightly. "Sire, you are presumptuous," she said coldly. "I have told you that this incident will be overlooked, but no more than that. Now, please, let us return to the house."

He did not move and she coloured again under his scrutiny.

"You are the most beautiful thing I have ever seen," he said finally, and her heart began to beat faster again. "How can I forget you?"

He moved suddenly as if to take her hand, but she drew back. "Monsieur, you do not know what you are doing," she cried, and there was distress in her voice. "You will regret . . ."

"No," he said harshly, "I shall not regret this meeting, nor shall I forget you. I had thought that we should not meet again after tonight, but I see now that this is not possible. I must see you again."

"No!" There was panic in Charlotte's voice as she saw the sudden sobering of the black eyes gazing into hers. "No, this cannot be. Sire, you do not understand."

"My name is Guy Ducroix," he said and moved towards her again. "And what is yours, my lady of the moonlight?"

"Charlotte?"

So engrossed had they been in their situation, that neither had noticed the newcomer, but at his voice they both turned sharply, and Charlotte's colour fled in fear as Cesare came to her side.

His hazel eyes were expressionless through his mask as he looked down at her and then at Ducroix, but his mouth was calm and he shewed no sign of anger, and taking courage, Charlotte gave a nervous laugh.

"Oh, my lord, you startled me, for I did not hear you. This is M. Guy Ducroix; we were dancing with the others, and M. Ducroix was about to escort me back to the Château."

Cesare's impassive gaze moved round the empty lawns, and Charlotte felt another pang of fear, for there was no one else in sight. Whilst she had been talking to Guy Ducroix, the other dancers had fled. She took a quick look at Cesare's face and said hesitantly:

"M. Ducroix, my husband, the Duc de Valence."

Ducroix's black eyes dilated suddenly, and his mouth was tense.

"Valence!" It was a whisper, and the tension in the air was tangible and frightening, then Cesare bowed slightly.

"I am happy to make your acquaintance, M. Ducroix," he said coolly, "and now my dear Charlotte, I think we should return, for the King asks for you."

The passionless eyes studied the face of Ducroix for a further second, and then he held out his arm to Charlotte who put a shaking hand on it, to allow Cesare to lead her back to the ball.

Ducroix stared after them, his face white and his eyes tormented; then he turned and stumbled away from the Château.

Charlotte expected some reprimand from Cesare for her indiscretion, but he said nothing, and the rest of the night passed off without incident.

In their chamber as they prepared for bed, Charlotte said hesitantly:

"Cesare. I fear I may have angered you this evening."

Valentinois turned to smile at her. "Cara, how could this be?"

She came to his side. "You found me with M. Ducroix in unusual circumstances, but it was not as it seemed. There were many dancers when I left the house, and I had not noticed that they had gone. When I . . . when we found they had left, M. Ducroix . . ."

She broke off, something in Cesare's steady gaze halting the words on her lips.

"Yes, cherie, M. Ducroix?" His smile was sweet, his face untroubled, but suddenly Charlotte's heart began to race.

"Cesare, I beg you to understand; it was nothing."

"Then why does it trouble you so, cara? I would advise you to put it from your mind, since it is a matter of no importance."

"Yes . . . yes, of course, but Cesare . . ."

"Yes?"

"M. Ducroix . . ."

"Yes?"

"You will not seek to . . . to . . ."

"To what, cherie?"

She met his tawny eyes, and still there was nothing in their depths but faint amusement, yet something about his manner made her mouth dry in terror. She could not understand it, for there were no external signs of anger or rage; nothing but calmness and tolerance, yet suddenly she feared for Guy Ducroix.

"He meant no harm, Cesare. I had not seen him before; I will not see him again. I beg you to forgive me for what happened; for what appeared to be . . ."

His brows rose slightly. "Appeared to be what, cara? It seemed to me that you were merely talking to one of the King's guests, and that he was on the point of bringing you back to my side. Why, then, does this incident distress you so much?"

She flushed, realizing that she was emphasizing the situation in such a way that Cesare's suspicions might well be aroused.

"Of course, I am foolish." She gave a faint laugh. "I am making too much of nothing. Forgive me, Cesare."

He put one arm round her and looked down at her.

"There is nothing to forgive, sweet. And did you enjoy the revels tonight?"

"Oh yes, Cesare. And the ceremony this morning. I was so proud when the King invested you with the Order of St.

Michael; so proud that I thought my heart would burst with joy."

He smiled slightly. "I am glad it did not, cherie, for I do not want your heart to be broken either by sadness or joy, but I thank you for caring so much."

He kissed her gently and moved away. "And now, cara, you must rest, for the night has been long, and you are weary."

She stared at him, her fears returning. Cesare had been a demanding lover, and she had responded with joy and gladness to those demands. Now he moved away from her, and there was something almost disinterested in his glance as he unbuckled his belt and removed the dagger from its sheath. She watched with growing fear his hand on the knife, but his face remained expressionless and she caught her breath.

"Cesare!"

He returned the blade to its sheath and looked at her.

"Cherie?"

"Why . . . why do you do that?"

"Do what?" He seemed genuinely surprised, and she bit her lip.

"I . . . I am sorry. For a moment, when you took your dagger in your hand, I was afraid."

His mouth moved in an unamused smile. "Did you think I sought your destruction with it, cara?"

He laughed. "No. It was nothing; I was thinking of something else."

She was silent, and he smiled again. "Go to bed."

"And you, Cesare, are you not coming to bed?"

"Later," he said slowly. "Later, sweet. I have things to do."

With that, he turned and left the room, and Charlotte's eyes were filled with tears as she prepared for sleep. Lying in the darkness she pondered on the events of the evening, and her mind was filled with nameless fears. Cesare had shewn neither anger nor concern for her presence with Guy Ducroix, and yet Charlotte felt instinctively that the incident had not left him unmoved, and her terror increased the next morning when she found Cesare had not slept in her bed.

She rose and dressed quickly, and made her way to the grand hall where the King's court had assembled, but of Cesare there was no sign. As soon as she was able to leave, she fled to the grounds in search of Cesare, but after twenty minutes of fruitless hunting, had seen no sign of his presence. She was about to turn back to the Château, when she heard a groan, and swung round in sudden fear, lest Cesare should have been injured in a fall from his horse. The sound had come from a clump of trees nearby, and cautiously she made her way towards them, leaving the bright May sun for the shadowy cover of the leafy canopy.

Lying by a tree stump, curled in an arc of pain, was Guy Ducroix, and with a cry of distress, Charlotte went to his side and tried to raise him.

He was ashen, with perspiration on his brow and round a mouth contorted in agony, and his hand was a sudden fierce grip on her wrist.

"Help me," he whispered, "help me." The black eyes were too glazed to recognize her. She was merely a human being from whom he sought aid in his extremity, and she put a hand on his burning forehead.

"M. Ducroix! What has happened? You are hurt, but what befell you? An accident? Did you fall from your horse?"

He shook his head as a spasm of pain shook his frame.

"No . . . no . . . not a fall." The black eyes closed momentarily, only to open again as another convulsion twisted his supine body.

"Oh sire, can you not tell me what is wrong, so that I may seek aid?"

Ducroix lay silent for a moment, then with an effort pulled himself together and looked at her, and for the first time recognition came into his gaze.

"The lady of the moonlight," he said in a whisper. "What are you doing here? And does the Duc know you are here?"

She shook her head. "I was looking for him when I heard

you cry out; oh, M. Ducroix, what ails you? You are in great pain. Have you been hurt?"

Ducroix' mouth curled again in pain, but the worst of the attack appeared to be passing, and after a moment he was able to pull himself up to sit on the fallen log nearby.

"I know not what ails me," he confessed. "Probably too much wine last night, or perhaps some food which was tainted."

Their eyes met, and in that second both recognized something which passed between them like a thread of terror.

"M. Ducroix." Charlotte's voice was small and still against the sounds of the summer morning. "Did you drink any wine late last night, or this morning?"

He laughed faintly, despite the fresh spasm of nausea which distorted his mouth. "You know only too well how much wine I had last night." He straightened himself with an effort. "Why do you ask this, madame?"

Charlotte did not reply, for they both knew why the question had been asked then Ducroix said quietly:

"You must get back to the house, madame. He must not find you with me again. You must not place yourself in jeopardy for me. I beg you, return to the Château, and forget what you have seen."

"I cannot leave you like this." Charlotte's eyes were distressed. "I must get help for you. Wait here, M. Ducroix, and I will see what I can do."

"No!" He was violent. "No, you must not do this, for if the Duc de Valence should discover you in your attempts to aid me, he will——" he broke off.

"Cesare will not hurt me," she said quietly, and his mouth moved in a slight mocking smile.

"Oh my lady of the moonlight, how little you know of your noble bridegroom. Do you really imagine your youth and beauty would save you if you stood in his way, or crossed his imperious will?"

"Sire! You must not talk to me thus about the Duc. And you do not know him as I do. Much unkind gossip has been spread about him, and in France he is believed to be depraved and wicked, but this is not so. He has shewn me kindness and gentleness."

She stifled the sudden fear she had felt when she had looked upon her husband's quiet face on the previous night.

"You do him much injustice when you believe these vile rumours."

There was pity in his eyes as he looked at her.

"I had not realized, madame," he said gently. "You love him."

"Yes." Her eyes fell under his gaze. "Yes, I love him. He is not as men say. He is not an evil man."

Guy Ducroix made an effort to stand, and Charlotte helped him to his feet.

"I said last night that we should not meet again, but, in fact, we have, and for this blessing, I give thanks to God. But after this morning, we shall not see each other any more, and thus I can tell you that which I would not otherwise be able to say. Madame, the King of France and the Pope sold you to Cesare Borgia to further their plans for an alliance between France and the Papacy; you were merely a tool which they used for their diabolical plan. But the Duc de Valence was no such tool. He was a party to this infamy, and further, madame, rumour does not lie when it accuses Cesare Borgia. He is a man without a soul. As yet, he has done little, but I tell you, madame, he will; he will. I recognize the quality of this man. He is not a pawn to be manoeuvred by Louis and the Holy Father for their purposes. They have created for themselves a monster, and they will both live to rue the day they used Cesare Borgia in their efforts to gain power."

Charlotte's eyes had widened in anger and fear as Ducroix spoke, and now she answered him hotly.

"You are wrong, M. Ducroix; very wrong. My husband is no monster. He seeks to do no one any harm."

"What about his brother, the luckless Duke of Gandia, madame, or have you conveniently forgotten his premature demise?"

"It is not known whose hand slew the Duke of Gandia," she

returned with spirit, but a far off echo of her words to Louise Duprés came to her at the mention of Gandia's murder.

"Is there doubt in your mind about this?" Ducroix was scornful. "Gandia stood in Valentinois' path; whilst he lived, the Cardinal of Valencia could not free himself from his ecclesiastical prison, but once Gandia was dead, Cesare lost no time in escaping the bonds of the Holy Church, and you, madame, have the felicity of becoming the first woman to wed a Cardinal."

"Stop, stop!" Charlotte buried her face in shaking hands. "I beg you, stop."

"I have finished, madame. I have said all there is to say. If you are wise, you will now return to the Château and forget you have seen me this morning, and certainly do not mention it to the Cardinal."

She met his scornful eyes. "Do not call him that. He is no longer a Cardinal, as you well know. He was released form this office, and is now a layman. Why do you persist in this. . . ."

"How can a Cardinal become a layman, madame?" Ducroix' voice was contemptuous. "The whole Catholic world laughs at this device the Pope used to free his belovèd son from the unwelcome bonds in which the Church held him, but in the eyes of God, madame, he is still a Cardinal."

"I will not listen to you," she said angrily. "What you say is born of spite and jealousy. Cesare is a layman, and was free to wed, for he had Papal dispensation for this act. And now I shall go, but since you are still obviously ill, I will do what I can to help you."

"You cannot help me, madame," said Ducroix shortly. "I am beyond aid now."

"No! Do not say this. Cesare does not wish you any ill. Last night, I explained what had happened, and he dismissed it as a matter of no importance."

"And you believed him when he shewed no concern, madame?"

Despite her desire to impress upon him Cesare's good-will, Charlotte hesitated, and Ducroix nodded.

"Yes," he said quietly, "I understand. Now go, lest your husband comes upon us again. For then I would stand no chance at all."

Charlotte brushed aside her fears. "Sire, if you will remain here, I will have a horse sent to you. Will this aid you?"

He looked at her with a slight smile. "You would do this for me, in spite of all I have said about your husband?"

She nodded. "I would do anything to help anyone in distress, M. Ducroix. You will wait here?"

"Yes, and I thank you, Madame, for your kindness. But ask yourself why you do this thing. Why you seek to aid me, if, as you say, your husband is the victim of slander and lies. Why do you seek to help me flee from this place, madame, if you are so sure of the Duc's goodwill?"

She closed her eyes, unable to answer him, and he managed to get to her side, one hand gripped against his body as pain clawed at him again.

"Forgive me, I should not torment you in this way, for you are gentle and kind, but I do so only to warn you, my lady of the moonlight, that you are in the hands of a man who may one day break your heart."

Charlotte's eyes were stricken as she turned from him and made her way out into the blazing sunshine, and her feet were attended by wings of fear as she ran to the Château. Fortune was on her side, and she managed to reach Louise Duprès without being intercepted by any of the King's entourage, and without encountering Cesare, and breathlessly she explained the circumstances of the previous night, and the presence of Guy Ducroix in the grounds.

Louise listened in growing consternation, and at the end of Charlotte's tale, gave an exclamation of dismay.

"Charlotte! What coil is this you have made? Where is the Duc de Valence? If he should hear of this. . . ."

"He must not," said Charlotte quickly. "I have not seen him this morning." She avoided Louise's enquiring eyes. "Now, Louise, there is no time to be lost. I beg you, get a horse and food and have them taken to the place where M. Ducroix waits. He must get away before. . . ."

Into the small pause, Louise said quietly: "Before the Duc de Valence finds him, Charlotte? Is this what you mean?"

A tear ran down Charlotte's cheek. "I . . . I . . . do not know, Louise. I only know I wish to help M. Ducroix leave this place. I cannot tell you why, but I fear for his life. He has been terribly ill; something he drank, perhaps."

Her eyes met Louise's and a visible shudder passed through her. "We do not know what caused this, but he would be better away from Blois. I beg you, Louise, help me."

Louise looked at her with pity. "Oh, Charlotte, if only it were you that I was helping to escape from Blois."

Charlotte raised her head. "I do not want to leave Blois," she said firmly, and a little colour returned to her cheeks. "My only desire is to stay here with my husband. Yet I would not want M. Ducroix to suffere because . . . because. . . ."

"Because Cesare Borgia turned his eyes upon him," finished Louise, and laughed shortly. "Charlotte, I beg you have a care in your dealings with the Duc. He is a dangerous man for all his charm. You think you love him, but. . . ."

"I do love him," said Charlotte angrily, "now Louise will you help me or not?"

"Yes. I will arrange for the unfortunate M. Ducroix to escape the wrath of the Duc, but there seems to be little that I can do to help you, Charlotte, for you are determined to ignore the risks you run, despite the proof you yourself bring to me."

Seeing Charlotte's distress, Louise's face softened, and she laid her hand on Charlotte's arm.

"Fear not, chère ami, I will help your gallant, and spirit him away. Now I beg you compose yourself, for should you meet the Duc like this, his suspicions will be aroused."

Charlotte nodded and her mouth trembled. "Yes, I will go to my chamber. I thank you, Louise, for your help. And you are wrong about Cesare, I know you are."

Louise Duprès shook her head as she watched the Duchesse de Valentinois go, and then turned in search of help for Guy Ducroix.

At the banquet that night, Charlotte sat next to Cesare, who seemed completely to have regained his good humour, and his smile was as warm and gentle as ever as he toasted his bride.

"You are lovely as always, cara," he said, and raised his goblet. "I am the most fortunate of men to have won such a prize."

She smiled, some of her fears having being lulled by the news that Louise had brought her of Ducroix' escape from Blois on a borrowed horse.

"Cesare," she murmured, and he took her hand.

"I would that this evening were over, so that we might be alone," he went on, "then I could tell you how much it means to me to have you at my side."

She blushed becomingly, and his hand tightened over hers.

How wrong she had been to doubt Cesare, and how foolish her fears had been. Clearly M. Ducroix had eaten some bad food or tainted wine, and had become ill, and she had leaped to the conclusion that this sudden illness had been caused by Cesare in his anger at the events of the previous night.

How wrong she had been to listen to M. Ducroix slanderous attack on Cesare, and to Louise's absurd fears.

She cast a side-long glance at Cesare's face. How could they accuse him of a string of crimes and evil deeds when neither of them knew him as she did. They listened to rumour and believed all that they heard, but she, who knew Cesare, should have known better than to listen for one second to the spiteful lies they had repeated, and she felt a flood of shame wash over her that her defence of her husband had not been stronger.

She was about to speak again, when a messenger entered the hall and made a low bow to the King. She saw the King frown at the boy as he spoke in quiet tones, and a silence fell as Louis hit the table in front of him with a clenched fist.

"Dieu! 'Tis monstrous that a man cannot travel on the business of the King without attack from bandits and rogues."

"Sire?"

The King turned to the Chevalier d'Almané who had spoken.

"Guy Ducroix has been set upon by robbers and slain," he said shortly. "He was a loyal subject and a man I trusted." He turned to one of his captains standing behind his chair.

"You will find out who was responsible for his death." His face was white with anger. "I will put him to death in a way which will teach men not to tamper with the servants of their King."

Charlotte's colour had drained from her cheeks at the King's words, and as one in a trance she turned to look at Cesare.

He was regarding Louis in mild surprise, but beyond that, there was no expression on his face. Her tongue touched her dry lips and she tried to speak.

"Cesare. . . ."

He did not look at her.

"Why did Ducroix leave Blois at this time?" Louis turned again to his captain. "I gave him no orders to go."

"Highness, I do not know." The captain's brows were bent in a frown. "To my knowledge, he had no mission to accomplish."

Louis muttered angrily, but after a moment, dismissed the incident, and started to discuss the forthcoming trip to Italy with those about him.

Charlotte looked at Cesare again. "Cesare."

He glanced down at her. "Chèrie?"

"M. Ducroix . . . did you know he had left Blois?"

"I? No, why should I know this? I did not know him, nor his business. Why do you ask, Charlotte? Is it a matter of interest to you?"

The hazel eyes held hers, and in them she saw reflected that which turned her heart to stone as she watched Cesare's mouth curve in a slight, satisfied smile.

CHAPTER FIVE

EXACTLY twelve months from the date he had sailed to France, Cesare Borgia returned to Italy. He attended upon Louis XII at his entry into Milan, and visited his father, the Pope, who was tearfully joyous at his son's return, but Cesare was merely biding his time. He had little interest in Louis' claim on Milan, and his mind and energies were concentrated upon the first impresa he intended to undertake, that of the possession of Imola and Forlì.

It irked him in no small measure that the troops needed to quell these vassal states were Louis', but despite the burning ambition which possessed his soul, he had kept under firm control his thirsting desire for an army of his own. This would take time; meanwhile, he accepted with outward calm the fact that he merely acted as Louis' lieutenant, whilst the control of military operations rested, at least nominally, in the hands of the Cardinal of Rouen and Yves d'Alègre.

The young Captains who had pledged their lives to his cause were less philosophical, and fretted with ill-concealed impatience at the superiority of the French, but Cesare laughed at them and bade them learn to wait.

"For," he said to Pietro Santa Croce, who had just thrown his sword across the room in an excess of anger, "if I am content to use Louis' army for the time being, why should you rail against this course?"

"But, sire," protested Giulio Alberini, in support of Santa Croce's intolerance, "this is no way to release us from the yoke of France, for we sink deeper into the King's debt and further under his control."

"But not for long," said the Duke quietly, "not for long, Giulio. 'Tis true that for the moment, Louis' forces are all we have for the task we undertake, but I did not rid myself of my Cardinal's chains to become servant to the King of France. Did you doubt this?"

His hand rested lightly on the hilt of his sword.

"Did you not listen to me when I told you why I sought freedom from the Holy Church? But this needs time, as I told you then. I am prepared to spend this time to achieve my ends, and thus you must share my patience."

He looked round the group with amused eyes.

"I know you long to be free from the hand of France, and so you will be, in good time. First we will take Imola and Forlì; then Pesaro, Rimini, Faenza and Piombino, and when I have the Romagna in my hand . . . then. . . ."

His amber eyes were half-closed and he was very still.

"Then, I shall be done with Louis."

"But where shall we get troops, sire?" Domenico Sanguigna's brow was puzzled. "How will the conquest of the Romagna help us, for we shall need troops to control these states; we shall get no army from them."

"You are wrong, Domenico," said Valentinois softly. "That is precisely where I shall get my army; from the Romagna."

The young men's impatience and irritation melted, and despite their bewilderment, they drew nearer to the Duke, attracted as ever by the inflexible purpose they saw in him, and the complete assurance they found in his words and bearing.

"But, sire, how can this be? These are rebel states. They will fight against you, and when you have subdued them, you will have to keep them in a state of subjection. You cannot rely upon their acceptance of your sovereignty."

Cesare smiled. "Again you are wrong." He turned to look at Gianbattista Mancini. "It is the Tyrants of Imola, Forlì, Rimini and the rest who will fight me; their subjects are not loyal to them, for they have suffered greatly under the yoke of these butchers. They will not sacrifice their lives for men who have starved and beaten them into submission. No, there is only one way to hold a state and that is by making it content, and this I propose to do. When I take a state, I shall reform its laws, and strengthen its civic life. I will give men order under my rule, and sufficient food for themselves and their families. I will lighten the crippling taxes, and give them land to work and till. I will give them justice, and make free men of them, Gianbattista, and from these free men, I will draw my army."

There was a moment's silence, for this concept was entirely new to Cesare's Captains, who had hitherto accepted without question that a state must be ruled with an iron fist, and ground under the heel of its master.

"Freedom, my lord?" Bartolomeo da Capranica was incredulous. "You will give the peasants freedom? Sire, such risk!"

Cesare laughed. "Freedom is a relative word, Bartolomeo. Fear not, these states will never doubt whose word is law; which master they serve, nor the folly of rebellion. They are a wild, rowdy mob, but I will subdue them, first with force and brutality, if I must, but then I will give them that measure of liberty which will secure their loyalty to me."

He turned and moved to the door. "Now, I must seek an audience with the Holy Father, for he is anxious to know my plans, and I pray you, have no doubt about the outcome of my proposals. This is not some wild scheme created in the fevered brain of a madman. I know what I am about, as you will see, and I tell you that 'ere long, we shall achieve that which will free us from France, and from all foreign powers. Trust me, for I shall not fail."

And with that he left the bemused and amazed young men to ponder amongst themselves on the startling policies he had uncovered to them.

" 'Tis a dangerous path the Duke takes," said Bartolomeo doubtfully, "such men are not used to freedom; they will become drunk on it, and rebel against his Highness."

"There is no other way to subdue such men than by the sword," agreed Giulio Alberini, "yet there was something in my lord's voice——" he broke off, unable to explain what it was about Cesare's words which had captured his imagination, and Santa Croce nodded.

"Yes, there was that about my lord's words, and I, for one, believe he will succeed, for, sires, remember this; there has not been such a man as this before. My lord Valentinois has in him a strange power; he is not as the Tyrants now ruling in the Romagna. When he says he will do such and such a thing, then I am filled with a conviction that he will attain his ends. And what he says is true. If a man could hold a state by means other than force; if he could contrive to hold men's loyalty by means other than cruelty and violence, then, signores, he would indeed have an army, for all men would support and fight for such a man."

Slowly the others nodded, the idea which had at first seemed so foolish and wild, gradually catching their minds and spirits and Bartolomeo laughed.

"Dio, yes, yes! I do not know why I doubted him for a moment, for he was born to succeed. I have never seen in any other man what I see in Valentinois. Come, sires, let us be done with doubts and impatience. If my Lord of Valence can wait, so can we."

He poured wine for his companions, and raised his goblet. "Signores, to our success."

"To Valentino," amended Domenico with a smile. "for his success will be ours."

He drank deeply, and his brother Captains followed suit, renewed in their determination by Cesare's words.

Meanwhile, Cesare made his way to the Pontificial Chamber where Alexander awaited him with keen impatience. As the doors were opened to receive him, those present bowed low to the Pope's son as he walked in his confident, easy manner to the Pontiff's throne.

For a second his eyes met his father's, which filled with tears of emotion, and then Cesare bent his knee. Alexander could scarcely contain himself as Valentinois kissed his ring, and almost before Cesare's obeisance was finished, the Pope rose, and clasped his son in his arms.

"Cesare. Cesare, my son." He held the Duke close for a

second, and a measure of hardness left Cesare's mouth as he regarded his father with something like affection.

"Holiness, I rejoice that I find you well," he said, and Alexander nodded.

"Yes, yes, I am well; but you, Cesare? You? How are you, for it has been so long since we have beheld you? Is all well with you, and what of France and your bride, Cesare? How is she?"

Alexander was as excited as a child as he plied his son with questions, not pausing for answers, and Cesare smiled faintly.

"All is well with me, Holiness, and Charlotte was in good health when I left her. Her child is expected in the Spring."

The Pope's eyes filled again, for he had been overwhelmed by the news which had reached him that Charlotte was pregnant, and he longed to have her in Rome, so that his grandchild could be born in the Vatican.

"You must tell me all your news, Cesare. What is she like, the sweet Charlotte? You are satisfied with her, eh?" The Pope's black eyes were knowing. "She pleased you?"

Cesare shrugged. "She is a pretty child." He seemed indifferent, and the Pope's full mouth drooped.

"You do not love her, Cesare?"

"She is my wife," said Valentinois, coolly and his eyes were forbidding, but the Pope was not to be put off.

"Why did you not bring her with you, Cesare, for I long to see her, and to have the child here in Rome. Why could she not come with you?"

"I left France with Louis for the reduction of Milan, Holiness," reminded Cesare a trifle bleakly, "I could scarce take a pregnant woman to war with me."

His voice had an edge on it, and the Pope regarded him silently for a moment, and then smiled cheerfully for he thought he saw something in Cesare's expression which belied the carelessness with which his son had dismissed the subject of his bride, and he considered that there was plenty of time for the fair Charlotte to be brought to Rome, as he was determined she should be, for he wanted more grandsons to strengthen the Borgia dynasy; more men like Cesare, his belovèd son.

The dark eyes were moist again as he looked at Valentinois' immaculate uniform which he wore with such authority. Yes, more sons like Cesare would ensure that the House of Borgia would grow in strength, but there was plenty of time, for Charlotte was barely eighteen. Once Cesare had taken the Romagna, then he would send for Charlotte. He nodded to himself in satisfaction. Yes, then Cesare would have more time for her.

"And now, Cesare." The Pope became businesslike. "You are ready for the first step?"

Cesare nodded. "Yes, Holiness. On the 9th November we shall leave Milan, whence I go tomorrow, and make the first move in our subjection of the rebel fiefs."

"And Louis has furnished all the troops needed for this?"

Cesare's teeth shewed briefly. "He has certainly furnished most of them, Father, for the Papal Forces are but a handful and insufficient for the suppression of one castle, let alone a state. But this is not important. We shall soon have our own army, then we shall have no further need of French mercenaries."

Alexander looked momentarily apprehensive, for although he had planned the first impresa, that vast conception which was to bring back to Papal control its defiant fiefs, he knew in his heart he had no weapons with which to control Cesare. He had fathered a tiger in this young man, who had dictated his own terms from the day on which he finally demanded his release from the Church, and he had an uneasy feeling that what Cesare now planned was not what he, Alexander, had originally envisaged. The apprehension died as he watched his son's calm face.

If Cesare now planned some variation to his father's original scheme, he planned it with a cold dispassionate mind. There would be nothing reckless or ill-conceived about Cesare's move, for the determination in the Duke was supported by an intelligence and astuteness of high order, and Alexander relaxed slightly, and the smile returned to his face.

Although strictly speaking it was Louis who undertook the subjugation of Imola and Forlì and the other rebel states, in fulfilment of his agreement with the Pope, it was Cesare who would ride at the head of the army and who would mould and manipulate the course of the struggle, and the Pope had little doubt that once the impresa began, the control which Louis and his officers believed themselves to hold, would soon pass to Valentinois.

" 'Tis good to have you back, Cesare, but must you leave for Milan so soon?"

There was something of a plea in the Pope's words, but Cesare was curt.

"There is no time to tarry in Rome, Holiness. There is much to plan and arrange."

The Duke did not elaborate, and the Pope quelled his disappointment and turned the conversation to other matters, but his heart was heavy for he would have liked to have held his son at his side for a little longer, and with something of self-mockery he admitted silently that whilst in Cesare's absence he could convince himself that he was still master of Rome, in Cesare's presence, this delusion burst like a bubble, and he knew that he had finally lost control of his brilliant son.

Early in November, on a day which was misty and clouded with rain, Cesare left Milan, accompanied by the Marquis of Mantua, a distinguished soldier, who was not best pleased to be saddled with an unfrocked priest who had never seen the colour of war, and on whom he now had to attend in what might well prove to be a major military operation. Francesco Gonzaga, Marquis of Mantua, son-in-law of Duke Ercole of Ferrara, was a broad impressive figure on his splendid chestnut mount, his strong hands firm on the reins. His brown eyes under thick brows shewed the irritation in him at the need to wet-nurse this Papal bastard in his grandiose plan to subdue the Romagna, and he was brusque when he spoke to Cesare.

Valentinois, fully aware of Mantua's disapproval, smiled slightly to himself, but gave no sign that he had noticed his companion's ill-temper, and when he replied to Gonzaga's abrupt questions or comments, his voice was tranquil and untroubled, a fact which caused the irate soldier more disquiet, for he saw nothing in the handsome Duke which gave any hope that he would stand firm in battle.

"He will run at the first sight of blood," said Gonzaga contemptuously to his fellow officers, "he should have stayed in the Vatican and contented himself with the designing and planning of his jewels and costumes."

Cesare's extravagant gems and proclivity for unusual and expensive dress had not gone unnoticed, and Gonzaga could not take seriously a soldier who was in the habit of wearing velvet, silk and diamonds in such profusion.

Cesare and Mantua took the Via Emilia through Piacenza to Parma, where Gonzaga proposed to leave him, whilst Cesare was to continue to Reggio and Modena to meet the infantry under the Baily de Dijon. There the Duke was to come to terms with the Commune of Bologna to permit the troops free passage over the Regno and through Bolognese territory.

"He is no more fit to settle terms for the moving of an army than is a serving wench," said Gonzaga angrily to Captain François Montand. "He is a raw, callow youth, and the famous impresa of the Holy Father is likely to begin and end at Modena."

Montand, who was occupying a tent with the Marquis in the roughly constructed camp, was silent. He had shared Gonzaga's unease when he heard that he was to join the Pope's son, particularly as, unlike Gonzaga, he would not be leaving the Duke's train at Modena. He had also agreed with Gonzaga's vitriolic contention that a young man of twenty-three, who had hitherto divided his time between the College of Cardinals and the scented beds of Rome's most beautiful harlots, was unlikely to be of any use in combat, and he recalled with a grimace the futile attempts of the Duke of Gandia to make a name for himself on the battlefield.

His expression of derision when he had first met Cesare was sustained no longer than a minute. A shrewd judge of men, Montand experienced something of a shock when he looked into the clear, cold eyes of the Duke of Valence. Young he might be, and inexperienced in war he undoubtedly was, yet Montand knew instantly that this was no perfumed fop before him. In the Duke's unwavering gaze he read the relentless determination which the Pope had seen before him, and in the firm line of the well-shaped mouth he saw the control and power which had overriden the Pontiff's will.

"I doubt this," he said finally, in answer to Gonzaga's scathing comment. "I think you underestimate this man."

"Man!" The scorn had not lessened. "He is but a boy; a child who has done nothing to earn the name man."

The Marquis struck the table in front of him in fury.

"What has he ever done that has amounted to ought?"

Montand was thoughtful. "According to his enemies, he killed his brother," he said slowly, "and in such a way that none could prove it. And 'tis said that the Pope fears him. What manner of boy is this, who destroys his own flesh and blood and reduces the Holy Father to such terror that he does not seek to punish the murderer of his favourite son?"

"Pah! If he did kill Gandia, and none knows this for sure, he merely hired an assassin to do the deed, and as for the Pope's fears, he is but an indulgent father. All know how he dotes on his bastards. This does not prove anything."

Montand stroked his chin, and his eyes were still pondering the problem.

"He has something in him; I cannot tell what, yet when I look at him, I think——" he broke off, and laughed slightly. " 'Tis just a feeling, yet look how he attracts men to his side. He brings with him the cream of the best families in Rome; Orsini, Capranica, Santa Croce, Alberini and others."

"Bought for him by his father," snapped Gonzaga, but Montand shook his head.

"No. Money could not buy what those men feel for Valentinois. There is more in this man than meets the eye. I feel . . ."

Again he stopped, unable to explain in logical terms what he did feel when his mind turned to Cesare Borgia. He sensed, as other men had done, some inexplicable force which could not be translated into words, and he shook his head in puzzlement.

"I know not," he ended quietly, and Gonzaga's face took on a slightly choleric hue, but before he could utter the withering comment on his lips, there was a commotion outside the tent, and the sound of voices raised in anger.

With a curse, Gonzaga rose from the camp bed on which he had been seated, and followed by Montand, strode out into the encampment, and his expression of fury increased as he saw two men struggling by the camp fire.

He opened his mouth to shout an order, but before he could be heard, the Duke of Valence went up to the men, who fell apart, panting and grunting with their exertions. Valentinois looked down at them without speaking, and slowly they pulled themselves to their feet and shuffled uneasily in the dust.

"What is this?" enquired the Duke finally, and his voice was soft, yet a slight shudder went through the men.

They were silent for a moment, then Cesare's riding whip flicked gently against his supple leather boot, and one of the men rubbed a hand against his mouth, raw from a vicious blow from his opponent.

"Sire . . . my lord. It was nothing."

"Men do not fight for no cause," observed the Duke calmly, "what cause was yours, and I advise a clean confession, lest my anger be aroused."

Montand watched fascinated. The two men were rough Gascon soldiers, who feared no man and who were brave, valiant fighters, yet in front of Cesare Borgia, the young man who knew more about silks and pearls than swords and mortars, they were curiously subdued.

The older man's feet shuffled again. " T'was a wager, my lord," he said finally, but none of his fear had dissipated.

"Oh? And what was the wager?" The Duke was still passive.

Again there was silence, and Montand glanced quickly at

Gonzaga, who was frowning, but, oddly enough, making no move towards the group.

"I am waiting," said Cesare, and there was something under the words which made the two men jerk uneasily.

"Sire," said one eventually, "we made a wager that the winner of our bout could beat any Italian condottiero in the camp."

The Duke's mouth moved slightly, but not in amusement.

"I see." He eyed the two for a second more. "And who is the winner of this bout? You?" He looked at the less battered of the two, who nodded.

"Yes, sire, I would have won this encounter."

"Good." The Duke smiled, and the man shivered suddenly. "Good. Now that you have won the first part of the stake, we will complete the second. You shall meet an Italian condottiero, and we will see the quality of your strength and skill."

The man stared for a moment, then something of relief shewed in his eyes, and he broke into a grin.

"Willingly, sire, willingly. I will take on any man in fair combat."

He clenched his hands, and the muscles in his forearms stood out in heavy knots. "And which man shall I fight sire, to prove our merit?"

"And with whom have you made this hazard?" enquired the Duke, his eyes still on the two men. "Who has made the other part of this wager?"

The man looked up quickly at Valentinois' tone, but read nothing but serenity, and the momentary twinge of fear died.

"Why, sire, the Italian troops here. They claimed they could beat our champions, and thus it was agreed that the best of our men would meet one of theirs, so that we could prove their boast was an idle one."

"I see. Well now you will have the chance to prove whether it was idle or not."

The Duke drew off his gloves and handed them to

Bartolomeo da Capranica who stood slightly behind him, and began to unbuckle his sword.

The man's eyes widened in amazement, and Montand gave a faint exclamation.

"Mon Dieu! He is never going to fight this peasant himself?" he said to Gonzaga. "He will be torn to pieces. He is no match for that brute."

Gonzaga's brows were knitted in a frown. "No, he cannot stand against this man, for he has neither the strength nor the experience, yet he does not appear to lack courage."

Montand, despite his amazement and apprehension, smiled slightly.

"And this surprises you, my lord."

Mantua nodded, his frown deepening. "Yes, this surprises me. I did not think he had it in him, yet it is an idle gesture, and as I forecast, the impresa is going to end here as far as Cesare Borgia is concerned, unless I stop this."

He made a move towards the Duke, but Montand's hand came down in a tight grip on his arm.

"No, my lord, let be. Let this contest continue. If Cesare Borgia is a weakling, let us know now. If not, no harm is done. Let be, sire."

Gonzaga hesitated uncertainly, but the decision was taken from him, as Cesare flung his belt from him and waved Capranica and his companions away with a sharp decisive gesture.

"Now," he said to the Gascon, and there was a smile on his mouth. "Now, sire, let us see whether you can make good your proud boast."

The man's yellowed teeth shewed in a grin of pleasurable anticipation as he beheld the tall slender figure before him, for although he saw the tapering white fingers his adversary stretched out, in his impatience to begin the reduction of the man who had challenged him, he had failed to note the breadth of the Duke's shoulders under the well-cut uniform.

The tension in the camp was high. All present had gathered in silent excitement round the two men, and Gonzaga and

Montand, held by the same strange emotion, drew nearer too as the struggle began.

The Gascon made the first move. He turned suddenly to one side, and brought his heavy fist down to the Duke's head. If the blow had fallen, it would surely have broken Valentinois' neck, but the Duke moved so swiftly that those watching scarcely saw the motion, and a second later, the slim steely hands were fastened about the soldier's throat.

The man grunted and brought his own hands up to clamp round the Duke's wrists, exerting all his strength to loosen the hold about his neck. For some moments the silent struggle continued, and the watching troops' amazement grew as they saw the pressure applied by the Gascon, which appeared to have no effect on the Duke's grip. Then, when it seemed that Borgia could no longer sustain the hold, he suddenly released the man's throat, and with a quick upward thrust, hit him with all his force across the face, and his opponent was flung backwards like a sack of grain.

Cursing and swearing, the Gascon got to his feet and threw himself at the Duke, who again twisted out of his way, and brought a clenched fist down on the man's spine in a shattering blow which flattened him in the dust, and brought a cheer from the Italian supporters.

Montand and Gonzaga watched in amazement as the Frenchman pulled himself up again and caught the Duke about the waist in a bear hug which would have crippled a normal man. Borgia's hand fastened under the man's chin, and slowly, and with terrifying purpose, forced the Gascon's head back until it seemed his neck woud snap, and the hold round the Duke's waist was released. The Gascon shook his head in fury and bewilderment, and with a snarl, he struck the Duke, his two hands clasped to form a human hammer. Cesare took the blow on the shoulder and staggered slightly, and seizing the advantage, the soldier grabbed the Duke round the neck and pulled him down.

There was a murmur from the assembled crowd, and Montand frowned. The huge Gascon had the Duke pinned to the ground, and it seemed that his dead weight would make it impossible for one of Cesare's build to shift the mass of flesh and release himself, yet even as he watched, the bulk of the soldier was slowly but surely shifted upwards, and Cesare rolled sideways in a lightning movement and leaped to his feet. Again there was a gasp of amazement, and Montand said in a whisper:

"Dieu, not only courage, my lord, but the strength to back it. I have never seen ought like this before."

Gonzaga did not answer. His eyes were no longer scornful, but his frown had not relaxed.

The Gascon hurled himself at Cesare again, one arm raised to strike a death blow, but as it descended, Valentinois flexed his muscles and sprang. He caught the sinewy limb in a vice-like grip, pulling the man down, so that his arm was brought abruptly across the Duke's upraised knee.

The soldier screamed in agony as his arm broke with a sharp snap, and he fell writhing to the ground. There was a subdued noise as a hundred breaths were released from the taut throats of the watchers; then the Italian soldiers let out a shout of triumph, and Cesare turned to Bartolomeo da Capranica.

"My sword," he said, and his Captain came forward, his face white with excitement, his eyes alight with admiration and something akin to worship.

"Sire," he began, when Cesare gestured him to silence.

"Attend to this man; he is a good fighter and t'would be a pity to lose his services."

He turned to go, and then catching sight of Gonzaga and Montand, pulled on his gauntlets and moved over to them.

"Your man is strong, Captain Montand," he said, and Montand pulled himself out of the bemused state into which he had fallen.

"Y . . . yes . . . my lord. He is a champion amongst the men, yet you, sire . . ."

"I do not engage in battles I cannot win, Captain Montand," said Cesare slowly, "either by the camp fire or in the Romagna."

The hazel eyes moved to Gonzaga and held the latter's startled brown ones captive.

For a moment the two men stared at one another, then the Marquis of Mantua nodded.

"That I can see, my lord. I had not thought . . ."

"You had not thought I was equipped to deal with the conquest of the rebel states," finished Cesare, smiling slightly. "Yet you will find, sire, that nature has endowed me with all I need for this endeavour. Do not confuse me with my brother, who was no soldier. I may lack experience, but I do not lack strength of purpose."

"That I can also see, sire." The frown had gone from Gonzaga's brow, and for the first time his eyes were friendly as he looked at Cesare.

"Sire, if I have——" he broke off, uncertain how to continue his apology to Valentinois.

"No harm is done." Cesare's smile acknowledged the unspoken regrets of the Marquis. "We shall understand one another better after this, I think."

He gave a slight bow and left the men staring after him.

Gonzaga gave a short laugh. "I was greatly misled in my reading of the Duke's mettle," he said finally, "and I account myself normally a good judge of men. The rumours we have heard of the Pope's son blinded me to his true qualities, and nothing I saw at first led me to suppose that he was made of such stuff."

Montand smiled to himself, for he had read beyond the tales and gossip, and had seen something in the Duke which had prepared him to some extent for Cesare's victory over the Gascon, although even he had been surprised by the physical strength exhibited by Valentinois.

"Yes, he is well equipped to lead an army," he said meditatively, "he will not turn and run as Gandia did. He will stand and fight, but he will not fight with blind courage. He will use his brain, this young man, for he has more than muscle at his command, and in but a short time, Italy will ring with the sound of Cesare Borgia's victories."

'You seem very sure of this, Montand." The Marquis

looked at his companion curiously. "He has shewn courage and strength, certainly, but this does not necessarily mean he will make a great commander."

Montand shrugged. "No, I agree, one fight with a Gascon soldier does not prove Borgia is an outstanding General, yet I tell you, sire, we shall live to hear all Italy acclaim him. I cannot tell you why I feel this; I only know that today we have seen a man who was born to lead; born to success. Mark my words; he will earn his place at the head of the Papal Army."

"Perhaps." Gonzaga would not commit himself by agreement, but he was no longer filled with contempt, and there was respect in the glance which followed Cesare's figure across the camp.

"Perhaps, Montand. We shall soon see, for now Borgia has to take Imola and Forlì, and we shall then see how he stands up in battle."

Montand nodded, and he for one had no doubt about the outcome of the test which lay ahead of Valentinois.

CHAPTER SIX

WHEN Alexander and Cesare embarked upon the first impresa, that of the subjugation of Imola and Forlì, many voices were raised in protest at what appeared at first sight to be an act of unprovoked aggression, without excuse or justification. In fact, however, the Pope was entirely justified in his action, and, indeed, the cunning Pontiff seldom moved unless he could prove beyond a shadow of a doubt his legal right to do so. Thus it was in the case of the vicariates of Imola and Forlì, now held by Caterina Sforza for her sons.

Pope Sixtus IV, a feeble irresponsible man of advanced years, had managed to wrest back from the Duke of Milan the city of Imola, which he then passed to his nephew, Girolamo Riario, on the occasion of his marriage to Caterina Sforza. Later, when Pino degli Ordelaffi died, Sixtus, with no great effort on his part, managed to appropriate Forlì and pass this also to Girolamo, for he had great affection for his nephew, and no small degree of admiration for his spirited and lovely wife.

After the lapse of seven years of savage rule, during which time the inhabitants of Imola and Forlì suffered considerably, Girolama died at the hand of an assassin, and Caterina, as forceful as she was beautiful, assumed immediate control of the vicariates for the Riarii heir. When Innocent VII succeeded Sixtus IV, the long-suffering populace turned anxious eyes on the Pope, in the hope that he might rouse himself to demand a return to the Holy See of the two states appropriated by the Riarii, but Innocent VII was a man who shunned arguments and quarrels, and wanted no trouble with the war-like Caterina, and meekly allowed the rights of the Church to lapse with no murmur of protest, and with the passing of time, the Riarii conveniently forgot the true rights of the Church, and reigned supreme in the confiscated states.

Caterina married again, Giacomo Feo, but he suffered a similar fate to her first husband, and when his mutilated body was flung from the battlements by a band of rebels, Caterina's answer was swift and terrible. She led her troops in a brutal destruction of the homes, families and livestock of the rebels concerned, and having revenged the luckless Feo, married again for the third time.

When Alexander first issued a Bull declaring that Imola and Forlì had failed to acknowledge the sovereign rights of the Holy See, and to pay their proper dues, thus forfeiting their freedom, Caterina resisted this claim with all the vigour at her command and had followed this defiance with an attempt to poison the Holy Father by sending him a parchment in which was lodged an envenomed splinter. This endeavour having failed, she sent her children and valuables to Florence, and set about strengthening the Rocca of Forlì against the onslaught of the Duke of Valentinois.

She kept with her her eldest son, Ottaviano, and him she sent to Imola to urge the Council and people to fight the invaders with all their might, but as the people of Imola and Forlì had suffered considerable wrong-doing and savage cruelty under the unjust yoke of the Riarii, Ottaviano's mission met with no success, and the Countess had to accept, with fury and rage, the fact that if she resisted Cesare, she resisted him alone.

Angered though she was, the thought of fighting the Borgia with only a handful of loyal men and the protection of the impregnable Rocca, worried Caterina not at all, for the rigours of her earlier life, allied to her natural strength and determination, exhilarated and encouraged her defiance. She considered that she was more than a match for the French, and certainly able to quell the impudent demands of a brazen youth, whose reputation was as well known in Forlì, as in Rome.

Her immediate advisers were more concerned, for they were aware of the strength of the French forces, and the purpose of Alexander, but Caterina would listen to none of their warnings, and personally supervised the fortifying of the Rocca where she intended to make her stand against the invaders, and something of her splendid spirit and courage lent her soldiers and courtiers the necessary valour to support her rebellion.

Meanwhile, Cesare, escorted by the cavalry under the Baily de Dijon, met at Castelfranco with the two Commissioners from Bologna, and with increasing admiration, François Montand listened to the Duke's negotiations with those worthy officials for the safe conduct and free passage of the Papal Army through their territory.

Cesare shewed a degree of administrative efficiency which Montand found extraordinary in a man, presumably unversed in these matters, and he stopped to wonder why it was that gossip and rumours about the Pope's son seemed to be solely related to the way he dressed himself or the mistresses he took, when they might well have been concerned with the outstanding ability he shewed in all his undertakings, and it occurred to the cynical Montand, that Cesare himself might have fostered and encouraged these rumours which served so well as a cloak for his true activities, lulling his opponents and adversaries into a completely false sense of security.

Imola, as Caterina soon realized, was not prepared to fight for her, and on the 24th November, Achille Tiberti invited the inhabitants of the town to open their gates to the Lieutenants of the King of France, and without further hesitation, this invitation was accepted, although the Rocca itself was still held for Caterina.

Three days later, despite the fact that the fortress was still in alien hands, Cesare entered Imola, thus taking the first step in his plan for supremacy.

Cesare and the army moved on through Faenza, where he met and received a warm welcome from Astorre Manfredi, the young ruler, who was so soon to know Valentinois better, and then went on to Forlì, which quickly surrendered to Tiberti.

Caterina was furious at the weakness and lack of spirit

shewn by the people of Forlì, not taking into account for one moment the suffering of the people under the Riarii rule, who welcomed the Duke's envoy with gladness, for whatever Cesare Borgia's rule was like, they were more than convinced that it could not be worse than their present lot.

After the formalities had been observed, and the Council at Forlì had been appeased and satisfied by Cesare's terms and promises, the Duke entered Forlì.

It was dusk, and the rain was falling in torrents. Through the gloom, the noise and flashes of the spasmodic firing from Caterina's Rocca mingled with the sound of the marching of the infantry in Cesare's train, now some eight thousand strong, and the dull thud of the hooves of the two thousand cavalry under the French Commanders.

The infantry were hired mercenaries, mostly Swiss, German and Gascon, and Cesare was by no means satisfied with their quality or behaviour, for although they were rough and effective fighters, they behaved like savages, and their cruel and inhuman treatment of those they conquered angered Valentinois in no small measure, for it was a denial of all that he intended in his conquest of the Romagna.

Riding at the rear of this formidable column were Yves d'Alègre and Cesare himself. The Duke wore full armour and carried his lance at rest, and before the King's two Lieutenants, the Gonfalon of the Church was borne on high, to emphasize again that the capture of Imola and Forlì was undertaken in the name of the Holy See.

The magnificent trappings of crimson on Cesare's white charger bore for the first time his new coat of arms, incorporating the lilies of France with the Borgia Bull, and the Duke's eyes were calm and confident as he rode into the fire of Caterina's opposition.

Cesare and d'Alègre lost no time in their preparations for the bombardment of the Rocca, and in a short span, had set up two batteries, the larger to the south-west of the town, which came to be known as the della Montagna. This formidable range of guns lay against the side of the City facing the foothills of the Apennines, and its lethal teeth grinned hideously at the defiant Rocca. The second, and smaller battery, was placed on the opposite side of the City near the Capuccini, and when he was certain that the batteries were properly set up, Cesare, who lacked faith in his French companions, and saw no reason to waste men's lives unnecessarily, sent a message to Caterina, informing her that he wished to see her with a view to negotiating terms of peace.

Caterina, upon receiving the message, gave a terse laugh, and expressed herself in violent terms, but nevertheless agreed to the parley, and Cesare, still wearing full armour and accompanied by a General's escort and gaily clad heralds, rode up to the Rocca.

For the first time Caterina met Cesare face to face, although there was some distance between them, for Caterina wisely remained on the battlements to talk to her enemy.

She looked down at the silver-clad figure on the huge steed, and even at that distance, something about the Duke made her catch her breath. The visor of his helmet was raised as he called to her in greeting. She lowered the sword she carried and came forward to the edge of the battlements, her chain-mail making her a spectacular figure, with corn-gold hair streaming down to her broad shoulders, her gentian-blue eyes angry and defiant.

"Well, Borgia," she said raising her voice to combat the noise about them. "What now? Do you come to surrender?"

Cesare smiled slightly, for he had a considerable degree of admiration for this woman who defied him so bravely, but his regard for her courage did not scratch the surface of his unbending resolve.

"No, madonna, not that, although t'would be a privilege to surrender to one so fair and bold."

Caterina's laugh was scornful. "Words, Borgia, words. What do you come for, if not to surrender?"

"I come to discuss terms with you, madonna, for I see no purpose in bloodshed when there is no call for this. Do you want your men destroyed for no reason?"

He put out a hand to still a restive move by his horse, and looked up at Caterina again.

"Madam, this is a battle you are destined to lose. You have seen the numbers of my forces, and the city has already surrendered. What point is there in this resistance, for if you do not give me access to the Rocca willingly, I shall take it by force."

"If you can," flashed Caterina angrily. "This Rocca will not fall like a ripe plum into your avaricious grasp, Borgia. It is well known that this stronghold is impregnable. You will not claw your way through its walls no matter what weapons you use."

Cesare was terse. "I shall take the Rocca, madam, no matter what comes. It is for you to say whether I take it by peaceful means, or whether I must hack my way through the blood and bones of your men to seize it. Well, what do you say?"

"I say that I will see you in perdition before I yield to you. I do not trust you, or your father, and the terms you now bring are no doubt as false as all your dealings. You have taken Imola, because I was not there to defend it, but you will not take Forlì so easily."

"I have already taken Forlì," said Cesare shortly, "only the fortress remains, and I will take that in due course, in peace, or in bloodshed. It is up to you, madam."

"Then take it in blood—if you can!" Caterina shouted her final challenge and turned from the battlements.

Cesare shrugged slightly, and signalling the heralds and escort, returned to his headquarters.

On the 28th December, Cesare opened fire on the Rocca. The powerful della Montagna had seven cannons and ten falconets, loud of voice and sharp of tooth, which began a violent and unceasing barrage against the Rocca. Of the cannons, the long-barrelled guns, the largest was at Tiverina, a maiden of death with a nine foot long barrel and a six inch bore, which hurled a stone ball with deadly accuracy against the defenders' walls. The onslaught was answered with zest and fury by Caterina's guns, and she trained her venom on the battery at Capuccini, causing considerable damage, but still Cesare pounded the fortress without cessation.

The deadly cannons were not the easiest weapons to use, for it was a slow and tedious business to reload the heavy field pieces, and the men needed constant encouragement to keep up the pace which was so vital to the attack.

Cesare was no military theorist, who directed the encounter from a discreet distance. He stayed with the guns day and night, and the artillerymen were astounded at the depth of his knowledge and competence. He could re-load the cumbersome field-pieces as swiftly and efficiently as any man, and quickly gained the respect and trust of those who served him.

His complete fearlessness in the face of the spite of Caterina's guns, and his apparent ability to forego sleep, rest, and food, amazed the French officers. who found it difficult to maintain the standard set by the Duke, and any scorn they might have felt at the commencement of the campaign, died quickly as the siege wore on. Courage and tenacity of this order were not learned by practice; these he had been born with, and his companions recognized very quickly the measure of the man who led them.

During one brief pause, when Caterina's guns were silent, and Cesare's batteries were being re-loaded, Cesare walked across to a tent which had been set up at a safe distance from the Rocca, and flung himself down on a camp bed. His page brought him wine, and he relaxed like a cat; easily, and with no need to unwind the tension normally generated by battle, for he was as calm in combat as he was when he selected the jewels he proposed to wear for a banquet.

He wiped the grime of battle from his forehead.

"This stubborn woman is responsible for much unnecessary death, and she will pay her debt to me in time."

His voice was grim, and Capranica smiled crookedly.

"She has magnificent courage, Highness. I had not thought a woman would take this stand, and hold it, in the face of opposition such as ours."

"Courage, yes, but folly too. She merely delays our victory; she knows this, yet her obstinate pride makes her resist without thought for the men she sacrifices. She shews herself to be a poor general, for a good soldier does not squander the lives of his men for no cause."

"A poor general, but a splendid woman, sire," laughed di Mariano as he wound a rag round an ugly gash in his forearm. "This you must agree, my lord."

Cesare glanced at him.

"See that that wound is properly attended to," he said briefly. "Yes, she is a woman of courage, I admit; the Madonna Caterina. Yet soon I will take possession of her, and the other Madonna she holds jealously to her breast."

"The other Madonna, sire?" Capranica looked up sharply. "I thought her daughters had gone to Florence. Who else does she hold in her fortress?"

Cesare smiled slowly. "No woman, Bartolomeo, but the Madonna di Meldola."

The others stared at him, and he laughed slightly.

"You have not heard of it?"

Bartolomeo shook his head. "No, sire, I for one have not. What is it? A treasure? A statue of the Virgin?"

"A treasure, certainly, but not a statue. The Madonna di Meldola is a miniature, so small that it can rest easily in the palm of a woman's hand, and it is surrounded by jewels of such beauty and value that the eyes are dazzled to behold it. This is the great treasure that Caterina Sforza holds with her in the Rocca, and which I shall wrest from her, with her Keep, when we break through her fortifications."

"But surely, my lord, she would have sent this to Florence, for we know she has despatched her valuables to that city, lest they fall into your Highness's hands."

Cesare shook his head. "No, she would not let this go, for there is a legend that when the Madonna di Meldola leaves the Rocca, the fortress will fall into enemy hands, and thus Caterina will keep it with her, at least as long as it takes me to reach her."

Di Mariano looked at the Duke curiously. "You have seen this treasure, sire?"

"No, but I have heard men talk of it, and of its beauty and

supernatural power, and I look forward to adding it to my own collection of works of art as a souvenir of my encounter with Caterina."

The Duke rose, his Captains leaping to their feet as he did so.

"Come, we must return to the batteries, for there is no time to tarry here. We must pursue this battle without respite, for thus will Caterina's spirit be broken on the wheel of our determination."

He turned to the tent flap, when it was jerked back to admit Giulio Alberini.

Cesare raised an eyebrow, when it was jerked back to admit Giulio Alberini.

Cesare raised an eyebrow at his Captain's hasty advent, and Alberini gave a quick salute.

"Sire, we have taken a prisoner. A lad who has escaped from the Rocca, and who claims asylum with us from the tyranny of the Riarii."

Cesare frowned. "A prisoner? How did he escape? It seems to me that the measures Caterina takes to keep me out would effectively keep in any of her own men. Are you sure this is not a trick, Giulio?"

Alberini shrugged. "'Tis not impossible, of course, sire, but his distress seems genuine, and he has been badly treated, that is obvious. I have ordered that he be tended and given food, but kept under close guard."

The Duke's eyes were thoughtful. "I see. Well, if 'tis a genuine plea for help, he will give us much assistance, for he will have information which will be useful to us. Later I will see him myself, but now we must attend to the guns. Come, sires, there is no time to be lost."

For the next few hours the battle raged. Cesare's batteries threw screaming stones in unending succession at the walls of the Rocca, to be answered by the venom of the Rairii guns, and through the twilight the noise of death and destruction was an ugly accompaniment to the sound of the soft rain which continued to fall. Caterina's losses could not be assessed, but Cesare grimaced in exasperation when his Captains reported his own casualties, and he swore under his breath when he learned of the number which had died in the last encounter.

Towards midnight the exchange died down, and Cesare, moderately satisfied with the damage he had done, if angered by the price he had had to pay for his success, returned to his tent and sent for the refugee from Caterina's stronghold.

The boy came into the lantern-lit tent between two soldiers and accompanied by Giulio Alberini, and Cesare raised his eyes from the maps spread in front of him to regard his prisoner.

He was some nineteen years, but sturdily built, and his shoulders and legs were strong and muscular under the torn rags he wore. His hair was dark and ragged, his eyes a curious pale brown and too knowledgeable for one of his age, but his mouth shewed his youth, and he hesitated as he met the Duke's gaze.

Cesare leaned back and surveyed him silently for a moment, then he gestured the soldiers to release him.

"Well, sire. And what business have you in my camp?"

The boy rubbed his wrists and his eyes fell before the compelling stare of the Duke. Then he pulled himself together and looked back at Cesare.

"Sire, I seek refuge from Caterina Sforza."

"So I gather." Cesare shewed no particular enthusiasm for this information, and the quill between his long fingers tapped a trifle impatiently on the rough table before him.

"Come, sire, a little more must be known about this. How did you contrive to leave so well-guarded a fortress as Madonna Caterina's Rocca?"

The boy shuffled uneasily. " 'Twas not easy, Highness, but the guards were careless and preoccupied, for the Madonna Caterina needed all men on duty at the batteries, and only one man was left to tend the prisoners."

"And?" The Duke was still sceptical.

"He was easily overcome, sire." The boy's shoulders

straightened in remembered victory. "Then it was simple to get from the cells where we were kept . . ."

"We? Who else was with you, and where are they now?" asked the Duke sharply, and his prisoner coloured quickly at Valentinois' tone.

"Sire, some three or four other men, but they were old and could not get beyond the walls of the Rocca."

"I see. Go on." Valentinois' quill began its light tattoo again, and the boy swallowed with difficulty, uneasy before the searching glance of the Prince, but he coughed gently and began his tale again.

"My lord, when your batteries opened fire, the Rocca was thrown into a panic, and all attention was on the guns. I jumped clear of the walls on the opposite side from the batteries and managed to clamber down to safety, and from thence I made my way here."

Cesare's gaze did not waver. "And your name?"

"Lorenzo Savelli, Highness; from Milan."

"And why did Caterina hold you prisoner?"

"I came to Forlì as a hired soldier, sire, but the Madonna Caterina discovered that my father had been one of the band who defied the Tyrant Giacomo Feo. My father was killed when the Madonna Caterina destroyed the rebels." His eyes fell and he caught his lip in momentary anguish.

"And yet you returned to Forlì to serve the Riarii cause?" asked Cesare softly, and the boy raised his eyes again.

"Yes, my lord."

"Why?" The voice was softer still, and Savelli flushed.

"It was in my mind, sire, that if I were one of the Madonna Caterina's hired soldiers, I could more readily effect her destruction."

"I see. You sought revenge for your father's death?"

The pen was stilled. "And Caterina discovered this?"

"She found out who I was, sire, although there was no proof that I sought her ill yet it did not stop her . . ."

Lorenzo broke off and his colour rose slightly again.

"Did not stop her from doing what?"

Savelli did not answer, and Cesare's gaze travelled slowly

over him, then he rose and crossed the tent and with a sudden twist, pulled the shabby jerkin from the boy's shoulders.

Alberini gave a faint exclamation as he saw the savage weals across Savelli's back, but Cesare said nothing, returning to his place behind the table.

Finally he nodded. "I see." He looked at Alberini.

"See that Messer Savelli is given food and clothes, and later I will have questions to ask you, sire. You may be of considerable use to me in this war I wage against your enemy."

"I will do what I can, Highness," said Savelli, recovering slightly from the Duke's overpowering presence. " I will do whatever I can to assist you, sire."

"Good, good." The Duke waved a dismissal, but when the soldiers and Alberini has escorted the boy from his presence, his eyes were even more thoughtful, and on the following day when Alberini came to him again in some agitation, his surprise was not so great as Giulio had imagined it would be.

The bombardment had continued all the morning, and Cesare was still in the batteries when Alberini approached him, his face white under the streaks of dirt, and the Duke left the gun he was helping to load to listen to Giulio's tale.

"My lord, I think we may have uncovered a plot of some kind." He pulled off his gauntlets and wiped a bloodstained hand over his sweat covered brow.

"This boy, Savelli, tried to leave the camp, and when he was taken, it was found that he had on him a casket of considerable value, and he refuses to say where he got it from, or what it contains."

Cesare's glance was impatient. "Are we so ill-equipped that we lack the means to persuade his tongue?"

Giulio laughed ruefully. "No, sire, but I thought you would prefer to handle this matter yourself, for the boy said——" he broke off uncertainly, and Cesare frowned.

"He said what?"

"He said that if we touched the casket our lives would be forfeit, for it was a treasure of such value and holiness, that mere mortals could not look upon it and live."

Cesare stared at him. "Dio, Giulio, and this stopped you? Have you become so chicken-hearted that the threat of some peasant boy checks your purpose?"

Alberini flinched at the Duke's contempt, but his voice was calm as he answered his master.

"No, sire, and I think you know this is not so. It occurred to me that there would be only one such treasure left in the Rocca, and for this reason, I thought you would prefer to deal with the boy yourself."

Cesare gave a faint sigh. "Your pardon, Giulio, I had forgotten. You are quite right, of course. If Savelli has a treasure of any value, it will be the Madonna di Meldola, and I ask your forgiveness for my words."

He laid a hand on Alberini's shoulder, who smiled warmly at the Duke's ready apology.

"Come," went on Cesare, "let us see this reckless youth, and hear what else he has to say, for it seems to me he has a glib tongue, and we must be on our guard, lest this treasure slips through our fingers."

Leaving orders for the re-loading and re-firing of the mortars, Cesare accompanied Alberini to the tent where Savelli had been taken. On the table in the centre of the tent lay a small golden casket of superb workmanship, and on its lid and on the sides was an intricate pattern formed by diamonds, rubies, sapphires, and other gems. Cesare looked at the box silently for a moment, then at Savelli, who was once more held between two of Cesare's guards. The Duke sat down behind the table and placed a finger on the lid of the casket.

"A pretty thing, Messer Savelli. You did not think to mention this to me at our first meeting."

Savelli's eyes were blank. " 'Twas of no concern to you, sire. This belongs to me."

"So?" The Duke was ironic. "And when did you become possessed of such a rarity, sire? Is this the wage Caterina pays her hired soldiers?"

The boy's mouth tightened, but he did not answer, and Cesare smiled.

"I think not, Messer Savelli. This was what you took from Caterina's treasure chests before you left the Rocca, was it not? I applaud your impudence in plucking from the Countess her most prized possession."

The boy's eyes were suddenly suspicious. "I do not understand you," he said quickly. "'Tis but a box. A pretty thing, but not of such value."

Cesare's finger continued to trace a pattern on the casket lid.

"No? Yet I estimate this box alone would keep you in prosperity for many years, sire. But it is not the box which you stole, is it, Messer Savelli, but the contents. That is what you wanted, is it not?"

He flicked the lid open suddenly, and there was a gasp of dismay from the boy.

The others drew closer, and Cesare stared down at the box. Inside the velvet lined casket lay an oval miniature, surrounded by a rim of diamonds, rubies and pearls, interlaced with gold filigree work of great beauty. The painting itself was of surpassing loveliness, and the silence in the tent was a tribute to the skill of the man who had painted it.

Cesare's smile deepened. "Yes, an exquisite trifle, Messer Savelli, and I can well understand why you wanted to take it with you."

His eyes fell again as he studied the miniature more closely, and his hand stretched out to lift it from its case. As he did so, he glanced up again, and for one brief, frozen second, saw in the eyes of his prisoner a look he had not thought to see.

The fear, the hesitation, the anguish were gone. In those odd, pale brown eyes was a look of triumph of such venomous intensity, that Cesare's hand was transfixed. The stillness was a thick blanket about the group, and as Cesare's eyes held the boy's, the look of victory faded from Savelli's gaze, and his face was ashy white.

"Pick it up," said Cesare, and his voice was a whisper of

sound, yet it cut through the deathly stillness like a trumpet.

The boy did not move, and Cesare's hand dropped.

"Pick it up," he repeated, but still Savelli made no move.

"No?" Cesare leaned back. "I see. Captain Alberini, I beg you lift this bauble from its casket, and do so with care, for if I am not mistaken, we may at last be coming to the true reason for Messer Savelli's visit to our camp."

He snapped his fingers, and Giulio drew on his heavy leather gauntlet, and taking a short knife from his belt, slipped it under the miniature and raised it from the crimson velvet bed. As he did so, there was a faint click, and a thin needle sprang out from the top of the jewelled frame, and Cesare gave a short laugh.

"Yes. Indeed, this would have been a valuable treasure had your plan worked, sire, for it would have rid Caterina Sforza of her conqueror, for make no mistake, sire, I will take Caterina Sforza as surely as I have taken you, and this trinket. She will rue the day she set her hand against me, and I will exact full penance for this act of treachery, from her, as well as from you."

He rose, and slammed the lid of the box down.

"Take him away," he snapped. "You know what to do with the enemies of the Church, Captain Alberini; see that Messer Savelli is given no further opportunity to plot against the Holy See, and then return to the batteries, for now we will intensify our efforts to reduce this pile of rocks behind which Caterina Sforza crouches, and when I enter the Keep, she will answer to me for this."

At the tent door, he turned to look at Savelli.

"So near to success, Messer Savelli, and such care you took to deceive me, even to the lengths of being flogged to convince me of your sufferings at Caterina's hands, but it was not enough. It is a little late to give you lessons in strategy, for you will not live to benefit from them, but one golden rule should always be observed in battle, be it between armies or between two men. One should never let an adversary know one's thoughts. That was your mistake, for I read in that single glance of yours, all I needed to know about your intent, and this has destroyed you, and will destroy Caterina."

He jerked his head to Alberini, and strode out of the tent, leaving Savelli pale and shaken, and he had no words left as Captain Alberini's hand descended on his shoulder.

CHAPTER SEVEN

CESARE went back to the batteries in a cold rage. He had been sufficiently incensed by Caterina's stubborn refusal to accept defeat, and although the number of men he had lost was not vast, he was miserly of men's lives, and hated to lose one unnecessarily, and in his view, all his present losses were completely pointless and due entirely to Caterina's pig-headedness.

Added to this absurd stand she had taken, was her effort to kill him, but even as his mind dwelt on this incident, his anger left him, and a faint smile touched his lips. As Caterina's plan had failed in its purpose, he could afford to regard it dispassionately, and he had to admit it had a certain amount of merit.

Had she sent her emissary into his camp, openly carrying the casket, it was certain that suspicions would have been aroused, and no one, least of all Cesare himself, would have touched it without extreme caution, but as Savelli had come, first as an ill-treated and nervous refugee from Caterina's cruelty, and then appeared to be an ambitious adventurer, who wished to flee from Cesare's camp with a priceless treasure, none had guessed at first that his true intent, and that of the woman whom he served, was to focus Cesare's attention on the miniature in such a way that he would handle it without hesitation.

Cesare reflected grimly on the narrow margin of safety which had remained when he glanced up to see that look of triumph on Savelli's face. Death had been very close at that moment, and Valentinois' mouth was no longer amused as he called a messenger to him.

His orders given, he walked out into the camp and sent for his Captains.

"I will try once more to bring a conclusion to this senseless slaughter," he said, and Capranica stared at the Duke in astonishment.

"Sire! You will parley with Madonna Caterina again? Surely, my lord, after her attempt on your life, this would be unwise."

"Perhaps." The Duke shrugged slightly. "But so is losing men, for no good cause. I am prepared to expend the lives of my troops when I have to, and when there is reason to do so. Here, there is no such reason. I will try again to make this virago understand how foolish this resistance is."

"Highness, she may try another trick. Let me go to her this time."

Cesare smiled faintly at Alberini's anxious face.

"It is possible, Giulio, but Caterina will only parley with me, and if there is risk, I must take it myself."

"No sire!" The vehement protest from Mario di Mariano increased the Duke's amusement.

"Come, come, Mario. Do you imply that I am no match for the Madonna Caterina?" He clapped di Mariano on the shoulder and laughed.

"Your fears are needless, Mario. I am more than capable of defending myself against Caterina. Now, come get my horse and summon the heralds, for I have sent a messenger to the Countess, and it would not do to keep a lady waiting."

"My lord." Caprinica was frowning. "Your armour."

Cesare shook his head. "No, not this time. I have sought a brief truce with the Madonna Caterina, and she will honour this, up to a point."

His Captains were silent, their faces reflecting their concern and anxiety for Cesare's recklessness, but they knew him too well to pursue their protests, for his Highness was apt to be impatient with argument, and none of them were prepared to risk the Duke's anger falling upon them.

Valentinois rode out of camp on his white steed, accompanied by two heralds and one attendant, and he was as calm and at ease as if he were taking his customary morning ride. It was mid-afternoon, and the January gloom hung like a veil over the countryside. The rain which had been falling all day had now stopped, but the ground over which the horses pounded was a thick cloying mud, and even the gay attire of Cesare's heralds seemed drab in this setting. As he arrived at the Rocca, he found Caterina had lowered the drawbridge, and accompanied by two of her Captains, she crossed the moat to meet Cesare.

As they came face to face, Caterina signalled her escort to return to the Rocca, and Cesare studied her with interest.

At closer quarters she looked older. From the top of the Rocca she had seemed to retain her youth, but at the distance of an arm's length her hair, though thick and fair, had lost some of its original gloss and golden sheen, and although her eyes were still a deep blue, there were fine lines round them, and there was a slight slackening of the jaw-line which betrayed the years. Her skin was thick and white and the excitement and anger generated in her by her struggle, gave her a wild-rose colour which, with her firm, well-moulded figure, made her still an attractive woman.

Valentinois, as responsive to beauty as his father, bowed low, and kissed the hand she extended to him.

"Well, Borgia?" Her voice was clear and strong, and Cesare detected no note of humility in it. "What now? Do you come to seek a reconciliation?"

Cesare smiled, but again he felt a sharp quickening of anger at her haughty tone.

"That is my intent, madam," he said calmly, and shewed nothing of his irritation. "For, as I told you before, there is no object in throwing men's lives away."

"My men regard their lives well lost in the defence of the Rocca," said Caterina coldly, and Cesare's brows rose slightly.

"Do they, madonna; I wonder?"

The blue eyes flashed. "You doubt my word, Borgia? You think my men would not die for me, if needs be?"

Valentinois eyed her steadily.

"Any man would be honoured to die for you, madonna, but do they really regard their lives well spent in the protection of this heap of stones which, in truth, is already lost?"

He flicked his whip contemptuously towards the towering Rocca, grim and grey in the quickly darkening day, and Caterina's mouth tightened.

"Whilst I live, the Rocca is not lost, Borgia. I am not afraid of you, for the raging ambitions of you and your father will not shift me from my position. I will make my stand against you here and shew you how empty your visions are. I will not bow before your dominance."

"You, and all Italy, will bow before me 'ere long," said Cesare, and although he had not raised his voice in the slightest, the intrepid Countess slowly whitened, for there was something in Valentinois' words which struck a shaft of fear into her indomitable courage.

He was so confident; so sure, and so cold. If he had shewn any trace of anger or passion; some indication that the man she fought was but an ambitious youth, with an insensate dream which drove him on to fight with such tenacity. But there was no such indication. He was cool, dispassionate and unmoved, and Caterina felt a tremor of something she had never experienced before.

She quelled the emotion sharply, and glanced back at the Rocca. Then she met Cesare's eyes squarely again.

"And what reconciliation have you in mind, and on whose terms is this to be arranged?"

"On my terms, Madonna," he replied smoothly, "did you doubt this?"

Again her colour rose, and he smiled.

"May we not at least discuss this together?"

She pushed a strand of hair from her brow.

"There is nothing to lose by this." She hesitated a second and then held out her hand to him again.

"I beg you to come with me to the Rocca, for there is a state of truce between us, and you will come to no harm."

Cesare paused fractionally, then gave a slight bow, and Caterina turned and walked back to the Rocca.

As the Duke put one foot on the drawbridge, there was a sharp grinding noise as Caterina's men started the clumsy apparatus which raised the drawbridge, and for a second

Cesare's cyes met Caterina's blazing blue eyes across the gap between them, and they were alight with malice.

Valentinois took a flying leap as the drawbridge moved slowly upwards.

From the safety of the far side of the moat, he laughed, and quickly mounted his waiting horse.

"Ill-timed, madonna," he called, "ill-timed, for your men misjudged their move."

The light was fading quickly, and Caterina's figure was a white blur across the moat.

"Now, madam," he was terse. "I am done with talking. Twice I have given you the opportunity to reach an honourable conclusion to this encounter, but you will have no third chance. Now, I will take you and your Rocca by force, and by God, madam, you will live to regret your short-sightedness."

With that, he turned his horse's head, and signalling to his heralds, returned to camp, and strode into the tent where his Captains awaited him.

"Sire!" Bartolomeo's face was white, for the incident at the moat had been reported to him by one of his men who had stalked silently after the Duke's party.

"That was a risk which you should not have taken."

Valentinois smiled coldly. "I am a soldier. I take what risks are needful. But now," the amber eyes were angry, "now we will shew that proud virago what is the cost of her defiance. Come, we will prepare for the assault without further delay, for we have wasted enough timc at Forlì." He looked at Capranica.

"Tell your men to bring up the fascines which we have concealed in the woods." He jerked his head in the direction of the sweep of hills behind him, where, under the thick clumps of trees at their foot, his men had stored such things as his Highness had not required for immediate use.

"There are barges in the river yonder," said Cesare to Pietro Santa Croce, "take them, and block the moat. Then tell the artillery Captains to move the cannons to the new positions we discussed last night, and upon my signal, open fire. I am done with words; now Caterina will feel my claws."

He strode out of the tent, leaving his officers to deal with his orders, and in a short time, when all was prepared, Valentinois gave the signal which began the last encounter at Forlì.

For six days the battle raged. Cesare's fire was heavy and damaging, but Caterina was as stubborn as the Duke, and a flash of her golden hair, or the white cloak she wore, could often be seen on the top of the battlements as she urged her men to return Cesare's venom.

But despite her valour and determination, the violence of Cesare's attack gradually took its toll, and one by one the guns on the battlements of the Rocca were silenced, and piece by piece the upper part of the stronghold crumbled under the steady blows.

"We shall be ready to use the infantry in two days," said Cesare to his Captains as they assembled on the morning of the seventh day. "Tell the men, for this will give them encouragement and stiffen their resolve."

And two days later, Valentinois made good his prophesy as he stormed the Rocca on the afternoon of Sunday the 12th January. Caterina, resolute to the end, manned the breach Cesare had achieved, but by then her guns were few and her men tired, and the fire with which they answered the Duke's challenge was not strong enough to hold the crumbling Rocca.

Caterina retired to the centre chamber of the Rocca with one or two of her Captains and servants, and prepared to defend the heart of the torre maestro, should the Duke cut his way through the outer shell, and she held in her strong right hand a sharp sword which she was more than capable of using should the need arise.

Cesare himself went up to the breach to urge his men forward and in spite of the defensive guns, the Swiss mercenaries flung themselves over the moat, now choked with barges, timber and masonry, and into the Rocca. The standard of the Rocca was hacked down by a Swiss soldier who gave a loud jeer as he flung it into a pile of burning wood, only to cry again a second later as a knife bit deep into his back. The hand fighting which ensued was bloody and savage. In the failing light, the fires and torches provided a glow against which the most lethal and bitter struggles took place.

Men clawed and hacked at each other with sword, knife, lance, or whatever weapon came to hand, and when these fell from bloodstained fingers, nails bit and gouged at the enemy in primitive and violent passion.

Caterina came to the doorway of the central Keep to watch the horror laid before her, and gave a sharp order to her men to fire the magazine stores, but the resulting chaos of explosion and smoke was the final straw which defeated her own men, and gradually her troops were driven back and were hemmed into narrow spaces where effective fighting was impossible, and when he could see that Caterina's forces were completely divided and spent, Giovanni di Casale, one of Caterina's Captains, took matters into his own hands and raised the white flag.

Caterina, screaming her rage at his treachery and cowardice, was seized by a French foot soldier, as Cesare and Yves d'Alègre, who had now rejoined him, crossed the moat into the Rocca.

As Cesare and d'Alègre rode across the smoke laden ditch and into the Keep, the Gascon and German mercenaries, now completely assured of victory, engaged in a spate of atrocities which was beyond description, and which caused Cesare's mouth to curl in anger, but he had no time to deal with them then, for he had other matters on his mind.

He and d'Alègre found Caterina in a chamber in the centre of the Rocca to which the French troops had taken her, and she was as proud and defiant as ever, her white gown blackened and bloodstained, and her corn-coloured hair darkened by the smoke and dust which covered thet whole Rocca.

Cesare walked over to her and ran his eye over her dishevelled appearance. She straightened her shoulders proudly.

"Well, Borgia?" Her tone had lost nothing of its defiance. "What next? You have taken the Rocca, through the cowardice and treachery of one of my own men; now, doubtless, you propose to take my person."

She shewed no fear, and again Cesare felt a slight flicker of admiration for his gallant adversary, but he merely bowed.

"That is so, madonna. I now take you. To Rome, as the prisoner of the Holy Father."

Cesare's quick ear noted the exclamation of dissent from d'Alègre, and knowing the Frenchman's exaggerated ideas of chivalry, he had anticipated some resistance to the idea of Caterina becoming his prisoner, but he gave no indication that he had heard the protest.

Caterina gave a short laugh. "The Pope's prisoner! But what of you, Borgia? Do you not claim my person for yourself? Do you not claim your rights as a conqueror?"

There was no tremor in her voice, and, indeed, she seemed to have about her a certain air of restrained excitement as she met Cesare's eyes with a bold stare.

Again Cesare heard the faintest protest from d'Alègre, but he smiled gently at Caterina.

"Madonna, if you mean what I think you do, you may rest your fears. You will be escorted to Rome with the same respect and privileges as I would accord my own mother."

For a brief moment there was silence in the chamber, as Caterina's face whitened under Cesare's insult, then she stepped forward and hit him across the face.

The sound was shocking in the quiet room, but Cesare did not move, and gradually the anger in Caterina's eyes died, and despite herself she shivered slightly at what she saw in her captor's face.

Finally Cesare stirred. "Take the Madonna Caterina to her chamber. Keep her there. In a short while we shall be leaving the Rocca; see that she is ready to accompany us."

He turned away, leaving the men to obey his commands, but d'Alègre followed him out into the dust choked hall and said sharply:

"Sire! You cannot take the Madonna Caterina prisoner. It is unthinkable. What sort of war do you wage, that involves taking captive a woman, and a woman who has shewn so much courage and spirit?"

Cesare pulled on his gloves and regarded d'Alègre thoughtfully.

"My instructions from the Holy Father are to take Caterina Sforza to Rome as my prisoner, and this I propose to do. As to the kind of war I wage d'Alègre, my war is absolute and total, and I will stop at nothing to achieve what I have to do. I have no time for your sentimental feelings for this woman. If a woman stands against me, barricades herself in her Rocca and fires on my men, killing considerable numbers of them, then she puts herself outside the realm of chivalrous protection. If a woman chooses to fight me, Captain d'Alègre, so be it, but she will receive no different treatment in her defeat than would a man, and I advise you not to stand in my way lest you too receive a lesson in the way Italians make war."

D'Alègre was white with fury. "I need no further lessons from you, sire, for I have seen your methods to-day. Only a peasant would fight this way. In my country, men do not make war on women."

Cesare's mouth was terse. "A peasant, eh? You take great risks, Captain d'Alègre, and not only in battle."

"I am not afraid of you, Borgia, nor your reputation, tarnished though it be. You will not harm one of his Majesty's officers; you would not dare."

Cesare moved forward a pace, and his eyes held d'Alègre's.

"Would not dare, Captain d'Alègre? You would be well advised to think before you speak in such rash tones to me. There is nothing I would not do to accomplish what I have set my hand to. And if this involves the capture of a woman who has defied me, and the destruction of a Captain, not loyal to my cause, then, Monseigneur d'Alègre, I would not hesitate for one second, and I beg you to remember this."

D'Alègre's mouth was rigid with anger, and his eyes stormy.

"You are a barbarian, Borgia," he said furiously. "An Italian peasant with no idea about the proper usage of war, and I regret that his Majesty's orders require me to serve with you."

The Duke was still, but he gave no further indication of anger, and his voice was light when he answered the enraged Frenchman.

"This exchange is hardly furthering our purpose, d'Alègre. You should be on your way to Forlimpopoli, and I suggest you assemble your men and leave without further delay. You may go with a quiet mind, for I have no intention of harming Caterina. I may be a barbarian Italian peasant, but I have no fancy for the possession of this ageing virago."

His sneer made d'Alègre's colour mount again, but he had no more to say, and with a brief salute, turned on his heel and flung out of the hall, leaving Cesare to gaze after him with an expression which was far from kindly.

But Cesare's troubles with the French were not finished, for on the day before he proposed to leave Forlì, he was confronted with the Baily de Dijon's demand that Caterina should be released.

The Duke was at his headquarters in the Palazzo Numai, where Caterina was also housed, when the Baily de Dijon stormed into the library. Cesare was working on despatches to Rome, and looked up in surprise as the tall Frenchman came up to the table and struck it with a sharp blow.

Cesare leaned back in his chair and raised an eyebrow.

"And what is this, sire?" he enquired shortly. "What causes this disturbance when I am engaged on important matters?"

The Baily de Dijon gave a short laugh. "Important matters! Pah! You merely play at war, Borgia, for you would be powerless without the French forces. You are nothing without his Majesty's troops to back you."

Cesare laid down his pen and looked pensively at the irate soldier.

"So I have been told before," he said acidly, "but the fact remains that Louis' troops have been engaged in this impressa, and the Pope has paid the price for them. I fail to see, therefore, why I must be bombarded by your continuous complaints as to my ordering of the battle."

"Your methods are inexcusable," snapped the Baily angrily. "You have no conception of how to fight a war."

"I have a very good idea how to conduct a war," said Cesare softly. "It is not your way, but this does not make me either incompetent or a fool. One day, sire, you will see how I make war with my own troops, when I am no longer hampered by a body of men who divide their time between atrocities inflicted upon the people they conquer, and a ridiculous sense of chivalry which has not part in conflict. This is not war as I understand it, and I will shew you and your brother officers that the Italian usage of war is more effective, more realistic, and more lasting than your outmoded traditions."

The Baily's face was purple. "You! You think you can teach me how to make war, Borgia? How will you do this? By poisoning your enemies? For if this is so, I can well believe you might succeed, for from what I hear, you are well versed in this method of disposing of those who oppose you. Or perhaps a knife in the back of your adversary would come more easily to you. It should not be difficult, for if you could kill your own brother thus, it would take little effort to despatch an enemy that way."

There was a gasp of astonishment from the secretaries who were working with Cesare, and Mario di Mariano, the only one of Cesare's Captains present, drew his sword and came round the table to face the Baily di Dijon, his face white, his eyes blazing with something more than fury.

"Captain Mariano," said Cesare sharply, "put your sword away."

For a moment Mario made no move, and Valentinois stood up.

"Obey me," he said curtly, and gradually the light went out of Mariano's eyes, and slowly he returned the sword to its sheath and bowed stiffly to the Duke.

"Your pardon, sire," he said, and his voice was taut with the rage in him. Cesare made a brief gesture, and Mariano returned to his former position, and the Duke looked back at the Baily di Dijon.

"Have you anything else to say to me, sire?" he asked coolly, "for if not, I am busy."

The Baily scowled. "Yes, Borgia, I have this to say. My men and I propose to take the Countess under our protection. She surrendered in good faith to one of my soldiers, and this imposes an obligation upon me. I will not let her fall into your hands, to be taken to Rome as one of your prizes. She will come with me."

Cesare's hand was on his dagger, and for a moment there was a light in his eyes which denied the calmness of his manner.

"Sire," he said quietly. "My orders are to take Caterina Sforza to Rome, and this I will do, but if it will aid your conscience and quieten your fears, I will hold her as the King of France's prisoner, and will accord her all the honour due to one who has the King's protection. Will this satisfy you?"

The Baily relaxed. In truth, he was a little uneasy at the fury he had unleashed upon Cesare, for although he led the company under the King's orders, Valentinois was the Pope's son, and the King was committed to the impresa for Alexander. Furthermore, although he had contempt for Cesare's action in taking Caterina, he had marked the manner of Valentinois' ability in combat, which, despite his present abuse, had aroused his reluctant admiration, and he knew the Duke was not to be underestimated.

Gruffly he gave his assent to the proposal, and after suitable arrangements had been made, he left Cesare and his staff to continue their work.

Mario di Mariano could contain himself no longer.

"My lord! You let this insolent Frenchman talk to you in this manner, and do not seek retribution? I beg you, sire, give me leave to deal with him."

The Duke gave a short laugh and resumed his seat.

"Do not be a fool, Mario. This is no time to challenge the Baily di Dijon. We need him, and we need d'Alègre. There is no opportunity now of engaging in personal differences. We are conducting an impresa, and we need the French. I have told you this before, and warned you of the need for patience."

"He called you a murderer, sire!" cried Mariano. "Surely, even in war, one need not bear insults such as this."

"And d'Alègre called me a peasant," said Cesare calmly, "the one accusation is as untrue as the other. Now, Mario, put this from your mind, for it is not important. You must learn to accept the need to await the achievement of your will, be it success in battle, or the destruction of an enemy. As I will wait."

The Duke's expression was hard to read.

"I will wait as long as I have to, but one day, when I am ready, and when the stars are in our favour, I will answer the French."

He glanced at his Captain. "Dismiss it from your thoughts, Mario, as I will, until I am ready to deal with it. Now we must attend to these despatches."

And with that, Mario di Mariano had to be content, but as he watched the lines round the corner of Cesare's mouth, it occurred to him that only the iron self-control which the Duke so constantly exercised, had stopped the sudden and untimely death of the Baily di Dijon.

Later that day, Cesare went to see Caterina. She sat by the window gazing down at the darkening scene, and something in the droop of her shoulders gave indication of her low spirits.

The grime and dust of battle had gone, and her hair was clean and flowing, and her pale blue gown richly embroidered.

Cesare bowed and kissed her hand.

"Madame."

"Well, Borgia?" said Caterina with something of her old spirit, and Cesare smiled and sat beside her.

"Your French captors are most concerned and anxious about your welfare," he said. "And I have given them my undertaking that you will be regarded as the King of France's hostage, and accorded due honours."

"But still you will take me to Rome?" Caterina's mouth moved in a twisted smile. "It will not stop you doing that, will it?"

"No, madonna, it will not stop me."

She smiled again, this time with more humour.

" 'Tis a pity we fight on opposing sides, Borgia, for you have great determination and spirit."

"So have you, madam."

"But it did not help me in my encounter with you. Had the French forces come to take Imola and Forlì without you, I should be free. I should not face the humiliation of riding in your triumphal train through Rome as our prisoner. D'Alègre and the Baily di Dijon would not have held me as you do."

She sighed, and her eyes were sad.

"It seems to me that I have spent a life-time in conflict, and now it is to end for me as the hostage of one who, as he himself points out, is young enough to be my son."

The Duke gave a faint chuckle. "Forgive me, madonna; that was inexcusable, for you are a beautiful woman. I was angry because you made me expend my troops against your defiance."

"An apology, sire?" Caterina was mocking. "Is it possible that there is a streak of chivalry in you after all? Can Captain d'Alègre have been mistaken in his reading of your character?"

"No, he was not mistaken. He would free you; I will not, but my decision does not blind me to your appeal, madonna."

He laid his hands on her shoulders, and felt her tremble slightly.

"You have nothing to fear from me," he said gently, and she raised her chin.

"I do not fear you, Borgia, nor would I, if you shewed that you did not intend to keep your word to Captain d'Alègre."

"I believe you," he said, and he was smiling. "I think you would enjoy a further encounter with me, madonna, but on this occasion, at least, I propose to keep my word."

He bent his head and his mouth covered hers. For a long minute he held her in his embrace, then he released her and stood up.

"I bid you good night, madonna. Tomorrow we shall leave Forlì."

Caterina was staring up at him; one hand, not entirely steady touched her lips.

"You are a devil, Borgia," she whispered. "A devil without a heart."

"So I have been told before, madonna," he said cheerfully, "but you will be safe in my hands as I have promised you."

And with that he left Caterina, torn between rage and despair at her capture by the ruthless Duke, and a sudden feeling she did not understand, which had been aroused in her when Valentinois had taken her in his arms.

CHAPTER EIGHT

CESARE returned to Rome at the end of February, and this time as a conqueror. The excitement and enthusiasm surrounding the preparations for his reception were wildly out of proportion to the size of his victories, and Cesare was the first to appreciate this, for he had placed little importance on the taking of Imola and Forlì, regarding the operation as something in the nature of a skirmish, rather than a battle. Nevetheless, all Rome became infected by the feverish tension which grew and grew as the time got nearer to Cesare's arrival.

The Pope was so excited that he was quite unable to deal with any work and dismissed in high impatience those seeking an audience with him, and to the Cardinals in attendance upon him, he spoke in fond and proud tones of the Duke's success.

"Did I not say he would succeed?" he demanded, his black eyes alight with pride and joy, "did I not say that he would achieve anything he set out to do?"

None of those to whom he spoke felt it politic to remind his Holiness that he had gone to considerable lengths to keep his son from a military career, for Alexander had pushed from his flexible mind the earlier differences with Cesare on this score, and if he ever thought of Giovanni, his most belovèd son who had once led the Pontificial Army, he gave no sign of it as he stood on the veranda above the main doors of the Vatican, and waited for Cesare.

He sent Cardinals Farnese and Borgia to meet the Duke, and they took with them to the gates of Santa Maria del Popolo all the prelates, priests and officials of the Pontificial Court, as well as the Ambassadors of the Powers who happened to be in Rome at the time, and leaving this imposing suite at the Gate, the two Cardinals went on to greet Valentinois.

It was not until evening that the Duke actually arrived in Rome, but the vast crowds of people who pushed and jostled in the streets waiting for a glimpse of Il Valentino, counted the time spent in this way well worth while, for Cesare, with his unerring instinct for a spectacle, had prepared a lavish and impressive pageant to bemuse the city.

First came the mules and baggage carts, and as they appeared a ripple of sound moved like a rustling wind over the assembled multitudes, for at last the real excitement was about to begin. Following the baggage, Cesare had placed a thousand foot soldiers, dressed as for war, and led by two heralds, one in Cesare's livery, and one, a graceful compliment by the Duke, in the colours of the King of France.

Vitellozzo Vitelli's horse came next; well-trained, and well-equipped and flushed with victory, they moved in perfect accord, the proud animals' hooves chiming against the stones, the bridles sounding a musical note as they moved forward, and behind them, Cesare's personal guard rode. Amongst the guard were Alberini, Capranica, di Mariano and the others in Cesare's immediate entourage, and there were gasps of admiration for their splendour.

The gasps turned to cheers and shouts of joy as Cesare came into view. His high-stepping steed was magnificently caparisoned and its bridle and trappings trimmed with gold and gems, but Cesare himself affected plain black velvet, and the severe elegance, broken only by a simple gold chain round his neck, made him stand out amidst his colourful train in a startling fashion.

He did not acknowledge the cheers and cries of the crowds which pushed against the restraining guards along the route for a closer look at the hero, but kept his eyes fixed upon the road ahead, and there was no sign either of triumph or pleasure as he guided his mount forward. Despite his ability to produce spectacular pageants and shows, he never lost his own aloof manner, and this mysterious withdrawal made the people of Rome the more avid to learn further of him.

Behind the foot-guards which surrounded him, rode Caterina Sforza on a white horse. She was clad in a black robe, her thick fair hair caught back by a simple jewelled net, and her face was expressionless and hard. Cesare had fastened her wrists in shackles made of gold, lest anyone should mistake the manner of her coming. She was his prisoner, and he let Rome know it.

Behind her was the welcoming party, the Ambassadors, the Cardinals and others who had gone to greet Cesare, including his brother-in-law, Alfonso Bisceglie, and his brother, Jofrè, whose face was alight with pride and triumph that his brother, whom he revered to the point of idolatry should now return to Rome, a victor.

The crowds were thicker as the train wound its way to the Bridge of Sant' Angelo, for this was the time of the Papal Jubilee and Rome was crammed with pilgrims and visitors from afar and near, a sight which warmed Alexander's heart, not least because of the enormous sums of money which were pouring into his coffers; money which Cesare would need for his next campaign.

The guns of the castle of Sant' Angelo burst forth in strident salute as Cesare passed on; and slowly, because of the dense masses of people, the long procession reached the Vatican itself.

Alexander could not keep still. He leaped from his chair and paced about the loggia, exclaiming in impatience at the time the Duke was taking to arrive, and in exasperation he turned to his daughter, Lucrezia, who was waiting with him.

" 'Tis so long, Lucrezia," he complained fretfully, "why does he not come?"

Lucrezia smiled with gentleness, but her eyes were remote and far away, and her soothing words had no thought behind them, for her mind was fixed on Cesare's coming.

She was small and slender, her hair a light, bright gold, beautifully brushed and cared for and now surmounted by an exquisite jewelled band. Her skin was pale and without blemish, her eyes a clear blue and her lashes had been darkened by cosmetics. The red mouth was full and weak, but her nose was delicate, and the general impression was one of great beauty, and few noticed the flaw of the slightly receding chin, which gave her an innocent, defenceless look.

Her hands were clasped together in an ecstasy of apprehension and joy. She had waited so long for this moment; the moment when Cesare would return to Rome. She hated his absences, and although her heart was bursting with pride at his success at Imola and Froli, in truth she would like to have kept her brother securely locked in Rome with her, and she had shed copious tears when he had finally secured his release from his vows and had taken his place at the head of the Papal Forces.

Her relationship with Cesare was a curious one. What Lucrezia felt for Cesare could not be encompassed by the word "love", for her emotions were too complex to be explained so simply. Since childhood, he had attracted her in a compelling, inexplicable way, which she did not understand herself, and which often frightened her. Twice she had married, and on more than one occasion had taken a lover, but these were merely interludes between the times she was with Cesare, for her feelings for him were stronger and more binding than anything she had felt for the men who had possessed her, and it seemed to her that Cesare represented not so much love, as life itself, and that without him, she could not survive.

This passionate devotion to her brother had been the source of a number of scurrilous and scandalous rumours, and many assumed, without a second thought, that Cesare, who was known to stop at nothing, had possessed his sister in an incestuous relationship.

In fact, this was not so, but Lucrezia, who had none of the perception and intellectual capacity of her brother or father, found it hard to understand her longing for Cesare, and many times had cried tears of desperation at the hungry aching she felt inside her, which she could not explain, but which filled her with such fear and anxiety.

Now, however, the torments of the love she felt, were momentarily dispelled, and she waited with bated breath for the first sign of Cesare, and the glow in her cheeks and the look in her eyes was the happiness of a woman awaiting a lover.

Finally Cesare reached the steps of the Vatican and went immediately to the Pope to bow low, and then to fall on his knees to make his obeisance, and as he did so, those about the Pope, heard Cesare speak in the strange Spanish dialect which he used on occasions when he addressed his father. The Pope, with tears in his eyes, took Cesare in his arms and embraced him, then released him to allow him to greet the others who awaited him.

Lucrezia came forward, her hands outstretched, and there was something in her eyes which did not match the weakness of her mouth and chin.

"Cesare! Oh, Cesare!"

Valentinois gave a low laugh and caught her to him.

"Lucia, my love." He bent and kissed her on the lips, and all the hardness had gone from his eyes and mouth. "Belovèd, you are well?"

She nodded and clasped his hand. "Oh yes! Yes! Now that you have returned, I am very well. Oh, Cesare, it is so good to see you again."

He smiled and put his arm round her as he turned to speak to the others who came forward to speak to him, but Lucrezia's gaze never left his face, and she trembled within his hold.

At a banquet in the Vatican that night to celebrate Cesare's return, Lucrezia was radiant in cloth of gold, and sat entranced listening to the Duke's account of the taking of Forlì, and her small white teeth bit her lip anxiously as Valentinois described the final assault.

"But, Cesare, you might have been killed."

Valentinois looked at her with affection. "But I was not, my dear Lucia, and one cannot win battles without taking risks, as you must know."

Alfonso Bisceglie, Lucrezia's young husband, sat by her side, his weak petulant face set and angry. Whilst fully aware that the accusations of an incestuous relationship between his wife and her borther were false, he greatly resented the uncanny hold Cesare had over Lucrezia, and hated the strength and power which Valentinois possessed in such measure. Cesare's attitude to his brother-in-law was one of contempt, and he made no pretence of friendship, merely tolerating Alfonso as a necessary but tiresome burden. Alfonso glowered at Cesare's easy dismissal of danger, and his thoughts were warped with the desire to see this arrogant man destroyed, and he regretted with bitterness the fact that Caterina Sforza had not been able to put an end to Cesare's ambitions by one well placed shot from her cannons.

"But, Cesare, you have soldiers to fight your battles. Why must you go yourself into such dangers?"

Valentino gave a faint smile. "My dear, men will not fight for a man they cannot follow with pride. What sort of General would I be if I skulked in the safety of my tent whilst I sent my troops forward to face death? No, Lucia, this is not the way to lead an army. The man who sets out to wrest victory, must be prepared to give his life for this purpose. But you must put these foolish thoughts and fears from you, for I was in no danger. I am quite capable of guarding myself, I assure you."

Alfonso's mouth twisted in galling anger at the casual way Cesare brushed aside his part in the siege of Forlì, and it was at that precise moment that something came into his mind which caused a chill shiver to run through his frame.

Whilst Borgia lived, he would always hold first place in Rome, and certainly first place in Lucrezia's thoughts. Alfonso found her feelings for her brother beyond his comprehension, particularly as not a week before, he had learned of her apparent infatuation for one of Cesare's Captains, Gian Orestes, who had been slightly injured in an affray at Imola, and who had returned to Rome, not taking part in the defeat of Forlì.

Orestes was tall and straight and vital. His dark hair and eyes and his deep bronze skin were fatally attractive to the opposite sex, and Alfonso scowled when he heard of his wife's attention to this impudent condottiero, but to some extent was prepared to accept her infidelity, which at least left him free to court a particularly beautiful girl he had met not long before.

But whilst understanding Lucrezia's reaction to Orestes, he was baffled by the fact that she could be conducting an affaire with him, whilst at the same time laying her heart in such obvious devotion at her brother's feet.

He frowned and drank more wine. The frightening thought came into his mind again, and he savoured it delicately and fearfully as he sipped his wine.

What if Cesare should die? Not in battle, as a soldier, but by the hand of an assassin as Gandia had died? What if the proud and confident Generalissimo, in whom the Pope placed so much hope, were to be found dead one night? Alfonso's eyes gleamed under half-closed lids. How much easier life would be without the contemptuous and determined Borgia. Alfonso's mouth moved in an unamused smile. He knew well that Cesare would not hesitate to remove him if it suited his purpose, and it occurred to him that the Pope and Cesare might well consider that to further their plans, Lucrezia should be given in marriage to a more powerful prince, who could bring greater benefits to the House of Borgia. But if Cesare died, the Pope would not pursue these ends alone. Further, if Valentino died, this queer compelling and unbreakable hold he appeared to have over Lucrezia would be gone too, and he, Alfonso, might once again be able to recapture her heart and thoughts.

Yes, if Cesare were to die. Alfonso sighed gently and relaxed. He would give more thought to this. Not tonight, for the moment was not propitious, and the plan needed careful thought, for Cesare was not careless; but soon. Soon he would contrive some suitable means for putting this idea into form, and before long his hateful and detestable brother-in-law would suffer the same fate he had meted out to so many others.

Later that night, the Pope and Cesare were left alone, and talked for some time about the future, and the next campaign to be undertaken, and when their business was finished, the Pope sat back and sighed.

"Ah, 'tis good that you have returned, Cesare." He smiled lovingly at his son. "You have been greatly missed, and 'tis time you came back, for I fancy only your influence will turn Lucia's mind from her present folly."

"Folly?" Cesare looked up sharply. "What folly is this?"

The Pope's eyes held a brief flash of alarm. The difficulty in engaging Cesare's help was that his son's solution to the problem was likely to be violence and death and this was not what the Pope wanted on this occasion, for he had no desire to upset Lucrezia unduly, nor to stain the name of Borgia with further ugly rumours.

"Now, now, Cesare, no need for such heat," he began, when Cesare sat up in his chair and said tersely:

"What folly?"

The Pope squirmed slightly in his chair, and for a second wished he had not embarked upon this course, yet it was something which had to be stopped, and all his entreaties and pleas to Lucrezia had been fruitless.

"Lucia believes herself in love," he said finally, and gave a slight laugh. "She is young, Cesare, and I suspect Alfonso does not spend enough time with her to ensure her affections do not wander, yet. . . ."

"With whom?" asked Cesare briefly, and the hardness which had been absent since his arrival in Rome was back.

Alexander's grimace became more pronounced. "Now, Cesare, I beg you to be calm about this."

"I am calm," said Valentinois shortly. "With whom does Lucrezia believe herself to be in love?"

Still the Pope hesitated and Cesare's lips thinned in anger.

"Holiness, I beg you to cease this prevarication. Who is this man?"

The Pope sighed. "His name is Orestes. Gian Orestes. He is, of course, a handsome young man, and one can understand. . . ."

"Orestes?" Valentinois' voice was a whisper. "Captain Orestes?"

The Pontiff looked uneasily at Cesare. He knew that whisper of old.

"Yes, but Cesare. . . ."

The Duke got up and walked over to the window and for

a moment stared out into the blackness of the night, and Alexander watched him with growing apprehension.

Then Valentinois turned from the window and came back into the room. All traces of anger had gone from his face and his eyes were expressionless.

"Put this worry from you, father," he said, and his voice was as calm as his bearing. "I will attend to it."

"But, Cesare, how," began Alexander, when Cesare raised one hand.

"How, is not important, father. Put it from you, I say. This is something I will deal with."

The Pope's eyes were worried. "Cesare. . . ."

"I will talk to Lucrezia," went on Cesare in the same unmoved fashion. "She will listen to me, I think, but if she does not. . . ."

For a moment there was silence between the two men, each fully understanding the other, then Cesare bowed low to his father.

"I bid you good night, Holiness, and I thank you again for what you have done for me, which has enabled me to undertake the conquest of the Romagna."

He kissed the Pope's ring, and withdrew, leaving the Pontiff torn between relief that the problem of Lucrezia's absurd infatuation for a condottiero was no longer his, and dread of the methods Cesare would employ to bring about a solution.

Cesare strode through the corridors of the Vatican to Lucrezia's apartments, and woke a startled guard dozing outside the doors.

He brushed aside the twittering serving maids and went straight to Lucrezia's bedchamber, and found her sleeping, her face childlike and innocent in the repose of slumber. Of Alfonso there was no sign, and Cesare went to the side of the bed and put a hand on his sister's shoulder.

She awoke with a slight start, but the fear in her eyes died quickly as she saw the Duke, and she sat up with a glad cry.

"Cesare! Dearest Cesare." She brushed her pale gold hair over her shoulder, and her eyes were eager.

"Oh, Cesare, my dear."

Cesare sat on the side of the bed. "Lucia." He made no

further move to touch her, and something in his aus[tere] manner made the light in Lucrezia's eyes die, and there was a trace of nervousness in her voice.

"Cesare? What is it? Why do you look like that? Have I done ought to displease you? Oh, I pray this may not be so, for I would not willingly do anything against your wishes."

For a moment Cesare was silent, then he said bleakly:

"What is this I hear about Captain Orestes, Lucrezia? What manner of nonsense is this?"

Her face whitened. "Orestes? How . . . how did you know? How did you hear of this so soon?"

He laughed shortly. "Did you imagine it would remain a secret in the Vatican? Don't be a fool, Lucia. Every move we make, every word we speak, every thought we have, is duly reported, not only to Rome, but to all the powers in Europe. Reported and distorted. Now, answer me, what is this absurd rumour I hear about you and Orestes?"

She pouted, although her face was still pale, and her defiance was assumed.

" 'Tis nothing, Cesare. Simply a way to fill the long lonely days when you are not here."

"You have Alfonso."

"Alfonso!" Her voice was curiously harsh. "I do not want Alfonso. I never wanted him. You and father thrust him upon me to further your ambitions, and it was you who spread the rumour about that I loved him greatly, but this was not so, and you knew it. You knew I did not care for him, but still you forced me into his bed. Do not blame me, therefore, Cesare, if I seek amusement elsewhere."

"Elsewhere, perhaps, Lucrezia, but not with a condottiero in my pay. What are you thinking about? You are the Pope's daughter, and my sister. You have no business with a common foot soldier."

The colour came rapidly into her cheeks and for once her blue eyes had an expression in them; that of anger.

"He is not a common foot soldier. He is a Captain, and a brave man, and I consider that if you are to choose my husbands, I have a right to choose my lovers."

Cesare's eyes were cold. "You will not choose your lovers from the ranks of my army, Lucrezia."

"I will choose them from whence I please, and you will not stop me. I do not dictate to you how you select your mistresses, and it is well known, Cesare, that you do not always look to Rome's best families for your amusements. What about Fiametta? She was a prostitute from the slums, yet it did not stop you from going to her bed. Do you set one standard for yourself and another for me, Cesare? Orestes is amusing and handsome and a satisfying lover. Why should I give him up, whilst you continue to find your diversions amongst kitchen maids?"

Cesare raised his hand and struck her hard across the face, and she fell back against the silken cushions with a cry.

"You will give this man up immediately," he said curtly, "and if I find you have not obeyed me, I will take steps to see that my commands are heeded."

Lucrezia held her aching cheek, and her eyes filled with tears.

"I do not want to give him up," she said in a choking voice, "for I am lonely. Do you ever stop to think of that, Cesare? I do not think you do. In fact, I do not think you stop to think of me at all. If you did; if you were here, with me in Rome, I would not need Orestes, nor any man, for I should have you."

Cesare stared down at her. "I cannot stay in Rome, Lucrezia; you know this full well. I did not give up my vows to remain in the Vatican to amuse you. I am a soldier, as I have told you before, and my destiny lies on the battlefield, not in your bedroom. But you will obey me, or I will bring about my ends by other means."

Lucrezia's eyes were suddenly frightened.

"Other means?" she whispered. "What other means, Cesare? What do you mean?"

"I suggest you do not wait to find out," he returned coolly. "I have told you to give this man up, and you would be wise to do so, then no harm will be done."

"And if I refuse?" Something of her previous defiance returned as she looked at her brother's stony face.

"I shall see that you do not refuse," he said briefly. "Y have disobeyed me before, Lucrezia, and have regretted it. I suggest you do not put it to the test again, for you already know the outcome."

For a moment they stared at one another; each angry, each determined to have their own way, and then Lucrezia turned to the pillows and started to cry. Her sobs shook her slight frame and Cesare frowned.

"Don't," he said finally. "Don't, Lucia."

He leaned forward and pulled her up and turned her tear-stained face to his. "Enough, Lucia, enough. There is no need for this, and you know it. Now, stop these tears and attend to me."

He wiped the tears from her cheeks. "Listen to me, Lucia."

He held her against his breast, and she clung to him.

"You are not free to take lovers such as Orestes, Lucia. You are my sister, and I will not allow you to behave like a common harlot. You have a great part to play in our destiny. You can do much to help us, and I know that you will not hesitate to fulfil your role. I realize Alfonso is dull for you, and I have been considering this."

The amber eyes were reflective, and Lucrezia pulled away from him, her own eyes wide.

"But whatever your future may be," went on Cesare, ignoring the question in her gaze, "Orestes has no part in it."

He released her. "He can only do harm to our cause and you must be done with this affaire at once, Lucia; do you understand?"

Her tears had stopped, but her eyes were still puzzled.

"What did you mean when you said you had been considering Alfonso?"

He smiled faintly. "I will tell you soon, Lucia, but not tonight. Now, do I have your promise to be done with this ridiculous infatuation of yours?"

The red lips tightened again in anger. "It is not an infatuation," she said sulkily. "Why should I not have Orestes, if you refuse to stay with me, and are bent on war?"

Cesare's eyes grew cold again. "I have told you why," he

said shortly, "you are behaving like a spoilt child, Lucrezia. I do not believe for one moment that you love this man, and if I were of a mind, I could prove this."

She shivered as he caressed her shoulder, but as she saw his sardonic expression, she twitched away from him.

"You are without heart, Cesare," she said angrily, "and you play with me simply to secure my obedience to your wishes; to ensure the success of your plans. I will not be your tool."

He leaned forward slightly and touched her forehead with his lips, then rose to his feet.

"Remember, Lucia," he said, and there was iron under his soft tones. "You are not to see this man again. If you do; if you do not heed my commands, I will deal with your disobedience in my own way."

With that he turned and left her, a prey to fears and anger.

If he had stopped to coax her, he could easily have brought her round to his will, for she was a pliant tool in his hands when he used his charm and persuasiveness upon her, but on this occasion he had not bothered, and had been terse and harsh in his demands, and Lucrezia was angry.

She resented the wars which took Cesare from her; resented the mistresses he took so indifferently; resented the brief time he spared her when he was in Rome, and, most of all, resented his present dictates regarding Gian Orestes. Her eyes were stormy as they stared into the darkness, and regardless of the risk to Orestes, she resolved on this occasion, at least, that her will would prevail over Cesare's.

Cesare went back to his own apartments and his secretary, Agapito Gherardi da Amelia, who awaited him there, saw immediately the fury under the Duke's outward control.

Despite the late hour, Agapito was still working, and Cesare came up to the table, spread about with despatches and papers, and gestured Agapito to be seated again.

"Tomorrow," he said slowly, "I want to know all that there is to know about Gian Orestes."

Agapito's bright brown eyes were surprised. "Captain Orestes?"

"The same." Cesare's mouth was hard. "It appears that the good Captain has spent his convalescence in Rome in a somewhat unusual manner."

"Highness?"

The Duke turned to look at his secretary, a round, comfortable man with a placid face and a quick, responsive mind, who was devoted to Valentinois.

"He has apparently engaged the interest of my sister." The Duke was terse. "Indeed, I would say he had gone a good deal further than this, and she is being foolishly stubborn about the matter, and refuses to put an end to this nonsense."

Agapito stared in amazement. "The Madonna Lucrezia, and a Captain in your army, sire?"

"Precisely." Cesare's hand was fingering the end of his dagger. "Precisely, Agapito. That is why I wish to know more about him. Tomorrow, you will take steps to get me all the information available."

"And this is all, Highness? You do not wish me to . . ."

"No." The Duke was definite. "Not yet. I will settle this in my own way, in my own good time. All I need now is more information about this man. See that I have it before noon tomorrow." He picked up a despatch from the table and looked at it with unseeing eyes.

"Lucrezia is not usually so determined," he said thoughtfully, "and one might almost think she cared for this man."

"Is this possible, my lord?" Agapito watched the Duke's still face with concern, for he knew that under the Duke's apparent carelessness, he had a deep love for his sister.

"It is possible, but in fact, I do not think it is so. I think Lucrezia is merely defying me for some reason. And it is true that she is bored with that clod, Alfonso. He is another who must engage our attention before long, for he is useless, not only to Lucrezia, but also to our cause, and the Pope and I have plans——" he broke off, and laughed slightly.

"But we go too swiftly, Agapito." His eyes were calm again. "One step at a time, and with caution. First we will deal with the temerity of Gian Orestes."

He left Agapito frowning. Agapito had watched with a measure of compassion the devoted love which Lucrezia shewed so openly for her brother, and although he knew Cesare returned this affection, he did not make it obvious as often as Lucrezia would have wished, for his attention was usually engaged on his own plans.

CHAPTER NINE

For the first few days after her stormy interview with Cesare, Lucrezia waited with fear for her brother to move. Each hour she expected to have news that Gian Orestes had been found in the Tiber, or in one of the dark squalid alleys which threaded their way like black ribbons through Rome, but no such tidings arrived, and gradually Lucrezia began to relax.

She sat in front of her mirror watching the deft hands of her maid brushing the long silken tresses which were her greatest pride, and which many women in Rome had tried to copy with the use of bleaches and dyes, without ever achieving the magical glow of Lucrezia's soft golden hair.

She gave a deep sigh and her maid looked anxious.

"Madonna is not well?"

Lucrezia smiled wanly. "Oh, yes. Nothing ails me, Lucetta, but my mind is troubled. I fear——"

She broke off; even to her servant who was so close to her, she was not able to discuss the terror Cesare had aroused in her.

Lucetta, thin, spare and advancing into middle age, gave a snort.

"As well you might, madonna mia. Such behaviour!"

She had nursed Lucrezia as a child, and did not mince her words, treating her just as she had done in the nursery.

Lucrezia flushed. "You do not understand, Lucetta. You do not realize what it is like being married to a dullard like Alfonso, particularly when the whole world believes it to be a love match, thanks to Cesare."

Her voice held a note of bitterness, and Lucetta frowned.

"Hush! Guard your tongue, madonna; even the walls have ears."

She glanced nervously over her shoulder, for although she

treated Lucrezia with such familiarity; petting and scolding her alternately, with love in her heart, she had no such feeling for the Duke of Valentinois, who filled her with cold fear every time his careless glance fell upon her.

Lucrezia shrugged. "Cesare will not harm me," she said, but the cloud still lurked behind her eyes. "But Gian; oh, Lucetta, I fear for him, for my lord Duke is angry that I have shewn him favour, and demands that I see him no more. But this I cannot do, for I love him, and he returns my feelings. Why should I sacrifice this small happiness at Cesare's command, simply because he does not approve of Gian's birth?"

Her voice had grown petulant, and her mouth was sullen as she picked up a perfume bottle and touched her throat and ears. Gian had been ardent and loving, and Lucrezia, determined to withstand her dominant brother, had convinced herself that her feelings for the young condottiero were as warm as his own.

"He shews no discretion in his own affaires; why then should I?"

The bottle was suddenly hurled from Lucrezia's hand in fury, and she twisted round to face Lucetta.

"Why should I heed his demands? He is not willing to put aside his ambitions to pay attention to me; why, then, should I tolerate this interference with my own plans?"

Lucetta blanched with terror at her mistress's angry words, and held up an imploring hand.

"Oh, madonna, I beg you, use caution!" Again she cast a nervous look to the door. "If my lord should learn of your defiance, he would be greatly angered."

A shiver passed through Lucetta's gaunt frame.

"He will not tolerate rebellion, madonna."

Lucrezia rose and removed the silken wrap.

"Help me with my gown," she said shortly. "And I am not afraid of Cesare hearing my words, for I have already told him how I feel. I will not bow to his will in this matter."

Lucetta's fingers were unsteady as she drew the rich velvet gown about Lucrezia's slender figure and arranged the sweeping folds of the skirt.

Lucrezia adjusted the low-cut neck, bound with pearls and diamonds, and her hands drew the fine gold hair over her shoulders.

"Come," she said impatiently. "The net, Lucetta, for I am to meet Captain Orestes and I do not propose to keep him waiting whilst I listen to your fears and protests."

Lucetta, still white and anxious, fastened the pearl trimmed headpiece, and touched the shimmering tresses with the brush.

"I beg you, madam, take care. I know that my lord Duke cares greatly for you, but he is a formidable man, and if he finds you have not heeded his orders, he will not let the matter rest. Use care, I pray."

Lucrezia eyed herself in the mirror with satisfaction, and some of her irritation and sulkiness vanished at the gratifying vision which met her gaze. She enjoyed her beauty, knowing that it gave her power over men, and her temper could always be soothed by the sight of her reflection in the glass. A faint frown touched the pencilled brows. If only her beauty could hold Cesare in the snare it held other men. The frown vanished, and she gave a light laugh.

"Come, I am ready, Lucetta," she began, when the door opened and one of her ladies in waiting came in and curtsied low.

She was slim and dark, with large brown eyes veiled by sweeping black lashes which touched exquisitely moulded cheeks of soft apricot colour. Lucrezia was not a jealous woman, and had the same appreciation of beauty as the Pope and Cesare, and was normally perfectly content to surround herself by women of equal charm to her own, but something in the girl who bowed before her, stirred a strange feeling of anger in her. She was so self-possessed and cool, and so beautiful, and Lucrezia's tone was a trifle cold as she turned to look at her.

"Well, Maria?"

"Madonna," the girl rose and her lovely mouth moved in a faint smile. "The Duca is here to see you."

"The Duke?" Lucrezia's heart beat a fraction faster. "You mean . . ."

Before she could complete the sentence, Cesare was in the

room. Lucrezia's colour rose slightly and her eyes were brighter.

"Cesare." She held out her hand to her brother, who bowed and came to her side.

"Lucia." He kissed her cheek and smiled.

"You look very beautiful, cara. For whom is so much loveliness created?"

Lucetta's face was grey, but Maria's eyes were faintly malicious as she watched the rose tint leave Lucrezia's cheeks.

"I . . . I . . . merely prepare for the banquet tonight, Cesare." Lucrezia did not meet her brother's eye, but he continued to smile faintly, and there was no trace of the anger that Lucetta feared so much.

Indeed, since his terse words to Lucrezia a few days before, he appeared to have dismissed the subject of his sister's indiscretion with Captain Orestes, and had not referred to the matter again, and his manner to his sister was as warm and affectionate as ever.

"Then our guests may account themselves fortunate," he said and put his arm round her shoulders. "'Tis a pity Alfonso does not appreciate the gift fate has bestowed upon him."

He turned and for the first time his glance fell on Maria Amati, waiting quietly for her mistress to finish her exchange with the Duke.

Cesare's brows rose slightly, and something kindled at the back of his eyes as he took a long comprehensive look at the girl.

She did not flinch, and bore his scrutiny with complete equilibrium, her mouth moving again in the faintest of smiles, her brown eyes meeting his with a certain boldness, tempered with admiration.

She had been watching the Duke since his return to Rome, and whilst under no illusion about the man she now faced, had set her hand to captivating Valentinois, for she saw many advantages in having a lover who wielded so much power, and whose slightest word had the force of law.

Cesare's hand dropped from Lucrezia's shoulder.

"Ah, I see you have enlarged your entourage, Lucrezia," he said suavely, "and to so much advantage."

He moved a step nearer to Maria, and she bowed low to the Duke, who studied her beautifully moulded body through half-closed eyes. "Yes, indeed, to much advantage."

He held out his hand to Maria as she rose, smiling slowly.

Lucrezia's mouth tightened. The instinctive feeling she had had about this girl had proved right, and her stony glance noted the satisfied gleam in the brown eyes which met the Duke's appreciative gaze. No wonder Maria Amati had been so pleased to serve her, for thus she drew nearer to the Duke. Lucrezia said stiffly:

"Maria Amati, Cesare, from Florence. She has come to serve me, and this she does well."

Maria was unmoved by Lucrezia's sharp reminder to her brother that she was but a lady in waiting, and her eyes were warm and inviting.

"I am glad that I please the Madonna Lucrezia," she said, her voice low and husky, and Cesare's hand tightened imperceptively over hers.

"Rome is greatly blessed that it should have so many fair women to dazzle it," he said, and Maria gave a slight chuckle which made Lucrezia's nostrils pinch in anger.

"My diamonds, Maria," she said curtly. "Fetch the necklace I wear with this gown, for it is time we joined the Holy Father."

Cesare released the girl's hand, and for a moment they looked at one another, and Lucrezia felt bitterness bite deep into her, as she recognized her brother's unspoken invitation to the wanton girl who moved sinuously away from him to fetch the diamonds from their casket. There was no doubt in Lucrezia's mind as to Cesare's intent, for although no words had passed between him and the girl, beyond a few pleasantries, Lucrezia knew her brother well, and was fully aware that Cesare had been instantly attracted to Maria, and would not be slow in following up his interest with something more tangible and satisfying.

Lucrezia's lips were thin with rage. How dared Cesare dictate to her about Gian when he so obviously proposed to take this brazen girl to his bed? She turned away so that the Duke should not see the anger in her. How dare he demand her obedience to his will, when he was prepared to take any woman who attracted him, regardless of her station? Her heart was beating faster, and her hands, concealed by the folds of her white velvet gown, were clenched so that the nails bit deep into her palms.

This settled it; no matter what Cesare's orders were, she would continue to see Gian, and as soon as this boring banquet were over, she would slip away to meet him by the sundial which was their rendezvous, hidden as it was by the trees and summer house beyond the formal gardens of the Vatican.

She was shaking with anger, but was wise enough to conceal it from Cesare, who now turned back to her.

"You are ready, Lucia?" he asked, and she nodded, waiting for a moment to allow Maria's hands to fasten the dazzling necklace about her slender throat.

"Yes, I am ready, Cesare," she said and her voice was steady again as she laid her hand on his proffered arm. At the door, Cesare glanced back at Maria, and again an unmistakable look was exchanged. As the door closed behind them, Maria's mouth curved in a smile of satisfaction and pleasure, her hands moving in a sensual caress on her body.

Late that night, Maria lay on her bed, a shaft of moonlight gliding through the window striking her slender, rounded form, lightly clad in a silk robe. Her thick dark hair, freed from its restraining net, fell about her creamy shoulders, and one slim hand fingered the end of a strand which strayed on to her breast.

The night was quiet, the stillness broken only by the sound of an occasional owl and the restless murmur of crickets. Maria smiled gently. Time was passing and she was still alone, but the smile on her mouth did not waver, for she had no doubts about the meaning of the Duke's look, and it would not be long before she would be able to take the first step towards her goal.

She hated her rôle as Lucrezia's lady in waiting, for she

considered she had not been born for subservience to a pale faced, straw-haired whore, whose only claim to importance was the incidence of her birth and the power and strength of her brother. She moved slightly in irritation as she remembered the haughty orders she was compelled to obey to satisfy Lucrezia's whims. Many times since she had come to Rome to join Lucrezia's court, she had felt she could not bear her situation, but the thought of Cesare's impending return had supported her, and she controlled her wild desire to slap the imperious mistress she served, and flee the Vatican.

No, it was worth it; the slights, the snubs, the sharp orders, the insolence. They would all be repaid in time; every last one. Maria relaxed, her annoyance gone. Soon, when she had captured Cesare's heart, she would be done with Lucrezia and her petty demands. Cesare would take her from the Vatican, and she would be free from all that had infuriated her for the last few months, and who knows, she thought maliciously; who knows how easy it would be to repay some of those pricks and irritations when she was the mistress of the most powerful man in Rome; nay, the most powerful man in Italy.

Her heart jerked slightly as she heard the latch of her door click, and the strand of hair fell from a hand which, for once, was not entirely steady.

Cesare came to the side of the bed and looked down at her. In the half-light he was tall, remote and rather frightening, and for a second her heart was not easy. Apart from the advantages of becoming the mistress of a man of Cesare's calibre, Maria had been greatly attracted by his beauty and personal charm, but as she stared up at the Duke, she felt for the first time, something of the fear which others had experienced when they looked upon that cold, handsome face.

He wore a dark robe, trimmed with sable, and in the semi-darkness there was something unearthly about the stillness of his bearing.

She stirred and felt her pulse flutter.

"My lord," she whispered, and one hand stretched out, half in welcome, half in supplication.

Still Cesare did not move, and Maria raised herself on one elbow to meet the calm, amber eyes.

"Sire," she began again, when he bent and caught her fiercely to him, and her fears and qualms were smothered in the intensity of his passion.

As he released her, she gave a faint laugh.

"My lord," she said in her deep throaty voice. "I had not thought to find you here."

Her hand stroked his shoulder. "I am greatly honoured that you choose to come to me."

Cesare's mouth was ironic. "You knew I would come," he said softly, "you were expecting me, were you not?"

She chuckled again. "Sire, would I dare to presume that you would find me desirable?" The hand strayed to his cheek. "I greatly hoped that you would find me attractive, but . . ."

Cesare laughed shortly. "You knew," he said, brusquely dismissing her pretence. "You knew well that I would come to you."

She wriggled slightly, and her eyes laughed into his.

"I hoped," she confessed, and the fingers moved again in light seduction, "and now you are here, my lord."

Cesare regarded her silently for a moment.

"Now I am here," he agreed finally, and his hand pulled aside the silken robe as he swept her ruthlessly into his arms.

On the 29th March, Cesare was officially appointed Captain-General of the Pontifical Forces and Gonfalonier of the Church. Men said he had killed to free the path to this office, but none had proved it, and the Sacred College had unanimously supported the Pope when he expressed his desire to give legal recognition to the rôle Cesare had played so well in the field. As always, the Pope had his eye on the law. Cesare had taken Imola and Forlì without the formality of this appointment, and Alexander was determined to remedy the situation as quickly as possible, and at the same time to bestow on his belovèd Duke, the Golden Rose, a much coveted symbol of the Church Militant and Church Triumphant, given to those who had served Her with distinction, and this, the Pope considered, Cesare had done in good measure.

The Cardinals led the Pope's path into St. Peter's and the great church was packed with people who sought a glimpse of the mysterious and fascinating Duke. There were soldiers, and courtiers, ambassadors of the great powers, scholars, artists, poets, and Cesare's own court, but in addition, there were presses of ordinary men and women, eager for a sight of the spectacle which was unfolded before their eyes.

The Pope's chair was lowered by the bearers as he reached the High Altar, and in his solemn, stately manner, he removed his Tiara, its jewels agleam under the light from the candles on the Altar, and after a moment of quiet prayer, he took his place on the Pontifical Throne.

After the Cardinals had made their obeisance, Cesare came before his father. He was dressed in cloth of gold and ermine, and his father shivered slightly as Cesare knelt before him. All the love and pride he had once felt for Gandia was now centred on Cesare, and his passion was made the easier in that Cesare was so obviously destined for success, whereas Giovanni, for all the Pope's insistence to the contrary, had not been equipped to fill the rôle his father had chosen for him.

Under the beauty and elegance that was Cesare's was all that was needed to wrest victory for the Church and Alexander was well aware of it, but as he looked down upon his son's tranquil face, the same tremor of fear lurked beneath the affection and exultation. With Gandia he had felt safe and confident, for to Giovanni his word had been law, and he had controlled and guided the situation without difficulty, but with Cesare there was no such safeguard. There was something in this strong, graceful man before him which made light fingers of fear touch the Pope's spine.

He dismissed the frisson of dread impatiently, and began the prayer which preceded the investiture. The mantle of the Gonfalonier was placed round Cesare's shoulders, the scarlet and ermine cap settled on his tawny head, and the Duke bent low to kiss the Pope's feet, before taking his place amongst the Cardinals.

After the celebration of Mass, the banners of the Church and the Commander's baton were placed in Cesare's charge, and he swore the oath of fealty to the Pope and to St. Peter, before the two armour-clad deputies took charge of the banners and fastened them to the lances they held ready for that purpose.

The Golden Rose was then presented to the Duke for the service he had rendered the Church, and after solemn prayers and the Pope's blessing, the spectacular ceremony ended, and the office for which Cesare had waited so long, was his by right of law.

When Cesare returned to the apartments which had been set aside for him in the Vatican, there were many who had come to congratulate him and wish him well, and his manner was gracious and charming as he thanked those who had come to pay their respects.

He turned from the effusive ambassador from one of the lesser powers to find himself confronted by his sister-in-law, Sancia, whose lip curled as she made her curtsey to his Highness.

"Sancia." The Duke's bow was as chill as his manner, for he had developed a marked dislike for the woman he had once sought with such fervour, and his increasing distaste for her brother, Alfonso, did nothing to make his feelings towards her more kindly.

"Cesare." She rose and her eyes were hard and mocking.

"So, you have achieved your will." Her voice was light, but there was venom in it as she stared at the Duke.

"Yes. In part, at least."

"Oh? There is more that you seek, my lord? And who will have to die that you may achieve your next step?"

Into the small silence, Cesare said quietly:

"You are fortunate, Sancia, that there are others present."

"So, my lord? And what if we were alone? What would you do then?"

Her grey-blue eyes were very bright, and her cheeks were flushed with suppressed temper.

"Would I too be found in the Tiber, sire, like my luckless brother-in-law?"

Cesare's hand was caressing the dagger at his waist, and his eyes were frigid.

"Do not imagine, Sancia, that because you are my brother's wife, I am not able to deal with your insolence." His lips moved in a brief, mirthless smile. "But then, I am sure you do not overlook the risks you run in talking to me in this fashion."

"I am not afraid of you, Cesare. Men cringe from your anger as if you were an avenging god, but to me, you are just a man, and your threats do not move me to fear."

Cesare's eyes wandered slowly over her, and despite herself, a faint spasm of something touched her, but she met his eye boldly.

"No?" His voice was as pleasant and bland as ever. "Then perhaps, Sancia, it is time I gave you a practical demonstration of the folly of incurring my anger."

With that he bowed and turned away from her, leaving her shaking slightly with rage, and with something else which she refused to acknowledge.

Maria Amati was amongst those present, and although she still remained in Lucrezia's service, she was convinved that before long she would be able to persuade Cesare to establish her in a villa of her own, away from the hateful restrictions of the Vatican and from the demands of the tiresome Lucrezia.

She smiled as Cesare came up to her, and something of the terseness of his expression abated as he saw her.

"My lord," she murmured as she curtsied to him. "I was so proud; so proud." Her black lashes shielded her expression of triumph as she saw Lucrezia out of the corner of her eye. Lucrezia had been furious when she learned that her fears concerning Maria and Cesare had been realized, and had been particularly demanding and dissatisfied since her spies had reported Cesare's first visit to her lady in waiting.

Maria was very glad to have the opportunity of shewing her tedious mistress that her lover was prepared to acknowledge her in public, and the gaze she turned upon the Duke was ardent and inviting, and Cesare's anger dissipated completely as he took her hand.

"Maria." His voice was soft, and he kissed her fingers, his eyes holding hers in a glance of blatant intimacy.

"Sire, you will come to me later?" The black lashes fell again in mock demureness and Cesare laughed.

"Doubtless, madonna, doubtless."

"Cesare, 'twould be so much easier if I were not chained to the Madonna Lucrezia's apartments, for 'tis a prison from which I long to escape."

"So you have said." The Duke's tone was dry, for Maria had not lost any time in pressing Cesare to take her elsewhere, a plea which as yet, he had not heeded.

"But, Cesare . . ."

"Enough, Maria!" The Duke was impatient again, and Maria's colour receded slightly.

"Forgive me, my lord." Her wide brown eyes met his, and there were tears in them. "I beg you to pardon my folly in worrying you at this time, but 'tis only that I care so greatly, and," she stifled a small sob, "that I love you so much . . ."

The lashes fell again, and a tear trickled down her cheek, a useful accomplishment which Maria had perfected some years before, and one which had served her well in her dealings with men.

Cesare's hand covered hers again. "Do not cry, sweet, for I understand your feelings. We will talk more of this later. Now, be done with tears, for they should not be allowed to mar a cheek as lovely as yours."

She smiled at him; a small pathetic smile, which made Lucrezia's colour rise dangerously, for she read very clearly the mesh this hussy was winding about Cesare, who, for all his astuteness and penetrating intelligence, appeared to be wholly convinced by the wiles and tricks of this black-haired trollop.

But as Cesare moved on to speak to others who waited to greet him, he was smiling quietly to himself, and not for one second had he misunderstood the little scene Maria had played out before him.

He found her exciting and sexually satisfying, but she moved his heart not at all. She would remain in his favour only for so long as she continued to please him. The first sign on her part of rebellion, or an attempt to dominate him, would see her end.

Not understanding this in any small degree, Lucrezia returned to her own apartments and gripping her hands together in a frenzy of rage and jealousy, she took her first step towards the destruction of the impudent serving girl who had dared to cast covetous eyes at her brother.

Her first move was to send for her chamberlain. He was a thick-set, clumsy featured man from a village outside Rome, who had risen to his present post by sheer determination and ruthlessness, but he served Lucrezia loyally and devotedly, and before him she laid her problem.

"What am I to do, Rafael?" she cried in exasperation. "This girl has the Duke bewitched, and I feel in my bones that she intends me harm. Besides, what harm may she intend towards the Duke himself? And now that he is Gonfalonier of the Church, he has many high tasks to perform, and should not be exposed to such risks as this. What am I to do to protect myself and the Duke?"

Rafael Buorossi looked into his mistress's clear innocent eyes, and saw nothing of the feline anger which lay under them. The Borgia cause was his, and his task was to serve the Duchess of Bisceglie and her brother, Cesare, and to this end he bent his energies.

"If she were harmed, the Duke would be filled with anger," he said slowly, "for at the moment, the girl finds much favour with his Highness."

"That is true," said Lucrezia bitterly, "and if ought befell her, he would know where to look. No, nothing must happen to her, Rafael. We must think of something else which will turn the Duke away from her."

"She could be found guilty of a plot against his life," said Rafael meditatively, but Lucrezia shook her head again.

"No. That would be too difficult to arrange, and Cesare would not believe it. Why should she plot against his life; it is to her advantage to keep him alive, for once he was dead, she too would be finished. No, that will not do."

They mused in silence for a moment, then Rafael said pensively:

"If his Highness believes himself in love with this girl, there is one sure way of arousing his fury, madonna."

Lucrezia looked up quickly. "And this is?"

"If she were found to be unfaithful to him." Rafael's thick fingers stroked his grizzled beard. "What man would tolerate a woman he favoured being found in the arms of another man?"

Lucrezia's eyes widened. "But, Rafael, she would not . . . she would not dare. Nor, I am sure, does she seek such pleasures elsewhere. Why should she when she has Cesare?"

There was something in her eyes which Rafael did not understand, but he smiled gently.

"She might not be a willing party, Madonna, but the Duke would not know this. If he found her with a man, would he believe in her innocence?"

Lucrezia began to smile, and her eyes sparkled with glee and malice.

"You are right, Rafael. The Duke would not believe her, but how can this be contrived?"

"It should not be too difficult, madonna. Will the Duke go to the girl tonight?"

"He will," said Lucrezia, the pleasure fading temporarily as her anger returned.

"Then, madonna, tonight, when the Duke goes to her chamber, he will find himself forestalled."

"But, Rafael, what man would be so reckless as to visit Maria Amati, knowing her to be my lord's mistress? No man would dare take this chance, for he would know that it would mean his death."

"No man who knew the girl was the Duke's paramour would dare, madonna, but what if the man did not know?"

The hope came back into Lucrezia's eyes. "If he did not know? Rafael! You know of such a man? But how? All Rome knows of this absurd infatuation of Cesare's for this . . . this whore."

"All Rome, perhaps, madonna, but there is a man who has arrived but today in the city to seek his fortune in the Duke's army. His name is Gioffre Ascano, and he is a hot-blooded fellow, who has already expressed his need for some diversion." Rafael gave a short laugh. "He has money to burn, and will not be afraid to spend it to satisfy his needs. I shall tell him that Rome's most beautiful harlot has agreed to receive him, for a price, and the price will be high. This will lull his suspicions. I will then arrange to admit him to the Vatican by one of the side doors. 'Tis known that the Duke does not visit Maria until midnight, and thus at ten minutes to the hour, I will contrive to smuggle the gallant Captain Ascano to Maria's room. When the Duke arrives, he will find that his mistress is otherwise engaged, and this should secure her removal."

"But the man? Captain Ascano? What of him?"

Buorossi shrugged. "There are plenty of soldiers of fortune, madonna. My lord Duke will not miss one of them, nor will the course of the Duke's next impresa be swayed by the loss of one man."

Lucrezia giggled and her hands clapped together in ecstasy. "Yes, Rafael, yes, yes! 'Tis a good scheme, and you can arrange this? You are sure nothing will go wrong? That my lord will not realize that it is of our contriving?" The anxiety returned to her eyes as she contemplated Cesare's reaction should he learn the truth.

"No, no, madonna." Buorossi was soothing. "Rest your mind, for I will move with great caution, and the Duke will never know the author of this plan, for he will kill the man instantly, if I know his Highness. And now, madonna, I must go to make the arrangements with the good Captain Ascano."

He saluted smartly and left Lucrezia crooning happily over the prospect of ridding herself of the hateful girl who had so attracted Valentinois.

Gioffre Ascano, a gay, reckless blade from Venice, was an easy prey for the wily Buorossi. He had come to Rome to sell his sword to Cesare, attracted as were so many young men of the day, by the personality of the Pope's son, and he was more than pleased to learn from Buorossi that for a purse of gold, he could visit one of Rome's famous courtesans.

"And is she truly fair, sire?" he asked as he sipped wine

with Buorossi in a local tavern. " 'Tis not some raddled old witch you are seeking to sell me?"

Buorossi laughed shortly. "Faith no! Maria Amati is a creature of great beauty, and all Rome will envy you, for she does not readily give herself."

Ascano's eyes were watchful. "Why then does she favour me thus?"

Buorossi shrugged lightly. "Who knows with women? When I learned of your desire to amuse yourself tonight, I mentioned the matter to a maid, a woman I know well." He leered at Ascano, who was still eyeing him with suspicion. "The girl told the Madonna Amati, and she, who is always attracted by men who live by their sword and their wit, expressed interest, and a desire to see you. She is tired of the ageing Roman prelates and courtiers who normally seek her favours. She wants a young vigorous man to amuse her for a change. And why not? She is herself young, and so fair, signore. Ah yes! You are fortunate. I only wish I had the opportunity you are afforded." He sighed longingly. "But, alas, I have to content myself with the maid."

The doubt and wariness slowly vanished from Ascano's eyes. "I see. Well, who am I to deprive the Madonna Amati of a night's pleasure?" He laughed. Faith, yes, I shall enjoy this encounter before I set my hand to serve the Duke. And you will arrange this, signore?"

"I will arrange it," agreed Buorossi readily, and in his satisfaction and youthful arrogance, Ascano did not see the gleam of something else in his companion's eyes as he drained his beaker of wine.

As Maria waited for Cesare that night, she planned her next step in achieving freedom from Lucrezia's service. She realized now that more care must be taken in this matter, for she had seen the Duke's irritation that morning when she raised the subject, and cursed herself for broaching the subject at the wrong moment. Despite this set-back, however, she was determined that Cesare should set her free, and her agile mind was busy with the manner in which she would entrap the Duke, when she heard the click of her door.

She started slightly, not realizing that the time had passed so quickly, and half raised herself to greet Valentinois.

"Cesare, belovèd," she began, when she found herself pulled into the arms of a man she had never seen before, and her heart began to race in panic.

She struggled fiercely in his iron grip, and spat her fury as his mouth sought hers. All her experience and knowledge of men and situations of this kind had not prepared her for the suddenness of the attack, and the intruder was strong and not ready to yield his advantage. She tried to cry out, but his kisses covered her smothered scream, and his hands were hard on her body as she writhed under his weight.

Her senses started to swim, and she felt the room slipping from her, when there was a hard step in the room and the door slammed violently behind the newcomer.

Startled by the noise, the man pulled himself up and Maria fell back, half-fainting, to the bed, as Cesare came up to them. The Duke's face was devoid of expression as he looked at Ascano, and then at Maria's ashen face.

"I fear I intrude," he said finally in a silken voice which made Maria's blood freeze in her veins. "I must crave your pardon." He bowed slightly and turned to go, when Maria cried out in agony.

"Cesare, Cesare! No! No!" She pulled herself up with difficulty, and held out an imploring hand. "Do not leave me, I beg you; oh, I beg you! This man burst into my chamber and attacked me. Oh, Cesare, help me! Help me!"

Cesare swung round sharply. "Attacked you?" His voice was cold, and she sobbed, this time with genuine fear and misery.

"Oh, Cesare, help me, help me. He threw himself at me. I could not fend him off; I could not protect myself."

She turned to the pillows, and her tears were real for the first time for many years.

Cesare's mouth was savage. "How did he get into your chamber, madonna, if not by invitation?"

He glanced at Ascano, who was standing in frozen horror by the post of the bed, the situation gradually sinking into his paralysed mind, for he had recognized instantly the tawny-haired man who had come, so obviously expected, to Maria Amati's bed.

Maria's cries did not abate, and Cesare leaned down and pulled her up.

"Stop it," he ordered tersely. "How did this man get here?"

"Oh, Cesare, Cesare, I do not know. I heard the door; but I thought it was you. I called your name, but he . . . he . . . oh God, Cesare, Cesare . . ."

She turned her head and buried in on the Duke's shoulder.

Cesare looked at the man. "Your name?"

The question cut the silence of the chamber, and Ascano's tongue moved uneasily over terror-dried lips.

"My . . . my lord," he began in a harsh whisper. "I do not understand this . . . I do not comprehend . . ."

"Neither do I," said Cesare shortly. "But I will, sire, I will."

He straightened up, and Maria fell back against the cushions, her eyes still agonized.

"Your name? And from whence do you come?"

Ascano swallowed hard. "Ascano, sire; Gioffre Ascano from Venice. And I came to offer you my sword for your next campaign, for there is none I would choose so readily to follow than you, sire."

"Even to this bedchamber?" Valentinois' tone was scathing, and the man's face grew a shade greyer.

"My lord, you cannot think . . . you cannot believe that I knew . . . that I knew the situation?"

Ascano held the bedpost in a hand shaking with a fear no battle he had fought had ever aroused.

"Sire, I did not know. I was told that I would be well received here, provided I had sufficient gold. I had no reason to doubt this, my lord."

His eyes could not meet the fury of Cesare's, and his knuckles grew whiter as his grip on the bedpost increased.

"You were told you would be received?" Cesare's voice was barely above a whisper. "By whom were you told?"

Ascano swallowed again. "By a man in a tavern, sire. A man I met earlier today."

"You know his name?"

Ascano shook his head, mute with the terror which the Duke had inspired in him, and Cesare's eyes narrowed suddenly.

"What manner of man was he, signore?"

Ascano bit his lip. "A man of some fifty summers, my lord, and grey of hair and beard. His eyes were dark, his face swarthy, and he had a scar on his forehead."

"A scar?" Cesare's voice was softer still. "A scar in the shape of a crescent, signore?"

Ascano looked up quickly. "Yes, sire, that is so. He is known to you, my lord?"

Cesare's hand left its habitual place on his dagger, and he gave a faint sigh. "He is known to me," he said slowly, and his eyes turned to regard Maria, whose tears had abated, and who was now listening to the exchange with eyes wide with fear.

"Why, that is . . ." she began, when Cesare raised a hand sharply.

"Silenzia!" He turned to the man.

"Signore, in normal circumstances I would kill you for what you have done, but I am content that you were used to strike at me, and that you were unaware of what you undertook when you came to this room tonight. I have a reputation for justice, and 'twould be against my principles to kill you for something you had no part in, but you would be well gone from this city, signore, and before the dawn breaks, for if I find you still in Rome tomorrow, anger may rule my reason. Begone, sire, and thank the gods that I interrupted you when I did, for otherwise you would not have lived, innocent though you might be."

He gave a sharp gesture, and Ascano fled the chamber, his heart pounding unbearably, and Cesare turned back to Maria.

"You knew nothing of this?"

"Oh, Cesare, how can you ask this?" Her tears started to fall again, but he was impatient.

"No more tears madonna, you have cried enough, and do not persuade me that this is a circumstance you have not encountered before."

"Cesare!" It was a cry of panic as he turned to the door. "Oh, Cesare, do not leave me, I beg you, please . . . please . . ."

"I have things to do, madonna," he said formally. "Do you imagine I will tolerate this situation. No, there is a price to be paid for this."

"But, Cesare . . ." She pulled herself up and ran to his side. "I beg you, Cesare, please. . . please . . ."

He looked down at her for a second. "Allay your fears, madonna. I have no quarrel with you, and tomorrow I will come to you again, but now," the hazel eyes were bleak, "now I have other things to do."

CHAPTER TEN

THE chill winds of March gave way to Spring and then to Summer. During the weeks that passed, Cesare turned his attention to the gathering about him of a well-trained, well-disciplined army, for he was determined to be rid of Louis' troops as soon as possible, and the time was not yet ripe for the assembling of a force from the Romagna. Such was his name and reputation, that he had no difficulty in attracting to his banner many who lived by their sword, and who were only too happy to pledge their lives to the cause of a man who was so generous in the payment he made to his condottieri, and whose fame had spread to the far corners of Italy. He attracted also the well-born young Romans of the great families of the day, and his personal guard was a brilliant galaxy, a fitting complement to his own dazzling presence.

Cesare was impatient to take to the field again, for his eyes were on Pesaro, Faenza and Rimini, but Louis was still engaged on the Pisan war, and Valentinois had to wait for the conclusion of this engagement before he could hope for the French troops he still needed to aid him. Whilst he waited, Cesare drilled his ever-growing army, and amused himself with the many pleasures to be found in Rome at the time of the Papal Jubilee.

Lucrezia, now served by another chamberlain of Cesare's choosing, had recovered from the failure of her attempt to rid herself of Maria Amati, who was still in the Duke's favour, and she contented herself with a quiet defiance by continuing to see Gian Orestes, whom Cesare appeared to have dismissed from his mind. That Cesare should so carelessly ignore Lucrezia's disobedience in this respect did not strike her as a matter of major importance, for she consoled herself with the thought that he had other things which held his attention, and gradually, as the weeks passed, she had been able to persuade herself that her brother had forgotten Orestes' presence in Rome.

But Cesare had not forgotten, nor for one second did he dismiss the impudent Captain from his mind. His anger was of the kind which smouldered slowly over a long period, and his revenge was not always so instant as when he took Rafael Buorossi to the Vatican dungeons and put him to death in a cruel and savage fashion.

Cesare's personal Court had also grown enormously, not only by the presence of the officers he gathered about him, but also swelled by numbers of artists, sculptors, poets and men of letters, whose generous patron he had become, and the Pope had cause to wring his hands on more than one occasion as he contemplated the liberality with which his son spent the money collected in the Vatican Treasury.

He was moved to remonstrate with Cesare one sunny afternoon in June whilst they watched a bull-fight which had been arranged for the pleasure of the Pope and the Duke. The Pontiff and his party occupied a garlanded box at the front of the steeply rising tiers, and the crowds were as excited by the presence of Valentino, not often seen in public, as they were by the prospect of the struggle in the ring.

"Cesare, you are reckless in your spending," said the Pope testily. "You are throwing ducats away in such a manner that none will be left to equip your army when the time comes to move against Pesaro. You must curb your generosity, for the Papal coffers are not bottomless."

Cesare's eyes were on the arena, where a slender youth matched his wits and skill against the bulk of the huge black bull, lowering its head in forbidding style as it weighed up the ability of its adversary.

"I cannot be expected to support my Court on a pittance, Holiness." Cesare's voice was disinterested. He did not regard the raising of money as any part of his task; this he left to the Pope, who had hitherto been extremely successful in this field. "Do you expect me to live like a pauper?"

"But, Cesare." The Pope tried to conceal his irritation at his son's off-hand contempt for money. "Do you not realize how difficult it is to raise the sums you need? Surely some economy. . . ."

"No." Cesare did not turn his gaze from the sight below, but his voice was crisp and decisive. "I will not live like a peasant, Father; it is for you to see that Rome provides the necessary ducats I need for my army. You do not usually have such difficulty in this regard."

The Pope clicked his tongue impatiently and turned to look at Lucrezia, sitting between Alfonso and Sancia. It was really impossible to reason with Cesare over money, and he wondered, for a fleeting moment, whether there was any future in trying to pursuade Lucrezia to talk to her brother, but even as the thought came to him, the Pope dismissed it again, for he had no illusions as to the stronger will involved, and Cesare would merely laugh at Lucrezia's efforts.

There was a sudden cry from the packed terraces. The Pope glanced back at the arena, and craned forward sharply as he saw the bull charge the matador. The crowd's sigh seemed to come from one throat as the torn, broken body of the young fighter was flung into the hot sand, suddenly stained red.

Cesare leaned back as men rushed into the ring to rescue the dying man, and to force the triumphant bull back into its pen.

"He was no match for the bull," said Cesare regretfully. "Alas, so few of our young men seem able to equal the strength and skill of these bulls from Naples."

He turned to Alfonso, and his mouth was contemptuous.

"The one strong and effective thing about Naples is its bloodstock, for its bulls are incomparable, whereas its men. . . ."

He left the rest unsaid, and Alfonso's face whitened in fury.

"One day, my lord, you may have cause to reconsider your words."

"This I doubt," said Cesare lazily, and his glance was scornful. "Unless, of course, you propose to descend to the bull-ring and prove me wrong, Alfonso. Well, what do you say?" His eyes were mocking.

Sancia gave an exclamation, and Alfonso coloured slowly.

"I . . . I . . . have no training, my lord. I could not kill a bull."

"Nor yet a man, Alfonso, and so I account myself safe."

Bisceglie's mouth was harsh, and he said no more, but Sancia, angered by Cesare's derision, was not so silent.

"And what of you, my lord," she asked in a voice high with rage. "We do not see you undertaking the task you would wish upon my brother. Why do you not shew us lesser mortals the ease with which you can kill a bull, or have you no stomach for such chances?"

The Pope was sharp. "Sancia! That will do. Cesare cannot risk his life in the bull-ring to please you; he has other tasks to perform, and you will not rouse him to such folly by your taunts."

"Other tasks, Holiness?" Sancia's mouth curled spitefully. "Other battles where men can die for him, you mean? Where my lord need take no personal risks, and where his precious life can be safeguarded whilst his men earn his glory for him?"

The Pope was getting angry. "I will have no more of this, Sancia," he began, when Cesare rose to his feet.

"You want the ears of a bull as a trophy, Sancia?" he drawled, "then I will be happy to oblige you."

"No!" Lucrezia's cry was frenzied. "Cesare, no! no! You will be killed."

"Not I, Lucrezia. 'Twill be the bull's ears Sancia will get, not mine, much as she would prefer the latter."

He turned on his heel and left the terrace, the Pope's cry of protest falling upon deaf ears.

Five minutes later, Alexander and his party watched Cesare ride out into the arena, one hand clasped lightly round a thin lance, and if the Pope and Lucrezia were filled with fear and dread, Alfonso and Sancia held their breath in gleeful anticipation, for it seemed at last as though there might be a chance of ridding themselves of their hated enemy, and, by a quirk of fate, through the agency of a Neapolitan bull. Sancia's colour was high, her grey eyes ablaze with the lust of hate as she saw the attendants release the first bull from the pens at the side of the arena.

The great creature lumbered noisily into the centre of the sand-strewn area, nostrils flared, its breath hot and angry as it sought its enemy. The Duke's horse whinneyed in fear, and tried to back away, but Cesare's hand was firm on the reins, and his voice comforted and encouraged the terrified animal, coaxing it to stand against the menace of the horned assassin facing it.

The bull pawed the ground impatiently. It was as if it recognized in his adversary something less easy to destroy than those normally sent against it, and the small bright eyes were gleaming with venom as it turned and made the first charge. Cesare's control of his horse was perfect. The animal moved like a dancer under the guidance of the Duke's strong, steady hands, and after the first few essays the bull's temper began to rise at the failure to panic its opponent into a false move which would give the vital advantage.

The harsh breathing increased and it flung itself away again, scuffling the dirt under restive feet as it turned for another assault.

The bull charged full tilt at Cesare, determined to kill, or to force him to retreat in an admission of defeat.

The densely packed tiers were hushed in a deathly silence under the hard blue sky. The Pope's fingers were unsteady on his Rosary as he watched his son. He knew his undoubted skill in the art of bull fighting, but these animals from Naples were savage and seldom beaten, and every time Cesare entered the ring the Pope felt the coldness of death enfold him, and was constantly exhorting the Duke to give up this dangerous pastime.

Lucrezia's face was buried in her hands, her eyes tightly shut, for she could not bear to watch the destruction of the man she loved so dearly.

The hooves of the maddened bull thundered across the rough arena, but Cesare stood his ground. The Pope closed his eyes in prayer as his stubborn son refused to bend to the animal's will, and then opened them just in time to see the finale of this battel between beast and man.

As the bull was within inches of him, Cesare pulled his mount aside in a movement which was sheer poetry, and the lance he had held so negligently, suddenly became a terrifying weapon of destruction as he drove it hard down into the animal's neck. So strong and vicious was the thrust that the vast bulk of the bull was immediately checked, and slowly, but surely, the creature sank to its knees, and its eyes glazed over as the last of the hot June afternoon was lost to it for ever.

The cheers which rang through the crowded balconies were deafening. Lucrezia dropped her hands, and the Pope said a hasty prayer of thanksgiving to the Blessed Virgin, but Sancia's white teeth bit her lip in anger and frustration, for not only had Cesare survived, but he had given a matchless display of skill, strength and courage, which could do nothing but enhance his reputation.

Her heart quickened again as she realized that Cesare had not finished, and once again the hush fell as the dead bull was dragged from the ring, and a fresh one loosed against Valentinois.

The second bull did not have the same measure of courage as the first, and Cesare killed it with ease, as he did the third and fourth which the attendants sent into the arena at his direction. The fifth took longer to despatch, but the outcome of the struggle was, in fact, a foregone conclusion from the moment the bull thundered into the ring, and it was only a matter of time before it too lay prostrate at Valentinois' feet; useless carrion which had so short a time before been a living, death-dealing force.

There was a ripple of surprise throughout the assembly as Cesare dismounted, and sent his sorely-tried horse back to the safety of the stables, and at a shouted command from the Duke, an attendant came into the ring, bearing a double-edged sword, which Valentinois took from him, surrendering his blood-stained lance.

"Oh no!" Lucrezia's cry was wrung from her heart, and the Pope paled as he realized Cesare's intent. Sancia and Alfonso exchanged a glance of hope. A hope that despite the superb exhibition given by the Duke, death might still await him in this hot, tension-ridden arena under the glare of the Roman sun.

If the silence had been deep before, it now had the stillness of the grave, as for the last time, the wooden doors were pulled open and the sixth bull stormed out into the dust.

"Now," whispered Sancia under her breath. "Now, my lord; see what you can make of a bull when you meet him on his own terms. Face to face."

Her fingers were tearing the silken handkerchief in an agony of excitement as she watched the opening gambit between the man and bull below her.

They were well-matched. Both were at the peak of physical fitness; both thoroughbreds, made for battle and possessed of that rare courage which has literally no fear at its roots. They faced one another with pleasure and respect; each recognizing, and paying tribute to, the other's spirit and quality, and Cesare's mouth moved in a slight smile as he waited for his enemy to make its first move.

And move it did. It rushed the Duke; a compact, devastating mass of flesh, bone and muscle, bent on death, but as it reached its target, Cesare turned slightly to one side with the minimum of movement, which brought a breathless sigh of admiration from the tense crowd. The bull snorted and backed away, angered by its opponent's refusal to acknowledge fear. It hurtled forward again, and once more the Duke turned aside with the same economy of motion and effort.

Four times the animal launched itself at the cool poised man who stood against it, and then gathering all its strength, it made one last desperate bid to crush the arrogant figure standing in its path.

As it tore across the blood-stained sand towards Cesare, the crowds half rose in their seats, for all were aware that the final moment was almost upon them; the time had come when bull or man must yield mastery to the other, and so perfectly were they matched, that none could guess who would be the victor in this duel of death. This time Cesare did not turn aside, but as the cumbersome beast reached him, he jumped back in a lightning movement, and one second later the heavy sword struck the bull with such force that the huge head rolled across the dirt at Valentinois' feet, completely severed from the carcase, which dropped lifeless into the dust.

For a split second, the silence was unbroken, then a cheer

rang out which rent the quietness like a thunder-clap, and the cries and acclamations of the ecstatic crowd surged round and round the arena in ever-increasing volume.

Cesare bent down and with two sharp movements, slashed off the ears of the bull, and raising his sword in acknowledgement to the frenzied mob, he returned to the Pope's box, and without a word, flung the blood-soaked ears on to Sancia's lap.

Lucrezia was sobbing, the tears pouring down a face torn by the fears which had wracked her whilst she watched her brother challenge fate, yet glowing with the pride she now felt at his stupendous victory.

"Oh, Cesare, Cesare." She rose from her seat, and he caught her to him, laughing at her tears.

"Carissima! Tears for the victor? Come, come, this will not do, cara. Will you drown me as a reward for my endeavours?"

His arm was round her, and his mouth touched her forehead. "Do not cry beloved," he said softly. "I have done what I set out to do. I have proved that a man from Rome can vanquish a bull from Naples."

His eyes met Sancia's for a brief second, and with an exclamation of disgust and rage, his sister-in-law threw the bleeding fragments from her lap, and stumpled out of the box, followed by Alfonso, strangely white and tense as he saw the quiet triumph on Cesare's face.

June wore into July, and Cesare remained in Rome.

One night, after a banquet at which Cesare had entertained his staff, he retired to his private chambers with some of his intimates, and stretched out on a low couch by an open window.

"Faith, I declare your banquets are more exhausting than your battles, sire," said Bartolomeo da Capranica as he flung himself down in a nearby chair and wiped a hand across his brow. "That red-head was most demanding."

"I trust you will resist the enemy with more vigor than you resisted her," laughed Santa Croce, "for it seemed to me that you put up no fight in that quarter, Bartolomeo."

"It was hard to stand against so much charm and beauty, and I did not notice you spurning the attentions of that raven-haired wench who found you so irresistible, Pietro."

Santa Croce pulled a face at his companion as he poured wine from a tall silver flagon and handed the goblet to Cesare.

"Well, 'tis best to make the most of what fortune sends now, for I doubt we shall receive such a warm welcome in the Romagna." He glanced at Cesare. "Is there chance that we may soon move, sire?"

"Not yet." The Duke took the wine with a smile of thanks, and glanced at his companions with a warmth he shewed to very few. "You must possess your soul in patience, Pietro, but do not despair, for 'ere long you will have all the battles you seek, and in plenty, for whilst some states will not oppose us, there will be some who will attempt to withstand our forces."

He turned to the Master of his Household, Ramiro de Lorqua.

"And how many joined us today, Ramiro?"

De Lorqua was a thick-set, burly man, with a short black beard and hot dark eyes, and his hands were large, strong and ruthless in conflict or in the control of the forces under his charge, and the men were wary about arousing his anger, which in any event was kept on a short chain.

"Two dozen, my lord," he said with satisfaction. "Five cavalry officers, and six artillery experts amongst them. A goodly haul today, and I have news that others will be coming from Ferrara and Milan tomorrow."

"Good." The Duke nodded. "Mario," he glanced over at di Mariano who was laughing with Gianbattista Mancini and Giangiordano Orsini.

"Sire." Mario moved towards the Duke's couch, but before he could reach it, the door opened and a page entered, stopping short in the doorway, his face colouring up, one foot rubbing nervously against the other as he was confronted by the Duke's elegant officers.

"What is it, boy?" asked de Lorqua shortly. "Come in, come in. Don't stand hovering in the doorway like that. What is your message?"

The boy shivered at de Lorqua's harsh voice, and Cesare smiled.

"Come," he said quietly, and the stripling moved uncertainly to his master's side.

He was some twelve years; thin and wiry, with ruffled gold curls and a pure white skin, now flushed with the embarrassment he felt as he faced the man whose very name caused men to pale in terror.

"S . . . s . . . sire." The boy bowed, and hesitated again.

"God's blood, boy, get on with it!" snapped de Lorgua testily, "has the tiger got your tongue? What message do you bring?"

The page's eyes darkened in fear, and his colour deepened.

"My . . . my . . . lord," he began again, when Cesare held up a hand.

"Peace, Ramiro, there is no need for such speed; the lad will tell us in good time. "Now," he looked back at his page. "What is your name, for I do not think I have seen you before?"

The boy's flush subsided and something of his fear left him at his master's friendly voice and easy manner, and he half smiled at Valentinois.

"Leo, my lord. My name is Leo, and I have been in your lordship's service but two days." He shitfed uneasily again, and his eyes were downcast.

"Well, Leo, you are welcome." The Duke's voice was still kindly. "Now, you have a message for me?"

The boy looked up, and finding nothing fearful in his master's gaze, nodded quickly.

"Yes, Magnificence. A man has come to see you. He seeks audience with you on a matter of urgency, for he says your life depends upon it."

There were faint murmurs from the others, and Cesare's glance sharpened slightly.

"And what man is this, Leo, who comes with words of such importance. His name?"

Leo heard the imperceptible change in the Duke's tone and his face whitened.

"S . . . sire . . . sire . . . his . . . his name . . . his

name. . . ." The boy swallowed, his stuttering silenced in fear as Cesare's eyes held his own.

"Come." The Duke's voice was gentle again. "His name, Leo?"

"Matteo Petucci, sire." Leo managed the words with an effort, and Giulio Alberini came forward with a quick oath.

"Petucci! Why he is one of Alfonso Bisceglie's men. Boy, are you sure of this?"

The page trembled as he looked up at the tall sun-tanned man who towered over him, and a nervous tongue flickered over his lips.

"S . . . sire, yes, yes. I am sure, Matteo Petucci; he said it was a matter of vital importance to his Highness."

"Very well, Leo. Have him brought to me," said Cesare calmly, "If he brings messages of such significance, then we must see him. Bring him hence."

He waved a hand, and Leo bowed and sped thankfully from the room, whilst Alberini frowned thoughtfully, and one hand adjusted the sword he wore at his side.

"Petucci. I wonder what he is about. Sire, this may be an attempt on your life." His eyes were worried as he looked at the Duke, who laughed and took another sip of wine.

"I hardly think so, Giulio. A man would have to be bereft of his wits to attempt to kill me when I am surrounded by a dozen of my Captains. No, I doubt this, but there may be some plot involved I agree. We shall soon see when the good Messer Petucci arrives."

"Alfonso would dearly like you dead, sire," said Capranica slowly. "There is little he would not chance to be rid of you; and his sister. . . ."

"His sister would sell her soul to the devil to destroy me," finished Cesar shortly. "Yes, Bartolomeo, I am aware of my lack of popularity in that quarter, and I am of a mind to see that this irritant is removed from my path, for I have more important things to do than concern myself with Alfonso of Aragon."

The doors swung open again and Leo returned with a man who came slowly forward to bow low before the Duke.

Cesare smiled at the page. "You have done well, Leo. I am glad to have you in my service."

The boy's face lit up, and from that moment he was the Duke's slave, for Cesare had more than one way of reaching his ends, and whilst he was savage and bloody in war, he held the loyalty of his own men and his servants by entirely different methods.

When the doors had closed once more behind the page, Cesare studied the man who waited quietly before him.

He was of medium height and thin; the brown hair was lank against a small round skull. His eyes were narrow and dark, his skin of a yellow pallor, and his mouth was weak. These things the Duke noted quickly before he spoke.

"Well, sire, you seek my ear on a matter of some importance?" His tone was light. "What is this news you bring to me, which affects my safety?"

Matteo Petucci glanced quickly round the group of men who had drawn nearer to the Duke. Whilst sharing Cesare's view that the man would not attempt assassination in such circumstances, they were not prepared to take any chances, and Petucci saw in their watchful eyes a suspicion and wariness which boded no good for any who would seek to harm the Duke.

He bowed again to Cesare. "That is so, Highness. It has come to my ears that an attempt will be made on your life, and this right soon. Thus, I had no choice but to come to you to warn you."

"No choice?" Cesare's voice was still unworried. "All men have a choice Messer Petucci. You have chosen to come to me, and doubtless you had a good reason. And who is this who seeks to destroy me?"

"Alfonso Bisceglie, my lord." The man was not ruffled by the Duke's words, nor did he lose his poise, as another faint ripple went through those assembled as he named the would-be murderer.

"Alfonso Bisceglie." The Duke was reflective. "Ah, yes. And you are one of his men, are you not, sire?"

Petucci nodded. "I was, my lord. I have been in the Duke of Bisceglie's pay for some two years."

Cesare's brows rose slightly. "And yet now come to me to warn me that he means me mischief? Why is that Messer Petucci? Have you grown tired of service with my esteemed brother-in-law?"

Although the tenor of the Duke's voice had not altered, there was a faintly suspicious note beneath the words, and the hazel eyes were a shade colder as they surveyed the man.

Still the man shewed no trace of nervousness, and with perfect aplomb, he nodded.

"Tired indeed, Highness, for I seek to better myself, and this I will not do in the pay of such a man as Bisceglie, for he is a weakling and a coward."

"Harsh words, Messer Petucci," observed Cesare, and raised himself from his reclining position on the couch. "But I had not noticed that Alfonso had changed so much in the last two years. Why now do you seek to be rid of him?"

Petucci shrugged. "Sire, I have for a long time realized that I served the wrong master, but until now I saw no reason to seek a change, although I was far from satisfied with the man I followed."

"But now?" The Duke rose from the couch and put aside his goblet. "Why now, Messer Petucci?"

"Now, my lord, I have the opportunity of serving you by warning you of Bisceglie's intention to kill you, and thus, I hope, you will be moved to offer me employment as a reward for my information."

"But what guarantee have I, Messer Petucci, that if I take you into my service, you will not serve me as you now seek to serve Bisceglie? What surety is there that you will not desert me when it suits your purpose, just as you would now desert Alfonso?"

The man gave a crooked smile. "You have no guarantee, Highness, but when a man serves the greatest, there is no incentive to change his loyalty."

Cesare gave a faint laugh. "A diplomatist. Well, Messer Petucci, what is this plot you would uncover to me? What does Alfonso Bisceglie plan to effect my destruction? You have details, sire?"

The Duke's voice was sharper, and Petucci straightened automatically.

"Sire. Yes, I have details. It is known that your lordship makes a practice of walking in the Vatican gardens at dusk, and often alone or with, perhaps, one or two men at your side. On one such night, there will be a man with an arbalest; he will be concealed in the bushes, and when your lordship passes by, he will loose his bolt."

"And when is this planned?" Cesare rested one hand on his hip as he paced in front of the man. "What night has been chosen for this folly?"

"The night of July the 20th, Highness."

"Why then?"

"No reason was given, my lord, save that on that night his Holiness plans a banquet, and 'tis known that it will be such that it will bore your Highness, and you will probably seek refuge from the tedium by walking in the grounds earlier than usual."

Cesare laughed shortly. "I see. How well Alfonso reads me, at least in this respect."

He stopped his pacing and came back to stand in front of the man, who raised his eyes fearlessly to meet the Duke's austere face.

"You must go back to Bisceglie, Messer Petucci."

For the first time, a flicker of fear crossed the narrow white face, and the hands at the man's side suddenly clenched.

"My lord! You do not believe me?"

"I did not say that. I said you must return to Bisceglie, for if you do not, he will guess that you have come to me, and thus his plans will be altered. Does anyone know you have come here tonight? You were not followed?"

The tremor of nerves disappeared and the man's gaze returned to its former calm. "No, my lord. No one is aware of my presence here. And I was not followed."

"Then go back to Bisceglie's quarters and say nothing. And watch your step as you walk through the Vatican, for every wall has a hundred eyes and a hundred ears, and although Alfonso and I are separated by but a short distance, it can be a long way, Messer Petucci; a very long way."

The man's face became a shade whiter at the Duke's words, but his demeanour remained as assured as before.

"I will remember your words, sire, and will use great caution in my return to the Duke's chambers."

He hesitated. "And, my lord, after . . . after . . ."

"After I have dealt with this matter, Messer Petucci, I will send for you. If what you have told me is true, and if you have indeed brought me true words, then you will not find me ungrateful. Now go."

He turned away, leaving Petucci no choice but to make his obeisance and withdraw, although he would dearly have liked to know more about the Duke's intentions concerning his reward and his future, but he was not a fool and could see the moment was not propitious.

After he had gone there was a moment's silence, then Cesare said softly:

"If this is true, and I have reason to believe it is, then I think the time has come to make a move to settle this issue between Alfonso and myself once and for all."

"Yes, indeed," said Alberini hotly. "And I beg you, my lord, that you will allow me to rid you of this man who dares to seek your life."

Cesare smiled at Alberini's indignant face. "Thank you, Giulio, but that would be a clumsy way of achieving our ends. There are other methods."

"But, my lord." Capranica was short. "We have no time for finesse in this matter. Petucci may be right about the date, but this is not certain. Suppose Alfonso moves in advance of this? Sire, we cannot delay. Giulio is right; this is a matter which must be settled now."

"Oh, it will be settled." The Duke's eyes were dreamy. "It will be settled, Bartolomeo, but in my way."

He returned to the couch and lay down, one hand reaching for his goblet again. "More wine, Ramiro. Yes, it will be settled, but I will arrange the details, and I think I have a way of doing this which will settle more than one score."

"Sire?"

"There are two men I would be rid of," said Cesare as de

Lorqua filled his goblet with clear sparkling wine. "One is my brother-in-law, Alfonso; the other is Gian Orestes."

There was a moment's silence whilst the others reflected on the crass folly of the man who had defied the Duke and dared to seek the love of his lovely sister.

"Yes," went on the Duke, an ugly smile on his mouth. "Gian Orestes." He looked up at the others. "Ramiro, send a message to Orestes. Tell him I wish to see him, and do not alarm him. Your approach is to be a friendly one, and you will contrive to see that he has no need to fear such a visit to me. I want him to come willingly, and I want him to understand that I mean him no harm. Is this understood?"

Ramiro nodded, but he was puzzled. "Yes, sire, that is clear, but I do not understand."

"You will, Ramiro, you will." The Duke's smile turned to one of satisfaction.. "Arrange this as soon as you can, for I would now put an end to these matters which have caused me concern, and thus my mind will be clear to attend to affairs of more importance."

Two days later, Gian Orestes came to the Vatican to see the Duke of Valentinois, and although Ramiro de Lorqua's invitation had been warm and friendly, and despite the fact that Cesare had made no previous attempt to stop his relationship with Lucrezia, there was a small inner worry in Orestes as he was shewn into the library where the Duke was working with Agapito da Amelia.

He saluted smartly, and Valentinois laid down his pen and leaned back in his chair. For a long minute he looked at the man who had taken his sister, and under the iron self-control, there was something so savage and lethal that had Orestes seen but a glimpse of it, he would have fled the room in terror. But no such hint shewed in the Duke's impassive gaze, and his manner was pleasant and affable.

"Captain Orestes, you are welcome, for it seems to me we should have met before."

Again Orestes felt the quiver of something very near to fear, but Cesare waved him to a chair.

"I beg you be seated, for there are things we must discuss. Things of mutual importance and advantage to us."

Orestes sat down facing the Duke and glanced at Agapito.

Seeing the look, Cesare smiled. "All I do is known to Agapito. I have no thought or feeling he does not know about, Captain Orestes. I would not have you concern yourself about his presence. Now."

The Duke sat up, and picked up a quill, running one finger along its length.

"Captain Orestes, it has come to my ears that you find my sister not unpleasing."

Orestes felt the sweat stand out on his brow, but he contrived to steady his voice as he answered Valentinois.

"Highness, that is so, for she is the most beautiful woman I have ever seen, and has completely won my heart. Sire, I realize that you must think me presumptuous to seek the favour of the Duchess in this way, but in truth I could not resist her, for she overwhelmed my mind and spirit."

The serenity of the Duke's eyes did not falter.

"But of course, Captain Orestes. I fully understand the reason why you found Lucrezia so appealing. She is, as you say, of great beauty and charm, and what man worth the name could stand against such loveliness?"

Orestes furtively wiped the palm of a hand across his doublet, and the small smile at the corner of Cesare's mouth noted the fear which held the man before him in its grip.

"Yes," he went on sympathetically. "This I fully understand, Captain Orestes. But," he paused and Orestes' glance quickened at the sharper note in the Duke's voice.

"But, Captain Orestes, the situation cannot be allowed to continue as it is. My sister is the wife of Alfonso of Aragon, and whilst I can well appreciate that she does not relish this role, she is his Duchess, and whilst he lives——" The Duke broke off and the smile deepened. "Whilst he lives, Captain Orestes, your position is unfortunate."

Orestes took a deep breath ."Highness, I realize this, and if there was ought I could do . . ."

Cesare's glance was encouraging. "Well, as I say, whilst Alfonso Bisceglie lives . . ." Again there was a tiny pause.

Then the Duke's teeth shewed in a brief moment of amusement. "If, of course, he were no longer alive . . ."

Orestes' eyes widened suddenly as he understood Cesare's intent.

"If he died, Magnificence?"

Cesare shrugged. "If he died, sire, then matters would be different, of course. Lucrezia is young and has had a dull time with Alfonso. 'Tis time she had a man to wed who could satisfy her needs, as I am sure you do."

The Duke's expression did not change, but Agapito saw the slender white fingers clench on the quill, which snapped with a light click, and his watchful eyes noted the lines at the corner of his Highness's mouth which spoke volumes to those who knew him well.

Orestes, not knowing the Duke, heard only his words, and his interest was aroused.

"If Alfonso Bisceglie died," he breathed and leaned forward slightly. "What then, my lord?"

Cesare's shoulders moved again in the faintest shrug.

"Could I stand between such love as you and Lucrezia feel for one another? No; she is very dear to me, and as she wants you, Captain Orestes, then I would have to acquiesce in the match."

"The match! Sire, you mean you would consent to our marriage?"

The Duke nodded and leaned back in his chair again.

"I would have no choice, for Lucrezia can twist me round her little finger, and she knows this. No, I would have to consent. Some title would be necessary, of course." He turned his head to gaze out of the window. "But this would not be difficult."

Orestes' eyes were bright and his fears dropped from him.

"Highness, I am overwhelmed. I do not know what to say. I cannot begin to tell you . . ."

"But, Captain Orestes," Cesare's glance turned back from the window to the excited condottiero. "Alfonso Bisceglie is still alive, and whilst he is, there is little than can be done to further your union with my sister."

For a second Orestes was crestfallen, then his eyes lit up again.

"But if he were to die, my lord?"

"Then, sire, the way would be clear."

Orestes clenched his hands. "Highness, if I could contrive to bring about this desirable end?"

"You?" The Duke was sceptical. "How could you do this?"

"T'would not be impossible, sire. Indeed, t'would be easy with such a reward for the labour." He bent forward, his manner eager and excited. "Sire, I could rid us of the Duke Bisceglie with little difficulty."

Cesare regarded him through narrowed eyes. "You would need to use caution, sire, for he is well guarded."

"I have men, my lord; men who are more than a match for Alfonso Bisceglie's guard."

"And when would you bring about this endeavour?"

"Soon, sire, soon. Indeed, there is no cause for delay, for the sooner we are finished with Bisceglie, the sooner I may claim the Madonna Lucrezia."

Agapito felt the tension in Cesare, and for a second feared that the instinctive reaction to the reckless Captain would over-ride his cunning plan, but his alarm was unfounded, for Cesare merely nodded.

"That is true, and I would like to see this achieved to-morrow night, for I am as anxious as you to make an end of this matter. Can you make your arrangements by then?"

Orestes nodded, his eyes confident, his manner suddenly more assured and certain. "Yes, this I can do, sire. My men are ready to meet my instant command, and t'will not be hard to discover the Duke's movements."

"No, it will not be difficult," agreed Cesare, "for I can tell you something of Alfonso's habits. 'Tis his custom to leave the Vatican at about nine o'clock, for then he and his companions make their way to the Borgo, there to seek the pleasures of the prostitutes who ply their wares for such fools as Alfonso. But, Captain Orestes." Cesare's voice was hard. "No word of this must reach the Madonna Lucrezia's ears."

He rose, and Orestes snapped to attention.

"I wish you good fortune, Captain Orestes," he said mildly, and only Agapito saw what lay beneath his courteous words. "For you will serve us both well if you succeed in your venture."

"Never fear, my lord, I will succeed." Orestes saluted and withdrew, and Cesare gave a terse laugh.

"Yes, by God, he will succeed, and so will I." The calmness was gone, and Cesare's hand struck the desk in fury. "I will succeed in ridding this world of carrion such as Orestes. He will not live long enough to enjoy the fruits of his endeavour. He will pay the price for his effrontery in seducing Lucrezia."

The Duke swung round, his eyes blazing, and Agapito looked at him in consternation, for the occasions on which Cesare shewed his true feelings were rare.

"But, sire, if he kills Alfonso Bisceglie, how will you withdraw from your bargain?"

The Duke was silent for a moment; when he spoke, the fury in him had died.

"After he kills Alfonso," he said softly, "he too will die."

"If you raise your hand to him, my lord, all Rome will know, and the Madonna Lucrezia . . ."

"There will be a struggle as Orestes' men attack Alfonso's. There will be nothing unusual in Orestes' death."

Agapito frowned. " 'Tis possible, of course, that he might die in the conflict, but this cannot be guaranteed."

"Oh, yes, it can, Agapito; yes, it can."

"But, my lord, how?"

Cesare turned a gaze on his secretary which chilled Agapito's blood.

"When Gian Orestes attacks the Duke of Bisceglie's party, Agapito, I shall be there; unseen, but a careful watcher of events. When Alfonso dies in the affray, I will repay my debt to Captain Orestes, and much pleasure it will give me."

Agapito frowned and gathered the papers from the desk.

"I beg you, do not take risks, my lord."

Cesare smiled coldly. "When I fear to take risks, Agapito, my use to the Holy See is at an end. But there will be no risk here. By my plan, Orestes will kill Alfonso, and the blame will attach to him; and I will kill Orestes, but none will know this, and so we shall reach a satisfactory conclusion to these tiresome affairs."

"But the Madonna Lucrezia?"

Cesare's eyes smouldered. "I have other plans for her," he said slowly, "and if she misses the good Captain Orestes, 'tis a fitting punishment for her disobedience."

Agapito said no more, and Cesare turned and strode out of the room, leaving his secretary to shake his head and continue his work, whilst his mind worried quietly about the part his master proposed to play in the destruction of the two men who had crossed his will.

CHAPTER ELEVEN

DESPITE his other preoccupations, Cesare found time that afternoon to ride out to visit Laura Montefiore, for in truth he was getting a little weary of Maria Amati and her constant demands that he should take her from the Vatican, a plea which he had so far ignored, and it crossed his mind that it was time that he took steps to sever his relationship with Lucrezia's lady in waiting, for whilst she had amused him and afforded him many hours of pleasure, she now shewed signs of wishing to hold him in too tight a grip, and this Cesare was not prepared to tolerate.

He rode swiftly through the city to its outskirts, and dismounted at Laura's house, and was quickly admitted by her servants to her presence.

It was the first time they had met since his return to Rome, and his gaze lightened as he looked at her, for he had not forgotten how lovely she was, and he held out one hand with a smile.

"Laura."

She curtsied formally, but made no move to take his hand and the Duke raised one eyebrow.

"Oh? You are not pleased to see me, Laura?" He came forward and looked down at her. "I had thought to find a warmer welcome."

She rose and her expression was as cold as she dared make it in his presence.

"My lord, you are always welcome in my house." Her eyes were hostile, and Cesare's glance was mocking, for he knew exactly why her manner was so chilly.

"This I am glad to hear, cara. I have brought gifts for you, my love. See, does this please you?"

He drew from his pocket a string of exquisite pearls and a diamond and ruby ring of staggering size, but even these did not thaw the ice. Cesare shrugged and tossed the jewels carelessly into a nearby chair.

"I am grateful, my lord," said Laura stiffly, assuming a formality she did not feel, for she would dearly have liked to claw his derisive face, but even in her anger, she was too afraid of him to shew this fury.

"I have missed you, my sweet," said Cesare lightly. "I trust you have also awaited my return with impatience."

He took her hand and raised it to his lips, but she jerked it away and hot colour flooded her pale cheeks, and her caution was dispelled.

"I have awaited you, Cesare," she said shortly, "for a long time, but I can scarce believe you have missed me, for I am told you have had other matters on your mind, and other distractions to hold your attention."

Cesare's amusement deepened, for he found her even lovelier in a temper, and the colour in her cheeks and sparkling eyes quickened his desire for her.

"Come, come, Laura. Jealous? There is no need. Have I not come back to you?"

"Have you, my lord?" The frosty glare did not lessen. "And I wonder why. Did Maria Amati have no time for you today?"

Cesare shrugged negligently. "You should not listen to rumours, Laura; it will only bring you unhappiness. Now stop this childishness and come here."

She stared at him, her anger mounting.

"For you to amuse yourself with, my lord? But surely, if Maria is otherwise engaged, the Madonna Lucrezia would be happy to fulfil all your needs."

For one frozen second of time there was silence between them, then Laura screamed as the Duke's riding whip slashed across her face.

She fell to the ground, and ignoring her sobs, Cesare bent, pulled her savagely to her feet, and shook her viciously.

"Do not ever speak to me like that again," he said through clenched teeth, "or by God, madam, I will give you a lesson you will not forget."

His hands left her shoulders, and her trembling fingers fled to the ugly weal he had inflicted upon her.

She shivered at the violence she saw in him, and would have stepped back, but he caught her arm and jerked her closer to him.

"I did not ride out here to listen to your absurd accusations," he said curtly. "You presume on our relationship when you dare to question my actions, madonna. You need discipline."

She was shaking with fear as she watched the unusual fury in Valentinois' face, and her defiance and challenge dropped from her as she held out a hand in entreaty.

"Oh, Cesare, Cesare, forgive me," she whispered. "I beg you, forgive me. I did not mean the things I said. I was angry because you did not come to me before, for I love you greatly. I did not think what I was saying; I could only remember that you promised to return to me, but that you took another in my place and I was filled with bitterness. Oh, Cesare, forgive me."

Her eyes pleaded with him and all the colour had fled from her face as she met the livid anger behind the Duke's gaze.

"Cesare!" It was a whisper of terror, and his laugh was hideous as he took a step towards her.

"You would do well to consider with care what you say to me, madonna." The voice was icy, and she felt a sweat of fear break out on her body as he caught her wrist again and dragged her over to a satin covered couch by the fireplace.

"You may regard yourself as fortunate that I do no more than take what I came for."

She was flung down with scant ceremony, and her tears continued to fall as he possessed her without remorse and with brutality.

But in half an hour, Cesare's anger had disappeared completely, and he was gentle as he held her against him.

" 'Tis good to be with you again, Laura," he said, and one hand stroked her soft silver-gold hair. "I will not leave you alone for so long again, for it seems to me you need my firm hand more often."

She sighed gently. "Oh, Cesare, I pray it will not be so long. I waited for many months for you to return, and when you came back to Rome and failed to visit me, I thought my heart would break."

"Foolish one." His lips touched her cheek.

"Then when I heard . . ."

"Forget it, cara," he said, but she heard the warning note under his brief words, and raised her head.

"Forgive me, Cesare. I do not mean to question you, but . . ."

"Forget it," he repeated and raised her up. "Now, sweet, put on the pearls I have brought you, for they will match the beauty of your peerless flesh."

He adjusted his doublet as he watched her cross the room and twine the long rope of pearls round her slender neck, their milky translucence a glowing complement to her white breast.

"Cesare, they are exquisite. Oh, I thank you, my lord, and I beg you to forgive my ingratitude."

He smiled and came over to her.

" 'Tis forgiven. Now kiss me, Laura, for I must return to the Vatican, but I will come back and this time without so long a passage of time."

His hands tightened on her shoulders and his mouth was passionate on hers. When he released her, she was shaking slightly, and Cesare smiled.

"Yes, I will return, my love, and before long."

She watched him mount with the easy grace which marked all his actions, and the hand which touched her scarred cheek was unsteady. Under the pleasure and satisfaction his Highness had given her, there was a thin, steady thread of fear which never left her when she was in Cesare's presence. As she turned from the window, her eyes were clouded by the thought of his return, which would bring excitement and joy, but also the shadow of something else which could not be put into words, but which made her heart beat faster as she mounted the stairs to her chamber to review her latest encounter with her terrifying lover.

On the evening of July the 15th, Alfonso Bisceglie prepared for his evening visit to the Borgo with his companions, and there was an undercurrent of excitement in his manner as his servant helped him to don the crimson velvet doublet with the huge slashed sleeves, and the yellow silken hose which clung tightly to his shapely legs.

As he settled the velvet and plumed cap on his head, he smiled suddenly and turned to Marco, his portly body servant, who had come with him from Naples, and his manner was gay.

"Come, Marco, my cloak, for I must not keep the others waiting."

Marco smirked in his sly way, and laid the black velvet cloak across Alfonso's shoulders.

"You are in good spirits tonight, master," he murmured. "She is beautiful, yes?"

Alfonso laughed. "There is a girl, certainly; a red-head with a pleasing figure and a willing manner, but 'tis not that which raises my spirits, Marco, for if one woman does not please, there is always another."

"That is indeed true, master." Marco adjusted the folds of the cloak and stepped back to admire his handiwork. "And you, Highness, would have the pick of any woman your heart desired."

For a moment the smile faded from Alfonso's face. "Any woman?" His voice was bitter as he thought of his wife. When he had first been told he was to wed the notorious Lucrezia Borgia, he had been filled with rage and some fear, for he had had no desire to become a member, even by marriage, of a family with the kind of reputation the Borgias had earned for themselves. When he had first seen Lucrezia, his amazement had overwhelmed his distaste and alarm, for she was fair and beautiful and, at first glance, gentle and compliant, and his heart had been moved as he saw her walk towards him in the elaborate wedding gown which had been fashioned for her.

It was only later that he discovered her coolness and indifference, and although a child had been born, he was well aware that Lucrezia despised him and shrank from his attentions, and his mouth twisted in bitterness as he remembered her rejection of his ardour. If others were ready to start rumours about the Borgias, the Borgias were equally deft at starting rumours of their own, and Cesare had been characteristically competent in the story he spread about, that this was a true love match, and that despite the original reason for the union, purely political, in fact Lucrezia and Alfonso were deeply in love. Since it pleased men to believe such tales, Rome had readily accepted this version of the marriage, and the ambassadors of the powers had accepted without question the fable woven by Valentinois as a screen for the truth.

But although Lucrezia had made quite clear her own feelings for Alfonso, he had felt his pulse stirred when he first saw the slight blonde girl who was to be his wife, and this feeling had never died. Indeed, despite her scorn and her unfaithfulness, the desire he felt for her had grown, and he was convinced that once he could rid himself of her dominant brother, he could easily win her affection and respect.

The frown lifted. "No, Marco, 'tis not the thought of a woman's body which excites me tonight, but the prospect of freedom."

"Freedom, Highness?" Marco's small brown eyes were puzzled. "But you are free now, sire. You are King Federigo's nephew, and Duke of Bisceglie. Who would dare to hold you prisoner?"

The frown was back, and Alfonso's blue eyes were stormy. "There is only one man who could do this, Marco, and 'ere long, I will rid myself of this tyrant, and be my own master. I will leave this silken snare."

He turned to look about the richly furnished apartment.

"I have no desire to remain in the Vatican, for methinks each moment I spend under the roof of these assassins, my life is in danger. I would return to the Palace of Santa Maria, where it was arranged that I should dwell, until the Pope decreed otherwise." His mouth was ugly. "Even that much freedom they would not allow me, but under the guise of an invitation to spend a short time in the bosom of his family, the Pope has lured me into a trap so that my end may be the easier for his son to contrive."

Marco was startled. "Sire! You fear a plot against your life?"

Bisceglie's angry blue eyes turned to his servant and he laughed shortly.

"And would you not have such a fear, Marco, if you were the husband of the Madonna Lucrezia? Would you not tremble if your brother-in-law were the Duke of Valence?"

He twisted the cloak about his shoulder. "But 'tis no matter now, for soon I will make an end of this man who has reduced Rome to his will. Soon, I will reach conclusions with him, and then, Marco; then we shall be free."

The blue eyes lit up again, and Marco shivered.

"Highness!" The voice was fearful. "It is not your intent to seek to do harm to the Duke of Valentinois?" The podgy fingers were trembling as they busied themselves tidying the garments Alfonso had discarded. "Sire, this would be madness, for any man who plotted against the life of the Duke would be in dire straits should that plot be uncovered."

"T'will not be, Marco." There was confidence and certainty in Alfonso's voice as he moved to the door. "I beg you, do not fear for me, for all is arranged and there will be no danger for me; only for Cesare, but this he will not realize until it is too late."

He left the room with a jaunty step and joined his companions in the corridor.

"Signores." He greeted them gaily. "Let us be gone in search of entertainment to while away the days until this cloud is lifted from us. Alas, another five days to wait." He sighed in mock exasperation.

"But, my lord, it will be well worth our patience, since, when these days are sped, we shall see an end to an era of terror and fear."

Alfonso nodded to the speaker, a young blade who had joined his court when he came to Rome, and who had shewn his loyalty and affection in good measure since that time.

"That is true, Bernardo, and as we have waited so long,

'tis foolish to rail against the remaining days, yet I wish it were over."

For a second there was a cloud over his eyes, for despite the care with which he had made his plans and the faith he had in the success of the plot, every now and then he experienced a moment of disquiet, for he had not mistaken the measure of the man he now sought to destroy.

"Come, come," he said impatiently, brushing his own fears aside. "Enough of doubts. Let us get to the Borgo, for I am in need of relaxation, and I find the beautiful Sophia most obliging."

The others laughed and followed him to the door, exchanging notes on the women they were about to call upon. Outside, the night was soft and warm, and the clear moon bathed the steps leading from the Vatican with a benign light. Still talking and laughing, Alfonso and his companions descended the shallow stone treads, not bothering to cast a glance at the dusky shadows which flanked their path and circled round the grounds of the Vatican.

So quiet and peaceful was the scene, that the first step which met their unsuspecting ears was a harsh note which made them pause uneasily, but before Alfonso and his party could make a move, there was a sudden rush of men from the dark patches of the night, and they found themselves surrounded by a band some dozen strong.

Alfonso gave a cry and wrenched out his dagger, his companions following suit, and for a few minutes the hand fighting was savage and cruel.

Bisceglie succeeded in throwing off his assailant, and turned to see Barnardo's body fall across his path, the life blood staining the white doublet in grim certainty. He raised his arm to strike the man who had killed his companion, when he felt a poignard's cold point against his neck, and the next second he cried aloud as the steel cut deep. He tried to turn aside, but the deadly blade found its mark again, this time in his thigh, and then in his shoulder. His senses swam as the night closed in upon him, and his struggles grew feebler as his knees buckled under the murderous attack. He fell to the ground unconscious, and the man who had guided the knife to its mark, gave a satisfied laugh and turned to deal with another of Bisceglie's party. In the mêlée and confusion, made greater by a sudden cloud which crossed the moon's tranquil face and darkened the scene to almost total blackness, a figure moved from the outer shadows and joined the struggling group of men.

The man, tall and clothed in black, moved silently and with purpose to the centre of the crowd. Gian Orestes cursed as someone fell against him, and he thrust the intruder out of the way. The sudden dimming of the moon made it difficult to tell his own men from those of Alfonso Bisceglie's but he calculated the time had come to leave the Vatican, for he had already achieved his purpose, and had seen Alfonso fall to the steps under the lethal assault of his own poignard. He was about to give a sharp order to his men to withdraw, when he felt a forearm whip round his throat, cutting off all sound. He braced himself to throw off his attacker, and his heart began to pound as he realized that he could not shift by so much as an inch the iron hold his enemy had upon him. He kicked out with one foot, but the man behind him merely turned slightly to avoid the blow and the arm tightened again. Orestes' eyes began to bulge, and his face crimsoned under the intense pressure, yet not a sound escaped his tortured lips.

About him the struggle was dying down. Alfonso's men were either lying prone on the ground, or had fled the scene, whilst his own men stumbled down the steps to their horses, not realizing their leader was not with them.

He managed to raise one arm in silent, tearing entreaty, but the merciless hold did not slacken and his consciousness began to ebb. As the blackness of the night mingled with his own darkening senses, he heard a faint whisper in his ear, and in his extremity, he could not tell whether his attacker had spoken or whether it was the murmuring of his own frenzied imagination.

" 'Tis well done, Captain Orestes," said the voice, "a good job, and here is your reward."

He felt the steel go through his body, pressed home with violent strength, but the exquisite agony of the pain was something he had to bear silently, for his bruised and injured throat was no longer able to voice the scream of torment which rose in him. He felt his mouth fill with warm blood, and suddenly all the darkness was as one, as his lifeless body rolled down the steps to sprawl awkwardly at the foot of the stairs.

The man in black stood silently for a moment, looking down at the body, then he wiped his blood-stained dagger and returned it to its sheath and melted back into the shadows.

The attack upon Alfonso Bisceglie caused a sensation in Rome. The noise of the assault had finally reached the ears of the Papal Guard and Alfonso, badly wounded, but still alive, had been carried to his chambers in the Borgia Tower where he had been staying, much against his will, and such was his condition that a Cardinal was hastily summoned to give him the last absolution.

The Pope and Lucrezia were instantly informed, and despite her reluctance to fulfil her marital obligations to Alfonso, Lucrezia felt an unexpected pang of pity as she looked down at her husband's face as he lay still and white on the bed. The messenger who had informed her of the attack, had told her of the circumstances, and her heart was filled with dread, for there was something about the affair which she found hard to understand.

She knew well that Cesare had contempt and dislike for Bisceglie, but she had not thought he would go to such lengths, and furthermore, had her brother decided to kill Alfonso, Alfonso would be dead, not lying wounded, but undoubtedly alive. She shivered and pulled her robe tighter about her as she lay back against a bank of lace-edged pillows on her bed. Alfonso was now being cared for by the Pope's own doctors, and a messenger had been sent to Naples to Alfonso's uncle, King Federigo, and there was little she could do to aid her unfortunate husband, even if she were of a mind to do so, but the dread she felt in her heart did not stem from the sufferings of Alfonso, but of the circumstances of the attack itself and its author.

She turned her head sharply as the door of her chamber opened quietly to admit Cesare, and her heart beat unevenly as he crossed the floor to her side.

For a moment he looked down at her silently, and her mouth dried in terror as she saw the expression on his face.

"Lucrezia." The voice was a gentle contrast to the look in his eyes, and she swallowed convulsively.

"C . . . C . . . Cesare." Her hand trembled as she pulled the robe tighter still about her shaking form.

The light in her brother's eyes died, and he smiled.

"Poor little Lucia." He sat on her bed, and his hand covered her own trembling one. "Do not be afraid, it is all over."

"Over? What is over? You mean Alfonso is . . . is dead?"

The Duke laughed faintly. "Dead? No, Lucia, Alfonso is not dead. That is the voice of hope in your heart which you hear. No, he is badly wounded, but I think he will recover."

For a moment there was something in Valentinois' voice which made Lucrezia shudder anew.

"No," he went on, the note gone again. "No, I meant the assassin has been destroyed. The man who sought to make a widow of you is dead."

Lucrezia's eyes widened and under his hand she was quivering with fear.

"The . . . the man . . . which man?" Her voice was a whisper, and he looked at her kindly.

"No need for such concern, cara. As I say, all is over, and the murderer has paid the price for his crime."

"Cesare!" She was shrill as she sat up. "Who is dead? Who tried to kill Alfonso? Answer me, Cesare? Who was this man? Who?"

He seemed mildly surprised at her concern. "Why t'was Gian Orestes, Lucrezia. Captain Orestes." His expression did not change as her colour fled, leaving her face ghastly in the light of the candle set by her bed. "The motive is not hard to understand, my dear, for he was bitterly jealous of your husband."

Lucrezia fell back against the pillows, her mouth working in silent agony, and her eyes were filled with a pain which made Cesare's brows meet in a sudden frown.

"Come, Lucrezia," he said sharply, "you cannot, surely spare grief for the man who tried to kill Alfonso? He was a murderer, Lucia; he stabbed Alfonso, not once, but many times in his jealous frenzy, leaving him to die. Would you spare a thought for such a man?"

Her dried lips tried to form words, but none would come, and Cesare leaned forward and pulled her up, holding her slender, trembling body against his own.

"You must pull yourself together, Lucrezia," he said briskly, for your sorrow for this man will not be understood. People will not comprehend your tears for the man who tried to kill your beloved husband.'

Still she said nothing, and the Duke shook her slightly, and his voice sharpened.

"Lucrezia! Do you hear me?"

Her blank blue eyes met her brother's and she shuddered terribly.

"Oh Dio," she said finally. "Gian! Cesare, Cesare . . . why? Why?"

He raised his eyebrows. 'Why? Well, that is easy enough to see, Lucia. Orestes was jealous, as I have told you, and sought to destroy Alfonso, so that he could have you for himself. 'Tis natural, I suppose, for a man to seek to do away with a rival, even a husband, whose rights are beyond dispute."

He seemed disinterested in Orestes' motive, and Lucrezia's cry was tortured.

"No! No! He would not do this. Why should he, for he would know you would never let me wed him? Cesare, why did he do this?"

'I have told you." The Duke released her and stood up. "His motive seems clear enough; do not seek to make mysteries which are not there, Lucia. No, come, do not upset yourself further. The man is dead; there is no more to say."

'And how did he die?" Lucrezia's tears suddenly stopped, and Valentinois' eyes narrowed at the sharp note in her voice. "How did Gian die?"

"He was killed in the struggle." The Duke's voice was as soothing as before. "One of Alfonso's men, no doubt."

"No!" Lucrezia flung aside the bedcover and rose from her couch. "No, no, no! You know this is not true. Orestes was a soldier; Alfonso's men were dandies, fops, weaklings. They would not have been able to overcome one of Gian's strength. You know this is true. Who killed Gian, Cesare?"

He shrugged. "I do not know, Lucia. I only know that when the Papal Guard arrived, they found Alfonso wounded, with some of his men similarly injured, and Gian Orestes at the foot of the steps of the Vatican. He had been stabbed."

"In the back?" Her blue eyes blazed into his.

"So I believe." He was all indifference.

"Yes, in the back." She faced her brother for the first time in her life with strength and anger.

"You did this, Cesare. This is your doing. Gian was not killed by one of Alfonso's lap-dogs, for they do not have it in them to kill a mouse; they could not have overcome one of Gian's strength, and you know it. You killed him, Cesare. As you promised when I refused to put him aside at your command. You, Cesare, you . . . you . . . you . . . Murderer, assassin, butcher. . . ."

Her fists struck her brother's chest in the torment of her anguish, and her eyes were wild and deranged as she realized the full extent of Cesare's revenge.

For a moment the Duke did not move, then suddenly he caught her wrists, imprisoning them in his firm hold.

"Stop this," he ordered sharply. "You are overcome with hysteria, Lucrezia. And this I can understand, for 'tis a shock to learn that Alfonso has been wounded, but you must stop this nonsense, for t'will make you ill."

She screamed and tried to free herself from his grip and Cesare's mouth tightened.

"Stop it, Lucrezia, lest you engage my anger. Pull yourself together, and stop this folly."

She screamed again, and the Duke released her wrists and caught her shoulders, shaking her hard until her screams turned to sobs and then to silent, tearing grief.

He let her fall back on the bed and looked down, silent and angered, at her supine body, lying still and stricken.

Then he turned away, and there was irritation in his step, but as he returned to his own chambers, the anger died, for he had supreme confidence in his ability to control Lucrezia, and had little doubt that once the initial grief had worn off, he could again hold his sister in the same thrall as in the past, for he did not weigh seriously her feelings for the dead Orestes, who had merely flattered her ego and held her attention in temporary physical captivity. But this would pass, and once it had done so, he would bring to fruition the other plans he had for his sister's future; plans which would strengthen and bind his own power in the Romagna.

Time passed, and Alfonso recovered, aided by a physician his uncle had sent from Naples, and Lucrezia and Sancia nursed him with the help of trusted servants. The fury of Lucrezia's sorrow was spent, and she seemed uncaring of what went on about her, tending Alfonso with an apathetic indifference which some put down to shock, and others to her inability to shew feeling or concern for her husband.

Her relations with Cesare were strained, and on the few occasions they met, she avoided his eye, and was cool, but her coldness was well matched by her brother's frigid manner, for Lucrezia's continued grief for the dead Orestes was beginning to anger Cesare. He was not used to Lucrezia turning from him in this way, but it did not occur to him to make any overtures to her. It was for Lucrezia to come to him, and his icy voice when he addressed her, gave some indication of his implacable determination that she would eventually bend to his iron will.

During these days, Cesare found Maria Amati increasingly trying. Maria was both disappointed and angered at her failure to hold Cesare in the grip she had visualised when she had first met him, and he had refused flatly to allow her to leave the Vatican, which was her dearest wish.

She shewed her displeasure by alternate displays of temper, coldness and scorn, none of which moved the Duke to anything but annoyance, until one day, when she had reached the limit of her endurance, having heard of Cesare's repeated visits to Laura Montefiore, she flung at the Duke a spate of invective, piling on contempt at his failure to take to the field again, derision that he could not bend Lucrezia to his will, and finishing with an expression of her own weariness at his inability to hold her own interest.

They were in Maria's chamber, and the hour was late. It had had been a black day; left alone by Cesare and by her own companions, who had found her impossible to live with of late, all her anger and frustration was poured out upon the Duke, who, far from being unable to satisfy her, still had the power to excite her to dazzling heights, a power he had not chosen to exercise recently.

She stood in the centre of the room, her dark hair tumbled about her white shoulders, her brown eyes alight with fury, and her red lips twisted in temper as she spat her venom at the Duke.

He lay back in a chair listening to her, and there was no shadow of expression in the eyes which surveyed the enraged girl before him.

Finally, when her harsh words had finished, he stirred.

"You are becoming a bore, Maria," he said coolly, "and something of a problem to me, for I do not expect to be berated in this manner when I come to you."

"A bore!" She was shrill. "I should not have thought, my lord, that you saw enough of me for this to be the case."

"One short visit would be enough to convince me that this were so," he returned curtly. "You are foolish to arouse my displeasure in this way, Maria. Do you not know enough about me and my reputation to recognize this?"

"Your reputation!" She took a step forward. "Oh yes, my lord, yes! A reputation to be proud of indeed. They call you a murderer, an assassin and a fratricide."

"And this does not give you pause for thought?" The Duke's soft tone did not penetrate the girl's insane rage. "Does this not prove my point; that you are unwise to speak to me thus?"

"You propose to kill me too, my lord?" Her voice was taunting. "But this might be dangerous, might it not? Those who have so far met death at your hands, have had other enemies, and although rumour has accused you, sire, no proof has ever been found of your guilt, for there were always others upon whom blame could rest. But who else would kill me, my lord? None. If I die, all Rome will know whose hand was responsible."

"And you think this matters?" The Duke's quiet voice was contemptuous. "What matters it, that all Rome knows who disposed of a tiresome prostitute?"

Maria blanched with the passion of hatred in her, and she raised her hand to strike Valentinois.

A second later she lay prostrate at his feet, and Cesare looked down at her with a dawning anger in his eyes.

"That was an act of madness, Maria," he said bleakly, "and one for which you will pay dearly."

She gave a faint cry. All her fury was spent, and the full realization of her recklessness flooded through her as she raised herself on one elbow to look at Valentinois' still facc.

"Cesare . . . Cesare." She held out a hand and her voice was timid and pleading. "Oh Cesare, forgive me; forgive me. I was insane with jealousy, for you have not cared for me for so long, and I cannot bear your indifference. Oh, Cesare, please!"

He made no move towards her, but looked down at her with dislike.

"Get up," he said shortly, and turned away. "You behave like a beggar girl, and I am weary of these scenes. I will have no more of it. Tomorrow I shall make arrangements for the Madonna Lucrezia to have another lady in waiting, for I think your usefulness is at an end."

Maira got to her feet unsteadily. "Cesare! You cannot mean this. You cannot send me away. Oh, Cesare, no! I beg you, do not do this."

She caught his arm, but he pulled himself free.

"Enough!" He was sharp. "I have told you; I am tired of these tantrums. Tomorrow I will put an end to this."

Maria's eyes were wide with fear as she watched him cross to the door, then they narrowed and shc said tightly:

"Very well, my lord, make your arrangements, and I will make mine. Perhaps Rome will be interested to know what you were doing on the night of July the 15th, when Alfonso Bisceglie was attacked and Gian Orestes died."

Cesare turned at the door and looked silently at her.

Unheedingly she went on. "Yes, my lord; Rome might be interested to know that the death of Orestes was witnessed."

He came slowly back to her. "Witnessed?" He was not angry; hardly interested, but she laughed wildly as she faced him.

"Yes, my lord Duke, witnessed. I thought you were bent on another assignation, and I followed you. I saw you in the shadows, and I saw you take your dagger from its sheath and kill Gian Orestes. What do you say to that, my lord."

Her cheeks were flushed, her eyes bright and her hands rested on her rounded hips in insolent defiance.

Valentinois' mouth moved slightly, and the hazel eyes which looked down at her were hard to read.

"I see." His fingers were on his dagger, but his manner remained as serene as ever. "You have dangerous knowledge, Maria. I can see I shall have to settle my quarrel with you."

The hand left the dagger and caught her wrist. "Come here, cara." He pulled her to him, and she shuddered as his mouth covered hers.

When he released her, she was plastic in his hands, and her eyes glowed with happiness.

"Oh, Cesare, belovèd; belovèd. You have not kissed me like that for so long. I thought you did not care, and this angered me. I am sorry for the words I spoke; t'was only because I felt you no longer wanted me. But now. . . ." She wound her arms round his neck. "Now, Cesare, my words are lost in my love for you."

He smiled gently. "That is good, Maria." He took her face between his hands. "We must not quarrel again in this fashion. Now come, sweet, let us lose no time in further talk."

He drew her to the bed, and in her ecstasy, she did not see the look in the topaz eyes as the Duke bent to blow out the candle.

The disappearance of Maria Amati, lady in waiting to the Madonna Lucrezia, caused no sensation. Indeed, few people realized she had gone, least of all Lucrezia herself, still wrapped in sorrow for the dead Orestes, but even Lucrezia was stirred from her apathy when, on the 17th August, Alfonso Bisceglie, almost recovered from his wounds, was strangled in his bed.

The news of his death set Rome by the ears, and every

ambassador in the City fled to his desk to write despatches to his masters of the deed which had caused the uncaring populace of Rome to gasp in consternation.

This time there was little doubt as to who was responsible, and fearful eyes looked quickly away from the Duke of Valence as he walked through the Vatican to his sister's apartments.

His interview with her was short and terse.

She had had little love for Alfonso, the handsome young Neapolitan, and was content enough to be free of his demands, but even Lucrezia was shaken by the boldness of Cesare's move, for on this occasion he had hardly bothered to conceal his hand, and it was no secret that Michele da Corella, the sturdy Spanish soldier whom Cesare trusted so absolutely, had burst in upon the young Duke and finished the work which Gian Orestes had started a month before. To the gossips and those who spread rumours, Cesare had let fall the plot which Alfonso had tried to fashion for the Duke's destruction and Matteo Petucci had been more than happy to give validity to the tale, for Cesare had been generous in his reward.

"You are now satisfied," she asked as she watched her brother pace the room. "You have now destroyed Alfonso, and cut for ever the links with the House of Aragon. What now, Cesare?"

"Another alliance," he said briefly, "I have, as I told you some weeks ago, a plan which will strengthen our power, and you, Lucrezia, will help to forge this new link."

She turned her head to look out of the window, her heart too weary to argue or plead with her determined brother.

"I am going to Nepi," she said slowly. "I cannot remain in Rome any longer, for my heart is sick with grief."

"Go to Nepi by all means," said Cesare shortly, "but you will come back when I order it; when I have completed the arrangements I am making."

She did not look at him. "And if I do not?"

"Then I shall come and fetch you."

She looked at him quickly, and her eyes darkened in pain.

"Oh Cesare," she begun, but he held up an impatient hand.

"I have no time to argue with you Lucrezia," he said curtly.

"Make your arrangements and go to Nepi, but be prepared to return to Rome when I send a message to you. Now I must go, for I have much to do." He moved over to her, and for a second laid a hand on her shoulder. "Farewell, cara."

She made a move to detain him, but her hand met empty air. She saw the door close behind Cesare, and buried her face in trembling hands as the tears started to fall again.

CHAPTER TWELVE

At the beginning of August, Cesare was almost ready to move, and at his instigation, Alexander issued a Bull against the Tyrants of Faenza, Rimini and Pesaro, depriving them of their fiefs, which they held illegally, having failed to comply with the conditions under which they ruled them under the Holy See, and further, excommunicated them, as a sharp emphasis of his determination to remove them from their strongholds.

When Louis de Villeneuve, Baron de Trans, arrived in Rome at the end of the month to reach agreement with the Pope and Cesare as to the manner in which Louis XII would further aid them in the second impresa, all knew that the die had been cast, and no further doubts lingered in the minds of those on whom Cesare's searching gaze had turned. Louis' price for this further aid was Cesare's support of the French forces when they sought the conquest of Naples, and when this help had been promised, Louis made it clear to Venice that she would be well advised to withdraw her hitherto passive support of Faenza and Rimini, a step which that Republic hastened to take, since it had no desire to stand against both France and the Pope.

Indeed, so eager was she to make her position clear, that in due course she conferred upon Valentino the highest honour it was within her compass to give, the honour of Venetian citizenship and the inscribing of his name in the Golden Book. Cesare received the tribute graciously, and promised his firm support to Venice on the occasion of the next conclave.

Louis sent Yves d'Alègre back to Rome with six hundred lances and six hundred Swiss mercenaries, and Cesare rode out to meet the Frenchman, whom he had not seen since their terse exchange at Forlì. D'Alègre reined his horse to a halt as the Duke came up to him with his escort, and for a moment the two men eyed each other silently. Then Cesare smiled and raised his hand in greeting.

"We are well met again, Captain d'Alègre," he said, and his gaze was friendly. "I have much need of your skill and valiant men."

D'Alègre saluted the Duke. His anger at Cesare's action in taking the Countess Sforza prisoner had dissipated, particularly as the Duke had acceded the point and had held her as Louis' honoured hostage. Rumour had reached his ears that when Cesare rode into Rome, Caterina was in his train, but d'Alègre was not a fool, and he recognized that a running feud with Valentinois was a wasted exercise. His orders from the King were to give Il Valentino support and help in his campaign, and this was what he intended to do to the best of his ability, and he put aside any doubts he had harboured as to Cesare's methods, as he returned the Duke's smile.

"Glad I am, Excellency, to be of assistance to you," he said, and urged his mount forward slightly. "I am told you are almost ready to commence the campaign."

"That is so." Cesare's hand tightened on the reins as his horse stirred restively. T'will not be long now. These men you bring with you, make my total force some ten thousand, and Vitellozzo Vitelli's artillery is strong and well-trained, and will serve us well. But come." He waved a hand to d'Alègre's escort. "You must be in need of food and rest; later we will talk, for there is much for us to discuss." He turned slightly in the saddle. "Bartolomeo."

Capranica moved up to the Duke's side, and Cesare smiled again at d'Alègre.

"You are acquainted with Captain Bartolomeo da Capranica, I think. He is now my camp master, and will see to the needs of your men. I have placed a house near the Vatican at your disposal, and there is ample lodging for your forces. Now, let us be on our way."

He turned his horse's head, and led the way back to the centre of Rome, where he parted from d'Alègre on the friendliest of terms, pressing upon him an invitation to sup with him at the Vatican that night.

D'Alègre settled himself in the well-appointed villa provided for him, and inspected his men whom Capranica had housed in their own quarters with great despatch and efficiency, and then strolled along the banks of the Tiber with Captain Réné d'Auton, whom he had sent to Rome in advance to get a measure of the situation.

"It seems the Duke has made his preparations well," observed d'Alègre, and d'Auton nodded.

"Indeed, sire, this is so. He has a gift for attracting men to his side, and furthermore, when he has them, he knows how to use them."

There was enthusiasm in d'Auton's voice which made d'Alègre's eyebrow tilt.

D'Auton chuckled as he saw the quizzical light in his companion's eyes. " 'Tis so, sire, I can assure you."

They moved slowly through the throngs of people who still flooded Rome, and gradually drew away from the centre of the city to the quieter outskirts, where they paused by a small bridge spanning the dark waters of the Tiber.

"An extraordinary man," said d'Alègre reflectively, "part courtier, part criminal."

"But all soldier, sire."

D'Alègre shot a quick look at d'Auton. "I trust you have not fallen under the spell of this man, for this would not be a wise thing to do."

D'Auton laughed reluctantly. "No sire, I realize this, but 'tis difficult not to share the enthusiasm of those who serve Valentinois, for he is a singularly efficient man."

"Efficient, but dangerous," said d'Alègre quietly, "I sometimes wonder if the King realizes just how dangerous, for he aids the Duke in something which may one day stand against the throne of France."

D'Auton gave a quick exclamation. "Sire! No, surely this is not so. Valentinois seeks only to reclaim the Papal fiefs in the Romagna; not more than that."

D'Alègre's mouth moved in a sardonic smile. "Yes, d'Auton, I can see the Duke has reached you."

"Sire!"

D'Alègre smiled grimly at D'Auton's indignant face. "Réné," he said gently, "this man has fooled you if you believe his ambitions stop there. If he succeeds this time, as he doubtless will, he will turn his attention to other targets."

"Such as sire?" D'Auton was frowning.

"Tuscany; Florence; the central states of Italy. Perhaps the whole of Italy itself."

D'Auton's gaze was incredulous. "You cannot be serious?"

D'Alègre shrugged. "Why not?" He looked again at his companion. "He is capable of endless ambition, and is possessed of a ruthlessness one does not often see, but that day is far off, and there is no need for us to concern ourselves with Valentinois' future plans on such a day as this."

He glanced up at the azure sky, stippled with delicate feathery clouds. "No, the future must take care of itself, and France is strong. Doubtless she can withstand this Italian adventurer if she has to."

He rose abruptly from the grassy bank on which they had been sitting.

"He is uncomfortably shrewd, this man. But never mind; we have been sent to aid him, and this we must do, but we would do well to watch his Highness, lest we get enmeshed in the net of ingenuity he weaves with such skill.

As Alexander had predicted, more money was needed, for Cesare's army was expensive to maintain, and in September the Pope created twelve new Cardinals, who had to pay over to the Holy See the whole of one year's harvest from the benefices they secured as the price of their Cardinal's hat, and this very considerable sum eased the financial pressure on the Pope, and enabled him to furnish his son with the ducats he required.

As the golden Autumn died, and October came blustering in, Cesare left Rome, taking in his train the result of his unceasing efforts of the past few months, a highly trained, well-equipped, professional army, and on his way to Orte, he stopped at Nepi to see his sister.

Lucrezia was in her chamber when her steward came to tell her of Cesare's arrival, and the colour fled from her cheeks as she listened to the man's excited words.

Lucetta was with her, making ready the gown Lucrezia was to wear on the following day, and her face grew bleak and grim as she heard the tidings, for she dreaded the presence of Valentinois more than the thought of Satan himself, and her fingers trembled as they touched the deep velvet pile of the black gown she held in her hand.

Lucrezia steadied her voice and dismissed the steward, and turned to Lucetta.

"Oh, Lucetta, I am afraid."

The maid came to her side, and caught her hand between hers.

"There, there," she soothed, brushing aside her own terror. " 'Tis nothing for you to fear, sweet."

"But, Lucetta, he may still be angry with me."

"Then why should he come here?" Lucetta's voice was calm. "If this were so, he would not tarry here, for he is bent on the capture of Pesaro."

Lucrezia's eyes did not lose their anxiety, and she scarcely paid a second's thought to the fate of Pesaro, which had been her home whilst she had been married to Giovanni Sforza. Her sole concern was the disposition of her brother, and she stiffened as she heard a firm step outside the door.

"Lucetta! He comes." Her hand gripped the arm of the chair, the knuckles standing out white as bone.

A moment later the Duke stood in front of her, and all the tension drained out of her as he held out his hands.

"Belovéd." His voice was soft, his eyes gentle, and with a little cry, Lucrezia rose and fell into his arms.

Over her shoulder Cesare's eyes met the white-faced serving maid's, and he nodded.

"You may go," he said coolly, for he knew how much this gaunt, ugly woman disliked him. "I would be alone with the Madonna Lucrezia."

She hesitated for a second, reluctant to leave her mistress with this man whom she distrusted, but seeing Cesare's face harden, she left the room hurriedly, for he was quite capable of enforcing his orders in a sharp and painful fashion.

When she had gone, the Duke held Lucrezia at arm's length and studied her face, now wet with tears.

"You have no need for tears, cara," he said, and drew a silk handkerchief from his tunic. "No, be done with this sorrow, for I have little time to stay here, and I would have you merrier than this whilst I am with you."

She cheered slightly, and caught the hand engaged in wiping her cheek.

"Oh Cesare, Cesare."

He smiled at her, and all the magic and fascination he had for her caught her anew in its web.

"Oh, Cesare, I am so glad you have come."

He drew her to the window seat. "And have you recovered from your grief," he paused, and there was a trace of malice in his voice, "at Alfonso's untimely death?"

She winced slightly at his words, but nodded. "I have recovered, Cesare."

"And when do you propose to return to Rome?" He glanced out of the window. "For this place does not seem a fitting setting for you, my dear."

She bit her lip. " 'Tis quiet and peaceful, Cesare, and I needed to recover."

"Of course," he said smoothly, "t'was very proper that you should mourn your husband in this fashion, but it is now time you put these things from you, for 'ere long you will have another husband."

Here eyes widened and a touch of colour crept into her pale face.

"You have said this before, Cesare, but you have not told me to whom you seek to wed me. Who is this man?"

"Alfonso d'Este," said Cesare briefly. "Ferrara's heir."

"But, Cesare. . . ."

"An alliance between the Duke of Ferrara's heir and the Pope's daughter will be of inestimable value to our cause." Cesare ignored the protest he saw rising on Lucrezia's lips, and put one hand over hers. "He will be a worthy consort for you, my dear, but there is plenty of time for this yet. First you must return to Rome, and forget these sorrows which have been filling your mind."

"But, Cesare." Her eyes were doubtful. "What sort of man is he? Will the Duke of Ferrara agree to this union? How will you achieve this?"

He smiled, his eyes cold and blank. "Ferrara will agree; he

will not be able to afford to do otherwise, and you may safely leave me to achieve this, Lucrezia. Have you ever known me to fail in anything to which I set my hand?"

She shook her head, numb with misery, for she wanted no part of this scheme of Cesare's in which, once more, she became the pawn of her brother and father in their ambitious designs.

"I am not ready for marriage again," she said weakly, knowing before she looked at the Duke's face how little heed he would pay to her words.

"Nonsense," he said briskly. "You are young. You cannot spend your life shut up in this place. It is right that you should wed again, and since this is so, it is fitting that your next husband should be suited to your position. Now, Lucia, do not be tiresome about this, I beg you. You will find Alfonso more than satisfying, I am sure."

"And if I do not?" For a moment there was a spark of defiance in her manner, but Cesare's quiet laugh stilled it as he put his arms round her.

"Oh, but you will, cara, you will, I promise you. Now come, do not let us spend this short time we have together arguing. We parted last time in anger; this time I would leave you differently, for you are precious to me, and I want your love to go with me when I leave for Orte."

She met the steady hazel eyes, and a pulse quivered in her throat as once again she drowned in the gaze her brother turned upon her.

"Cesare." The whisper was half plea, half surrender, and his arms tightened about her.

"Good girl," he said softly, and bent his head to kiss her trembling lips.

When he released her, all her resistance had left her, and she held his hand tightly as he outlined to her his plans for the forthcoming conflict with Pesaro, Rimini and Faenza, and her heart swelled with pride as she watched her brother's confident face and heard the crisp sure words he used to describe his plan of destruction for the rebel states.

"You will take care, Cesare," she said finally when he had

finished. "There is much danger for you, and I pray you will exercise caution."

He laughed and patted her hand. "Oh I will use discretion," he promised, "but, as I have told you on more than one occasion, I do not hide in my tent whilst my men take risks for me, no matter what Sancia may say." His eyes hardened as he thought of his sister-in-law, whose hatred of him had increased a hundred-fold since her brother had died at Cesare's hand.

"No, I know, I know." Lucrezia moved uneasily. "Yet, Cesare, I fear for your safety."

"Do not, sweet. I was born under a star of good fortune, and men acknowledge this when they call me filius fortuna, and with reason. I beg you; do not distress yourself with fears for my safety, for I am well able to care for myself, and when I return to Rome, I shall expect to find you fully restored and happy again, not grieving for me. Come, cara, let me see you smile."

She swallowed her dread and misgivings and raised her head to obey Valentinois' command.

"Good." He kissed her cheek lightly and rose to his feet. "I must see Bartolomeo about the supplies, then I will return and we will sup together 'ere I leave."

He raised her chin with a gentle finger, and for a long minute held her eyes with his.

"You are very dear to me, Lucia," he said finally, and she caught her breath in a sob as the door closed behind him.

When Cesare left Nepi, he swept on as quickly as the elements, which were now wholly bad, and his considerable train, would allow him. Balgioni and Palo Orsini, two condottieri of great renown, led the four thousand strong infantry, and Vitellozzo Vitelli controlled the artillery; the six cannons, the columbrine, and the nine sakers, but the transporting of these heavy pieces was no light task, and Vitelli spent many uncomfortable hours in torrential rain, cursing and swearing at his men as they tore the guns from the soft mud which sought to envelop them. The seven hundred men at arms, with their mounted complement, completed the force, but in addition to his soldiers, Cesare took with him a vast number of camp followers, smith, foragers, armourers, cooks and other servants, and it was a formidable body of men which moved relentlessly into the Romagna, where Ercole Bentivoglio awaited him with more men at arms and five siege cannon.

Cesare's first encounter was at Fossate, a grim hill fortress which he came upon as he crossed the Apennines at Gualdo. Here he paused to demand the surrender of the fortress and the release of the prisoners held in the vast dark dungeons below the rocky pile. The Castellean refused the Duke's demand, and Cesare sent for Capranica, Taddeo della Volpe and Ugo da Moncada.

"You will take your men," he said to them, when they came to his tent, small and cramped, but affording some protection from the rain which had fallen incessantly since the dawn, "and you will destroy Fossate. When you have released the men imprisoned there, you will tear the fortress down, stone by stone, rock by rock, and then you will set fire to the surrounding citadel and territory."

Ugo da Moncada, a distant relative of Cesare's, who had been delighted to join his distinguished cousin in the impresa, looked startled.

"My lord! So small a citadel? Is it worth so much effort?"

Cesare laughed shortly. " 'Tis probably the most important thing we shall do for many a long day Ugo."

Moncada's bewilderment grew. "This fortress, sire? Of such importance? I do not understand, for it does not hold the key to our success."

Cesare smiled. "It is the key to my determination, Ugo. If I do not make abundantly clear my intent in this first encounter with opposition, men will not take seriously my vow to reclaim the rebel states. If I let Fossate's rebellion go unpunished, I shall find more resistance and more defiance at Pesaro, at Rimini and at Faenza. No, Ugo, we will raze Fossate to the ground. Nothing will remain but the smouldering, charred timbers and broken stones to bear silent witness to our will."

He had not raised his voice, nor had his quiet manner changed; he could have been discussing a pageant he was proposing to stage, and Ugo's eyes darkened slightly as he began to understand the measure of the Duke's violence. Taddeo della Volpe, more used to Cesare's humour, nodded, and Cesare looked at Ugo again.

"Here we will shew men the price to be paid for opposition, lest others have it in their minds to stand against us." His smile was still pleasant. "I will destroy Fossate."

And destroy it he did. His men stormed the fortress, released the prisoners, and systematically tore down its walls, then turned their attention to the citadel, which they burned and plundered, the shrieking, terrified inhabitants fleeing from the horror which the Duke visited upon them.

Despite these difficulties, the effect of Cesare's march was beginning to tell.

Pandolfo Malatesta in Rimini waited with increasing nervousness as he learned of the Duke's progress, for he was well aware how his own people detested him, and was fully conscious that they would not support him in resistance against the Duke, even had he stomach for such venture. Venice, at Louis' insistence, had removed her protection, and Malatesta realized immediately how dangerous was his position, and set his mind to working out the most advantageous terms of surrender. He sent his wife Violante, and his children, to Giovanni Bentivoglio's court, thanking his stars that his father-in-law was able to receive them, and when this was done, he sought shelter himself in the fortress built by his grandfather, Sigismondo.

Whilst Pandolfo's mind was turning on these affairs, the Council of Rimini wasted no time in sending a message to Cesare, offering to surrender, but it was not long after this despatch had been sent, that Pandolfo himself sent a messenger to the Duke offering him the town and citadel.

Cesare accepted the city, and his Lieutenant-General in the Romagna, Bishop Olivieri, signed the articles of surrender in the Duke's name on the 10th October, whilst Malatesta was granted safe conducts for himself and his immediate court, and since parsimony was not one of his faults, Cesare also granted the defeated Pandolfo three thousand ducats for his expenses, in return for which Malatesta left behind him his artillery for

Cesare's use. After more bargaining, Olivieri and Pandolfo agreed that for the latter's relinquishment of the forts of Sarsina and Meldola, and the castle of Montagna, he would receive a further generous sum, and when these affairs had been settled, Malatesta quickly removed himself from the scene of the Duke's operations, and Cesare was master of Rimini without firing a single shot.

In Pesaro, Giovanni Sforza was making frantic attempts to resist his hated ex-brother-in-law, but, like Malatesta, he was loathed by his own people, and his appeal to neighbouring powers had been in vain.

Realizing the hopelessness of the situation, Sforza fled Pesaro, and on the 27th October, Cesare, at the head of two thousand men, rode into Pesaro, lance at rest. Before him rode heralds proclaiming his style, and the white banners with the red Borgia bulls fluttered over their heads as they moved in good order into the City.

He was acclaimed and welcomed by the people of Pesaro, who had nothing to lose by receiving him willingly, for they had been unmercifully treated by their former lord, and considered that any change was bound to be for the better.

When Ercole d'Este, the Duke of Ferrara, sent to Cesare's court at Pesaro, Pandolfo Collenuccio, a famous poet and historian, the Duke responded to d'Este's graceful compliment in despatching an envoy of such eminence by housing Collenuccio in fine style and bestowing upon him many gifts. They talked long into the night, and the scholar was amazed at the lively turn of the Duke's mind, which was fully capable of switching from matters military to the arts and literature, but Cesare did not miss this opportunity of paving the way for the proposal he was nurturing in his fertile brain, that of the union of d'Este's heir and his sister, Lucrezia.

Having settled his new territories, appointed lieutenants to represent him, and assured himself that all was in order, Cesare began his march on Faenza, arriving outside its walls on the 10th November, but here he stopped, for, unlike Rimini and Pesaro, Faenza did not surrender as the sound of the Duke's trumpets hit the air outside their city.

Astorre Manfredi, the Tyrant of Faenza, was sixteen years

old. He was slim and delicate, with pale gold hair and a transparent skin which shewed a pink flush in the cheeks, not due to health. His blue eyes were troubled as he sat in Council with his advisers and considered the situation.

"If I were to leave Faenza, t'would save the city," he said slowly, "for Borgia will only destroy the town if we resist. My lords, it is not my desire to see my people ravaged by the hand of Valentinois. I think I should withdraw without delay, for we cannot hope to win against the Duke's forces."

The elders on the Council nodded in sympathy, recognizing the motive behind their young lord's words.

'The people do not want this, sire," said one eventually, and his hand stroked his long beard as he looked at Astorre. "They will fight, sire, for they have great love for you. Further, we know your grandfather, Bentivogli of Bologna, will lend aid, despite the Pope's demand that he should not lift a hand to help you. With this support, sire, we can at least try to withstand Borgia."

The boy's flush deepened. "You think there is a chance?"

"There is always hope, sire, and right is on our side. I think we should fight this ravening brute. Winter comes, and Borgia will find it difficult to maintain his forces in the snow. I think we have every chance, and every man, woman and child in Faenza will resist to the death."

Thus, when Cesare's demand for entry into the city was made, he found the gates closed fast against him, and with a gesture of impatience, he opened fire on one of the bastions, maintaining the bombardment night and day until some days later, the savage pounding caused one of the towers to hurtle down into the moat.

Cesare was in his tent having breakfast with some of his officers when the tower collapsed, and immediately complete chaos reigned, for the men, seeing the opportunity of storming the breach, surged forward in hopeless disorder.

The Duke, guessing the cause of the noise and disturbance, left his tent and sped to the breach, where he used both whip and voice to restrain the premature attack on the city.

It took a full fifteen minutes for Valentinois to restore order, and to drive his over-enthusiastic troops back to their positions, and when he was satisfied that he had them under control again, he started back to the tent.

"These men need more discipline," said Cesare angrily to Capranica and Mario di Mariano as they made their way from the breach. "Bartolomeo, you will see to it that in future they do not dispose the course of battle themselves, but await my orders. Is that clear?"

"Yes, my lord. I regret that this should have happened, but the men are enthusiastic and anxious to be about the business of conquest."

"They will not succeed that way," returned Cesare sourly, "If every man is going to fight his own way, we may as well lay down our arms now. You will investigate this matter, Bartolomeo, and see to it that such a thing does not occur again."

He brushed the dust from his tunic and turned to speak to Mario di Mariano, when across the noise and bustle of the camp, a sharp whine cut through the sounds about them.

Di Marian twisted sharply, then with a cry he flung himself at Cesare, pulling him down to the ground as a screaming stone-shot hurtled past them, missing the Duke by an uncomfortably small margin.

Mario's face was white as he pulled himself up, but Valentinois was unmoved as he got to his feet and caught di Marian's shoulder.

"My thanks, Mario. Your vigorous intervention has saved my life; I will not forget it." He glanced over his shoulder. "Come, I do not think this is a good place to continue our discussion; let us repair to the tent."

Before they could reach the sanctuary of the tent, however, they were intercepted by Taddeo della Volpe, returning from the breach where he had been assisting the Duke to stem the tide of onrushing soldiers. He looked grim, and Cesare paused in his attempts to remove the mud from his uniform.

"Taddeo? You seem disturbed; you have news?"

Della Volpe nodded. "News, indeed, sire, and bad. Onorio Savelli has been killed by one of our own guns."

"What!" Cesare's hand was stilled. "Savelli? But how? What happened?"

"Our guns continued to fire, sire. They had not realized that the breach was being assaulted by our own men, and they did not pause in their bombardment. Savelli was killed by a cannon ball which exploded near to the place where you were standing only moments before."

Cesare's mouth was tight with displeasure. "As I said, Bartolomeo," he said curtly, "these men must learn to obey orders and not manage the affray as they please. Their folly has cost me a good officer."

"And almost your own life, sire," said Mario uneasily. "More care must be taken to see that you are not exposed to such risks."

"Nonsense." Cesare was sharp. "One cannot fight a war without risks, and I do not propose to have the conduct of this battle coloured by plans for my personal safety."

He glanced at Mario's crestfallen face, and suddenly his irritation left him, and he smiled.

"In any event, Mario, such precautions are not necessary when I have men such as you at my side to stave off the haunting face of death. Now, come, let us finish our breakfast, for starving never helped men to win a battle."

But victory was elusive, and when the snows came, enveloping hte countryside in a blizzard, Cesare abandoned his attempt on the city and withdrew his forces to Forlì, blocking the supply roads as he went, and leaving sufficient men in outlying villages to ensure the beleagured town had no respite from the artillery he had left behind. From Forlì, Cesare moved to Cesna, his capital, where he stayed until the following March and then, judging the time to be ripe for a renewed attack, he turned his attention once again to Faenza.

CHAPTER THIRTEEN

In Faenza food was running very short, despite the fact that those possessed of an abundance of wordly goods had shared these with the poorer people, and had lent Astorre Manfredi money to pay his soldiers in their fight against the Duke of Valentinois.

The women of Faenza also played their part, helping the defending soldiers by carrying stones to the top of the ramparts for the men to hurl down upon the invaders' heads.

By mid-April, Cesare's guns had opened a breach in the walls and the assault which followed was frightening. The defenders poured burning pitch from the top of the towers, and stormed the advancing troops with heavy rocks and boulders, yet still Cesare's men moved forward, but when the daylight faded, Cesare called off the attack, knowing that to continue it would merely cost him men's lives for no purpose.

Far from being angered at Faenza's resistance, Cesare's admiration for the gallant little city grew by leaps and bounds, and he said openly that had he a full army of men of the quality of those in Faenza, no conquest would be beyond him. But despite his high regard for the courage of the city, he did not stop his pounding of the walls, and slowly but surely the spirit and valor of the defenders was sapped by lack of food and sleep and the exhausting efforts they had made in the last few months.

Finally, one man broke the sustained courage of the people of Faenza and deserted. He came into Cesare's camp, filthy and stained by mud and dust, and was brought to the Duke's tent between two slightly contemptuous guards.

Cesare received him coldly, and the man was uneasy as he shuffled to the centre of the tent, his eyes glancing nervously from right to left, for he sensed the animosity around him.

"Well?" The Duke's voice was colourless as he eyed the man up and down. "Why have you come to me?"

The man, a dyer named Grammante, coughed nervously.

"My lord Duke," he began, then paused to cough again, for his throat had suddenly become rusty and dry under the bleak gaze of Valentinois.

"Yes?" Cesare gave him no help, and his scorn was patent as he waited for the man to tell his tale.

"I can tell you, my lord, how to storm the citadel." His eyes flicked sharply from side to side again, as he felt the tightening of the atmosphere, and the quickening attention of Cesare's Captains.

"So?" The Duke maintained his monasyllabic contribution to the conversation, and the man's face lost such colour as it had boasted when he had first come into the Prince's presence.

"I would serve you well, Potency," said Grammante, suddenly all fawning eagerness. "It is obvious that Faenza cannot stand against a force such as yours, my lord, and I would do what I can to help you, sire."

"And how can you do this!" There was no interest or belief in Cesare's question, and the man rushed on, words tumbling over one another in his attempt to convince the Duke of his intent and goodwill.

"S . . . sire, there is a point in the citadel's defences where there is a marked weakness. I know this point, my lord, and if your lordship's guns were turned upon this section of the wall by the north-east turret, you could not fail to gain entry into the city."

Cesare's eyes were half closed as he leaned back on the camp bed.

"What makes you bring this information to me, Messer Grammante?" he asked finally. "Why do you not seek to resist me as your gallant comrades have done?"

The man flushed slightly under the coating of dirt which marred his pock-marked face.

" 'Tis a hopeless cause, my lord. Why should I serve a defeated boy and his reckless supporters? No, Potency, I would give my support to you, for with you, there is victory and success."

"Also justice," said Valentinois very softly, "and justice is what I propose to mete out to you, Messer Grammante."

The man's face whitened again as he stared at the Duke.

"My . . . my lord, I do not understand."

"All things will be made clear to you, sire," promised Valentinois grimly. "Captain Santa Croce," he turned to Pietro who stood by his side, quietly scornful as he listened of the traitor's words.

"Take this man and hang him. And hang him outside the walls of Faenza where the good citizens may mark the measure of our contempt for him."

The man gave a hoarse scream. "Sire! No! No! Why do you do this thing, for I have given you information which will enable you to capture this rebel city. Why do you seek to kill me for this, my lord? Is this justice?"

"It is my justice," said Cesare shortly, "take him away, for he sickens me."

The man was dragged out of the tent, moaning and struggling, and Cesare's brief laugh was devoid of humour.

"Carrion," he said curtly, "Captain Tiberti. Despite my feelings for this man, his information cannot be wasted for we have spent enough time on the reduction of Faenza. You will comemnce the bombardment of the section of the wall described by his traitor, and you will maintain this attack until we breach the wall sufficiently for troops to enter in force."

And so the final assault began, and the Duke's guns pounded the weak section of the wall for eight hours without respite, until Astorre Manfredi, looking round at his exhausted men and ruined city, sent his ambassadors to the Duke of Valentinois to offer his surrender.

The price Cesare paid for this final assault was high, for he lost many men, including Achille Tiberti, who had died when one of the guns he was loading exploded. When Cesare had been told of his death, he had frowned and was strangely silent for a while, for he had had a great affection and esteem for this loyal officer of his.

When suitable terms had been arranged, including a clause

permitting Astorre Manfredi and his bastard brother, Gianevangelista, to go wherever they chose, Astorre and some of his courtiers came to Cesare to pay their respects.

The boy Tyrant came into the Duke's presence in some fear, for although the latter had assured him of his good will, and had signed a treaty to the effect that his freedom was assured, Astorre was well aware of the Duke's reputation, and there was a sense of dread and foreboding in him as he was ushered into the chamber where Cesare awaited him.

He moved slowly forward to bow to the Duke, and as he raised his head, his lower lip trembled slightly as he gazed at Valentinois.

Cesare smiled in a friendly fashion and held out his hand. "You are welcome, my lord," he said. "I am truly glad that this struggle between us is over, and I compliment you again on the gallantry and bravery of your men and women, which has won nothing but admiration in my camp."

Astorre flushed in embarrassment and he stammered some words of thanks, allowing Cesare to lead him to a chair.

"We will now set about the repairing of your city, my lord," went on Cesare, "and I give you my assurance that no reprisals will be sought for the damage caused by your good people. Very real damage, I would add, sire."

Astore raised his head quickly, but found Cesare smiling and he relaxed with another little quiver of confusion.

"And we must talk of your future too." Cesare turned to a nearby page. "Wine, Carlo, for my lord."

"My . . . my . . . my future, my lord?" Astorre's eyes were anxious again and Cesare held up a soothing hand.

"Your future, which you yourself will determine, sire, for this was one of the terms of the treaty between us. You are free to go where you will. All Italy is at your feet, and it is for you to choose where you will spend your life. However," the Duke took a golden goblet which the page held out to him. "If it should be your desire to stay in my train, you would be more than welcome, for I should consider it an honour to have a man with me who had shown such courage in resisting my forces."

Manfredi sipped his wine and over the rim of the goblet his eyes searched Cesare's face, which shewed nothing but kindness and concern.

"You mean this, my lord? I may stay with you, or go, as I wish?"

"Of course. Have I not said, sire; these are the terms of the surrender we signed. The choice is yours, and 'tis not a choice you have to make immediately. You are tired and worn by the struggle which has ensued. I would counsel you to remain here with me for a few days to rest and regain your strength, and when you are thus refreshed, you will be better able to decide what course to pursue."

Astorre smiled suddenly. "You are very kind, my lord; it was not what I expected from a man such as you."

He was very young in his involuntary admission, and Cesare smiled.

"And what had you expected?"

The Manfredi coloured again, and he hung his head.

"Forgive me, my lord; I should not have said that."

"You are free to say anything you wish," said Cesare with amusement, "and I would like you to tell me what it was you anticipated, and do not fear that you will cause me either pain or anger, for I am well used to abuse and hard words. Come, sire, what did you expect?"

Astorre wriggled uncomfortably in his chair. "S . . . sire . . . I . . . I . . . know not . . . not really. I expected you to be filled with fury at my rebellion, and I thought you would seize me and hang me from the battlements, even as you did the traitor Grammante, for you are not renowned for mercy."

Cesare threw back his head and laughed in delight, and Astorre crimsoned.

"Forgive me, Magnificence. I fear I have been impertinent," he began, but Cesare raised a hand to stop his shaking voice.

"Nonsense. I asked you, and you have told me. You have not offended me, sire. Some more wine?"

Astorre shook his head and gave Cesare a nervous half-smile.

"No thank you, my lord."

"You will sup with me," said Cesare, and it was not a question. "I would know more of you and your people, for whom I have a high regard, and I hope that you may learn enough about me to encourage you to stay in my train, for in my task, I could use men of your quality."

Overcoming his nervousness and embarrassment at Cesare's praise. Astorre raised his head again and ventured a question.

"Your task, Potency? This is to seize back the fiefs which the Holy-Father claims are his?"

Cesare's brows elevated a fraction at the phrasing of the question, but let it pass as he answered the boy.

"That is only the beginning, as you will see if you stay with me."

He gave the warm dazzling smile with which he had won so many in the past. "I shall not stop with the repossession of the lost states of the Holy See, for I have a vision, my lord, of something far greater and far more enduring."

He leaned forward in his chair, and his eyes held Astorre's in bondage as he spread before the boy his dreams of a land no longer torn and divided, but held under one strong rule, and Manifredi's eyes grew rounder and rounder as he listened to the persuasiveness of Cesare's ambitions.

By the time the splendid feast, which Cesare's servants had prepared, was over, Astorre Manfredi's mind and heart were prisoners of the Duke's personality, and as he bade Valentinois good night, his manner was a mixture of subdued excitement and determination, and those about them, heard the note of hero-worship in the boy's voice.

"Sire, I hope you will allow me to stay with you," he said eagerly. "For I would deem it a great honour and privilege to serve with you in this task you have set your hand to."

"I shall be more than happy if this is your pleasure," said the Duke gently, "but the time has not yet come to make your decision. First you must rest, and give consideration to these matters, for it is unwise to determine one's future on the spur of the moment. Reflect upon all the aspects of the proposal, my lord, and then, if you are convinced that this is the right course, make your will known. And now I bid you good night, for it is time you got some sleep, for I doubt that you have had much of late."

When the boy had gone, Cesare went back to his companions, and Mario di Marinao looked at the Duke in some amazement.

"I am surprised my lord," he said hesitantly, "that you should seek to welcome the Manfredi to your court, for if he lives, his people might one day seek to reinstate him at Faenza. Is there not such a risk?"

Cesare nodded. "If he were to live there is indeed such a risk, but he will not live, Mario; at least, not for long."

There was a moment's silence in the chamber, only the crackling of the burning logs in the huge fireplace breaking the stillness.

"You will kill him, my lord?" Capranica's voice was uncertain, and Cesare smiled at him, and there was irony in the glance he gave his Captain.

"I will kill him, Bartolomeo," he agreed. "For the policy of a Prince in regard to the preservation of a state he captures must be quite clear in this respect. No one must be left alive who could have any legal claim to that state. This, surely, is something which is self-evident."

"But why then, sire, do you seek to win his loyalty to you, and to persuade him to stay with you? Why do you not kill him now?"

"The time is not ripe," said Cesare slowly. "We must appear to honour the treaties we have made, and shew ourselves to be loyal to our word. Astorre Manfredi will choose to stay with me." There was complete assurance in Cesare's voice. "Later, when the moment is propitious, I will see to it that Faenza has no legal claimant to challenge my hold on that city."

Alberini nodded. "Yes, my lord, 'tis the only road of safety, yet. . . ."

"There is no alternative," said Cesare briefly, cutting across Alberini's hesitation. "There is no time for sentiment or emotion in the creation of a Kingdom, Giulio. The goal is clear and we must march straight for it, cutting down that which stands in our way. We cannot be swayed by thoughts of mercy and compassion."

"Yet you did not kill Caterina Sforza or Malatesta, my lord?" Alberini's voice still had a shadow of doubt, and Cesare gave a faint laugh.

"You are missing the point, Giulio. Caterina Sforza and Malatesta were of no importance, and represented no risk to me, for their people hated them heartily, and would much prefer to have the government I have provided for them. But Astorre Manfredi is much loved. If needs be, the people of Faenza would fight for him again, when their wounds are healed and when they have had time to gather together more money, more arms, more men. No, Giulio, Astorre Manfredi is a threat to me; Caterina and Pandolfo were not. Thus, the latter I can afford to spare; the former I cannot."

Alberini nodded slowly. "Yes, my lord, I see the wisdom of this now. Forgive me if I appeared to question your judgement, but I did not understand."

"You are forgiven, Giulio," said Cesare tolerantly. "Now let us have wine, for we have much to celebrate, sires, and this is only a beginning. As I promised you in Rome, we shall have great victories, and we are on the threshold of success. Let us drink to this."

Cesare did not linger in Faenza to establish his position. Castel Bolognese was his next target, where Bentivogli waited apprehensively for the Duke to shew his hand, but this was not Cesare's way. There was no preliminary warning. So swift was Cesare's exit from Faenza, that he was in Bentivolgli's territory before that quivering Tyrant had time to gather his wits. Whilst Cesare's envoy went ahead of his army to demand surrender, Bentivogli despatched his own ambassadors to the Duke to inform him that his Council were considering the matter, but as the envoys came upon the Castel San Pietro, they found Vitellozzo Vitelli and his soldiers were already there, and further, that the Duke had plucked the castles of Guelfo, Medecina and Casalfiuminese in his whirlwind path.

Thoroughly scared and discouraged, Bentivogli remembered, a little late in the day, Louis' advice to him not to stand against Borgia, but to come to terms with him, and thus, realizing that his Council had already sent its intention to surrender to the Duke, Bentivogli made his peace with the formidable Duke, allotting him money and lances, and the promise of aid in any of his ventures during the ensuing twelve months, save a move against the King of France.

Cesare, in return, surrendered the castles he had taken, and gave the Tyrant his promise that he would intercede with the Pope, so that none of Bentivogli's previous rights and privileges should be lost to him.

At this point, Alexander, released from Cesare's immediate and overwhelming presence, asserted his authority and sent a peremptory message to his son, commanding him to return to Rome immediately, and in no circumstances whatsoever to interfere or disturb the Florentines, but Alexander was in Rome, and Vitelli and Orsini were with Cesare, and their voices were strong and clamant.

"My lord," said Vitelli in earnest and imploring tones. "I seek no more from Florence than justice for my brother's death, and the release of his Chancellor, still held in that city under duress. I beg you, my lord, consider my plea and let us take passage through Tuscany, so that I may right these wrongs."

"Yes, indeed, Magnificence. I beg you to hear us in this request, for I too seek justice from the Ten." Orsini had no interest in Vitelli's quest, but greatly desired to bring about the reinstatement of the Medici, and provided Cesare agreed to take his troops through Florentine territory, he cared little what reason the Duke gave.

Valentinois listened carefully to what they had to say, and whilst he had no particular desire to invade Tuscany, nor in this instance to disobey the Pope, he considered he owed Vitelli and Orsini some return for their ready response to his earlier call for aid in the reduction of the Romagna, and finally gave way to their entreaties, and sent a message to the Signory of Florence, seeking their permission to return to Rome through their territory.

Agapito brought Florence's reply to the Duke whilst the latter was composing a pacifying reply to his father.

"Ah!" said Valentinois as his secretary made known his mission, "and what does the Signory of Florence have to say in answer to my request?"

Agapito's smile was dry. "Highness, the Ten have agreed, and obviously with some reluctance, to your Potency's passage through their lands, but you are expressly required not to enter any city or town but to keep to the open country."

Cesare raised one eyebrow. "Oh? And what other demands do they make?"

Agapito's smile became even more dry. "They require, nay sire, demand, that you should not bring Captain Vitelli or Captain Orsini with you, for they are persona non grata with their Excellencies." He coughed gently. "This is a trifle awkward, my lord, for you will recall we are already some twenty miles inside Florentine territory."

Cesare gave a short laugh. "This fact had not escaped me, Agapito, but I do not accept these terms. It is not for Florence to dictate to me who travels in my train. I choose my own Captains for my own reasons and if Florence does not approve of my choice 'tis too bad, for it will not alter my course."

"But, my lord." Agapito was wary for he could see Cesare was irritated. "We have entered their lands without their prior approval, and . . ."

"Unfortunate," broke in Cesare curtly. "Do you suggest I should turn tail and flee because these . . . these traders send these impudent terms to me?"

Agapito pulled a discreet face and withdrew as quickly as he could, but two days later, and two days nearer Florence, he returned to Cesare to tell him that the Florentine Ambassador, who had been making his way to Cesare, had encountered the Duke's party in his own territory, and was expressing high indignation at this fact.

Cesare's mouth twisted slightly. "Bring him hence," he ordered, "I shall have no difficulty in explaining to the envoy the reason for my move," and to the half-angry half-fearful ambassador he made his position clear.

"You are surprised to find that I have not waited for your Masters' reply," he said as he faced the envoy. "But why you should be I cannot think, for your Signory has shewn itself hostile to me. Do they expect me to accept these insults—the aid they gave to Forlì and again to Faenza—without a murmur? Do they imagine I will overlook their attitude?"

The ambassador, a short, plump man with snow white hair and a ruddy complexion, looked at his Grace with some indignation.

"Sire, this is not so. My Signory have given no aid to your enemies, either at Forlì or Faenza. You have no call to lay this charge at my masters' door."

Cesare, who was striding back and forth in simulated anger, whirled to face the man, who backed slightly as the Duke's eyes burned into his.

"You accuse me of lying?" snapped Cesare. "I tell you Florence gave aid to my enemies. I do not trust your Government, Sire, and they have greatly offended me by their attitude. I will stand no more of it."

He resumed his pacing, whilst the envoy spluttered in subdued fury, for whilst he recognized only too clearly that the Duke's rage was as false as his claims that Florence had stood against him, there was little he could do about it.

"I want a treaty with your Masters," said Cesare presently, coming to a halt once more in front of the Florentine. "An agreement so worded that the Ten cannot wriggle through it to suit their convenience. You are aware, sire, that I seek the capture of Piombino, and I would be assured that Florence does nothing to help this city as she did Forlì and Faenza, and I will have this assurance in writing."

Snarling inwardly at the insult, the envoy bowed stiffly.

"I will inform the Signory," he said through gritted teeth. "Are there any other demands your lordship wishes to make?"

Cesare looked at him suspiciously, but the ambassador had by now regained his self-control and his face was expressionless.

"I seek justice for Captain Vitelli and Captain Orsini," said the Duke shortly, "for they have been ill-used by your Masters. And further, as a token of your Signory's future good-will to me, I want a condotta of three hundred lances, together with artillery to aid me at Piombino, and a yearly stipend of thirty-six thousand ducats for three years. Tell your Masters that, sire, and be quick with their reply, for my patience is worn out."

The man gasped in amazement as the Duke laid down his outrageous terms, but he knew the position of Florence was extremely dangerous, and being a man of some cunning, he could well see that the quickest way of getting rid of Cesare and his unwanted troops would be to agree to anything he demanded, even in writing if needs be, for there was no cause to think such promises had to be kept.

He bowed slightly, and giving the Duke an assurance that his message would be taken immediately to the Ten at Florence, he withdrew, leaving the Duke smiling slightly.

The next day Agapito came to the Duke with another despatch from the Pope, repeating his orders in even stronger terms, requiring Cesare to leave Tuscany without delay.

"His holiness is disturbed," ventured Agapito, his eyes on the bleak line of Cesare's mouth. " 'Twould be as well, perhaps my lord . . ."

"His holiness is easily moved," said the Duke and let the paper drop on to the table. "Yet, in fact, I have no particular desire to remain in Tuscany, but first we will demand the artillery which has been promised by the treaty, and some part of the stipend, for these will be useful to me at Piombino. Send Captain Santa Croce to me." He turned away, leaving Agapito to hurry out in search of Pietro, but when the latter returned to Cesare some two days later to report his meeting with the Florentine envoy, his face was rueful.

"Well?" Cesare eyed his Captain coolly. "What success, Pietro?"

Santa Croce took a deep breath, for he knew his master was likely to receive the tidings he bore with some anger.

"None, Highness. None at all." He hurried on, trying to ignore the lines which sketched anger at the corner of Cesare's mouth.

"The Florentines expressed surprise that I should demand part of the money due at this time sire, for they said there was nothing in the agreement which would suggest that it should be paid immediately."

"And the artillery?"

Santa Croce winced slightly at Cesare's tone, but he shook his head. "They would give me no definite answer sire. They twisted and turned with such dexterity that I confess I found myself at a loss to know what their intent might be."

"Save that this intent is not to produce the artillery now," said Cesare, and the hazel eyes were half-closed. "Yes, I see. Well, so be it. We shall leave Tuscany, without the guns and without the ducats, but Florence has not heard the last of this. They will pay more dearly than they know for this attempt to cheat me; they will live to realize the high price of playing fast and loose with me."

Vitelli and Orsini, frustrated and enraged by Cesare's withdrawal, pestered and plagued his Highness to such an extent that Cesare was moved to something more than his usual quiet anger, and threatened them in no uncertain terms with swift reprisals if they did not quell their demands and obey his orders. Smarting under the injustice of the Duke's fury, his two Captains simmered with rage, but their respect for Cesare's reputation was more immediate than their desire for revenge against Florence, and they ceased their cries of protest and accepted the need to wait yet again for what they sought so eagerly.

Gathering his forces about him, the Duke made his way to Cecina, stopping for two days to make camp outside a small village near the valley, and whilst he was there, he noticed a young man talking with some soldiers by the camp fire. The men were exclaiming in astonishment at something the stranger was drawing on a sheet of parchment, and Cesare, his curiosity aroused, sauntered over, unseen by the group, to glance over the man's shoulder.

He watched with interest whilst a swift hand completed with a few expert strokes the lines of a bridge. Even on paper, the strength of it was obvious, yet there was nothing heavy or clumsy in its design; it was a flowing, poetic span from one pencilled bank to the other, and Cesare's eyes narrowed slightly.

"Admirable," he said, and the young man started, his pencil falling from his hand as he rose to face the Duke.

Seeing who addressed him, he bowed low, his face flushed at the Duke's compliment, and Cesare held out a hand for the parchment.

The man's unease increased as Cesare studied the drawing closely and then suddenly the Duke smiled.

"Excellent; on paper. Tell me, sire, could you build such a bridge of something more substantial than charcoal and parchment? Could this structure actually be brought to reality?"

"Y . . . yes, my lord," stammered the man in an agony of embarrassment. "Indeed it could, Magnificence."

Cesare nodded. "I see. And could you build it? If I gave you men and materials, could you supervise its construction? Could you plan its erection?"

"Y . . . yes, my lord, I could do this." The man brushed unruly hair from his brow, and bent to retrieve his charcoal pencil. "If I had the men, I could build a bridge for you."

"From whence do you come, sire? How do you come to find yourself in my camp?"

"I have come from Florence, sire, where I have been seeking employment, and before that I was in Milan."

"And you found no employment in Milan or Florence?"

The youth flushed again. "A little sire. I painted some portraits, and drew up plans for a fortress and some other buildings. I also designed a new gun, but none were interested."

"You have been industrious," said the Duke smiling a little. "How is it that you found no one concerned in your work? Are these your drawings?"

The Duke nodded towards a tattered folio by the man's side, and the boy bent and picked up the drawings, opening the folder, and his glance was shy as he met the Duke's enquiring eyes.

"Yes, sire. These are some of the things I have been working on, but no one seemed to need the plans I had drawn up, nor shewed interest in my drawings. I left Milan to seek my Fortune in Florence."

"And fared no better there?"

"No, Potency." The youth's smile was rueful. "In fact,

even worse in Florence, and I was glad to leave there, for I should have starved had I remained there longer."

The Duke was scanning the sheets of parchment with a keen eye, and there was a short silence, the soldiers withdrawing discreetly from the Prince's presence.

Presently Cesare looked up. "Milan and Florence seem to have been a trifle short-sighted," he observed and the boy coloured again, this time with pleasure. "I think your work has much merit. And what do you seek in my camp?" The hazel eyes were searching but encouraging, and the man swallowed his nervousness, one hand seeking to subdue the rebellious lock on his forehead.

"I sought you, my lord," he said frankly. "For I have heard . . . all Italy has heard of your lordship's patronage of the arts, and I thought that if I could but see you; if I could shew you my work, you might——" he broke off again, hardly able to put his dreams into words.

"You thought I might give my patronage to you. Yes, I see. But if I did, sire, it would not be to scribble away with things like this."

A finger flicked contemptuously at a portrait of a young woman lying in sensuous invitation on a low couch.

"I have no time for such things just now. But these," the finger moved again, and tapped reflectively on the sketch of the bridge and a drawing of a sturdy fortress, "these might interest me. Indeed they might."

The Duke looked up again. "What is your name, sire?"

The young man's eyes were bright with the hope the Duke's words had aroused in him, and he answered eagerly.

"Highness, my name is da Vinci; Leonardo da Vinci."

The Duke nodded. "Well, Messer da Vinci. I think I can use your services, for there is much work to do in the Romagna. There are fortresses to repair and some to build; there are bridges needed, and a new gun would always be useful, particularly to Captain Vitelli. Yes, sire, I think I can find you employment. See Captain Bartolomeo da Capranica, my camp master. Tell him you are joining my train as an engineer and architect, and he will see to all your needs. And Messer da Vinci."

Da Vinci's eyes, dazzled by his good fortune, focused sharply as the Duke's tone altered.

"Do not waste your time drawing pictures of women. Sleep with them if you will, but confine your talents to matters of more importance. Work hard, Messer da Vinci, and provide me with what I need, and you will find me a generous master, and who knows." The Duke paused again , and his eyes were amused. "One day you might be famous."

He turned away, leaving da Vinci to bow low, overcome by his luck and the opportunity presented to him, and as he watched the Duke walk through the camp, he quickly gathered his papers about him, and clutching a shabby knapsack in his hand, he made his way through the bustling crowds to find the camp master.

CHAPTER FOURTEEN

CESARE took Piombino without undue difficulty, although he did not wait himself to see the end of the siege he laid to that city, but assuring himself of the success of the endeavour, he turned his steps homewards, for the Pope was still pressing for his return, as Louis now claimed Valentinois' aid in his forthcoming assault on Naples.

Leaving adequate troops to conclude the capture of Piombino, Cesare made his way, without particular hurry, through the green countryside and came upon the enchanting Castel Villaro, set against smoky-grey hills and surrounded by a screen of tall trees.

A messenger rode out from the Castle to inform the Duke that Ramiro de Lorqua had taken possession of the stronghold two days before, and that all was prepared for his arrival. The Duke nodded with satisfaction, for he considered that a brief pause in this delectable spot would be a welcome change from camp life, and the somewhat strenuous weeks which lay behind him, and he rode into the courtyard to be met by his own guards, standing at rigid attention to welcome their master, and by de Lorqua, who saluted smartly, and led the Duke into the castle.

"Very pleasant," said Cesare looking round with gratification at the well appointed sala into which the Master of his Household had conducted him. "Very pleasant indeed, Ramiro; I congratulate you." He sat down in a tall carved chair and gave a faint sigh. " 'Twill be a relief to eat a meal free from dust and insects. I trust the servants have remained Ramiro; and what of the Duke of Villaro and his family? Where are they?"

"Fled, sire," said de Lorqua contemptuously. "At the first sign of our approach they were gone as with the wind, but the servants remained. I saw to that," he added grimly, and snapped impatient fingers at a page boy.

"Wine for the Duke," he said sharply, "and look lively boy, or there will be trouble."

The boy scampered away, terrified by the loud voice of the ogre who had taken possession of the castle, and Cesare rose to inspect a painting on the wall.

"A fine piece of work," he said after a while. "I shall welcome its addition to my collection. What else of value, Ramiro? Anything of use to us?"

"Indeed, my lord," said Ramiro with satisfaction. "There are many fine paintings, gold and silver ornaments, and some excellent plate."

"Ducats? Jewels?" Cesare was sharp, for his need for the latter was more urgent than his desire for ornaments, as his army was a constant expense.

"None that I could see, sire." De Lorqua's voice was irritated, for he too had hoped to find both money and gems. "I have searched the castle, but there is neither gold nor silver."

Cesare frowned. "They took it with them, perhaps?"

Ramiro shook his head and pursed his lips. "I doubt this, sire. I do not think they had time to gather any possessions about them, for our attack was sudden, and they barely had time to flee before our men were in possession of the castle."

"But Villaro must have had some money; some treasure. If they did not take it with them, it must still be here. Have another search made, Ramiro, for you know how I need ducats to keep this army of mine supplied." He sat down and accepted wine from the page who had now returned with a fine silver goblet on a delicately engraved silver tray.

"What else did your investigations reveal?" asked Cesare, dismissing the boy with a brief wave of his hand. "Ought of interest?"

"Nothing, my lord; at least——" De Lorqua broke off, and his brows were knitted together.

"What is this, Ramiro?" The Duke sipped his wine and watched his Captain's perplexed face. "What causes you such puzzlement? What did you find?"

"Only one thing I did not understand, my lord."

"And that was?"

"A room in the dungeons. An odd place." De Lorqua's frown had not lifted, and Cesare raised one eyebrow in enquiry.

"A room, Ramiro? This does not sound so unusual. What kind of room might this be?"

De Lorqua shook his head slightly. "Four bare stone walls, my lord, and nothing else."

"So? An unusual room. What is so strange about that?"

"The lock, sire. The lock on the door was new and well-oiled. 'Tis obviously in use."

"But for what?" The Duke laid his goblet down and his own brows were bent in a slight frown." Was there nothing at all in the cell?"

"Not a thing, Highness. No furniture, no implements, nothing. Just four walls."

"Four bare walls and a new lock. Curious." The Duke's eyes were thoughtful as he reached for his wine again. "I will come and look at this mysterious cell myself later, Ramiro. Meanwhile, see to it that a banquet is prepared for us tonight. And has Agapito arrived?"

Ramiro stopped his pondering and nodded.

"Indeed, sire, he has. He is in the library, arranging and cataloguing the books."

"Very proper," said Cesare with a smile. "I must make known my presence to him, for doubtless he has a hundred and one tasks for me to attend to. He is a tyrant, Ramiro, and gives me little peace."

Cesare rose, stretched and glanced round the sunny chamber again. "Yes, 'tis a very pleasant spot, Ramiro; I shall enjoy a brief stay here before I make my way to Rome to join D'Aubigny and his men. Come, take me to the library, and to the good Agapito, and later, we will explore your empty room, Ramiro, and see whether we can uncover its secret."

Later that night, Cesare went to the dungeons under the castle to look at the cell which had caused Ramiro de Lorqua some disquiet, and in the light of the flaming torches the accompanying soldiers held aloft, the Duke's keen eye scanned the barren stone walls and bare dusty floor. He ran a tentative hand over the roughly set stones which formed the walls, but apart from a coating of dirt, his fingers discovered nothing, and he frowned again.

"There seems nothing here," he commented finally, "yet I share your amazement, Ramiro, that the lock should be so well kept. Yes, 'tis very odd, but doubtless we shall discover anon what secret this chamber holds."

He cast a final look around him, and returned to the sala to join his officers who were testing the quality of the Duke of Villaro's wine cellars.

They rose instantly as he came into the room, but he motioned them to be seated, and in a short while they were engaged in a deep discussion on tactics to be employed in the third impresa, which Cesare had merely postponed whilst he paid his debt to Louis, bent on the destruction of the House of Aragon.

Presently Agapito da Amelia came to the Duke, and there was something thoughtful and preoccupied about his manner, which his perceptive master was quick to see.

"Well, Agapito? What causes this frown to mar your brow?"

The Duke was lying back in his chair, twirling the stem of a gold and crystal goblet between his slender fingers, and his voice was lightly mocking.

"Have you too found a mystery in this castle?"

Agapito hesitated, and seemed to find difficulty in answering Cesare, which in itself was a strange occurrence for the highly articulate secretary, and the general talk died down as attention was focused on the stocky, solid figure who stood before the Duke.

"My lord, it would seem so, although it is an order of strangeness which makes me doubt my own wits." Agapito shook his head slightly in perplexity. "Faith, sire, had I not known myself to be cold sober, I should have judged myself bewitched by wine."

"Indeed?" The Duke shewed a slight flicker of interest, for he knew his secretary to be an eminently sensible and practical man, lacking perhaps in imagination, but not one given to flights of fancy.

"And what is your particular puzzle, Agapito? Tell us, for it may be a worthy match to Ramiro's empty room."

Agapito, who had heard all about the cell and its incongruous lock, shook his head.

"No, sire, 'tis not of that order, for at least Captain de Lorqua's cell is really there for men to see, whereas I——" he broke off, and Cesare laughed.

"Dio, Agapito? Have you then seen something which is not there?" He turned to the others. "It seems I was wrong when I thought I came here for a brief rest, for first Ramiro uncovers me a puzzle in the dungeons, and now Agapito is seeing things which are not there."

He looked back at Agapito. "Well, Agapito, do not leave us suspended like this. What was it you saw, which was not there?"

Agapito laughed reluctantly. "Sire, I realize this sounds like the mouthings of an imbecile, but I am not a man given to imaginings, and when I entered your chamber not fifteen minutes ago, I saw something which I cannot explain in rational terms."

"Then explain it in any terms you will," said Cesare, "for you are filling us with impatience, Agapito. Now come, what is this which is not there, but which you have seen with your shrewd eye?"

Agapito gave another faint shrug. "I saw a page boy, sire."

The Duke stared at his secretary. "A page boy? But why should you not see a page boy? There are many about the castle, and there is no reason why one should not be in my chamber, for he may have duties to perform there. I do not understand you, Agapito, for your mystery seems to have no foundation."

Agapito's bright black eyes met his master's. "Sire, this boy wore a mask, and as I entered the room, he moved into the shadows and was gone."

The Duke's brows met sharply. "Gone? You mean he brushed past you to the door?"

"No, Highness. He moved away from me and vanished."

"Through the wall?" asked Cesare caustically. "Are you telling me, Agapito, that this boy, this strange boy who appears to like playing pranks, simply melted through the wall of the chamber?"

"Yes, my lord," said Agapito simply. "That is exactly what he did."

Cesare sat up abruptly. "This is ridiculous," he said shortly. "What sort of boy was he?"

Agapito raised his shoulders. "Just a boy, sire. Not very tall; slim, and nimble in his movements. Beyond that I could not see, for he wore a complete mask covering face and head. The mask of a clown with sad eyes and a grinning mouth."

"A clown, eh?" Cesare's lips tightened. "I see. It would seem that the servants in this castle need to be taught what service means, for I do not expect page boys to go about their duties adorned with carnival masks."

"Nor to vanish through a wall, my lord," said Mario di Mariano with a slight chuckle, for he did not take Agapito's tale very seriously. "Agapito, there must have been another door. Did you look?"

"Of course, Captain." Agapito looked a trifle indignantly at Mario's laughing face. "That was the first thing I did. I looked over every inch of the wall where I last saw the boy, but could find nothing. It appears to be a solid wall."

Di Mariano's amusement increased. "Faith, Ramiro, this beats your cell, which is, after all, but an empty room, whereas Agapito has found a vanishing trickster who can melt through walls."

Cesare was thoughtful. "You are quite sure about this, Agapito?" The mockery had gone from his voice, and he gave his secretary a very straight look. "There is no doubt in your mind that you actually saw this? 'Twas not a trick of light and shadow; something you imagined whilst your thoughts were elsewhere?"

Agapito shook his head. "No, Highness, there was no mistake. I may have had other matters on my mind when I entered your chamber, but I saw a boy, and I saw him fade from my sight into the shadows, and when I searched, he was no longer in the room. This was not a jape of my imagination."

His voice was firm, and Cesare nodded, for he believed him, knowing him well, and he lay back again and smiled slightly.

"Indeed, a most odd occurrence. I trust I shall not have my sleep disturbed by this impish page boy thrusting his way through the wall again."

"Sire!" Agapito turned to the Duke quickly. "You will not sleep in this chamber tonight?"

"But of course. Why not?"

"But my lord, this would be most unwise." Agapito's face had grown anxious. "As we do not know what this matter is all about, surely it would be wise for you to occupy another room. There is another fine chamber on that floor; I will go immediately to see to its preparation."

He half turned, but Cesare's hand stopped him. "Wait, Agapito. I beg you, do not disturb yourself. I shall sleep in the room, and there is no need for you to make other arrangements for my welfare. What harm can come to me?"

"My lord, this boy. . . ."

Cesare's teeth shewed momentarily. "Yes, Agapito, this boy. You think I am unable to cope with a page boy if the need should arise? You underestimate me."

Agapito bit his lip. "Sire, you know that was not my meaning. If this is some kind of . . . of. . . ."

"Yes, indeed, of what, Agapito?" The Duke's voice was soft and reflective. " Tis interesting to conjecture just what this is all about, but the easiest way to find out is to sleep there tonight and see whether our reckless youth returns."

Agapito shook his head unhappily. "Sire, I wish you would not. Something may happen which would mean your life was in jeopardy."

"Oh, come. Agapito! From a page boy? In any event, I shall be ready. Now, enough of this nonsense. Ramiro, give Agapito some wine, for if he can see vanishing boys without the aid of wine, who knows what visions may come to him when the balm of the grape has him locked in its hand."

He smiled at Agapito in a way which took all offence from

the words and his secretary grinned reluctantly and took the goblet from de Lorqua.

"Very well, sire, but I beg you take heed. There is something odd about this place. I would entreat you to have a care."

"I shall, Agapito; I shall," said Cesare, and his eyes were closed as he lay relaxed in his chair. "I always have care, Agapito; have no fear. And tomorrow I will regale you with all the happenings of the night."

Bartolomeo rose to his feet. "Sire, I propose to set a guard otuside the door of this chamber; you will excuse me whilst I make the arrangements?"

"No need," said Cesare without opening his eyes. "I require no guard."

"Sire, your pardon, but it is my duty to take such steps as I think necessary to protect your Highness. With your permission, I will now deal with this matter."

The Duke opened his eyes and looked at Capranica in amusement.

"As you will, Bartolomeo," he said gently, "and I thank you for your concern. Now gentlemen." He got to his feet, the others following suit. "I suggest we retire, for we have had a tiring time, and sleep will be welcome. Rest well, I beg you, and have no fears for me, for I shall come to no harm."

He inclined his head and left his Captains talking amongst themselves about the incident, whilst Agapito, still frowning slightly, made his way to his own room to ponder on the trick his hitherto wholly reliable eyes had played him.

At three in the morning, Cesare's chamber was dimly lit by the light of a hesitant moon, clouded every so often by wisps of cloud. It was very quiet, and the Duke lay relaxed and still under the silk covers of the huge bed. An owl flew past the slightly open window, its muted cry the only sound in the tranquil night.

In the dark corner of the chamber, not reached by the moon's silver balm, there was the faintest sound as part of the panelled wall slid gently back, and a slim figure put a cautious foot into the room. Satisfying himself that all was safe, the green-clad pageboy moved quietly and with purpose across the room to halt before a deep carved chest placed under one window, and with another quick glance over his shoulder, he knelt and opened the lid, taking care that not the slightest creak should disturb the man on the bed. The lid removed, the intruder gripped the shallow tray which fitted snugly into the top of the chest and lifted it clear, placing it gently to one side, then once again plunging his hands into the depths of the oak box.

For a minute or two the boy struggled with the iron bound box inside, but the weight made it difficult for him to raise it, and he got to his feet to get a better grip on his prize, but even this did not make easy his task, for the small chest was of great weight, and he paused in his effort to regain his breath. Finally he managed to shift the box and as he straightened up, a voice said in a quiet conversational tone:

"May I help you?"

With a sharp cry the boy let the box fall with a crash and he spun round to face the Duke.

Cesare rose from the bed, still fully clothed, and moved across the room, and as he did so, the guards which Bartolomeo da Capranica had placed outside the Prince's door, began to hammer on it and call to the Duke.

The Duke cast a look at the page, who had backed away into the shadows, then crossed to the door and opened it, quietening the men's fears and assuring them of his safety; then he closed and locked the door again, and came back into the room.

"Come here," he said, and the boy came forward hesitantly, his hands taut at his side, his face still concealed by the clown's mask so accurately described by Agapito da Amelia earlier in the evening.

Cesare moved past the boy to look into the chest, where the iron box had fallen, the lid having opened as it dropped. His mouth moved slightly as he saw the profusion of jewels and gold ducats which spilled over the base of the chest.

"The Duke of Villaro's treasure, no doubt," said Cesare, and turned to the page again.

"Well, boy? What is your name, and what are you doing here?"

The page did not answer, his silence a strange contrast to the grinning leer of the painted face.

"I do not usually have to repeat my questions," said Cesare softly, and the boy gave a slight shiver at the Duke's tone, and one hand adjusted the mask as if to emphasize his determination to remain hidden from Cesare's gaze.

"I . . . I . . . came to get the box which you have seen."

"So I gather," said Cesare sarcastically, "but why?"

The clown's face was raised suddenly. "Because it does not belong to you. It is the Duke of Villaro's, and I seek to return it to him." The voice was muffled by the mask but the defiance was obvious.

"So?" The Duke was dangerously quiet.

"Yes, indeed this is so. You have stolen the Duke's castle. You shall not have his gold in addition."

"No?"

Again there was a slight tremor, but the boy did not back away from the Duke. "No. It does not belong to you."

Cesare smiled bleakly. "It does not belong to you either. How did you get into this room, for you caused my good secretary some alarm when you vanished through the wall earlier this night? How did you make your entry?"

The boy's head dropped again, but he did not speak and Cesare's slim brows met in a sudden frown.

"I would remind you that I have ways of making you impart this information," he said shortly. "I would advise you not to test my patience further, for already you have disturbed my slumbers, and I have no desire to spend the rest of the night asking questions which are not answered. Now, tell me, and quickly, how did you get into this chamber?"

The page still made no move, and with an impatient gesture, the Duke stepped forward and stripped off the mask and his eyes narrowed slightly as in the shadowy half-light he saw the face beneath the painted canvas.

"Well, well." The Duke smiled and flung the mask from him. "No page boy this, but a woman, and a beautiful woman at that. The mystery becomes deeper."

He moved over to his bed and lit the candles in the silver holder, and in the supplemented light, turned to look at his prisoner again.

"Yes, a very beautiful woman."

The girl flushed at his tone and took a half step backwards as Cesare approached her again.

"Well, madam?" His hazel eyes were inquisitive. "And what do you do in my chamber at this hour of night? You are, of course, welcome at any time, if you crave my company, but . . ." he broke off as the girl coloured and shook her head in emphatic denial.

"You do not seek my bed? No? I am desolate." The Duke was sardonic. "Then you seek merely the treasure? But why, madonna? Why does the Duke of Villaro send a girl to retrieve his ducats for him? Is he such a mouse that he cannot do this for himself? Where is his son? What of his servants? His soldiers? Why you, madam?"

The mockery was gone, and the Duke's tone was terse, and he moved a step nearer to the girl, pausing to take in the details of her white face as she stared up at him.

Her blue-black hair had been cut in the style of a page boy, but the beauty of the curved cheek and full mouth was wholly feminine, and the deep green eyes, now dilated in fear, were fringed with curling lashes which would have been completely wasted on a boy.

She bit her lip and tried to answer the Duke, and her voice was low and clear.

"I . . . I . . . am one of the Duchess's maids," she said finally . "When we fled the castle, there was no time to take ought with us, for your soldiers were almost upon us before we knew of their coming. Thus, when we reached the safety of Citta della Moreno . . . oh!"

She broke off in sudden horror, as she realized her words had betrayed the Duke of Villaro's hiding place, but Cesare held up a hand.

"I knew where Villaro was," he said casually. "I do not employ spies for nothing. The news of the Duke's resting place was made known to me almost as soon as he reached it. Now, you say you are one of his servants."

"Yes." She raised her head and met his eyes as boldly as she could, and the Duke's mouth curved slightly.

"A very faithful and dedicated servant," he commented finally, and she flushed again.

"And did you consider the consequence of your efforts, madonna? Did you stop to think what would happen to you if you failed in your endeavour?"

The green eyes had lost their nervousness, and met his without fear.

"I considered it, sire," she said and there was a proud tilt to her chin. "But I thought the risk worth while, for had I succeeded, I would have returned the Duke's treasure to him, and would have robbed you of that which does not belong to you."

"It does now," said Cesare, mildly amused by her spirit, "the treasure, the castle and the Duke's servants."

Again there was a faint movement behind her eyes, but the girl did not reply, and Valentinois laughed gently.

"Indeed, I have done well from my conquest of this castle, madonna. I had not realized until this moment just how successful I had been. But I still do not understand why Villaro should send a girl to do his soldiers' work. I would like you to explain this to me, madam, and also to answer my earlier question as to how you got into this room."

The girl flushed slightly. "The Duke did not know I was coming. Had he known, he would have stopped me, and I got into the room through a panel over there." She pointed to the wall behind Cesare and he nodded.

"Yes, I guessed 'twas something like that when I heard Agapito's tale, for he is not a man given to hallucinations. And you say Villaro did not know you had come here?"

"No." A pulse moved at her throat, and this time she did not meet Cesare's eyes. "I left Citta della Moreno undiscovered."

"Villaro will be touched to learn the depths of your loyalty," remarked Cesare, "for it is unusual for a servant, particularly a woman, to risk death, and perhaps worse, for a master of Villaro's quality." The sneer was deliberate, and the sudden spark of anger in the girl's eyes confirmed what Cesare wanted to know, and he smiled gently.

"You are Isabella Villaro," he said, and she flinched. "No servant, madonna, but the Duke's daughter. He is a fortunate man to have so beautiful and brave a daughter, but alas, madonna, you have in fact served your father ill by your move, for now I have the weapon I need to bring about my purpose."

Isabella Villaro put an uncertain hand to her brow to brush away a strand of dark hair, and her voice was not entirely steady.

"A weapon? I . . . I . . . do not understand."

"I can hold Villaro by force, if I want to, but I would prefer to have the Duke's surrender. This I can now achieve, for I shall send a messenger to your father, madonna, to tell him that I require his presence at the castle immediately to sign a treaty which will secure my hold on this city."

"He will not come," she said violently. "He will never surrender to you, Borgia!"

"Why not? He did not stop to fight me; he ran like a rabbit. Why should he hesitate to make final his relinquishment of the castle and citadel?"

"He did not have sufficient men to fight you," she said hotly, "but he will now be able to raise the necessary troops to evict you from the castle; he will not yield to you."

"He will," said Cesare confidently, "for I shall tell him that unless he returns immediately to sign my treaty, I shall kill you."

She stared at the Duke. "He will not believe you," she whispered. "He will not come."

Cesare laughed without humour. "Oh my dear Isabella, he will. There is no man in Italy who would not believe the worst of me, and when I tell your father that unless I get his signature on the document which I shall prepare, I shall first take you for my pleasure, and then kill you, he will believe me."

She was shaking slightly. "You . . . you would not do this."

His mouth twisted slightly. "Do not delude yourself, madonna, I would do anything to achieve my purpose, and my purpose now is the holding of this castle. If this entails your death, madam, 'tis unfortunate, but it would not hinder me."

She moistened dry lips and her voice was harsh. "They do not lie about you, Borgia, when they say you are a fiend. A man without human thought or feeling. You are, as they say, truly evil."

He nodded. "That is what they say," he agreed coolly, "but whether they are right in their condemnation, only history will be able to judge, madonna, for my path is not a purposeless road of destruction. I pursue a course for a definite reason which one day will be clear to all men."

She was not listening to him, and her eyes were hard.

"And if my father comes? If he signs the treaty? What then?"

Cesare shrugged. "You will both be free to go. I shall not seek to hold you, for I shall have achieved my ends."

"Do you expect me to believe you?" Her tone was bitter, and he smiled gently.

"It does not matter, madonna, whether you believe me or not. Time will shew that what I say, I mean. When your father has signed the formal surrender of Castel Villaro, neither you, nor he, will be of further interest to me, and you may go where you will."

"Without money or possessions, I presume?" she said acidly, and he gave her a quick look.

"Indeed, the treasure of Castel Villaro will remain with me, but you will not find me ungenerous, madonna, for whatever men may say about me, they do not accuse me of being mean. You will have sufficient money to live, madonna,"

"You are insufferable," she said stormily, and he laughed, this time with real amusement as he took her shoulders and gazed down into her angry eyes.

"And you are lovely," he said, and the girl's rage faded suddenly, and something else flickered behind her green eyes and her body tensed in his hold.

"No!" She tried to draw away from him, but his grip was firm, and his amusement deepened.

"No? Very well, at least not now. Not unless your father fails to comply with my command; then madonna, the story will be different, for what I have promised, I will do. Believe this, and let us hope your father has the good sense to recognize truth when he hears it, but, then, I am sure he will, for, as I say, my reputation is such that he will not mistake the meaning of my demands."

He released her and held out his hand.

"Come, I will take you to your chamber, for I think we will abandon the secret door for the time being."

She hesitated a second, but realizing the danger was past for the moment, she accepted his hand, and allowed the Duke to take her to her room, ignoring the amazed stares of the guards outside his door. In her chamber she turned to face him again.

"Is . . . is . . . there anything I could do to stop you?" She found it difficult to meet his eyes. "If you kept the gold and the jewels, and if you. . . ." Again he saw the faint pulse tremble in her throat, "If you kept me, for whatever purpose . . . you . . . you wished . . . would you then abandon this plan to send for my father?"

Cesare smiled gently. "You have much courage, madonna, but you misread me. If I wanted you, I would take you. What I want is Villaro's surrender, no more, no less. To get this I will do what I must, including both murder and rape, but I doubt, in fact, if such violence will be called for, for I have no doubt that when Villaro gets my message, he will come quickly, and you will not have to subject yourself to my unwanted attentions."

Her lips tightened. "I see. Nothing will move you from your intent?"

"Nothing, madonna, not even your generous offer." The sneer was back, and he bowed slightly.

"I bid you good night, madonna. Do not try to leave your room, for if you do, I will see that you are housed where you cannot make a further attempt to escape."

He glanced round the room. "Are there any other exits to this chamber?"

It was her turn to sneer, and her voice was bitter as she answered him.

"Yes, indeed, that is a question, is it not, my lord?"

He looked back at her quickly. "You would be well advised

to answer me, madam," he said curtly, and her scorn increased.

"Send for your men, Borgia," she advised, "let them test the walls and see if they can uncover a way in which I could even now slip through your fingers."

He looked at her silently for a moment, then he took a pace towards her and one slender hand took her throat between the long white fingers.

"Folly, madonna," he said very softly. "Never throw down the gauntlet unless you are fully prepared to pay the price of defeat." The fingers tightened and she winced in pain. "What other exits?"

She tried to turn from his hold, but the Duke's hand could not be budged.

"What exits?" he repeated and increased the pressure, one arm encircling her waist to steady her.

Her mouth moved silently, and for a moment he relaxed his hold and she swallowed with difficulty.

"Well?"

"N . . . none," she whispered painfully, and he nodded.

"Good." He still held her round the waist, but his hand had dropped from her throat. "Good. Now rest, madonna, for you have had an exhausting time. Tomorrow we will talk again. I bid you good night."

He bent and kissed her lips, and with a faint laugh was gone.

CHAPTER FIFTEEN

AT dawn on the following day, Cesare's messenger left the Castel Villaro for Citta della Moreno with Valentinois' message to the Duke, who received it with a cry of rage and fear, for unlike his daughter, he had no doubts about Cesare's determination, and was in deadly fear for Isabella's safety, and realizing Borgia held all the weapons for success, he prepared himself for the journey to his castle.

On the day following her discovery by Cesare, Isabella Villaro kept to her room, and made no attempt to escape the confines of her prison, but when another night had passed, she decided to make one last effort to stop Valentinois' plans for the complete subjection of her citadel, and in the morning, when the sun was high, she ventured downstairs and made her way into the garden.

There were many guards on duty, but none made any attempt to stop her, but she had no delusion about her chances of leaving the castle, and contented herself by walking a little way through the trees to a small wooded arbour where she sat down on a bench and reviewed her situation, which seemed to her to be entirely hopeless.

Presently she heard the sound of voices and quickly left the seat to hide in some nearby bushes as the men drew nearer to her. Through the dappled leaves, she saw two of Cesare's Captains come into view, and as they saw the bench, they halted and one sat down, his long legs stretching out as he relaxed in the warm sunshine, and for a while they were silent.

" 'Twill be a pity to leave this pleasant spot," said one finally, "but I fear we shall soon be gone, once my lord has finished his business with Villaro."

His companion chuckled. "Yes, and that business will not take long, once Villaro has signed the treaty."

"No, indeed. Just long enough for Ramiro to put an end to Villaro's life."

Santa Croce nodded. "Even so, Giulio, this still leaves Villaro's son to lay claim to this citadel. 'Tis not normally his Highness's policy to allow any one to live who could make legal claim to the land he conquers."

Alberini laughed. "Fear not, Pietro; the Duke has thought of this. He holds the Duke's daughter; soon the Duke himself will be here, and already plans have been put in train to deal with the son. You may rest assured that there will be none left to claim this jewel. My lord will have a signed surrender, and no tiresome claimants on his hands. A very satisfactory conclusion. Ah well, we must get back, for my lord wishes to consider the question of the artillery we shall need for the next campaign. Come."

He rose and together the two men left the arbour, and Isabella crept out from her hiding place, her face white, her eyes ablaze with the fury which Cesare's treachery has aroused in her.

How foolish she had been to believe his words when he had said that she and her father would be free once the treaty had been signed; how gullible to accept the word of a man of Cesare's stamp. And her brother, Lorenzo; what did the Borgia have planned for him? With sinking heart she realized that whatever infamy this might entail, it was probably already afoot, and no matter what she might do, it would be too late to save Lorenzo. She sank down on the bench again, and buried her face in her hands whilst her fevered brain tried to think of some answer to the problem confronting her. She did not doubt that her father would answer Cesare's demands, and would make his way back to Villaro, but now she knew that his signature on the terms of surrender would mean nothing, for as soon as the document was signed, Valentino proposed to kill him, and perhaps her, but not until he had. . . . Her mind stopped her thoughts, which were too horrible to bear, and she suddenly raised her head as an idea struck her.

Only one thing would save her father and herself, although it was probably too late to aid Lorenzo, and that was the death of Valentinois. If this could be achieved before her father arrived at the castle, then there would be hope of escape and the prospect of holding Villaro.

She made her way back to the castle, and her step was light with the renewed hope she felt, for although Cesare's death would be hard to achieve, a germ of an idea had taken hold of her mind, and she was busy with the details as she entered the castle. So intent was she upon her plans, that she did not see Cesare until she was almost upon him, and her breath was drawn in quickly as he bowed to her.

"I bid you good morning, madonna," he said. "I trust that you are in good spirits."

She curtsied quickly, and her reply was cold. "Thank you my lord, yes."

He watched her for a minute, then offered his hand.

"Come into the sala, madonna; I would like to speak to you."

She hesitated, but realizing this was no moment to shew defiance, she laid her hand on his arm, and allowed him to lead her to the sala.

"Come; sit by me," he said, and reluctantly she sat by his side on the brocaded couch, her eyes avoiding his.

"Well, it should not be long now before your father arrives, and you will both be free."

She raised her head, hating his smooth words which covered such black treachery.

"Indeed?" Her voice was still icy.

"And I will furnish you with all you need," went on Cesare unmoved, "for your treasure chest contained a goodly supply of ducats, some of which I can well spare for you and your father."

She contained her fury as best she could. "You are too generous, my lord," she said stonily. "Are you sure you can afford to let even one ducat go, for it must be an expensive matter, stalking the Romagna and seizing other people's estates. A lot of money must be needed to maintain your forces, sire."

"Indeed, this is so, but fortunately most of my conquests produce some prize which aids me, and, madonna," his light bantering tone dropped suddenly. "You would do well to remember that I have a legal right to take these fiefs, for they belong to the Holy See."

"So you say, my lord," she said contemptuously, "but this view is not shared by all."

"That does not make the facts untrue," he returned equably, and she gave him a look which was pure hatred.

"It must be satisfying, my lord, to be able to destroy, rape, murder and pillage in the sure knowledge that you have the blessing of the Pope and the Holy Church."

For a second there was something like anger in Cesare's eyes, but then his expression lightened again.

"Yes, indeed; a great comfort to me, madam."

The silence which ensued was uncomfortable, then Isabella stirred and smiled unkindly at the Duke.

"For all your cleverness, my lord, you have missed the true prize of Villaro."

"Oh?" He watched the glint in her eyes with interest. "And what may this be, madonna, that my eagle eye has failed to uncover?"

Her lip curled. "Why the real treasure of Villaro, of course. Did you really imagine that the contents of the small box was the complete fortune of my House, my lord?"

"In truth, it had seemed a trifle meagre to me, madonna, but then, you could have fallen on hard times."

His bland manner made her nostrils flare in anger, and she gave a short laugh.

"Hardly times as poor as that, sire. No, there is much more than that, and you have missed it, my lord, for all your astuteness."

Cesare smiled faintly, and was intrigued by what the girl was now planning in her beautiful head, for it was quite obvious to him that she had now embarked upon some scheme or other, designed for his destruction, else she would have given no hint of further valuables in the castle, and he led her gently on in the web of deception she was weaving.

"Really, madonna? This is indeed an interesting thought. And where is this miraculous treasure hidden, for my men have thoroughly searched the castle, and nothing was found."

"No, it would not be, for we know how to guard that which belongs to us."

"But you will tell me where it is, will you not?" he asked pleasantly, "for if this had not been your intent, you would not have mentioned it to me. And why, I ask myself, do you now propose to reveal to me this so secret hiding place?"

She shrugged. "In payment for my life, and that of my father."

"But I have already told you. Once your father signs the surrender, you will both be free to go as you will."

"I wish to ensure that this will be so," she said bleakly, "for your word is not always kept my lord."

"I do not see how surrendering the treasure of Villaro to me will help you, madam, for if you regard me as capable of treachery, what then is to stop me accepting your offer, and later destroying you?"

For the first time she really looked at Cesare, and her eyes were no longer angry.

"I do not entirely share the view that some hold of your character, my lord," she said slowly. "I do not think you are entirely beyond honour."

His brows rose slightly, and he gave her a keen look.

"I am flattered, madam," he said in a toneless voice. "but still I fail to see. . . ."

"I am prepared to make a bargain with you," she broke in, "and I am also prepared to take your word that you will keep this bargain."

"I see. And the bargain, madonna?"

"Tonight I will take you, and only you, my lord, to where the treasure is hidden. In return, you will give me your promise that my father and I will truly be free to go."

"And you will accept my unsupported word?"

"I will, my lord." Her voice was firm, and Cesare's mouth was derisive.

"You seem to have had a somewhat abrupt change of heart, madam," he observed dryly. "When we first met you had no such trust in me."

"I have had the opportunity of talking with you since then," she said, and glanced down at her hands clasped in her lap.

"I did not know you when I first pronounced my view; now I think I see what kind of man you are." She raised her head again to meet his stare. "Now, I will take your word, if you will give it to me."

Cesare was silent for a second as he sought to fathom the girl's plan, then he nodded.

"Very well, madam. You have my word."

Her eyes fell again so that he should not see the venom in them as he gave his false promise, then she smiled.

"Good, my lord, then we have a pact, and tonight, when all are asleep, we will go to the dungeons, and there I will uncover for you the secret of Villaro."

"In the dungeons, madonna? An odd place, surely?"

"But no, my lord, what could be safer than an empty room to keep one's treasure." Her eyes were hard and mocking, and Cesare's attention was suddenly held.

An empty room?"

"Yes, my lord. In an empty room in the dungeons below this castle is something which will amaze and bewilder you."

"You make my interest quicken, madonna," he said in a colourless voice. "And I greatly look forward to tonight. What time are we to visit this room which holds so much, so invisibly?"

She smiled, her lips curling in savage satisfaction as she held his eyes with her own.

"Come to my chamber at midnight, my lord," she said quickly for by then most will be sleeping, and we can safely make our way unobserved to the dungeons."

"Why so much secrecy, madam? If am to make this bargain, others will have to know sooner or later. Why not now?"

"No!" She was sharp. "Only you, my lord. The secret is for you alone." Her glance was anxious, but as he nodded, her fears died and she cast a demure look at him.

"You will excuse me now, sire?"

"Of course." He rose and bowed to her. "I will await with impatience our next meeting."

She left the sala, and Cesare moved to the window and stared out at the sunlit lawns.

Presently Giulio Alberini came to give the Duke a message, and Cesare said thoughtfully:

"Giulio. Has Villaro arrived yet?"

Alberini nodded. "Yes, sire, he came hence some ten minutes ago. Do you want to see him immediately?"

"Yes, and Giulio; I do not want his daughter to know he has come. They must not meet. Is this clear?"

"Sire." Giulio saluted and withdrew, leaving Cesare smiling slightly, and there was both satisfaction and amusement in his eyes as he waited for the Duke of Villaro to be brought to him.

At midnight, Valentinois presented himself at the door of the Madonna Isabella's chamber, and found her waiting for him. She was clad in a pale green velvet cloak, and the admiration in the Duke's eyes as he glanced over her was genuine.

"We shall need light, my lord," she whispered, "for it will be dark in the dungeons."

Cesare nodded and reached up to free one of the burning tapers which lit the passage-way.

"Come," Isabella moved quickly from him, and he followed, a small smile round the corner of his mouth as he watched her play, for despite the plots she hatched to his undoing, he found himself greatly attracted to her, both by reason of her physical beauty, and the spirit and determination she had shewn, and there was at least one of his promises he did not intend to keep.

They encountered no one on their journey to the dungeons, for Cesare's instructions to his staff had been explicit, and despite the dismay and disapproval of his Captains, his orders had been obeyed to the letter, and the Duke and Isabella reached the room, discovered by de Lorqua, without mishap.

"Here, sire." She turned to look at him, and by the warm glow of the flare, he saw her green eyes were bright with an excitement and hope he had not seen in them before, and the delicate colour in her cheeks indicated the importance of what she was doing.

He smiled. "The empty room, madonna?"

"Yes, my lord, but not so empty as soon you will see, for here is something which will cause all Italy to stand amazed."

"A bold claim, madam," he said as she turned the lock. "What riches have we here that could bring about such wonder?"

"You will soon see, my lord." She went ahead of him, and the small room came to life under the light of the torch the Duke held above him.

"There is a ring there, sire; fix the torch." She indicated a small iron sconce near the door, and Cesare slipped the flare into it, and waited for her to make the next move.

"There, sire," she held out her arms. "Here is the secret of Castel Villaro."

Cesare was very still, "Oh, madam? Yet still I see nothing."

"Oh, my lord, you will. You will. Soon, you will. See, over here." She held out her hand and led Cesare to the far wall.

"There is a loose stone here, sire," she said in a voice which had a quiver of something vital in its depths. "Can you feel it?"

She took his hand in hers, and laid his fingers on the crumbled grey stone.

"Do you feel it move, my lord?"

"Yes, it seems loose, madam, but I do not see. . . ."

"Press hard, sire, and you will see."

"I would know more before I take this step," he said slowly, "for who knows what I may uncover."

She laughed, her dark hair swinging free as she threw back her head in amusement.

"Oh, fear not, my lord. When you press that stone, it will release a hidden slab over there." She pointed to the wall on Cesare's left. "It will come down slowly and there reveal such treasure as will dazzle your eyes. Gold, silver, rubies, diamonds and more."

The green eyes were brighter than any jewel as she watched Cesare in the half-light.

"Come, my lord, are you afraid to press the stone which will bring you such wealth?"

For a long second they stared at one another in the

shadowy cell, then Cesare's hand moved to the stone and pressed hard.

The slab came down with screaming violence, stopping short of the floor by a mere inch, not to Cesare's left, but immediately in front of where he had been standing.

Isabella stared at Cesare, who had leaped clear of the stone in one lithe bound, and then back at the slab, and suddenly she started to scream.

Strapped to the inside of the slab was the body of a man, clothed in crimson velvet, which had once been pale amber, but of his face nothing was left, for it had been crushed to pulp, and only the mangled remains of a human being were left inside the torn garments.

Cesare made no move towards the girl, and presently her cries were stilled, and half-fainting, she groped towards the slab to look closer at the horror it held against its stone side.

"My . . . my . . . my father?" she whispered finally, and Cesare nodded.

"Your father indeed, madonna," he said, and his tone was terse. "Crushed, as you would have had me crushed. A fitting justice, I think."

"No!" Her tortured cry was wrung from her heart and she turned away to bury her face in her hands.

"No, oh Dio, no! No!"

Valentinois came round the end of the slab and pulled her sharply to him.

"Yes, yes, madonna. Your eyes do not deceive you. This is what is left of your father, thanks to you and your desire to destroy me. You plotted against my life, and this is my answer. I hope it satisfies you."

She stared up into his cold eyes and shuddered terribly.

"I . . . I . . . do . . . do not understand," she began in a whisper which was hardly audible. "How could . . . how did . . ."

"How did I know of the slab, madonna?" His eyes were as biting as his voice, and his grip on her arms tightened, but she was beyond feeling, and the pain he inflicted did not alter her glazed stare.

"Your father told me, madam. It was as simple as that."

"My . . . my father?" She swayed in his hold. "But how . . ."

"When you made your bargain with me earlier today, your father was already here. I knew your intent to be false; as false as your promises, and I had already seen this room; seen its emptiness and seen the new lock on the door, and so I sent for your father. At first he pretended ignorance of my questions, but then we went to the dungeons and came to this room. Finally, under persuasion, he told me of this little device, but like you, he lied as to where the slab would fall, but bloodstains are hard to move, madonna, and I had already seen on the floor the faint traces of redness from some luckless victim of your father's. I guessed, therefore, exactly where the slab would fall, and, further, I deemed the rate of its descent would not be slow."

Cesare paused and he gave her a slight shake. "You and your father were foolish to assume I was so gullible, madonna." His eyes were malicious.

"I continued my talk with your father, gradually manœuvering him into the position I wanted him, and so intent was he upon our conversation, which concerned your safety, madonna, that he did not see my hand move until it was too late. If you should be in doubt, madam, the end was very quick. He did not suffer. In one second there was nothing left but blood and broken bones. 'Twas then simple for my men to lay the Duke to rest on the slab, clean the cell and lay fresh dust on the floor to cover the blood-stains, and all was then ready for our visit tonight."

She sagged against him and he caught her to him to support her.

"Why is it, madonna," he went on, the trace of anger dying out of his voice, "that all Italy accuses me of infamy and violence, yet no man in his dealings with me, really takes into account what this means? They picture in their minds a devil who is possessed by satanic impulses, but in their encounters with me, they make no provision for dealing with them. Did you really imagine you could destroy me with your childish plan, madam? Did you truly think that when I possessed myself of a castle, I would not make a thorough search for its secrets? This room had already been noted, and it merely needed someone to unlock the key to the mystery; this your father did under pressure. Yet you went blindly on, not stopping to think of the kind of man you opposed." He laughed shortly. "Such folly, madonna."

She was sobbing against his shoulder, and he felt her body tremble against his.

"You have seen enough to convince you of the hopelessness of your task, madam?" he asked after a moment. "If so, we will return to my chamber, for it is chill down here."

He held her away from him and looked silently at her ashen face and dead eyes, then nodded.

"Yes, I think you are convinced. Good, then let us leave here." He turned away.

She did not move. Her body seemed locked to the spot and for a moment her eyes turned to look at the slab, then a tear coursed down her cheek.

"Come," he repeated impatiently. "Have you not studied your handiwork sufficiently?"

She tried to move, but could not, and with an unfeeling hand brushed the tear away.

Cesare went back to her and swung her up in his arms, and she lay still against him as he made his way back to her chamber, and laid her on the bed.

She closed her eyes and knew no more until she felt herself raised in the Duke's arms, as he held a goblet of wine to her lips.

"Drink this," he said quietly, and she felt the potent wine flow into her, and her head cleared slightly.

He let her fall back against the pillows.

"I advise you to sleep now, madonna," he said and she felt her eyelids droop. "I will see that you are not disturbed."

His voice trailed off into silence as unconsciousness swept over her again in a merciful shroud.

Back in his own room, Cesare sent for Capranica.

"That is over," he said shortly, and Bartolomeo looked up sharply, for there was a note in Cesare's voice which was unexpected.

"And the girl? Where is she, my lord?"

"In her room; she is sleeping."

"I will mount a guard, my lord."

"I doubt this is necessary, Bartolomeo," said Cesare, and he poured wine into two goblets. "She is unlikely to stir."

"She was courageous, sire," ventured Capranica finally, and Cesare's laugh was terse.

"She was a fool," he returned and drained his cup. "What of her brother? Has he been dealt with yet?"

"Yes, sire. There was some resistance, and we lost a few men, but the task is finished."

"Good. Tomorrow we will leave here for Rome."

"What is your lordship's intention towards the Madonna Isabella?" Bartolomeo had, in fact, little doubt as to his master's intention, and his question was purely perfunctory.

"She will come with us." Cesare filled his goblet again. "She and Astorre Manfredi; I will house them in Rome until the time comes to——" he broke off and drank again, and Capranica frowned slightly.

"I see, sire," he said finally, and Cesare turned to look at him.

"Yes, no doubt you do, Bartolomeo," he said. "Now go and make the necessary arrangements for our departure, for I wish to make an early start."

He dismissed his Captain and threw himself on to the bed, but if Bartolomeo harboured any thoughts that his master had had some spasm of regret at what he had achieved that night, or what he proposed to achieve in the future, he was completely mistaken, for as Valentinois lay still and quiet, he was not thinking of the stricken girl, nor the terrible sight in the cell below him. He was thinking of Camerino, the city he proposed to take when he had given Louis the help he had demanded, and nothing else clouded his mind as he began to plan his next move towards the unification of central Italy.

CHAPTER SIXTEEN

WHEN Cesare returned to Rome in June, he did it quietly, and without ceremony, and then locked himself up in the Vatican apartments set aside for him. Here he set about the business of putting into order the affairs of his newly won states, and the ambassadors who came to seek his ear, found it well nigh impossible to gain an audience, and more often than not went away disgruntled and dissatisfied.

Later that month, Alexander, having received the ambassadors from Louis of France, and from Ferdinand and Isabella of Spain, issued a Bull declaring Federigo no longer King of Naples. The Bull accused him of disobedience to the Church, and of seeking the aid of the Infidel in his military operations. These flimsy excuses veiled the true reason for the Pope's action, which was governed by the desire of the French and the Spanish to divide the kingdom of Naples between them, in which enterprise, Cesare was committed to aid Louis.

Although he would have preferred to continue with his own campaign, Cesare was by no means adverse to a scheme which would destroy Federigo, for he had not forgotten the latter's curt rejection of the suggested alliance with his daughter, and despite the delay in his own plans, he was content to divert his forces to this end.

Cesare sent a considerable force with D'Aubigny, the Captain-General of the French Army, when the latter rode out of Rome at the end of June, and in July, the Duke himself left to join his allies, whilst Gonsalo de Cordoba took his Spanish troops to Calabria as the French began to prepare for battle.

Strict though Cesare was with his troops when they moved through his own territories, he shewed no such concern as the army moved into Federigo's kingdom, and the Duke turned a blind, disinterested eye on the ravages inflicted upon the luckless peasants who stood between the ruthless soldiers and their target.

Two miles outside Capua, the invading forces met with their first check, as Prospero Colonna rode out of the city at the head of six hundred lances to try to stem the tide of the invasion.

A messenger came to tell D'Aubigny and Cesare of their impending arrival, and the Duke's eye quickened as he listened to the man's words.

"Capital!" he said, and called for his horse. "They will be a more worthy adversary than the peasants we have encountered hitherto. Mario, Giulio." He beckoned his two Captains to him. "Marshal your lances quickly, for we will now give Federigo's men a lesson they will remember."

D'Aubigny frowned. "You lead the charge yourself, sire?"

Cesare looked surprised. "But of course. I do not ask my men to attempt that which I would not venture myself. Besides," he adjusted a stirrup and looked at the Frenchman, "this is something I would not miss."

He leaped into his saddle and took a lance from his attendant.

"Come," he said, and he was smiling as he spurred his horse forward, drawing after him the troops he had schooled so carefully. They rode forward, quickening their speed as they pulled away from the main force, and within minutes Cesare gave a shout as he saw Colonna's lances ahead.

"Forward," he said, raising his voice above the noise of the horses' hooves and the jangling of their bridles. "Let us give Federigo a taste of what is in store for him."

He increased his speed so that he rode slightly ahead of his men, and his vigour and encouragement quickened the heart of every man who rode with him, and not a single one of his followers flinched as they flung themselves at the opposing forces.

The lance in Cesare's iron grip did terrible damage, but not for one second did his personal encounters with the enemy stop him urging his men on to further efforts, and so effective was his leadership, that in a comparatively short time, Colonna's men were driven helplessly back to Capua, whence

Cesare's men followed to finish their work of destruction.

Flushed with victory from the first engagement, the Duke's men were joined by D'Aubigny's forces and together they settled down to the systematic bombardment of Capua's walls and bastions.

After five days of unceasing fire, they broke through a ruined barbican and killed two hundred men who were valiantly defending the city, and four days later, the united army poured into Capua to write one of the most terrible pages in history.

The troops were completely out of hand, and none of the officers seemed to be able to stem the uncontrolled violence which broke out all over the small sheltered city. Men, women and children were slaughtered like cattle, and the screams of the dying were heard on all sides as the shouting, blood-maddened soldiers spread the mantle of death over the streets.

Cesare watched the troops' excesses from the loggia of a villa in the central square. His face was expressionless as he looked down at a group of Spanish soldiers who had dragged into the square a number of terror-stricken nuns from a nearby convent, and not by a flicker of an eyelid did he shew his thoughts as the men, jeering and laughing, stripped the habits from the unfortunate women and flung them to the ground to satisfy their lust.

Smoke was rising from many of the houses which had been fired by the invading forces, and beneath Cesare's feet the cobbled stones were already stained red, the torn and mutilated bodies of the citizens flung about in horrid confusion.

Pietro Santa Croce, who stood by Cesare's side, was less able to conceal his thoughts and his mouth was twisted in revulsion as he watched the scene below. His eyes followed the slight figure of a girl, no more than sixteen, as she fled mindlessly through the smoke and dust, her feet stumbling every now and then over the ravaged corpse of a neighbour. Behind her in hot pursuit were two Swiss soldiers, their eyes alight with predatory and unthinking desire.

"Sire!" Santa Croce could no longer maintain his silence, as he saw the girl falter again, and watched the soldiers gain on her.

"Can you not stop this? This is not warfare; it is cold-blooded murder! Is this the war of which the French have boasted so proudly? Is this the chivalry d'Alègre claimed we lacked? The rape of nuns, and children; the butchering of innocents? My lord, can you not bring this carnage to an end?"

Cesare's eyes did not leave the street below him, nor did his impressive face reflect the scream of agony which rose as the Swiss caught the girl, and pulled her to the opposite side of the road, dragging her down into the shadows thrown by the overhanging balcony of the nearby villa.

Santa Croce's hand was on the hilt of his sword.

"Sire! I cannot stand by and watch this done. Your leave, my lord; I will at least call halt to this encounter."

He turned to go, but the Duke's hand checked him.

"Will you also give back to the good nuns their inviolate bodies, Pietro? Will you restore the torn and severed limbs of those who lie in their own blood in the gutters? Will you draw a veil over the eyes of the children who have watched their mothers hacked to pieces, so that they shall not dream at nights? Will you cleanse the smell of death from the streets of this fair city?"

He turned to look at Santa Croce's face, white and tense, and gave a short laugh.

"No, Pietro, you will not. You cannot, and no more can I. And thus, since you cannot weave these miracles, I pray you, peace. There is nothing for you to do here."

"But, sire." Santa Croce came back to Cesare's side. "Is it not within your power to stop this now? Can you do nothing?"

Cesare shook his head slightly. "Nothing. This is D'Aubigny's command, not mine."

"The men would listen to you, my lord; they would heed your voice."

Cesare's voice was ironic.

"You think so? Against this turmoil; these screams and groans, these shouts of revenge and victory? No. They will heed no man's voice now. 'Tis too late; their blood is roused and they seek death and destruction. No man can turn them from their course."

Valentinois looked back at the street. The two Swiss were lurching drunkenly into the centre of the road, one clutching a wine bottle raised to his lips, the other fumbling at his disarranged clothing. Santa Croce followed the Duke's gaze and frowned sharply as he saw the girl lying still and quiet, free at last from the shuddering horror which had gripped her in icy fingers.

"She is dead," he whispered and his mouth was hard. "She had no chance."

"None at all." Cesare glanced at Pietro's angry face.

"When one adopts the trade of arms, one must accept the consequences, Pietro. War has many faces; none pleasant, yet some are more vile and unacceptable than others. Such a face is this."

He sighed faintly, and turned away from the edge of the balcony. "Louis determines to destroy the House of Aragon, and I am committed to aid him in this, and, in truth, I do not find the task unpalatable, for I have my own reasons for wishing to see Federigo's pride reduced." His eyes were hard, and Santa Croce knew he was remembering the curt manner in which Federigo had received his overtures not long before.

"Yet." The look was gone. "I would not design this." He half turned, and one hand indicated the shambles below them, "for there is no advantage in waging war like this, and I regret it."

He gave Santa Croce a faint, rueful smile.

"I once told my brother, Giovanni, that long after he was forgotten, I would be remembered, and so I will; for this, if for nothing else."

" 'Tis not your doing, sire," protested Santa Croce, "as you yourself have said, this is D'Aubigny's army."

Cesare nodded. "Yes, but it is known that I am here, and this is what will count when men recall this hour. Make no mistake, Pietro, my name will not be forgotten in Capua while time lasts; the very stones will cry out against me for what has been done today."

He was silent for a moment, then he shrugged.

"Ah well. As I have said, it is war's most brutal aspect, and when I set my hand to the sword, I did not shrink from what this meant. 'Tis no good crying halt now, for what has been started must be finished, and no man can recall the dead. Come, let us join D'Aubigny, for I judge this sack is almost at its end, and we must ride on to Gaeta and Naples. I would be done this campaign, for we have other work to do, and I would be about my task without delay."

He glanced again at Santa Croce, whose hand had fallen to his side, and there was a glimmer of sympathy in the Duke's eyes for his companion's reaction to the affray.

"Let us delay no more," he said quietly. "We must first seize power in the Romagna, then in Tuscany, and then . . . who knows?" He smiled. "We must take our swords, Pietro, and use them well, before time burns up the years, and I beg you, no regrets, for we shall have to pay the price of victory, and the cost will not be small. I will not wreak havoc when I can gain my ends by peaceful means, yet, if those I call upon to surrender should resist me, I shall not hesitate to put them to the sword as a sharp reminder to others of my purpose."

Santa Croce saluted, his fury and disgust all spent.

"I am prepared to pay what is necessary, sire; forgive me if I have shewn weakness this day, but . . ."

Cesare made a brief movement with one gloved hand.

"You owe me no apology, Pietro. What has taken place today in Capua is not a matter for pride, but it was necessary. Now, no more about this; our minds and hearts must go ahead to the finish of this task, and then we will be free to pursue our course untrammelled."

He walked past Santa Croce, and made his way to the street, his Captain following, and Pietro's face was as controlled as the Duke's as they stepped into the streets, now running with the blood of the slaughtered. Even the glance he cast upon the broken body of the girl was blank, and he barely saw the newly dead, lying in terrifying numbers on the rough stones about them, for such was the power Cesare Borgia had over his soldiers, that he never failed to overcome their doubts, and to seal their loyalty and devotion to his cause.

Not every inhabitant of Capua had been killed or maimed; one small group remained untouched, at least physically, and these were some thirty young women, all beautiful, who had been rounded up by the troops in their passage through the city. They had been gathered together in one of the few towers which had survived Cesare's bombardment, and were huddled together in whimpering terror as the lascivious sergeant-at-arms, with two of his grinning foot-soldiers, looked them over.

It was not until he was back in Rome that Cesare realized the women had been brought with his train, but having shewn his teeth in a brief, exasperated grimace, he merely observed that they were probably better off where they were than in the holocaust that was Capua.

Gaeta and Naples fell to the allies in a short space of time, and on the 3rd August, the ex-Cardinal of Valencia rode into Naples to unseat the man he had once crowned king, and the House of Aragon, which had spurned his hand of friendship, was in the dust.

Although he had many matters of importance on his mind, Cesare had not neglected his negotiations with Ercole, the Duke of Ferrara, for the marriage of his sister with Alfonso, Ferrara's son, for Valentinois saw many advantages in this union, not least that it gave him a friendly state on the borders of the Romagna.

Ercole drove a hard bargain, for despite the material benefits to be derived from the alliance, Lucrezia's reputation was not unknown, and the whole of Italy viewed with caution the activities of her unpredictable brother.

Finally, however, terms were settled to the satisfaction of both sides, and Cardinal Ippolito d'Este, and his brothers, Sigismondo and Fernando, came to Rome bringing with them a spectacular company who were to escort their brother's future wife back to him.

If Cesare's last entry into Rome had disappointed the populace, he made up for this lack when he rode out to greet his future in-laws, and there were cries and exclamations as his entourage rode out to Ponte Molle to welcome his guests.

The marriage was performed by proxy on the 30th December, and before the ceremony, Cesare went to see his sister, dismissing her servants with an impatient hand as he entered the chamber.

For a second his calculating eye assessed her gown, her jewels and above all her face, which was white and strained, for this marriage was not of Lucrezia's choosing, and it had taken all Cesare's persuasion to secure her agreement to it. Now he looked at the slight shadows under her wide blue eyes, and noted the droop of the full red lips, and his brows met in a faint frown.

"Cara." He went over to her and took her hands. "Why so sad? This is a day of joy for you, for now you are to be wed to Alfonso d'Este, and will be received in Ferrara with great pleasure and honour."

She did not raise her head to look at her brother, but the droop of her mouth became more pronounced.

"I do not want to go to Ferrara," she said, and her voice was a trifle petulant. "I want to stay in Rome with you."

He laughed gently. "I am not long for Rome, Lucrezia; 'ere long I shall resume my task, and will be gone from here."

"But you will return to Rome." She turned her head away. "You will not come to Ferrara, and I shall not see you again."

"What nonsense!" Cesare released her hands, and turned her face to his, and at last she looked into his eyes.

"Ferrara is not the end of the world, Lucrezia. Of course I shall come to see you; did you really think I would not? Did you imagine I could face life without seeing you again?"

He watched the sadness and irritation leave her face, and saw the glow his words lit in her eyes.

"You mean this, Cesare?" she asked eagerly. "You will truly come to Ferrara to see me?"

"I will truly come," he promised, and one hand stroked her cheek gently. "Never doubt it, Lucia."

She gave a little sob, and he held her to him for a minute, then said briskly:

"Come, my dear, all Rome waits for the bride. And you are radiant, my love. Alfonso is a lucky man." He saw the shadow in her eyes again, but before she could add further protests, he took her arm, and called to her servants. Then he kissed her cheek tenderly and left her to her maids, and if he saw the last desperate look of longing she cast upon him, he gave no sign of it.

After the ceremony, and before Lucrezia's departure to Ferrara in January, the Vatican was given over to intensive celebrations. The banquets were magnificent and breathtaking, the plays and masques never better, and Cesare was prominent in the part he played in the show put on for the benefit of Alfonso's brothers and their party. At night there were dances, and many ironic glances were cast at Cesare and Lucrezia as they moved in easy harmony together through the graceful Spanish dances they had learnt as children, but if there were faint sneers for Valentinois' part in this activity, there were none when the Duke displayed his prowess in the bull-ring, or in the jousts during the day, for none could match his strength and address, and there were gasps of admiration as the crowds watched the lithe young Duke, and in these moments the rumours of his darker deeds seemed to fall away, lost in the skill and agility he called so readily to his command.

Finally the celebrations were over, and the time came for Lucrezia to leave with the splendid escort which her brother had provided for her, and since there was now no escape from what Cesare had planned for her, she accepted her lot with more or less gracefulness, and bade the Pope and Valentinois farewell, shewing remarkable control for one who normally did not trouble to curb her emotions.

When she had gone, Cesare settled down to work again until the time came to escort his father to his newly acquired states, and during February and March they travelled to Caere, Corneto and Piombino, and then to Civita Vecchia, and thereafter returned to Rome to prepare for the third impresa, the course of which had been interrupted by the destruction of Naples. This impresa was aimed at bringing Camerino under the obedience of the Church, and the Tyrant Guilio Cesare Varano had already been deprived of his lordship, a move of which he had taken little note.

Whilst Cesare was busy with his officers and secretaries on the details of this proposed campaign, news was brought to him that attempts were being made to free Astorre Manfredi.

After the capture of Faenza, the young Manfredi had readily decided to remain with Cesare's train, for in the first few weeks after his state fell, he had developed a dog-like devotion to Valentinois which, if the latter did not actually foster, he certainly did nothing to discourage.

Astorre remained with Cesare after the fall of Faenza until he returned to Rome, and as Cesare listened to his agent's report on the plot to rescue the young Tyrant, his mind went back briefly to recall the last time he had spoken with him some months before.

Astorre had come to Cesare's chamber at the latter's command, and his young face was eager as he made his bow to the Duke.

"Sire, you called me?"

Cesare regarded him silently for a moment, and then waved him to a chair.

"Be seated, I pray you, for there is something which I have to say to you, and I bitterly regret the need for it."

Astorre's eyes darkened, but he took the chair indicated and his fingers gripped the arms as he waited apprehensively for Cesare to speak again.

When Faenza fell, I gave you a choice," said Cesare, and one hand tapped reflectively on the table in front of him. "I told you that you could stay with me, or go, wherever your heart dictated."

"That is so, my lord." Astorre flushed slightly. "But there was never any choice, sire. I had to stay with you, for you were all that I admired and honoured. I wanted only to be with you; to follow your command and to please you."

Valentinois looked at the eager boy in silence. There was much of pathos in the child-like worship he displayed, and very few men could have resisted the temptation to accept the uncritical loyalty offered by the devoted Astorre. But Cesare was no ordinary man. He never judged situations with his emotions, but only with his cold intellect, which weighed and assessed human feelings as impartially as it calculated all other factors in his campaigns. Where another man would have taken a chance that the boy would be no more trouble, and would have accepted with pleasure the unquestioning dedication and admiration, Cesare did not.

"You are right in one thing," he said finally, breaking the stillness between them. "There was never any choice for you."

Astorre looked faintly puzzled at the Duke's tone, but he nodded slightly.

"No, Potency, that is true, but . . ."

"Had you chosen differently, I would have done then, what I propose to do now," went on Cesare, ignoring the interruption. "You cannot be unaware, sire, of my methods. It is part of my unwavering policy to leave none alive and free who could, at a later time, claim legal right to the states I now take back in the name of the Church. Sire," his fingers stilled on the table. "You were much loved in Faenza, and for you, the men, women and children of Faenza put up a resistance the like of which I have not seen before."

Astorre's eyes brightened. "Yes, sire, my people shewed great courage, and I am glad of this, for now they are your subjects and will give to you the same devotion."

"Yes, they will, provided at some later time their minds are not seduced, and their old loyalties revived."

The boy frowned. "I do not understand, sire."

Cesare smiled bleakly. "No, I do not suppose you do, for you have not yet had time to judge the way men's hearts and minds are moved. Sire, it is my intent to bring under one strong united rule, all the states in central Italy, and to these states I will give a good government and an efficient civic structure. Thus they will remain content. But, my lord." The fingers started the light tapping again. "If in one state there should be but a handful of men who resented my rule, and if those men could produce the former lord and tyrant of that state, it would not be a great matter for the whole populace to be stirred into rebellion, fired by the thought of the reinstatement of he who previously claimed the right of lordship."

"But, Magnificence!" Astorre half raised a hand in protest. "They could not do this without my consent, and I would not agree to do anything which would cause you displeasure or anger."

"You would have no choice," said Cesare coolly. "You are a child; you could not resist the forces of rebellion once the seeds started to grow. If such a plan were fostered, you would find yourself enmeshed in its tentacles, and, sire." He paused and looked at the young man with remote eyes. "I cannot afford to let this happen. This is a chance I cannot take."

Astorre's hand dropped, and his face was paler.

"Sire, I . . . I . . . do not understand your meaning. Are you saying you do not believe I would be loyal to your cause?"

"You would not be able to be loyal to my cause if such a plot were hatched. You could not withstand the tide of events."

The Manfredi slumped back in his chair, and his eyes were tormented as he looked at the Duke.

"What can I say to convince you, sire," he said, and there was a tremor in his voice. "How can I make you believe me, when I say I would do nothing to your ill?"

"You cannot." Cesare was decisive. "You cannot judge the future, Astorre, for you are young and unaware of how strong would be the pressure put upon you to return to your state to defend your people. You would not be able to resist this in the final analysis; no one could. Therefore, I must now take steps to see that such a temptation is never placed in your path."

"And h . . . h . . . how will you do this, my lord?" The boy's voice was hardly above a whisper, and the pallor of his face had accentuated.

"I shall house you in the Castel Sant' Angelo," said Cesare and his smile was grim. "No matter how fervent the trouble makers of Faenza might be, they will not be able to reach you there, sire, for the castle walls are thick and strong, and my guards vigilant and watchful."

"You mean . . . you mean I shall be your prisoner?" The boy's voice was still slightly incredulous, as if he could not absorb the idea of his god turning his wrath upon him.

"You were always that." Cesare smiled faintly. "The only difference is that hitherto your prison has been less obvious, but now, as I have other tasks to perform, and must be away from Rome about my business, it is necessary that I ensure you are securely housed in my absence. Thus, your future home will be at Sant' Angelo. You will not find this too uncomfortable, sire."

The young Tyrant was staring at the Duke in increasing bewilderment.

"You will hold me prisoner? For how long, my lord?"

Cesare had turned his head to look out of the window, but at the question torn from tortured lips, he glanced back at the boy.

"For as long as I deem it necessary."

The Duke rose and took a step towards the stunned Manfredi.

"I regret, my lord, that we should have met in these circumstances, and that necessity makes of me a hard master. I would have had it otherwise."

For a second there was a flash of genuine regret in Cesare's eyes, then it was gone.

"I trusted you," said Astorre through dry lips, and his tormented eyes met the Duke's steady gaze. "You gave me your word and I trusted you."

"Honour is a luxury too costly for me," said Cesare coldly. "I would that I could live up to the standards you have set for me, sire, but I cannot. My task requires my undivided energy and purpose. I cannot turn aside for you, much as I might wish to do. I have to hold the Romagna, and there is only one way to do this, and if history calls me a monster, a criminal, a fiend, and a man without integrity or humanity, let it do so. Compassion and honour in this context are weaknesses in which I cannot afford to indulge. But when history judges me, I trust it will weigh in the balance my motives, for I do not pursue this course lightly. When I made my decision, my lord, I knew that to achieve my ends, I should have to do much which would bring wrath and criticism upon my head, but my ends were sufficiently important for these factors to be ignored."

Cesare's eyes held Astorre's. "My purpose is to unite Italy, and to make her strong and dominant. Men say I attempt this only to make a throne for myself, and for no other reason, but this is not so, although I do not expect to be able to convince anyone of this, nor do I propose to try. Let men judge as they will; it will not alter my intent. But, sire, the price of my endeavour is high, as you have already seen. Many will die before I have done, and men will revile my name, yet this will not stop me."

He relaxed slightly and gave a faint laugh. "Forgive me, sire, I fear I weary you."

His eyes were almost kind as he looked at the stricken youth.

"I will remember you, my lord. For your courage, and for your devotion to your people, and to me." He turned away and called his guards to him, and the young Tyrant was led from his presence, and Cesare, his mouth a trifle terse, sent for his other prisoner.

Isabella Villaro had none of Astorre Manfredi's illusions about Cesare, and when she was brought into his presence, her manner was cold and hostile, and the Duke gave a short laugh.

"Yes, madonna. You do not doubt my purpose, do you?"

"No, my lord, I do not."

"That makes easier my task of breaking to you the news of your future."

"Have I a future, my lord?" Her voice was brittle. "I should not have expected you to allow me to live."

He shrugged. "There is no particular hurry to end your life, madonna," he said indifferently. "You will be sent to Sant' Angelo, where you will remain as my prisoner."

"Until?" Her voice did not waver.

"Until I decide differently."

"I see. You condemn me to a living death." Her eyes were bitter. "It would be more merciful to kill me now, sire, for the years weigh heavily in such a prison."

"I am not renowned for mercy," he said blandly. "It will not suit my purpose to destroy you at this particular moment, and thus you will be housed in the castle as I have said."

She bit her lip, seeing her anger had made no dent in his unconcern, and Cesare's mouth curved in a faint smile.

"Yes, madonna, you hate me, but you should have used

more care when we first met. You tried to kill me; did you expect mercy for that?"

"I wish I had killed you," she cried with passion. "Dio! If I could have brought this about, all Italy would have rejoiced with me." Her green eyes were blazing and her colour was high. "Would that I could have freed this country from your hand, my lord."

"And let it sink back into a battleground for France and Spain?" He was scornful. "Have you no perception, madonna? Can you only see what is in front of your nose; have you no eyes for what lies beyond?"

She was startled at his vehemence, for his icy control was seldom broken.

Seeing her surprise, he gave a brief sardonic laugh.

"No, I see you have not. Well, madam, you will have plenty of time to reflect on my words, for there is little else to do in Sant' Angelo but ponder on one's mistakes."

He bowed slightly, and Isabella Villaro was taken out by the men who had waited at the door for his Highness to finish speaking, and Cesare looked after her with a trace of regret.

Valentinois came sharply back to the present as his spy finished his report, and he nodded.

"I was right," he said to Agapito, who sat by his side. "It is as I expected, and I was wise to keep the Manfredi under lock and key, but now, even this is not enough."

He waved the messenger away and called for Michele da Corella.

Agapito looked at the Duke's set face. "You think the time has come . . ." he began tentatively, and saw the lines appear at the corners of Cesare's mouth.

"Yes, it has indeed, Agapito. The time has come to dispose of Astorre Manfredi and, incidentally, Isabella Villaro, for both of them could cause unrest."

"It seems a pity," said Agapito slowly, "the boy is devoted; the girl beautiful."

The Duke nodded. "Yes, this is so, but these are incidentals, Agapito, as you fully realize. I have no choice, and this you also know.

His secretary nodded regretfully. "No, Potency, I see that, but still——"

He broke off as Michele da Corella came before Valentinois, and the Duke looked at him in silence for a moment. Then he stirred, and shrugged off any measure of reluctance which had beset him, and his instructions were curt and to the point.

On the following day, when the sun was high in the clear June sky, fishermen engaged in their tasks on the banks of the Tiber, came upon the bodies of a young man and a girl. The discovery of corpses in the River Tiber was no new thing, and the hardened fishermen pulled the bodies free of the murky waters with almost unmoved aplomb, but as one of them, younger than the rest, laid the body of Isabella Villaro on the soft green bank, he paused in regret as he looked at the swollen distorted face, and noted the savage marks about the slender neck.

His voice was sad as he gently brushed the sodden hair from the bloated face, and uttered the only epitaph Isabella was to receive.

"She must have been beautiful," he said quietly, as he stared at the sightless eyes. "God rest her soul."

The Borgia Prince

PAMELA BENNETTS

Of all the princes of Renaissance Italy, Cesare Borgia was the most powerful – and the most feared. Duke of Valentinois and Romagna, Cesare built his kingdom with his sword and his quick wits, brooking no opposition to his ruthless will. When his followers, the condottieri, rebelled against him and rival princes plotted his downfall, Cesare was forced to plan the destruction of his own men. And as he struggled with his enemies he found himself involved in a more personal battle . . . with the lovely Bianca di Marco, his hostage from the great battle of San Savarno. For despite their sworn enmity, Cesare and Bianca found themselves drawn inexorably together into a love match that defied both their political allegiances and their own fiery natures.

A Sphere Book 35p

The Black Plantagenet

PAMELA BENNETTS

Raised on the ideals of chivalry and trained from childhood to a soldier's life, Edward Plantagenet won his spurs at the battle of Crecy. Fighting beside his father against the French he became the idol of all England.

And none admired him more than his cousin Joan, the Fair Maid of Kent. Sent to Aquitaine to protect England's domain, he smashed the French army at Poitiers and returned triumphant, the King of France his prisoner.

Then his father arranged a marriage with the Duchess of Burgundy, and Joan decided it was time to use her wiles to arouse her handsome cousin.

A Sphere Book 30p

Warwick the Kingmaker

PAUL MURRAY KENDALL

Richard Neville, Earl of Warwick, has been relegated to a famous oblivion. The chronicles of his age recorded his deeds and registered his impact, but passing time has been cruel to whatever revelations of himself were left in his restless wake. Tudor writers were so intent on depicting the victory of Henry Tudor as part of the pattern of God's justice, that Warwick was regarded only as a bellicose baron in the hurly-burly of civil strife from which England had been rescued.

Paul Kendall has attempted to make good this deficiency. The result is a work of historical biography every bit as colourful and dynamic as its predecessor, RICHARD III. For the first time in literature, Warwick becomes a figure of flesh and blood, and a memorable human being.

A Sphere Book 75p

Elizabeth I, Queen of England

NEVILLE WILLIAMS

Neville Williams' portrait of Queen Elizabeth I, thoroughly based on contemporary scholarship and at the same time highly readable, will appeal to today's readers as widely as Sir John Neale's life appealed to the last generation and Bishop Creighton's to a previous one.

Here is an absorbing account of the clashes of interest between Elizabeth the woman and Elizabeth the queen, with the frankness that is now possible. The result is a real insight into the mind of this child of the English Reformation.

A Sphere Book £1.00